ALLIES & ASSASSINS

ALLIES & ASSASSINS

JUSTIN SOMPER

LITTLE, BROWN AND COMPANY
NEW YORK · BOSTON

Copyright © 2013 by Justin Somper

Little, Brown and Company

Hachette Book Group
237 Park Avenue, New York, NY 10017
Visit our website at lb-teens.com

Little, Brown and Company is a division of Hachette Book Group, Inc.
The Little, Brown name and logo are trademarks of Hachette Book Group, Inc.

The publisher is not responsible for websites (or their content) that are not owned by the publisher.

First U.S. Edition: May 2014
First published in Great Britain in 2013 by Atom

Library of Congress Cataloging-in-Publication Data

Somper, Justin.
Allies & assassins / Justin Somper. — First U.S. edition.
    pages cm
"First published in Great Britain in 2013 by Atom"—Copyright page.
Summary: "Sixteen-year-old Jared inherits the throne of Archenfield after his older brother, Prince Anders, is murdered. He relies on the twelve officers of the court to advise him but soon suspects one of them could be responsible for his brother's death and vows to hunt down the killer, who may be after Jared as well"— Provided by publisher.
    ISBN 978-0-316-25393-2 (hc) — ISBN 978-0-316-25394-9 (ebook)
    [1. Princes—Fiction. 2. Courts and courtiers—Fiction. 3. Assassins—Fiction. 4. Fantasy.] I. Title. II. Title: Allies and assassins.
                  PZ7.S69733Al 2014
                      [Fic]—dc23
                      2013017968

10 9 8 7 6 5 4 3 2 1

RRD-C

Printed in the United States of America

For Jenny Jenner

Lindeberg Line
WOODLARK

Wynyard Line
ARCHENFIELD

Blaxland Line
ARCHENFIELD

Erik (d) --- Klara

Tristan (d) --- Agnes (d)

Rodrigo --- Marguerite (d)

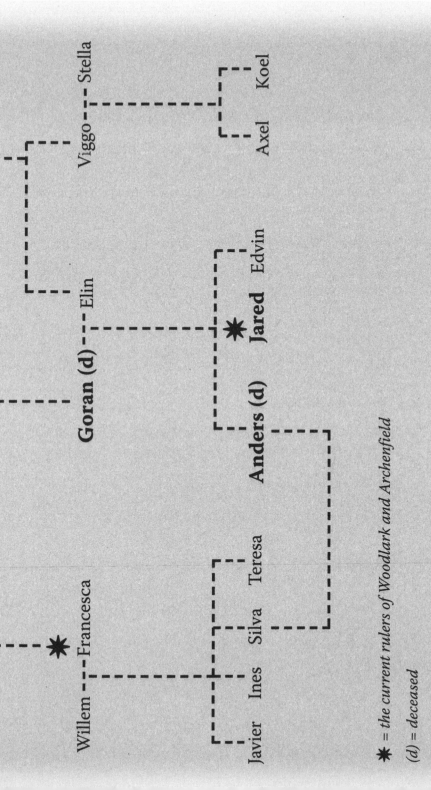

Willem –•– Francesca ✷

Goran (d) –•– Elin

Viggo –•– Stella

Javier   Ines   Silva   Teresa

Anders (d)

✷ Jared   Edvin

Axel   Koel

✷ = the current rulers of Woodlark and Archenfield

(d) = deceased

Bold = the princes of Archenfield

THE ARCHENFIELD HOURS

The Prince's Bell
The bell chimes once, for there can be only one true Prince.
We use this hour to give thanks for his multitude of virtues and for how he embodies all that is good and fair in our Princedom.

The Captain of the Guard's Bell
The bell chimes twice.
We use this hour to give thanks for the protection and peace the Captain of the Guard affords our Princedom.

The Cook's Bell
The bell chimes three times.
We use this hour to give thanks for the diverse and plentiful food that we eat three times each day.

The Woodsman's Bell
The bell chimes four times.
We use this hour to give thanks for our woods and forests and for those who tend them through the four seasons of the year.

The Groom's Bell
The bell chimes five times.
We use this hour to give thanks for the horses and other animals, on whom we all depend, and those who look after them.

The Poet's Bell
The bell chimes six times.
We use this hour to give thanks for the Poet's gift for finding words to tell the story of our Princedom.

The Falconer's Bell
The bell chimes seven times.
We use this hour to give thanks for the Falconer's ability to communicate with her birds and for the protection this affords us all.

The Huntsman's Bell
The bell chimes eight times.
We use this hour to give thanks for the skill and bravery of those who capture food for us to eat.

The Bodyguard's Bell
The bell chimes nine times.
We use this hour to give thanks for those who protect our Prince and thereby the Princedom.

The Beekeeper's Bell
The bell chimes ten times.
We use this hour to give thanks for the honey harvested from her hives and for the sweetness of life we enjoy in Archenfield.

The Physician's Bell
The bell chimes eleven times.
We use this hour to give thanks for those who know how to cure us and for the mysteries of our mortal bodies we have yet to comprehend.

The Priest's Bell
The bell chimes twelve times.
We use this hour to give thanks for the Priest, who guides our path through this life and shepherds us gently into the realm beyond.

The Executioner's Bell
The bell chimes thirteen times.
We use this hour to give thanks for the Executioner's axe, which is wielded with rigor and justice so we may all sleep safe in our beds.

The Edling's Bell
The bell chimes fourteen times.
We use this hour to honor our illustrious heritage and also to look forward to the glorious future of the Princedom.

The Prince and Officers of Archenfield

The Prince: Anders Wynyard (assassinated)

The Edling: Jared Wynyard

The Beekeeper: Emelie Sharp

The Bodyguard: Hal Harness

The Captain of the Guard: Axel Blaxland

The Cook: Vera Webb

The Executioner: Morgan Booth

The Falconer: Nova Chastain

The Groom: Lucas Curzon

The Huntsman: Kai Jagger

The Physician: Elias Peck

The Poet: Logan Wilde

The Priest: Father Simeon

The Woodsman: Jonas Drummond

DAY ONE

ONE

The Falconer's Mews, the Village of the Twelve

WITH THE LAST OF HER SEVEN FALCONS BALANCED on her wrist, Nova Chastain walked back out onto the balcony once more. Her gray-brown eyes glistened, as if wet with dew; her dark hair, hanging low beneath the small of her back, was gently tangled from her previous trips out onto the windblown balcony. Already she had sent six of her falcons on their way—carrying their somber messages to her six deputies at each of the border gates. The new day had barely announced itself, but already Nova was weary. Her head ached and there was a gnawing sensation in her stomach, though she had no appetite for breakfast. It felt like an age since they had brought her the terrible news, but she knew from the changing light that it had been less than an hour ago that the Prince's Bell had sounded; the single

1

chime that announced another Archenfield dawn. Albeit one that the Prince himself had not lived to see.

She had been watching, as was her habit, the budding of the new morning from her perch high above the village when the Captain of the Guard's messenger arrived. Hearing his cold, hard words, she had turned away—eyes already stinging—to watch the golden sunlight nudge away the pink residue of dawn. The view across the Princedom was as beautiful as she could ever remember, but today its very beauty felt wantonly cruel.

The Falconer could feel her bird's eagerness to take wing and follow its six fellows. It moved impatiently from side to side on the worn leather gauntlet that encased Nova's slender left arm, from her muscled bicep to the tips of her fingers. Nova had saved her favorite bird until last. She held Mistral close a moment longer, knowing that once the falcon took flight, she would be all alone with her grief. The Falconer's Mews, set atop its high tower, seemed a cold and lonely place when the falcons' roost was empty.

She conjured the image of her other six falcons—already in the air, soaring swiftly in their appointed directions across the Archenfield sky, carrying the bleakest of messages to the smaller mews at each of the gates:

Prince Anders has been killed. One or more assassins are on the loose. Close down the borders and take all other appropriate action.

After these two hard-won, barely savored years of peace, Nova knew what a gut-churning shock it would be to her comrades at each border mews to unfurl such an ominous note.

Stroking Mistral's small hooded head with the fingers of her free hand, Nova looked across the landscape spread out before her—the landscape she loved with a deep, visceral passion. She thought of how the news would travel swiftly, beyond the palace and the court, out to the settlements. Before the striking of the next bell, every man, woman and child might already share in the news of Prince Anders's assassination. Shock and grief would run amok, like the most aggressive forest fire—*no*, like a wind-borne plague. People who had never seen the Prince's face nor heard his voice would fall to the ground, keening in sorrow.

Unlike them, Nova had known the Prince: his face was as familiar to her as the sun; his voice as commonplace as the rustling of the trees. Imagining a world without him was as implausible as conjuring up a day without sun, wind or trees.

Nova attempted a steadying breath. She was one of the Council of Twelve—the council that supported the Prince in ruling the Princedom. She knew she must try to tamp down her personal feelings and keep focused on doing the job required of her. The Captain of the Guard's messenger had briefed her with extreme clarity and she had executed his bidding to the letter. Just as she always did. No one could take issue with Nova Chastain's dedication to duty.

She nuzzled Mistral one last time. There had always been a particularly strong bond between the Falconer and this bird. She had felt that she could sense Mistral's emotions—whether exhilaration or anxiety—and she was equally sure that the bird could intuit her own moods.

Now she removed the bird's hood and gazed down fondly at Mistral's jewel-bright eyes. They served as twin mirrors to her own disquiet. The bird's head began moving jerkily about. Whenever her birds were free from their hoods, it felt as if they were thirstily drinking in every aspect of their surroundings. Each day, she had the impression they were experiencing the world—its sights, sounds, scents and secrets—for the very first time.

The moment could be delayed no longer; it was time to set Mistral free. Nova gave a practiced flick of her wrist and the falcon extended her wings and took flight.

Watching her go, Nova felt suddenly weightless, giddy. She reached out both hands to grip the balcony. Snatching uneven gulps of air, she was distracted by signs of activity below her.

To the right was the dark blue-green forest, and beyond that, the silvery fjord. Turning her gaze in the opposite direction, she saw a cluster of figures in the glen—a hunting party. She strained her sight with the effort of identifying the figures, but her eyes soon budded with water again and her vision became blurred. She lifted a square of linen to her eyes to absorb some of the moisture. As she drew it away again, she saw a lone horseman riding out toward the glen.

She knew from the way he rode that it was Lucas Curzon, the Chief Groom. Lucas, her fellow on the Twelve, was one of the gentlest and noblest of men. He was a man of few words—to human companions at least. She had sometimes heard him, when he thought he was alone, deep in "conversation" with his horses.

Lucas must be taking a message to the hunting party. Piecing together the picture, Nova realized that Prince Anders's younger brother, Prince Jared, might be one of the hunters. Was it possible that the young prince did not yet know of his brother's fate? This thought sent a stabbing pain through her insides. She opened her mouth to cry out, but no sound would come. Her grief, she knew, was buried too deeply to be easily released. Holding her tender belly, she rocked to and fro for a moment, begging the pain to subside. But it was a stubborn hurt and she knew it would remain down inside her, submerged like a locked casket tossed to the depths of the fjord.

She knew this just as surely as she knew that dark and difficult times lay ahead. Not just for her and the rest of the Twelve but for all of Archenfield.

A sudden noise pulled her from her reverie. The north

door had blown shut with such force that one of the glass panes had cracked and shattered. A fresh pain searing through her head, Nova surveyed the fan of fallen shards.

It was best to go inside. For now, her work was done. She turned and approached the broken door. Though she opened it as gently as possible, more shards of glass fell through and shattered next to her boots. One of the fragments, carried perhaps on the wind, ricocheted up and embedded itself in the pad of her forefinger. She watched with horrid fascination as a bud of blood appeared there and kept watching as it grew in size. It was rather like watching a rose bloom.

As the blood began to spill over the side of her finger, she lifted it to her lips and drew the metallic taste into her mouth. In a strange way, it comforted her, offering her some kind of fellowship with Prince Anders. She imagined, once more, the life draining from the young and virile Prince. She closed her eyes, trying to shut out the vivid image. But there it was, lurking horribly behind her eyelids.

"Prince Anders," she whispered. Then, an even softer echo. "Anders." Her eyes were still tightly shut. She felt a single tear snake down her cheek and fall saltily upon her blood-stained lip.

TWO

The Glen

"HOLD FAST, SIR," KAI JAGGER, THE CHIEF HUNTS-man, instructed Prince Jared. "You and I will wait here."

They had dismounted from their horses and now stood waiting in the long grass as the two other members of the hunting party set off on foot toward the woodland up ahead. The grass was wet with dew and some remnants of the morning mist still snaked around them. Jared could feel moisture seeping in above the tops of his riding boots. It was unwelcome but—at the same time—the cold and wet made him feel that much more awake and alert.

He hadn't wanted to be dragged out of his bed to hunt this morning—he would never actively choose to be dragged from the comfort of his bed—but it was all part of his princely training. He knew there was no escape for him—any more than there would be for the stag.

Jared's crossbow was trained on the line of trees ahead—the line of trees from which, assuming Jagger's subordinates executed their part successfully, the stag would emerge directly into the firing line. Jared watched his companions—a man and a woman—advancing on the glade. He noticed the precise way they walked, staying close to the adjacent trees so that their green and brown uniforms blended in with the flora. It was becoming harder and harder for him to distinguish the hunters from the trees. What chance would the stag have?

He turned now to the man at his side. Much as Jared would rather be back indoors and under his bedcovers, if he *was* to be subjected to activity at this hour, at least Kai Jagger was an easy, undemanding companion. Jagger was not much given to small talk—or to any kind of talk really. Watching him now, Jared had the feeling that Kai's senses were far more engaged with the plants and animals surrounding him than with his human companion. This suited Jared just fine.

He couldn't help but feel intimidated by Jagger. Jared considered himself to be in reasonably good physical condition. Now that he was sixteen years old, his body seemed to be constantly evolving from that of a boy into that of a young man. With each day, he packed on harder muscle and noticeable gains in his strength and endurance—a metamorphosis that happened almost without conscious effort. But, in spite of Jared's growing strength, and indeed height, he always felt like a puny youth in comparison to Kai Jagger.

He was unsure of Kai's age—and had never dared to ask him. It would seem somehow too intimate a question—even though he was a prince and entitled to ask whatever question came into his mind. Surely Kai must be in his forties now. For as long as Jared had known him, the hair on Kai's head and beard had been bright silver. And yet his face, though ruddy from endless days exposed to the wind and sun, was smooth and for the most part unlined.

Kai was now one of the older members of the Twelve, having kept his life while others around him had been lost in the last war. It was no surprise that Kai Jagger had made it back from the battlefield unscathed. As a boy, growing up in the court, Jared had aspired to become something like Kai when he reached adulthood. But even now that he was sixteen, and in spite of his growing physical power, he sensed he would always feel like a stripling in comparison to Jagger.

"He should make his way out any time now, sir," the Chief Huntsman informed Jared, raising his own crossbow. Jared knew that the onus was on him to make the kill shot. Jagger was only readying himself to fire a second if the entry was not clean or decisive enough.

There was a sudden noise and Jared tensed, preparing himself for action, but he swiftly realized that the sound had come not from the woodland but from above. He glanced up in time to see a falcon flying overhead.

"Nova," he whispered. It wasn't unusual to see one of her falcons on the wing at this hour, but there was something ominous about the bird's arrival today. Or perhaps he was only imagining it. The prince took in, with awe, the way the bird climbed with seemingly minimal effort to a higher airstream.

Now he felt Kai's breath, warm at his ear. "Don't allow yourself to be distracted, Prince Jared," the Chief Huntsman told him. "Stay focused on the woods. You may only get one chance at this."

Obediently, Jared returned his full concentration to the woodland. The sun was growing stronger all the time and now a golden shaft of light struck a section of the trees. As it did, Jared witnessed a most curious—and impossible—sight: his father, Prince Goran, stepped out from between the trees and glanced toward him.

Utterly transfixed, Jared raised his hand in greeting. His father lifted his own hand, in mirror fashion. Jared found himself trembling. His father had been dead for two years now—slain on the battlefield before Anders had rallied the troops to the final, decisive victory. So how could Prince Goran be here now?

"Focus!" Kai Jagger told him. "Look! Here he comes. Take aim!"

When Jared looked again, his father had disappeared. In his stead, the sunlight now illuminated a stag.

The stately creature stepped out from the line of trees, as if drawn by the light. Their fellows had executed their part. Now it was up to *him* to finish the job. But the stag was such a fine, noble creature. And Jared was still in shock at the strange vision of his father. He hesitated, bow strung back.

"Now!" Jagger commanded him. "Do it now!"

No "sir," no "Prince Jared." No further pretense about who was in command here.

Feeling a cold sweat overtake him, Jared released the bow and sent his arrow racing toward the trees. And that's exactly where it took root—in the trunk of a tree.

Before the stag could run, however, a second arrow had taken flight through the air. And, of course, this one made perfect contact with its target. Kai Jagger's aim would never fail at this range.

The fatal arrow had plunged into the stag's neck. The entry was deep and the creature reared up for a moment, then fell slowly backward as the tip of the arrow buried itself deeper still, slicing through the animal's nervous system and almost instantaneously shutting down one faculty after another. Jared could see, almost feel, the waves of pain the stag was experiencing, until at last its ability to stand gave way and it crashed down to the wet ground, sending up a spray of dew. Jared was filled with a heavy sadness and was unsure if this stemmed from his own sense of failure or from such a close proximity to death.

Jagger sighed, resting a heavy hand on Jared's shoulder for a moment. "You must not allow yourself to be distracted, sir. I believe I have told you this before."

Without further conversation, they set off toward the dying prey. Their two fellows emerged from the woodland and made their way over to meet them. As the four hunters were reunited, the stag looked up wearily, then gave out its last defeated breath.

"Well done, sir!" one of Jagger's subordinates congratulated Jared. Evidently, she hadn't noticed that it was not Jared's arrow that had felled the stag.

Jared opened his mouth to correct her mistake, but Jagger's voice now cut across his own, rendering him silent. The Chief Huntsman gave brief instructions to his team and, in answer, they began stringing up the beast to transport it back to the palace. Jared averted his eyes.

Since being named as Anders's Edling, his heir, Jared had been subjected to these hunting exercises every week. It was not something he naturally excelled at, unlike his older—and indeed his younger—brother. It seemed that the middle Wynyard brother lacked the killer instinct. But if the unlikely day did come when he was crowned Prince of All Archenfield, he would have to be as precise and ruthless a shot as anyone in the Princedom. That was the plan at least. But this morning's outing had only proved how far from fruition that plan still was.

Jared knew that Anders wouldn't have fluffed that shot any more than Jagger would. How much more rewarding Jagger must have found it to train Anders in princely pursuits. Not for the first time, Jared thought how little he had wanted his brother to choose him as his Edling. If only Anders had chosen Cousin Axel instead. Axel was far more accomplished with a bow and arrow. He seemed to enjoy all sporting endeavors—especially those ending in death.

His reverie was broken by the drumming of hooves. He looked up to see the Chief Groom, galloping toward the hunting party at breakneck speed. The fields were still cloaked in mist and Lucas Curzon's horse seemed almost to be flying through the air rather than pounding over solid ground. Glancing to his side, Jared saw that Kai was standing alert. Did he know, or suspect, the Chief Groom's purpose? If so, he was giving nothing away.

Lucas brought his steed to a stop right at the foot of the fallen stag. He swiftly dismounted and stepped closer still. Jared held his breath, seeing pain in Lucas's expressive gray eyes. He could tell it was bad news, even before the Chief Groom fell to his knees before him.

"I'm so sorry, Prince Jared," Lucas began, his voice unusually husky. He took a breath and resumed more forcefully. "Prince Anders is gone." He paused, but only for an instant. "Your brother was found dead in his bedchamber. It looks like he was assassinated."

Jared was dimly aware of Kai Jagger asking a question and of Lucas Curzon turning to him and beginning to answer. He could see the Chief Groom's mouth moving, though as if in slow motion with no comprehensible sound emerging. Jared felt his body going through a sequence of convulsions. He remembered keenly the way the arrow had buried itself in the stag's flesh, causing deeper and deeper impact and chaos within. Now he was the stag and this terrible news was the arrow. His brother was dead. Now he, Jared, was not merely *a* prince. He was *the* Prince of All Archenfield, ruler over all the lands his forefathers had claimed for themselves and fought many wars to protect.

He felt a hand on his shoulder. His first thought was that it was Kai Jagger again. But looking up, he saw that Kai was still deep in conversation with Lucas. Kai's two companions stood on either side of him. In which case, whose hand was on Jared's shoulder? He turned and found himself looking into his father's face once more. The ghost—if that was what it was—did not speak, but Jared knew that his father was trying to comfort him, to tell him to pull himself together. He nodded, discreetly, so the others wouldn't see. Then he drew himself to his full height. As he did so, he realized with a fresh wave of sadness that his father had faded from view.

Jared felt giddy. Then nauseous. A deep churning sickness seemed to rise up from his entrails. Powerless to hold back, he opened his mouth and emitted a quite spectacular torrent of vomit all over his hunting boots.

THREE

The Palace

As the grooms led the horses off to the stables and the team of hunters dispersed, Prince Jared heard the three chimes of the Cook's Bell. Archenfield's sixteen-year-old ruler strode alone toward the back doors of the palace. He was dimly aware of activity going on around him—of the members of the Cook's team already out picking herbs and vegetables in the Kitchen Garden, scurrying to obey the forbidding Vera Webb as quickly as possible; of Emelie Sharp, the Beekeeper, placing a cover on one of her hives. Such actions spoke of order and continuity. But how could it be so? With the news of Anders's murder, everything within the Princedom was fractured.

Jared could feel his heart hammering with the anticipation of everything that awaited him inside the palace walls.

He saw that Logan Wilde was standing on the back steps, ready to receive him. Logan was another important member of the Twelve. His title—the Poet— could at first prove deceptive. Yes, he was capable of crafting fine poems and stories, but his position was as much political as ceremonial.

Logan now raised his hand. Jared nodded, looking with new eyes at the tall, slim man standing in readiness to greet him. As the Prince approached, Logan's dark closely cropped head bowed down for a moment in respect. When he raised his face again, there was warmth in Logan Wilde's hazel eyes. He was smiling at Jared, doing his best no doubt to offer reassurance. But Jared thought he could see signs of strain in the Poet's face. He knew that Logan had been one of his brother's most constant companions.

The Twelve were not simply the Prince's retinue and the comrades with whom he ran the Princedom; they were each devoted to their ruler. Jared was keenly aware that his older brother had inspired a strong sense of devotion within everyone from his officers to his subjects. The ripples of his death would spread far and wide. Jared already felt a heavy sense of dread at even attempting to walk in his brother's golden footsteps.

"I need to see him," Jared told Logan Wilde, as soon as the two young men were within earshot of one another.

"Yes, of course, Your Highness," Logan said. "I'll take you to him."

It felt strange to be addressed as "Your Highness" rather than "sir"—as if Anders, the true Prince, was standing just behind him, or they were acting out some skit. But this was real and Prince Jared knew he was going to have to get used to it; it was the least of the changes he must swiftly acclimate to. Logan pushed open the doors into the palace to allow Prince Jared entry. Together, they proceeded swiftly along the corridor.

"Who discovered him?" Jared asked, keen to marshal what facts there were.

"It was Silva," Logan answered. "As you know, the Prince and his consort have—had"—he corrected himself—"separate but adjoining quarters. She heard him cry out in the middle of the night and went to see what was wrong." Logan and Jared pushed through a heavy oak door, leading into the heart of the main palace building. "Needless to say, Silva is in a deep state of shock. Your mother and brother are with her now. I will take you to them—"

"I'll see Anders first." Jared cut Logan off.

"Yes, of course, Your Highness." Logan nodded. "Afterward, is what I meant. Prince Jared, you are aware that as Anders's Edling, you now assume a host of new duties, even before your brother's funeral and certainly before your coronation? Be under no illusions, from the moment Prince Anders's body was discovered, for all intents and purposes, you became Prince of All Archenfield."

Before Jared could answer, a pair of servants came around a corner, walking toward them. The man and woman looked surprised to see Prince Jared and, seeing the naked heartbreak etched on their faces, he realized *they* were looking to *him* to offer them strength and comfort. How on earth was he supposed to deliver that? He turned his head, feeling cowardly as he did so—as if he had failed the very first, small challenge presented to him as de facto ruler. He was relieved when they continued on their way.

Perhaps having witnessed his unease, Logan placed a reassuring hand on Jared's shoulder. The Poet's touch was fleeting, but still Jared drew some comfort from the gesture. They turned the next corner.

"Things will happen very quickly now," Logan told him. "Much will be asked of you. You are going to need an office—somewhere to receive people. The obvious solution is for you to move into your brother's quarters."

Jared scowled and shook his head. "I have absolutely no intention of sleeping in my dead brother's bed..."

"No, of course not," Logan said. "Not yet. But I assume you don't have the same reservations about sitting at his desk." His eyes met Jared's. "In a way, you could say it would forge continuity between the two of you, Your Highness."

Jared knew when he was beaten. "All right—yes, I'll use his desk and his office. But I'm sleeping in my own quarters until I decide otherwise."

That seemed good enough for the Poet, who nodded before continuing. "On the whole, I think it best we take one step at a time, but the big challenge will come tomorrow when you address the people from the palace balcony." Already, Jared's blood was running cold at the prospect. "You have two options. Either I can announce the news of Anders's death and you can follow with some rousing words…"

Jared stopped dead in his tracks, wondering how exactly he'd find rousing words with which to address the people. Pausing beside him, Logan seemed to have read his mind.

"Don't look so worried, Your Highness!" Logan said, offering him two sheets of folded paper. "I took the liberty of preparing something for you. As a starting point at least."

"Thank you," Jared said, gratefully taking the papers and tucking them safely into one of his pockets.

They had almost reached the main palace staircase, which cut up through the hall in a vast Y shape. The walls of the Grand Hall were lined with portraits of the royal family, past and present. Jared paused before a painting of his father, feeling the all-too-familiar jab of inferiority. He knew that his father had been no more than sixteen himself when the portrait was painted. It was years before he came to the throne, but you could see in the set of his eyes that he was ready, even then.

Looking at the image of Prince Goran, Jared was struck by how much Anders had resembled their father. It wasn't only that they both possessed straw-gold hair and blue eyes, while Jared's own hair and eyes were deep brown. There was something commanding about Goran's and Anders's faces, whether in life or in art. Each had possessed an unwavering certainty that he was destined to rule. Jared had never felt that way and, now that he held the reins of the Princedom, he felt less qualified than ever.

He looked over to see Logan Wilde, a few steps ahead, watching him. Surely the Poet must be thinking the same thought—that things had come to a pretty pass when some-one like Jared was in command of the Princedom. But if the Poet was thinking such things, he gave no sign of it. Instead, he gave a warm smile and gestured for Jared to follow him up the stairs.

They were passed by more servants, this pair weighed down with bundles of heavy black cloth. Jared realized that they had been given the job of covering all the mirrors in the palace. The same thing had happened two years before, following his father's death. He remembered his uncle Viggo telling him that the mirrors might trap the souls of the survivors. They would be covered for a full seven days.

It might only be a superstition, but it was a chilling one. Jared watched as the two women cloaked a large, ornate mirror in black. In spite of the niggling sense of unreality he was experiencing, something about the sight of the mirror, in its mourning garb, drove home to him that all this was real. A nightmare, perhaps, but not one from which he was about to wake.

"You mentioned two options before?" he said to Logan, attempting to focus on practical matters.

"Yes." The Poet nodded. "The second possibility is that you make the death announcement as well. But with some of the servants already aware of the news, it's only a matter of time before word spreads beyond the palace walls."

"What do you suggest?" Jared asked.

"I suggest we send messengers to the settlements," Logan answered, decisively. "That way, when the people come here, they will arrive already knowing that Prince Anders is dead. They will come to see what you are made of and how you will ensure that the Blood Price is paid."

"The Blood Price," Jared echoed.

Logan seemed to interpret the Prince's scant words as a question. His quick eyes met Jared's. "Whoever is responsible for Prince Anders's death must pay the debt with his, or indeed *her*, own blood." He cleared his throat before resuming. "It's a central tenet of how we do things here in Archenfield."

Jared nodded. Did the Poet really think he didn't know this? He had grown up at the heart of the court and, as such, knew the customs of the Princedom as well as anyone.

"I agree with you, Logan. We should send word announcing Anders's assassination ahead of my address. It makes things..." He was frustrated not to be able to readily locate the right word.

"Cleaner?" Logan offered, bright with purpose.

Prince Jared nodded. He realized that he had just given the Poet a command. Maybe there was a chance—albeit a slim one—that he really could hack it as Prince.

Glancing up, he saw they were now walking together along a galleried landing, the door to Anders's chamber in sight up ahead. Once more, Jared felt a chill and knew it had nothing to do with the temperature of the long gallery.

"The Prince's quarters have been secured by the Captain of the Guard," Logan informed him. "Elias Peck, the Physician, is currently examining your brother's body. Once his initial work is complete, the body will be taken to Elias's surgery for a fuller...examination."

"Not before I have seen Anders myself," Jared asserted again.

Logan nodded, though it seemed more an acknowledgment of Jared's wishes rather than an agreement to honor them.

Given that he was supposed to be Prince, Jared was starting to form the impression that he was not the one in control here. He had many unanswered questions about his brother's death, but somehow Logan Wilde had managed to steer their conversation away from the investigation into his brother's murder, toward the ceremonial necessities of the next day.

The door to Prince Anders's chamber was closed and guarded by the Chief Bodyguard, Hal Harness. Hal nodded cordially at Logan Wilde, then turned to Jared.

"I'm very sorry for your loss, Your Highness," he said.

"And I for yours," Jared found himself saying. "Prince Anders's death is a loss for each and every one of us."

"Indeed," Hal said with a nod. He remained standing in front of the chamber door.

"Step aside, Hal," Logan told him. "Prince Jared wishes to see his brother."

There was an awkward moment of silence. Hal's eyes met Logan's, but the Chief Bodyguard did not move.

"I said, 'step aside,'" Logan persisted.

"I'm under orders not to let anyone inside while the Physician is conducting his investigation."

Jared felt fresh tension rising in his chest. He was aware of his eyes narrowing in anger. "I'm not *anyone*..." he began.

"Let me deal with this," Logan told him. Before Jared could contribute anything further, Logan pressed on. "Hal, we understand that Elias Peck must be granted peace and quiet and solitude while he makes his initial examination, but *Prince* Jared must be allowed to see his brother's body without further delay."

Hal seemed to be considering the matter, but still he did not move from his post.

"Stand aside!" Jared cried out, angrily. "Or, so help me, I will make you!" He regretted the words the moment they left his mouth—well aware that saying them and backing them up with physical action were two very different things. Jared might be Archenfield's new Prince but, in any kind of a fight with Hal Harness, he would certainly be defeated. The Chief Bodyguard had the critical advantage of a few more years of age, several more pounds of significantly tauter muscle and—as if these alone were not enough—proficiency in forms of combat that Jared hadn't even heard of. All things considered, Hal was pretty much the last man in court with whom to pick a fight.

The stalemate was finally broken from within the chamber. The door opened a fraction and Axel Blaxland, Jared's cousin and Archenfield's Captain of the Guard, appeared in the doorway. Seeing Jared, he moved Hal Harness aside and extended a hand to the shoulder of his younger cousin. "Cousin Jared, there are no words to adequately express my emotions or with which to comfort you at a time like this." Axel's dark eyes met Jared's own.

As Axel withdrew his hand, Jared saw over his shoulder into the room. The door was only open a fraction, but it was enough to see his brother's supine body, and the Physician,

Elias Peck, leaning over it, then standing back and speaking to someone else in the room.

Jared was aware of Axel still talking to him and then Logan and Hal, but his own attention was fully focused on the chamber beyond. Now he saw a second person come into view.

He recognized the girl, though he couldn't remember her name. She was the Physician's niece and apprentice. Her hair was the most extraordinary color—a deep coppery red, which made him think of the trees in the palace gardens, dressed now in their autumn finery. The girl was making studious notes as her uncle made his observations. Elias Peck had been too engrossed in his work to acknowledge those at the threshold of the chamber, but now the girl looked up from her notebook and her lively gray eyes met Jared's. She smiled at him. It was an encouraging but sad smile, as full of warmth as the morning sun.

He nodded to her. She returned the gesture then lifted her pen again and resumed noting her uncle's comments.

"So we're agreed, then?" Jared now heard Axel saying.

"I'm sorry," Jared said, realizing his attention had drifted. "What exactly did we agree?"

Axel's dark eyes returned to his cousin. "That the messengers will also send word of when to come to the palace for your speech tomorrow. That Logan will confirm Prince Anders's death and then hand the floor over to you for a few well-chosen words. I believe that the Poet has written the speech for you?"

"I've simply jotted down some ideas," Logan interjected. Jared had other, more pressing concerns.

He turned squarely toward Axel. "I'll see my brother's body now," he said.

"Absolutely," Axel said. "As soon as Elias has concluded his initial examination, I'll send someone to find you."

"I'd prefer to see him now," Jared said.

Logan smiled warmly at him. Jared was starting to notice that the Poet was given to smiling warmly—especially when he wanted something.

"Your Highness," Logan said, "your mother asked me to bring you to her."

"My mother?" Jared said.

Logan nodded. "I believe I mentioned that she and Edvin are with Silva. I think it would be most comforting for each of them to see you now. We are, after all, not only confronting the assassination of a prince but the death of a husband, brother and son." The Poet closed his eyes for a moment. "I apologize," he said. "I hardly need to say such things to you, Your Highness."

Jared hesitated. There was undoubtedly truth in the Poet's words. "I'll go to my mother in a moment. It's important to me to see her and Edvin and Silva."

As Logan nodded, gently, Jared turned his head. "But

first, I will talk to the Captain of the Guard. *Alone.*" Against all his own expectations, there was authority in his voice. He sensed it and he could tell the others did too. He wasn't sure which of them was more surprised.

"Of course," Axel said, as if it had never been up for debate. "Logan, I suggest you wait here with Hal. Prince Jared, shall we step into the library? We can talk privately there." He gestured to a door farther along the corridor.

Nodding decisively, Jared walked past Hal Harness and Logan Wilde to the doorway. He sensed he had won his first battle. It was a small victory but a victory nonetheless.

FOUR

The Prince's Library, the Palace

"I DON'T WANT TO SEEM CONDESCENDING, COUsin," Axel said, as he ushered Jared into the library, "but you're handling everything remarkably well so far."

"Thank you," Jared said, simultaneously comforted and disconcerted by his cousin's kind words.

"All our lives have been turned upside down by the shocking events that occurred before sunrise," Axel said. "But your life, your world, most of all."

It was an adjustment for Jared to find himself alone in Axel's company. They had never been enemies as such but Axel had never seemed to take Jared seriously—in spite of, or perhaps because of, his position as Anders's Edling. It was no secret that it was a role Axel had wanted for himself.

But now, at last, his cousin seemed to be talking to him as an equal.

"Can you tell me," Jared asked, "how did my brother die?"

Axel nodded. "The Physician's first reaction, when he saw the body, was that Prince Anders had been poisoned."

"Was there anything particular that made him say that?"

Axel's jaw tightened. "Let's just say there were certain physical signs that indicated deadly toxins." He paused. "But he still needs to carry out a full examination of the Prince's corpse."

Jared's eyes sought out Axel's. "But you're certain my brother was assassinated? This couldn't, for instance, have been a terrible accident?"

Axel took a breath. "Your brother was the ruler of a Princedom—a Princedom gaining in power over its neighbors. Neighbors who have, in the recent past, made no effort to disguise their intent to bring death and chaos to the very heart of Archenfield. As you know, we have spies in all key neighbor states—Eronesia, Paddenburg, even Woodlark. Based on the intelligence they have been sending, it seems very unlikely indeed that Prince Anders might have died an accidental death. Your brother delivered peace to Archenfield but perhaps it was not the lasting peace he promised us." He shrugged. "But I am sure Elias will consider every possibility."

Jared shook his head. "I still can't believe that he's dead, let alone that someone could have killed him."

Axel nodded. "I feel the same way, Prince Jared. But, as popular as Prince Anders was here in Archenfield—and as strong as the alliance achieved with Woodlark by virtue of your brother's marriage—still we should not delude ourselves into thinking that the Prince did not have enemies." He paused, adding in a soft but nonetheless ominous tone, "And now that you are Prince of All Archenfield, you inherit those enemies, just as you inherit his robes and the crown of state."

"But who specifically could have killed my brother?" Jared asked. "And why?"

"It's too soon to answer that question conclusively," Axel said. "But I'm convinced of one thing. The Prince's assassination was planned from outside Archenfield."

This statement, made with extreme confidence, opened up many other questions in Jared's mind. But before he could ask them, Axel had resumed speaking.

"This is all being investigated, as we speak," Axel reassured him. "My teams will work night and day and they won't rest until we have an answer—for you and our family and for all of Archenfield. We *will* find Anders's killer. The Blood Price will be paid." His eyes bored into Jared's. "I promise you now, as your Captain of the Guard, this threat will be swiftly lifted from the Princedom and you will be free to commence your rule in peace. If, as I suspect, further plots are to be hatched in foreign courts, they will be stillborn. History will not repeat itself." His hand came to rest on Jared's shoulder. "I promise I will keep you safe."

Jared was touched by his cousin's words and reassured by the sentiment underpinning them. Nonetheless, he felt suddenly vulnerable.

"As I'm sure is blindingly obvious to you," he confided in Axel, "I feel totally unprepared for all this. It's stupid, isn't it? I've been Anders's Edling for two years. On some level, I must have known this was a possibility."

Axel's face did not show shock or even surprise. "I can quite believe that," he said. "Speaking personally, I imagined that Prince Anders's rule would be as long as Prince Goran's. And I expected a child of Anders to succeed him, not one of our own generation."

Jared smiled ruefully. "In so many ways, you'd have been a better choice of Edling than I. I hope the fact my brother chose me won't come between us now."

Axel shook his head, his eyes making direct contact with Jared's. "It was Prince Anders's decision to make, just as now it must be you who decides the right Edling to secure the future of the Princedom."

There was a poorly disguised note of coercion in Axel's words, and also one of unbridled desire. Jared felt keenly just how much Axel must want to be made his Edling. He waited, curious to see if his cousin might push the case further. He did not.

"I need you, Cousin Axel," Jared told him now. "I don't know how either the Twelve, or the people of Archenfield, will react to having a sixteen-year-old on the throne. You've so much more experience than I of how the Princedom works."

"All my experience is at your disposal," Axel said. "Like the rest of the Twelve, my first duty is to help you rule. But I am doubly bound to you. We belong to the same family. My family name is Blaxland and yours Wynyard, but we are two closely twining branches of the same ancient tree. You are my Prince, but you are also my brother. If you are under attack, I am under attack. If you bleed, I bleed."

"Thank you," Jared said, feeling a small release of tension, "for these words and kindnesses and for everything you are doing." His eyes met Axel's. "The very moment you have news of my brother's assassin, I want to know. Whatever the hour, come and find me."

Axel nodded. "One small piece of advice for you, Cousin Jared. Seize whatever space this day allows you to gather yourself together, for much will be asked of you in the coming hours and days. I will give you all the support you require, but try to summon up what strength you can from within." He put his hand once again on Jared's shoulder. "If your brother or father were still here, I think that's what they would want to say to you. Since they cannot address you now, these words, of necessity, come from me. We are their heirs, Cousin Jared. We will honor their names and, when called upon, match their heroic deeds."

FIVE

The Low Gallery, the Palace

HAL HARNESS, CHIEF BODYGUARD TO THE PRINCE, strode down the gloomy corridor. The sun had long since made its ascent, but it remained dark in the low-lying recesses of the palace. It was eerily quiet, as if it were the middle of the night when in fact it was the middle of the morning.

The torches on either side of the passageway had been lit and the crackle of their flames cut through the silence. Their flickering light cast shifting shadows on the stone floor as Hal continued on his way toward the corridor's end. His eyes were fixed on a heavy wooden door, reinforced with iron, up ahead.

Had anyone seem him, they would have formed the impression of a creature of utter confidence and unwavering conviction, a creature used to danger, in both confronting it and imparting it. People often made that assumption about Hal Harness, on account of his position at the Prince's Table but also on account of his obvious physical strength. It was an understandable mistake to make, but a mistake nonetheless.

As Hal's eyes zeroed in on the door, he felt his heart beating just a little too fast. "Calm yourself," said the voice inside his head. He took a steadying breath accordingly, then reached out to try the door.

It was unlocked and, checking once more to reassure himself that he had not been followed, he pushed the door open and stepped inside the palace armory.

The light was as scant in here as out in the corridor, with no windows but only row upon row of metal to reflect the glow of the central iron candelabra. Hal closed the door behind him. As he did so, he heard the sound of footsteps from deeper within the room. His eyes searched through the darkness and found Axel Blaxland, turning toward him, the handle of a double-headed axe gripped between the fingers of his left hand.

They stood there for a moment: Axel in attack pose, the whites of his eyes reflecting the sharpened steel in his hands. Hal stepped forward, weaponless, until he was standing directly before the other man. Smiling, Axel lifted the blade of the axe to Hal's neck. "It would be easy enough," he said with a chuckle, then stepped back and dropped the axe down through his hand, letting its twin heads rest on the stone floor.

Hal nodded. "It would be easy enough," he repeated. His eyes met Axel's. "I'm glad to have found you, sir. I've searched for you all over the palace."

"Should have started your search here," Axel said. "I often come here to think. There's something tremendously calming about all this cold, sharp metal."

Some of the tension in Hal's face dissolved. He found himself smiling. It said plenty about Axel Blaxland that he found sanctuary in a room devoted to instruments of torture and bloodshed.

"So," Axel said. "What can I do for you, Hal?"

Hal stepped closer still. "We need to talk," he said. "I didn't feel I could bring it up earlier."

Axel's eyes were like hot coals—intensely dark with sparks of light. "Bring what up?" he asked. "Be specific, Hal."

"About Prince Anders's murder," Hal continued.

Axel nodded. He turned and walked a short distance away, returning the axe to its place on a wooden rack. Then he walked along the racks, his hand brushing the hilts of other weapons, pausing as a particular sword seemed to draw his interest. Hal waited patiently for Axel's attention to return to him. At last, Axel's eyes turned to his. "Well?" he said, as if it were Hal and not he himself who had slowed their conversation.

"I didn't kill him," Hal said.

His words seemed, to him at least, to echo around the room, the sound bouncing from the face of one weapon to the next.

It was Axel's turn to smile. "I know you didn't," he said. "Anders was most likely poisoned, as I'm sure you know. And poison was never part of our plan, was it?"

"No," Hal said.

"Well then," Axel said. Reaching forward, he took the sword in his hand, slicing through the air at an invisible adversary.

Hal waited for Axel to still the sword, then continued. "I'm confused," he said.

"Confused?" Axel raised his left eyebrow.

"Was Anders's death part of the plan?"

Axel thought for a moment, then nodded. "Yes, of course, Anders's death was always part of the plan. First Anders, then Jared. You know how it goes. We prune the unwanted branches of the Wynyard tree. Nothing like a good bit of pollarding." He paused. "You're looking more confused than ever, Hal."

"I am," Hal confessed. "We had a plan. And now I'm not sure exactly what you're telling me."

Axel smiled again. "Ask me another question. Be specific!"

"Did you kill him?"

"No," Axel said.

"Did you instruct someone to kill him?"

A pause. Another smile. Then, "No, I didn't. Well, *of course*, I did. I instructed you. But, as must now be as clear to you as it is to me, someone beat us to it."

"I see," Hal said.

"It's quite amusing, don't you think?" Axel said. "And undoubtedly useful."

Hal's head was spinning. "Do you know who killed him?"

Axel shook his head. "Not yet. But, as I assured Prince Jared earlier, I have all my best investigators working on the case. It shouldn't be long before we weed out the culprit. And then..." He lifted the sword once more but did not complete the sentence.

"And then what?" Hal asked. "Do we resume Plan A at that point?"

"Plan A?" Now it was Axel who seemed puzzled.

"I mean," Hal said—before Axel could instruct him once more to be specific—"do you want me to proceed with the murder of Prince Jared?"

Axel looked utterly horrified at the thought. "No!" he said. "Murder Prince Jared? What a monstrous thing to say!" He couldn't hold back the smile pushing at the corners of his mouth. "No, we mustn't let anything happen to Cousin Jared. At least not until he has made me his Edling. And until we've discovered who else is in this game."

"And then?" Hal persisted.

Axel dropped the sword to his side. He stepped closer to Hal and rested his hand on the bodyguard's shoulder. "One step at a time, eh? A happy coincidence has saved us from having to sully our hands. Now we need to see how this situation plays out."

Hal shook his head. "This is all a game to you, isn't it?"

Axel's eyes narrowed. "Oh no," he said, darkly. "This is not a game. It's the most important thing in the world."

After another long pause, during which Axel seemed lost in thought, Hal cleared his throat. "What should I do now?" Hal asked him.

"You're the Prince's Bodyguard," Axel said, coming to and squeezing Hal's shoulder amiably. "Do your duty. Guard and protect him. Don't let him out of your sight for so much as a second. If the Prince goes for a piss, I want you there, watching his back. Nothing must happen to Jared, you hear me? Not so much as a scratch across that milky white face of his. Certainly not until he has named me as Edling. You understand, Hal?"

"Yes, Axel," Hal said, nodding. "I understand."

"That's good," Axel said, withdrawing his hand from Hal's shoulder. "I'm glad I was able to clear up your confusion. Now you'd better be going. Who knows what dangers could befall the Prince of All Archenfield while you and I stand here, gossiping like scullery maids. We have an assassin to catch."

SIX

The Queen's Quarters, the Palace

A MUSCLED, SCAR-FACED MEMBER OF THE HOUSE-
hold Guard was stationed at the door to Jared's mother's
chamber, sword at the ready. Jared got the message, loud
and clear: the Captain of the Guard was doing everything
in his power to demonstrate he had palace security under
control and there was no further risk of attack. But Jared
also knew that Axel could position a guard at the door of
each and every royal chamber if he chose to—assuming he
had enough foot soldiers to deploy in this way—but that
such a show of force didn't for one second take away from
the fact that someone *had* infiltrated the fortress and gotten
close enough to Prince Anders to assassinate him. And that
someone might still be within the inner sanctum, preparing
to launch the next attack. Although, as Jared thought about

it, it seemed far more likely that just as the assassin had effortlessly penetrated the innermost reaches of Archenfield, so too had he or she now slipped away. Prince Anders was dead. Mission accomplished. Game over.

These dark thoughts prompted Jared to gruffly bark at the guard. "Let me through!"

The hulking guard stepped briskly aside and, bowing low, began offering up words of consolation. He found himself voicing them to Logan Wilde, however, as Jared had pushed past into the chamber, where he was confronted by a vivid tableau of grief.

His brother's young widow, Silva, sat at the foot of his mother's four-poster bed, trembling. Queen Elin, Jared's mother, sat on Silva's left side while on her right was perched Jared's fourteen-year-old brother, Edvin. Jared had no reason to doubt that his mother and brother had been doing their utmost to comfort Silva. It was equally clear that they were failing in this mission.

He could see the obvious relief in his mother's and brother's faces that he had come to find them. Perhaps they thought he might rescue them from the impossible task of comforting Silva. He noticed that Silva had not raised her eyes to see who had come in: her gaze remained fixed on the intricately woven carpet on which her stockinged feet rested. It occurred to Jared that he had not seen his sister-in-law's feet bared like this before. Usually she was clad in the most elaborate shoes in court, but he saw that these had been removed, or discarded. Feeling somewhat uneasy, as if he shouldn't be witness to such a sight, he let his eyes linger on her feet. They seemed tiny—like those of a child or of one of the dolls that Cousin Koel had once devotedly carried around with her.

"I'm so sorry," Jared said, cautiously moving a step further into the room.

Now, at last, Silva glanced up. Her face had always been pale, but this morning it was as white as the bark of birch trees and rain-slick with tears. Seeing Jared, she shuddered. What state must she be in that just the sight of her dead husband's younger brother made her start? But, to Jared's surprise, Silva's initial shock rapidly faded and a smile broke across her sharp cheekbones. Slipping her hands free from Elin's and Edvin's grasps, she rose to her feet. Something in the way she did so reminded Jared of one of Nova Chastain's birds about to take wing. There was, undeniably, something avian about Silva, though she was surely more akin to a dove or a nightingale than the more predatory falcon.

Before he knew what was happening, she had thrown herself at him and wrapped him within her arms. Trapped there, Jared retained the image of Silva as a bird, imagining himself caught within the span of her delicate yet powerful wings. Silva clung to him as though he were the only piece of rock preventing her from falling from a very great height, her slender fingers digging into the flesh of his biceps. It was painful, but he did not try to wrest himself free. Instead, he glanced down at her face, finding it now strangely serene.

"You came back!" he heard her say. "You came back for us!"

Jared smiled tenderly at Silva, mainly because he was unsure what else to do. But then he heard his mother's strident voice, growing in volume and spiraling through the room like smoke.

"She thinks he is Anders! See how her grief tips into madness?"

Silva had buried her face in Jared's chest and he was able to look over the honey-gold crown of her head into his mother's and brother's troubled expressions.

"Jared looks nothing like Anders," Elin continued. "He never has. Jared takes after my family, the Blaxland line. Why, you might take him and Axel for brothers." Now, she turned to Edvin. "Not you though. You have the Wynyard coloring and build. You, your father and Anders—all hewn from the same ancient rock. Not Jared though. Why would she mistake Jared for Anders and not you?"

"I don't know!" Edvin shook his head, frowning at his mother. "What does it matter anyway? She's clearly deeply distressed. It's natural enough. I just wish there was more we could do to help."

What you can do is help pry this poor girl off me, Jared thought but did not say. Silva's fingers were still pinching his flesh, but it wasn't that so much as the weight of her that disconcerted him. Not her physical weight, of course, but the weight of her need, which seemed just as tangible. Surely she didn't genuinely believe him to be Anders, come back from the dead?

Her face burrowed farther into his chest, as though she were journeying ever more deeply into the delusion.

"Come now." It was Logan's soft voice. The Poet had come to Silva's side and was reaching out his elegant, almost feminine hands to her shoulders. "Come, Silva. This is not Prince Anders. It's his brother Prince Jared."

The Poet's words were as gentle as his touch, but now Silva shuddered once more and withdrew her grip, staggering backward in horror and the renewal of her grief. It seemed for a moment as if she might fall. Edvin surged forward, ready to catch his fragile sister-in-law.

"You're Jared," Silva said, observing him anew. Her voice was discordant, like that of an infant still unfamiliar with the proper cadence of language. "You're not Anders."

Jared knew that many others would repeat those three words in the days and weeks to come: even if they did not speak them, they would certainly think them. He might be the Prince—he might wear the crown of Archenfield—but he was *not* his brother. Already he knew that every time he heard or observed the sentiment, he would be brought back to this chamber and to the disappointment in Silva Lindeberg Wynyard's painfully beautiful eyes. He realized that he had already failed on some level—simply by not being his brother.

As Edvin and Logan settled Silva back onto the bed, Jared found that he was now trembling. He was unsure if it was his own grief for his brother beginning to express itself physically, or if Silva had left the imprint of her feelings upon him.

He was relieved to find his mother approaching. She reached out her arms, her dark sleeves enfolding him like night, and he stepped gratefully into the circle she made. But, even as she embraced him, it was clear that she was biting back her own grief and expected him to do the same. There was nothing soft or nurturing in his mother's embrace. Nor had there ever been. He and Edvin had joked on more than one occasion that they might as well hug one of the trees in the forest for all the human comfort they could derive from their mother.

Now Elin drew back and, placing her hands on his shoulders, signaled her retreat from personal matters, in favor of those pertaining to the Princedom.

"There is much to be done," she said, her voice familiar in its steeliness. "We must all be strong."

Jared found himself nodding and matching the strength of his mother's tone. "Yes, I agree. We must do everything we can to understand what happened to Anders—and how such a thing *could* happen, deep within the heart of Archenfield. We must act swiftly to eliminate any further danger to the court."

His mother nodded encouragingly. "There is to be a meeting of the Twelve upon the hour. We must both be there. Edvin too."

"That's not strictly necessary," Logan said. He had consigned Silva to Edvin's care and had now joined the others in the center of the chamber.

Jared turned to the Poet. "What do you mean? Not strictly necessary?"

Logan's tone was reassuring. "One of the purposes of the Twelve is to take care of the running of the Princedom at a time like this," he said. "There are protocols, even for such horrific and unprecedented circumstances as these." His head turned to include Edvin in his next comment, but Logan's bright eyes soon returned to Elin and Jared. "You are a family and you have suffered a terrible loss. You should take whatever time you need to help begin to close the wound." His voice dropped to little more than a whisper—

still it retained its force. "Silva's grief is rather more evident, but I know you must all be feeling the same sense of loss at Prince Anders's passing. The Princedom will wait while you mourn."

Jared was persuaded by the Poet's words, but it seemed his mother was not. "The Princedom will *not* wait," she said. "When you occupy our position, it's the mourning that must wait." Jared realized uncomfortably that her words were primarily directed at him, not Logan. "Archenfield and its citizens have expectations that must be met. It's the price we pay for the privilege of power." She glanced back to Logan. "Be assured we *will* be at the meeting."

Jared found himself drawing strength from his mother's iron resolve. She was wise, he realized, in ways he himself had yet to learn.

The four chimes of the Woodsman's Bell struck.

"Time has moved on more swiftly than we anticipated. The meeting is about to commence and we must be there." Elin turned to Jared. "You should change out of your hunting clothes but be quick."

Jared glanced down at the commingled traces of stag's blood and vomit on his boots. He suspected that was what his mother was referring to, though she hadn't said so in so many words.

"Come, let's find you some robes of state. You are Prince of All Archenfield now. Anders lives on in you."

"No," said a small but potent voice behind them.

They turned to find that Silva had risen to her feet and stood facing them, her eyes bright.

"What's that you say, child?" Elin asked.

Silva's eyes had a new determination about them. "Anders lives on in *me*."

"What exactly do you mean?"

Silva smiled sweetly, but she did not answer with words. Instead, she simply raised a delicate hand and placed it upon her belly.

SEVEN

The Council Chamber, the Palace

LOGAN WILDE HAD POSITIONED HIMSELF SEV-
eral paces ahead of the royal party as they entered the Council Chamber. Jared followed him in—flanked on one side by
Edvin and, on the other, by their mother. The others were
already there—the eleven remaining members of the Council
of Twelve were gathered around the imposing Prince's Table.

The meeting, Jared observed, already appeared to be well
under way. This fact had not escaped Logan Wilde's notice
either. As voices swiftly hushed and all eyes turned toward
the new arrivals, Logan addressed Axel Blaxland, who was
standing in prime position at the head of the Prince's Table.

"So you've chosen, once again, to break with protocol?"
Logan remarked. "Starting a meeting of the Twelve without
the Prince."

Axel's thick hands tightly gripped the top rail of the chair in front of him. "I wonder, Logan, is that what's really bothering you? Or are you in a lather because we started without *you*?"

"I *am* responsible for handling crises," Logan said, his voice every bit as commanding as the Captain of the Guard's.

"We are *all* responsible for handling crises," Axel countered. "As the Poet, your specific role is to find the right words to convey what we decide here to the court and the world outside."

Jared knew that it was neither the beginning nor the end of this particular argument, though he hadn't noticed such obvious friction between Logan and Axel before. He wondered—had it always been the case, but he had never troubled to notice? Now that the Twelve reported to him, he would need to pay much better attention.

Once again, he was grateful to hear his mother take command of the situation, addressing her nephew Axel with vinegary tones.

"It's a matter of debate whether you should have begun this meeting without the Poet." She stepped forward to the foot of the table so that although she was standing at one end and Axel at the other, all eyes were on her. "But it's a matter of decorum that you should have waited for the new Prince to take his chair."

At these words, there were nods and sighs along both sides of the table.

"She's right, of course," Jared heard Father Simeon say.

"We were just doing what we are required to do," protested Emelie Sharp, the Beekeeper. "Addressing the situation."

The Beekeeper was the youngest of the Twelve. Jared knew that she often kept her counsel but, when she did proffer an opinion, it frequently arrived with a sting.

"By 'situation,'" Elin snapped back, "you mean the assassination of my son, your Prince?" As Emelie's face flushed red, Elin turned to address the whole table. "Yes, well, if you had all been managing things as you should have, we wouldn't be faced with this 'situation' now." Her furious eyes settled upon Axel. "I'd have thought you'd have been only too grateful for my help."

Axel nodded, smiling—with little trace of warmth—at his imperious aunt. "We are always grateful for your help, Queen Elin. You have so much...experience to bring to the table." As Elin's eyes narrowed at the implied insult, Axel forged ahead. "And now perhaps you and Cousin Edvin would like to take your seats?" He gestured toward the dais.

"Certainly," Elin said, adding before she moved, "and perhaps you would like to claim your own seat so Prince Jared can take the Prince's Chair?" As her own barb found its mark, Elin took Edvin's hand and they approached the dais.

Attention in the room was now divided between Axel and Jared. Jared found himself hesitating at the foot of the table. More than any other object within the palace, the Prince's Table symbolized the Princedom and how it was run. The vast table had been hewn, centuries ago, from the sturdiest of Archenfield oaks and its age and solidity were a testament to the strength of Archenfield's government throughout the long and often turbulent history of the nation.

Several centuries previously, fourteen titles had been carved into the surface of the oak and hot pewter had been poured into the lines of the inscriptions. The nameplates, which designated the correct position at the table for key members of the court, were as clear today as the day the pewter had been set. Jared stared down at the words "The Edling." This marked the place, at the foot of the table, where he had sat at Council meetings for the past two years. Each place around the table bore a similar script, designating the correct position for the key members of the court. Currently, three seats remained empty—"The Edling," "The Captain of the Guard" and "The Prince." Jared gazed up the length of the table, noting how Axel's hands were still tightly gripping the Prince's Chair. Jared smiled to himself. His cousin could not have made his position any clearer. Axel Blaxland was not even the Edling, yet already he had his sights set even higher.

Filled with sudden purpose, Jared strode around the

perimeter of the table until he was standing shoulder to shoulder with Axel. Axel's hands still rested on the intricately carved cresting rail at the top of the chair. It seemed as if another impasse had been reached. Jared was unsure how to break it. Fortunately, he did not have to. Smiling at his cousin, Axel drew back the chair. "Please, Prince Jared, take your rightful seat," he said, willingly relinquishing his hold.

As Jared sat down for the first time in the Prince's Chair, he was suddenly aware of all the others rising to their feet. This they did in unison, quite soundlessly. He noticed too that his mother and brother, up on the dais, were also now on their feet. Jared was in no doubt he was the chief focus of the room. He had a sudden awareness that, from then on, he would always be the chief focus of every room he entered. It was not a comfortable epiphany.

"Thank you," he said, gesturing for them all to sit down. It felt strange to be sitting at the opposite end of the table from before. Staring down past the empty chair—waiting upon his decision to nominate his own Edling—his eyes were drawn to the vast mural on the wall beyond. He had been aware of the formidable painting before, of course, but this was the first time he had ever truly engaged with it. The mural told Archenfield's story, from its tempestuous beginnings to the peace brokered by his brother Anders's succession. He realized now that Anders's eyes must have scanned the same mural every time he had taken his seat at the Prince's Table. Had his brother, with his innate sense of entitlement, drawn comfort from this image? Jared could imagine Anders, unfettered by self-doubt, congratulating himself on the decisive victory over Eronesia. Anders had always felt himself to be preordained as the latest and greatest Prince of All Archenfield. Jared, however, found the mural intimidating. It made him feel as though the eyes not only of those in the room but of each and every one of Archenfield's previous rulers were scrutinizing him. Doubtless, his value had risen, almost alchemically, today—but his true worth was yet to be determined.

Jared was aware that the others in the room were now waiting on his lead. He knew that he had to take some kind of control—for his own sake as much as theirs. He cleared his throat. "There are urgent matters to address. Axel, perhaps you could summarize for the latecomers to this meeting where you had gotten to before our arrival?"

Axel, alone of the assembly, had remained on his feet, though now at least his hands gripped the back of his own designated chair. He nodded to acknowledge Prince Jared's question. "I was informing the others of what we have done to make safe the Princedom and seek out your brother's assassin." He paused. "Working outward, the palace buildings and grounds are all being searched."

"Yes," Elin noted in a piercing whisper to Edvin. "It's true one can't walk from one chamber to another without encountering a member of the Household Guard, dagger at the ready."

Ignoring his aunt's latest aside, Axel pressed on, "Our guards have extended through the grounds and beyond." He glanced at Jonas Drummond, the Woodsman, who picked up his cue.

"My team and I have activated the traps within the forest. Rest assured, it will not offer any fugitive safe haven. Quite the reverse."

There was the flicker of a smile on Axel's face as he continued, "Quite so. And the borders are all locked down too." He was addressing the information directly to Jared. "Nova sent one of her falcons to each of the gatekeepers as soon as we made the discovery..."

Elin cleared her throat. "Can you remind us all what time that was?"

"Just before sunup," Axel answered, without bothering to meet her gaze.

"So much time has passed already," Elin said. "Do you feel confident you have closed down every possible escape route?"

Nova spoke up. "I sent out my falcons, as the Captain of the Guard commanded me to—one to each of the border gates. They carried a message to lock down the borders and take all appropriate actions."

"Yes, well, that's very impressive," Elin said, somewhat dismissively. "Though I'm starting to form the impression that these actions were taken *before* word was sent to your new Prince. I realize we are in a state of emergency, but all the more reason to adhere to the proper order of things."

Nova was silenced by Elin's stinging attack. Axel stepped back into the fray. It was to Jared he addressed his words.

"We keep meticulous records of every man, woman and child who crosses our borders. I have possession of the current ledgers and there have been no border crossings during the past week." He paused for effect. "Therefore, Prince Anders's assassin must still be here in Archenfield."

"Assuming that the reports are accurate," Elin interjected. "And that our defenses are as inviolable as you say."

"You may be confident on both counts," Axel told her.

Jared had a question for Elias Peck, the Physician. "Do *you* feel confident you will soon be able to tell us how my brother died?"

The Physician nodded. "Yes, I have already narrowed down the range of options considerably. As soon as this meeting is concluded, I will return to my rooms to conduct a postmortem."

"Thank you," Jared said. There was something in Elias

Peck's manner that instilled utter confidence. "For my part, I feel happy to give you leave to return to your work now. It seems to me that there is nothing more important at this moment than your examination of my...of the Prince's body."

To Jared's surprise, Elias looked anguished rather than relieved. Axel's voice was heard again. "This will not be a lengthy meeting, Prince Jared, and Elias is not merely the Physician but a key member of the Twelve. It is right and fitting that he should remain here to cast his vote on other matters that may arise."

Jared was unconvinced but he saw no value in further challenging the ways of the Council at this juncture. "There's really only one question on my mind," he said. "I feel sure it's the same for the rest of you too." He took a breath. "Who could have wanted my brother to die?"

Father Simeon nodded. "You're right. That is the question on each of our lips. And we must work together, tirelessly, to answer that question."

"We are pursuing several lines of inquiry," Axel said. "In my opinion, the most likely scenario is that this was an act of provocation from one of our rival states."

Father Simeon frowned. "But we are at peace with our neighbors," he said. His eyes alighted on the mural once again as he spoke.

"Yes," Axel agreed. "As far as we *know*, we are at peace

with our neighbor domains. Our spies in foreign courts have reported nothing to the contrary."

"Then perhaps," Elin said, "you need to push your spies to dig a little deeper and a lot faster."

"Indeed," Axel said. "Previously, the most likely adversary would have been Eronesia. It's hard to think they could be ready to mount a fresh attack, but with allies, perhaps? We can never dismiss the threat from Paddenburg—not since those two demented princes succeeded to the throne. Previously, we might also have expected aggression from Woodlark but, for obvious reasons, that no longer seems a possibility."

"We shouldn't rule them out," Hal Harness said.

Jared's eyes turned to Hal, now his Chief Bodyguard. It was Hal's first contribution to the discussion.

The Prince shook his head. "I think we can safely conclude that Anders and Silva's marriage brought an end to all enmity between us and Woodlark." He frowned. "But, as I say, to the best of our knowledge, aren't we at peace with all of our neighbors?"

Axel nodded. "Yes, but Prince Jared, I'm afraid that peace is not guaranteed forever. This act—your brother's murder—could signal the beginning of a new threat."

Elin took the floor once more. "At one time or another, we've had to take arms against each and every one of our neighbors." She pointed to the mural. "Look there, if you need evidence that battles have always been a thread in the tapestry of our homeland."

Axel nodded somberly. "That time may have come once again."

"So be it." Elin was resolute.

Jared shook his head, feeling unsettled. "It seems strange, don't you think? In the two years that I have taken my seat at this table, we have often talked of our relationships with neighbor states. Under Prince Anders's leadership, much was done to cement the peace he won for Archenfield."

"You're right," Kai Jagger spoke up. "A political assassination would be strange now, given the state of our foreign relations." He paused. "But if Prince Anders was not murdered for political reasons, then why... and by whom?"

Emelie Sharp attempted to answer him. "Perhaps the answer lies closer to home. Perhaps the murder was motivated by personal reasons."

Jared noticed the effect the Beekeeper's words had upon his companions. The air of discomfort within the room was now palpable. He nodded. "Cousin Axel, I think you should consider a personal motive for the murder. However unthinkable it seems... if only to rule out the possibility."

To his surprise, Axel did not protest. "You may rest assured that every line of inquiry will be pursued, Prince Jared. I don't think anyone could ever accuse me of taking a soft line as the Captain of the Guard. My teams and I will be asking uncomfortable questions of everyone we need to. Including all of you in this room." He looked around the table. "If you have something to hide, you have everything to fear."

Jared was as surprised as the others by this shift. Hadn't Axel himself assured him earlier that his brother's assassin had come from outside Archenfield? Axel's latest words prompted outcry along the Prince's Table. Everyone began talking over one another. As the volume of chatter continued to build, Jared realized that it was his job—and his alone—to call the meeting to order. "Please, everyone!" The force of his voice achieved the desired effect. He saw that Axel had more to say and gestured for him to continue.

"I realize, of course, that what I just said was not popular," Axel said. "I didn't mean it to be. We must face facts— Prince Anders is dead. And it's my job to find out who is responsible. While I remain convinced that the attack was launched from outside the Princedom, we have to face the uncomfortable truth that our enemies have allies within our borders. Perhaps even within the palace walls."

"I'm sure we all understand," Jared said. He could not keep the sadness from his voice.

"You may be quite certain that I will uncover the truth soon enough," Axel declared, warming to his theme. "The assassin will be identified and the Blood Price will be paid."

The Blood Price.

The three simple words hung heavily in the air. The company remained silent for a time.

Turning to Jared, Axel reverted to a more businesslike tone. "You need to think about what you will tell the people. It won't be long before they make their pilgrimage to the palace grounds."

"I've already taken care of that," said Logan Wilde. It was, Jared realized, the first time the Poet had spoken since the fracas at the beginning of the meeting. A silent Bodyguard was entirely to be expected, but a silent Poet less so. Jared wondered if Logan was still smarting from his earlier argument with Axel, or if the Poet's mind was engaged on other matters.

Now the Poet smiled as he addressed the Captain of the Guard once more. "Communications are my responsibility, as you so eloquently reminded me before."

"Well." Jared turned to Axel again. "Is that everything? Should we release everyone to go about their business?"

"Not quite," Logan said. "There is the matter of arranging Prince Anders's funeral and your coronation, Prince Jared."

"Yes, yes!" Axel waved his hand dismissively. It was clear that he was only too eager to go commence his investigation. "You managed it seamlessly enough two years ago. I have every confidence in your ability to do so once again."

"Before you all go," Jared said, "I just want to say that today is a terrible day for each and every one of us. I do not believe—I cannot believe—that my brother's assassin is in this room. Nevertheless, the Captain of the Guard must steer this investigation in the way he determines to be the best. But please, everyone, know that we will get through this. We will get through the dark hours and these difficult days ahead. Archenfield may be reeling now, but she will rise again. She always has. She always will."

He hoped his words had succeeded in lifting the spirits of the assembly, if only temporarily. Had he passed his first test and made them see him as a viable Prince, or did they remain unconvinced? He couldn't be certain. He glanced around, searching for friendly faces. Some were easily found—there could be no mistaking the genuine kindness in Lucas Curzon's eyes. Others were considerably harder to decipher—he'd spent quite some time out in the wilds of Archenfield with the Chief Huntsman. Yet Kai Jagger remained as much of an enigma at the Prince's Table as he did out in the Glen and the forest. Jared realized with a jolt that he did not yet know which of the Twelve he could trust but knew that he had better not leave it long to find out. In truth, every single one of the Twelve was a stranger to him.

EIGHT

The Queen's Quarters, the Palace

ASTA PECK WAS QUIETLY THRILLED THAT UNCLE Elias's latest request had brought her deep into the heart of the palace, alien territory to her. She adjusted her position in the tall wooden chair by the window, lifting the cushion and propping it higher against her back. That way, she could both be comfortable and maintain a better view of the young woman sleeping in Queen Elin's bed. *We're only separated by a few years in age*, Asta reflected. *But, in all other respects, we are worlds apart.*

Asta had always been fascinated by the beautiful Silva Wynyard and, now that she was in such rare close proximity, she found it hard to draw her eyes away. Although Asta resided within the court—though not in the palace itself— Silva had seemed to breathe different air to Asta. She possessed an innate grace. The combination of her fair skin and her sleek gold hair, whether worn in braids or hanging simply between her narrow shoulders, made her seem less a being of this world and something far more ethereal.

It's good that she's sleeping, thought Asta. Silva certainly needed to rest after the tortures the still-young day had inflicted upon her. Asta had been able to piece together the story through the patchwork of conversations overheard earlier in the Prince's chamber. According to these, Silva had been woken in the early hours by Prince Anders crying out in pain and then hammering on the door that connected their two chambers. When Silva had roused herself, she had found her husband in a state of intense distress, taking refuge by a corner post of his bed, raving about an array of terrifying beasts stalking his bedroom and blood cascading down the walls. He had described each animal to her in horrible detail—the slimy scales and lashing tongues, the gnashing teeth and needle-sharp claws. The descriptions were horrific and more fitting with one of Father Simeon's sermons about hell than any creatures glimpsed in the forest or mountains beyond.

Asta saw the bedclothes move at last and Silva roused herself, sitting up and blinking her eyes for a moment as she came to terms with her strange surroundings. Asta waited for a moment, then said helpfully, "You're in Queen Elin's chamber."

At these words, Silva's head turned toward her. "Who

are you? Why are you here? Do they think I can't be trusted to be alone?"

"No," Asta said reflexively. "No, my lady," she corrected herself, remembering Uncle Elias's stringent instructions regarding protocol. "They thought you might welcome some company."

Silva smiled softly. "In truth, I'm rarely alone. Such is life at court." She gestured to one corner of the room, where one of Elin's maids was quietly and methodically taking dresses from her closet—perhaps choosing an appropriate one for the mourning period. "But I do appreciate the gesture. Forgive me if I ask again—who are you?"

Asta rose to her feet at the same time that Silva placed her own feet on the floor. "My name is Asta, Asta Peck. I'm the Physician's apprentice."

Just as suddenly as Silva's eyes had found her, now her attention strayed elsewhere. A silk robe—sky blue, patterned with spring flowers—lay on the ottoman at the foot of Elin's bed. Perhaps one of Silva's own maids had brought it over from her chamber earlier. Asta noticed that Elin's maid had slipped discreetly out of the room. She was alone with the Prince's Consort.

Silva moved toward the robe but stopped just short of it, her hands at her side. It took Asta a moment to realize that she was expected to take the robe and help her companion into it. Silva was used to being attended to. *Do what-*

ever you can to make her feel comfortable. With Uncle Elias's words ringing in her ears, Asta lifted the beautiful robe and held it open so that Silva could slip her slender arms inside. Asta briefly wondered if she was expected to tie the sash for her but was relieved when Silva took it and knotted it herself.

"I've seen you before," Silva said, as she turned once more to face her.

Asta nodded, feeling pleased that Silva had remembered her. "I live with my uncle. We haven't met properly but—"

"I mean today." Silva cut her off sharply. "I saw you earlier today, in my husband's chamber." She sighed. "Before they strong-armed me away."

"That's right. I was helping Uncle Elias."

Silva's eyes widened. "Examining my husband's body?"

"Yes, my lady," Asta conceded, knowing that this admission was bound to lead to further questions. Most of which she was not permitted to answer.

"Do you know what killed him?"

Asta paused. "It's too soon to say for sure," she replied, quite truthfully. "Though it seems the Prince was poisoned." She knew her uncle had his suspicions as to which poison had been used, but he wanted more time to consider both the physical evidence and the useful testimony Silva herself had provided. The specificity of Prince Anders's hallucinations had excited Uncle Elias in that they had considerably narrowed down the range of possible toxins. But this was not the moment to inform Silva of these facts, nor was Asta the appropriate person to do so. Aware of Silva's gaze now burning into her, Asta scanned the room for a distraction. Her eyes alighted on a tea tray on a low table close by the chair she had been sitting in earlier.

"Shall I pour you some tea?" she asked Silva, moving forward to gauge the temperature of the cast-iron teapot. "It's still warm. And there's honey, from the palace hives."

"The hives are all closed up now," Silva mused, as if to herself. "The colonies won't produce again until the spring." Her eyes met Asta's, brimming with sadness. "The seasons are so important, don't you agree?" She glanced momentarily out the window, then back to Asta again. "Outside the trees are all aflame for autumn. But, in spite of the rich colors, this is the season of decline and death."

She paused. "And yet, out of death springs new life."

Silva looked knowingly at Asta. Unsure what she was being told, Asta nodded, encouraging her companion to continue. Thankfully, she did.

"You know, no doubt, that I am carrying my husband's child?"

No, she had not known that! Nor, to her best knowledge, did Uncle Elias. Asta was as shocked as she was exhilarated by Silva's remark. She knew though that she must react in a calm, measured way. She lifted the teapot and began pouring tea into a china cup. It did not escape her notice that the china was patterned with the crest of Archenfield. Fragrant steam spiraled up; the tea smelled delicious. She added a good measure of honey, watching the amber liquid cascade down from the ridged olive-wood spoon into the brew.

"I know it's only tea," she said, holding out the cup and saucer to Silva. "But it's hot and sweet and it might soothe your nerves just a little."

Her companion did not answer directly. Instead, her eyes became agitated as she glanced from the cup back to Asta. "How do I know you're not going to poison me? I don't know you. I don't know who you are."

Asta was keenly aware of how wildly Silva's emotions vacillated from one moment to the next. It was understandable, but she knew she needed to tread carefully for fear of further unsettling her companion.

"You do know who I am," Asta said gently. "I told you before. I'm the Physician's apprentice. My name is Asta Peck."

Silva seemed to receive this as if it were new information. "Are you trying to poison me, Asta Peck?"

"No!" Asta protested, more forcefully than she intended. But it was not unreasonable that Silva should feel such paranoia. Frankly, after everything she had endured in the past few hours, she had no cause to trust anyone. "Look, why don't I pour a cup for myself and we'll both drink?"

Silva lifted the china cup to her lips and took a sip. "To die today wouldn't be the worst option."

Asta found her hand trembling as she picked up her cup and saucer. "Please don't talk like that. I know how bleak things must seem to you now. But perhaps, in time, you will come to see that you still have everything to live for."

"How can you say that?" Silva asked, her eyes darting hungrily to Asta's face for any trace of hope, however faint, to be found there.

"You're going to be a mother," Asta said. "You're going to bring your husband's child into the world." She noticed that, as she said the words, Silva's hand moved instinctively to her belly—though there was no visible sign of her pregnancy. Nonetheless, the contact she made seemed to soothe her for a moment. Then her eyes filled with panic once again.

"Is there a sedative in this tea?"

Asta shook her head. "No. Sedatives aren't a good idea for women in your condition."

"I'm so tired," Silva said. "I'm fairly certain they gave me a sedative before."

Asta nodded. "Yes, you're right. That was unfortunate—but I'm not sure they knew." Seeing the alarm in Silva's eyes, she added, "It's nothing to worry about. One dose wouldn't be enough to do any real harm."

Silva looked at her curiously. "You seem to be something of an expert in medical matters."

Asta felt her cheeks flush red with embarrassment. "Goodness, no, my lady. But I am studying with my uncle. I'm his apprentice. It's why I came here."

"Came here?" Silva raised an eyebrow.

"From the settlements," Asta said. "My uncle needed an apprentice and my parents thought I'd have better prospects here than at home."

Silva did not respond to this directly, but something Asta had said had clearly gotten her thinking. "You're an exile," she said. "Like me."

"I suppose I am, my lady. But a happy exile." Her eyes met Silva's, realizing that they had more in common than she had initially thought. "I do miss my parents and our friends and neighbors, but I love it here. The court is such a beautiful place to live."

Silva sipped her tea, then smiled wistfully. "You've never visited Woodlark, have you?"

Asta shook her head. "Not yet, no. One day, I hope..."

"It's far more beautiful than Archenfield," Silva said. "I miss it...very much sometimes."

"Do you go back often?" Asta inquired.

Silva shook her head. "I haven't been back even once since my marriage to Anders."

"Why not?"

"A good question," Silva said. "Perhaps because if I had gone back, I might have been sorely tempted to stay. And, to be honest with you, I'm not sure my husband would have liked me to have left Archenfield. Not that he'd ever say such a thing, not in so many words."

Asta was disconcerted by Silva's confidences. Of course, Anders's widow was in an intense state of grief and it was easy to attach too much importance to random information. Nonetheless, there was an edge to her voice that made Asta think that perhaps the Prince's marriage had not been quite the fairy tale it had been portrayed as.

"Did Prince Anders know you were going to have a baby?" she found herself asking.

This question brought a sudden smile to Silva's face. "Oh yes!" she said. "He knew. It was to be our secret, we decided—for as long as possible. It wasn't easy for us to have a secret, not in this court. Like I said before, we were hardly ever alone."

Asta nodded encouragingly.

Silva took another sip of tea, then put down her cup. "I can't remember ever feeling so tired as this. Do you think it's the baby?"

"It might just as likely be the impact of your grief," Asta observed, as she put down her own cup. She had noticed such things before, back in the settlements, where death had been an all-too-frequent visitor. A fresh thought occurred to her. "Tell me, when did you last have something to eat?"

Silva shook her head. "I really can't say. The past few

days, I've felt so sick, I've not been able to keep anything down. At dinner, last night, I couldn't even put the food in my mouth." She smiled, her face brightening. "Anders ate my food, as well as his own. I didn't want anyone to know of my sickness, so he covered for me, whenever he could. He was very kind to me after he discovered I was pregnant. It wasn't only last night he ate my dinner..." Her voice trailed off. Then her beautiful face turned paler than ever. "Oh God, no..."

Asta knew what Silva was going to say before she next opened her mouth.

"Do you think someone was trying to poison me and Anders died instead?"

Asta shook her head, then reached out her hand and laid it on Silva's arm. "I don't think that's what happened, my lady." Unwittingly she had pressed her hand against the pulse in Silva's wrist and she could feel her heart's wild thrumming. "Lady Silva"—it was the first time she had spoken her companion's name and it seemed to make an impact—"no one had any reason to wish you ill."

Silva was trembling more than ever and tears coursed down her face. When she managed to speak again, her words were staccato. "How. Can. You. Know. That?"

Asta gripped her companion's wrist tightly. "I'm sure it's true. You have enough to contend with today. You mustn't torture yourself with additional worries. You have to look after yourself and your baby. That's what Prince Anders would want, don't you think?"

Tears streaming down her face, Silva nodded. "You're right," she said. "But I'm so alone here. I just need someone to help..."

"I'll help," Asta said, instinctively.

There was a knock on the door, but before Silva could answer, it opened and Queen Elin appeared in her chamber. Her face was flushed.

Asta rose swiftly to her feet and curtsied. "Your Highness."

Elin acknowledged her with practiced formality. "Thank you for taking care of Lady Silva in my absence," she said. "You may go now."

Asta glanced back at Silva. Their eyes met for the briefest of instants. Asta saw many things in Silva's eyes at that moment. Grief. Fear. Loneliness. But, to her surprise, the thing she saw above all else was the desire for friendship.

"Your uncle will be grateful for your safe return," she heard Queen Elin say. Asta nodded and, head down, slipped out of the chamber. As she departed, she heard the Prince's mother address her daughter-in-law.

"You look desperately tired, my dear. We must get you back into bed. Sleep is the best thing for you. Best for that precious cargo inside you too."

NINE

The Physician's Ice
Chamber, the Village

ASTA STOOD NEXT TO HER MOTIONLESS UNCLE
in the small frigid chamber below his main surgery, gazing
at the exposed and naked corpse of Prince Anders. She felt
an involuntary shudder—not because of her close proximity to the corpse but because of the bone-numbing cold.
Clutching her notebook in one hand, she brought her arms
across her chest, intent on retaining what body heat she
might. The room's temperature was regulated by blocks of
ice, harvested from the fjord during the winter months—
and, if supplies ran low, from the mountains beyond—and
insulated with straw. The exact same system was employed
in the kitchens to keep Vera Webb's food stores cool and
comestible.

Asta was no stranger to the Ice Chamber. Since arriving

in court to study at her uncle's side, she had accompanied him down here on several occasions. "If you really want to ponder the mysteries of life and death," he had told her, the first time he had led her down the narrow stone staircase, "you will only learn so much upstairs in my surgery. The deeper secrets of our existence are to be found down here."

Up above, the Physician's surgery was crowded with objects—ranging from medical and surgical implements to human and animal skeletons and diverse organs stored in jars of preserving liquid. On her first few nights in her uncle's house, Asta's tortured dreams had taken her back to the surgery and its collection of macabre curiosities. In contrast, though it was permeated by death, the Ice Chamber had not yet caused her a single sleepless night.

It had been Asta's job earlier to light a sufficiency of candles so that Elias Peck might proceed with his work: the chamber was a conical structure with no natural light—hardly surprising, as the majority of its wall area was underground. As she had lit each candle, a fresh patch of the sparse domed room had come into view. In stark contrast to the Physician's surgery, this chamber was almost entirely devoid of furniture or decoration. It was a confined space and, for this reason, Elias only kept things there that he needed to perform his work—whether it was simply preparing a body for the funeral rites or, as in this case, proceeding with a thorough examination of it.

With its minimal furnishings, there was nothing here to distract attention from the table in the center of the room, nor from the marble-pale body that lay sprawled upon it, as if in the depths of slumber.

Asta had seen several other bodies laid out on the Physician's slab—men and women, young and old. The dead and naked body of Prince Anders was both strikingly familiar and yet profoundly different. Asta had not had many direct interactions with the Prince in life, but she had certainly had good opportunities to observe him, as she had accompanied Uncle Elias on his rounds of duty in court.

Prince Anders had always seemed to her a dazzling, larger-than-life presence in the palace and its environs. In this way, he was quite different from Jared, though perhaps that would change now that the younger brother had assumed his place as Prince. Whereas Anders had never seemed so much mortal but rather a demigod on temporary loan to Archenfield and its people, there was something fundamentally human about Jared.

She gazed at Anders's inert forearm, studying the lines of his veins and muscle as if she were preparing to commence a sketch. Here was Anders brought down—literally—to the same level as his subjects. The exposed parts of his body—and almost all of it was exposed—revealed a young man at the pinnacle of physical fitness. She could see the lean, worked muscles in his chest, shoulders, arms and legs. The taut flesh spoke of days dominated by outdoor pursuits— riding, hunting and, when necessary, combat. In life, this body had given him a cloak of invincibility. But here, as Elias had promised her, the truth was revealed. And the truth was that, however impressive his physique, Prince Anders's body had not been strong enough to fight the poison administered by his assassin. *Do you know why you were killed?* the voice in her head asked him. *What secrets are you keeping, perfect Prince?*

"Look here," Elias suddenly said, addressing her for the first time. It was as if he had emerged from a trance. He was pointing toward Anders's right foot.

Unwrapping her arms from her body, Asta stepped closer to the table and followed the line of her uncle's pointing finger. She was shocked by the pure horror of what he was showing her. The flesh of Anders's big toe and the next two toes beside it was shriveled and blackened. The toes reminded her of morsels of meat left cooking too long over a fire. The toenails ranged in color from rust to a greenish yellow.

"Is that gangrene?" Asta asked.

Her uncle nodded. "It's surprising that it's already so developed," he observed.

"And is it the same on his other foot?" Asta inquired.

In answer, Elias stepped to the corpse's other side

and encouraged Asta to follow. The equivalent three toes on Anders's left foot were similarly desiccated and discolored.

"The poison would have caused this necrosis," Elias confirmed. "You remember, of course, what necrosis is?"

"Yes." Asta nodded, rising to the challenge. "The death of the tissue cells, due to injury, disease or failure of blood supply."

Elias, never quick to offer compliments, nodded with satisfaction. "Necrosis is indeed caused by lack of blood supply. The poison would have interfered fatally with Prince Anders's circulation. That's one certain cause of death." He paused, looking at her for a moment with irritation.

"Oh, sorry!" she said. "Would you like me to make a note of that?"

"Yes, that would be most helpful," he replied, unable or unwilling to keep the note of sarcasm from his voice. Suitably chastised, Asta made the note in her book.

When she had done so, she glanced up to find her uncle had moved to Anders's midsection. He appeared lost in thought once again.

"Does the gangrene, and how far advanced it is, help you to narrow down which poison was used?" Asta inquired.

For a moment, her uncle was silent, his hand reaching out to adjust the sheet, which already seemed to her like a shroud. Then he drew back to his full height and his keen eyes sought out hers. "Yes," he said, "I believe there are two possibilities."

Asta felt her heart race at this news. Her pen was poised on the notebook, ready to take down her uncle's findings.

"The first possibility is ergot."

Asta made a note, then glanced back up at her uncle. It seemed to her that he was waiting for her to say something.

"Ergot," she obliged. "A fungal parasite that infests cereal grains, especially rye."

Elias smiled softly. When he spoke, there was a rare note of tenderness in his voice. "Sometimes I worry if my brother would really be happy at the things I am filling your hungry brain with."

She was both surprised and pleased at the compliment but anxious to move on. "Does ergot also cause gangrene?"

"Yes," he confirmed. "The poison exerts a paralyzing effect on the sympathetic nervous system, leading to this and other circulatory problems. So one class of symptoms would begin with itchiness and lead on to burning sensations and ultimately, as we have seen, necrosis."

Asta nodded as she continued writing. "So that fits."

"Yes," Elias said. "And ergot causes a second set of symptoms...and this is where Silva's recollections may prove particularly helpful. This poison causes severe convulsions, accompanied by vivid hallucinations. Typically, these might include wild imaginings..."

Asta's heart was hammering again. "He thought he saw animals stalking the royal chamber. And then blood running down the walls."

"He *did* see them, Asta. Neither you nor I would have seen them, but to Prince Anders, they were completely real. Such was the power of the hallucination."

Asta nodded. "So the poison might very well be ergot," she said. "It seems like a very good fit."

Elias continued. "The other possibility is savin. That could certainly provoke necrosis, as well as other physical symptoms we can observe on the Prince's body." He pointed. "These blisters you see here, for example."

Asta scribbled a note furiously. "Savin is a plant, isn't it?" She couldn't resist showing off. "A species of juniper."

"Someone's been doing her reading." Elias nodded. "It is indeed a plant, a bitter plant that, in high doses, causes convulsions and vomiting—both of which we know, from the Prince's widow, Anders experienced prior to death."

Asta jotted down her uncle's latest observations. As she did so, she thought of Silva. Poor Silva. The mere fact that Anders had been taken from her was horrific enough, but in such a violent and degrading way.

"It may interest you to know, Asta, that there are some

less scrupulous physicians who employ savin to encourage miscarriage."

Asta froze at her uncle's words.

"I apologize," he said. "I never think of your having a sensitive disposition. It's easy to forget you are a girl...a sixteen-year-old girl, I mean."

At any other moment, Asta would have enjoyed seeing him in the throes of such awkwardness, but now her mind was working furiously.

"It isn't that," she said. "I was thinking of Lady Silva. You know, of course, that she is pregnant?"

Elias looked askance at his niece. "No, I did not know that. And, I wonder, how do you happen to be in possession of that information?"

"She told me before, when you sent me to sit with her."

"And you didn't think that, perhaps, it might be helpful to tell me?"

"I'm sorry," Asta said in a small voice, aware that this was his second rebuke in as many minutes. "I assumed that you would know. I mean she told me that she and Prince Anders were intent upon keeping the matter secret, but you are the court Physician. I felt sure that they would have confided in you."

Elias shrugged. His expression was not a happy one. "It appears not." His attention shifted away from Asta again and back to the corpse.

Asta's keen mind was racing now and she could not keep her thoughts to herself. "On account of her condition, Silva has been too nauseous to eat much over the past few days. In order to protect their secret, Prince Anders had been eating her food as well as his own."

Elias glanced up at her again. "Do you have a question?"

Asta nodded. "Could Silva have been the intended recipient of the poison, rather than Prince Anders?"

Elias's eyes narrowed, as they often did when he felt uncomfortable. Asta had another question for him and she knew that it was likely to make him feel still more ill at ease.

"What if the poison was not intended to kill her but merely to prompt her to miscarry?"

Elias held her gaze for a moment. It seemed to her that he might be giving her hypothesis careful consideration.

"I think that it is not for us to contemplate who was the intended victim or what provoked the attack. My job is to establish cause of death…"

"But," protested Asta, "surely our job…"

"*My* job," Elias's raised voice cut across her own, "is to establish cause of death. Your only job is to take notes so that we may hand them over to the Captain of the Guard, who I am reasonably convinced is more than capable of conducting this murder investigation without your colorful musings."

Even for her uncle, this was a rather severe outburst.

Asta supposed that the pressure of the situation might be revealing itself, but she couldn't help but feel that he was also angry that she had been privy to Silva's secret before him.

"We will confirm to the Captain of the Guard that Prince Anders's death was caused by poison, with both savin and ergot as strong possibilities."

"Aren't you tempted to go for one over the other?" Asta asked. She knew she was pushing the bounds of her uncle's patience and temper, but sometimes she just couldn't help herself.

"No," Elias said, firmly. "I find there to be sufficient cases to be made for either poison. I will leave my findings there and let the Captain of the Guard build *his* investigation accordingly."

"But," Asta persisted, already knowing she was going to regret it, "we don't know if the assassin was intending to kill Prince Anders or Silva or both of them. We don't know if he or she was merely attempting to cause Silva to miscarry but too strong a dose was administered."

To her surprise, Elias did not look flushed with fresh anger as she finished speaking. "You're right," he said. "Those are all valid questions. And there are more besides. Was the poison swallowed via tainted food or was it absorbed through the skin? There are some small lacerations on the Prince's leg, which may be accountable as wounds received while hunting. The poison could certainly have been administered through these—via an ointment, say, or a contaminated bandage. If so, it is likely to have had a much swifter impact than if it was in his food. Then again, there are some who take ergot in mild doses to relieve headaches. It is possible that the Prince did this and merely took too many doses himself. In which case, there was no assassin at all."

Asta found her head spinning with all these possibilities. She had thought, and expected, that her uncle's examination would narrow down the possibilities of what had occurred. Instead, it seemed that a veritable Pandora's box had been opened and her brain was full of dark, fluttering shapes, each signifying a different kind of evil.

She stared at her uncle, feeling powerless in the face of this dead end. He gazed back at her, amused rather than angry. "What's wrong?" he asked.

She fumbled for the right words. "I suppose I thought that the body would tell us why he died and we'd begin to solve the mystery, but it feels like, if anything, we've opened up an infinite number of possibilities."

Elias shook his head. "I told you before, Asta. It is my job to establish cause of death. This I have done, with help from you and Lady Silva." He glanced down at the Prince's corpse. "A dead body cannot tell us why it is dead but, with luck and a certain degree of knowledge and experience, it can tell us how it became so. Now we must depend upon the knowledge and experience of others to carry the investigation forward." He smiled. "I feel you exaggerate, by the way, when you say there is an infinite number of possibilities. Try to maintain perspective."

Sometimes, Uncle Elias was such a scientist. All right, so there was not an *infinite* number of possibilities, but he had himself identified a fair few. Asta couldn't help but dwell upon them. And, as much as she was beginning to sift through the possible scenarios now, she knew herself well enough to know that this was only going to get worse.

Her heart was thumping and she felt faintly sick; she knew exactly why. Somewhere deep inside herself, she had decided to solve the mystery of Prince Anders's assassination. And nothing and no one, from her uncle to the Captain of the Guard, was going to deter her from that path, wherever it happened to lead.

TEN

The Captain of the Guard's
Office, the Palace

KOEL BLAXLAND WAS CURLED UP IN THE WORN leather chair in the corner of her older brother Axel's office. In front of her was an intricately carved oak screen that she was able to look through, without being seen. This was not the first time she had secreted herself away there—it was a surprisingly cozy, and generally rather informative, bolt-hole. Still and silent, she watched as the door to her brother's office opened and her brother strode in, followed closely by their father.

"So how can I help you, Father?" Axel asked. Not only his tone of voice but every aspect of his body language revealed his impatience.

"I wanted to speak to you," Lord Viggo said, rubbing his beard as he often did when he was brooding over something or other. He walked over to a side table, atop which stood a decanter of aquavit, next to some glasses. He turned to Axel; his eyes—the same intense gray-blue—were bright. "Shall we have a drink?"

Axel shook his head, sharply. "I don't have time, I'm afraid. The Physician is due at any moment with his post-mortem report."

Lord Viggo smiled, reached for the decanter and poured two glasses of the liquor. He lifted one in his hand and took a hit of the drink, then handed the other glass to Axel. "As your grandfather Erik was fond of saying, one of the key lessons in life is identifying what is important and what is urgent. The two are not the same. Whatever other pressing business calls you, this conversation still falls into the important category." He clinked his glass against Axel's.

Axel set his glass down on the edge of his desk without drinking from it. "Father, I'm sorry to be blunt, but I really do need you to come to the point. We're in danger of being interrupted at any moment."

Careful not to make a sound, Koel leaned a touch closer to the screen. Watching her brother and father maneuver around each other was like observing wild beasts stalking one another in the forest.

Still refusing to be rushed, Lord Viggo drained his drink and smacked his lips. "It's impressive, don't you think?

Someone got right to the heart of the court in order to assassinate the Prince."

"Yes, Father, and it's my job to identify that person and ensure he, or she, pays the Blood Price. I must make safe the Princedom."

Lord Viggo nodded, rubbing his beard once again. "That is indeed, on the surface, your job. But, son, you must keep your eyes on the bigger prize."

Axel sighed. "Don't you think I know that?"

Lord Viggo winked at him and slapped his shoulder. "I never think it hurts to remind you. This unexpected situation is rich with possibilities for you. It's vital that you make the maximum capital out of these events. Every move you make now counts."

"I'm aware of that," Axel said. Koel could see the pressure of the situation etched across her brother's face. He was twenty-five years old, yet he looked as if he had all the worries of the world on his shoulders. In certain ways, she supposed, he did.

Lord Viggo brought his face up close to his son's. Axel grimaced—whether from their father's breath or his invasion of personal space, Koel was unsure—and stepped back a pace.

"This is the moment our family has been waiting for," Lord Viggo declared. "The moment of change. For too long my sister and her spawn have held sway in Archenfield.

And, tell me, what good has that done the Princedom? Two Princes dead in the same span of years. That's not stability by any measure."

"No," Axel agreed.

"The Wynyards have had their day and been proved unfit to rule. Once the crown is raised by the steadier hands of the Blaxlands, it will be strong enough to repel any attack." Lord Viggo grabbed his son by the arm. "All my hopes—the hopes of all your living family and your ancestors—rest in you, boy."

Axel carefully loosened his father's grip. "No pressure, then."

Lord Viggo laughed. "Ha! You thrive on pressure. Always have. You got that from me. Your mother is shockingly intelligent, cultured, but she's a softer creature—like your sister. They are like pearls, Axel—rare and precious. It's up to you and me, son—brutes that we are—to get the job done."

Koel frowned. It was no surprise to hear herself discussed and dismissed in such a fashion, but still it rankled. The worst of it was that she had no doubt her father thought he was paying her a compliment of the highest order.

A sudden rapping on the chamber door snapped all three of them to attention.

"That will be the Physician," Axel told Lord Viggo, seizing the empty glass from his father's grip. "Time to go." Marshaling his father toward the door, he barked, "Enter!"

Koel glanced toward the chamber door. Elliot Nash, Axel's thickset deputy, came in first, shaking hands with Lord Viggo. Nash was followed by Elias Peck and his apprentice, Asta, the niece who had arrived from the settlements some six months earlier. Koel surveyed the girl with interest. Asta Peck was sixteen—a year younger than Koel herself. She was pretty, albeit in a way more suited to the woods than the inner sanctum of the court. Asta's flamed-red hair made Koel think of raging forest fires.

"Thank you for the visit, Father," Axel said, as Lord Viggo lingered on the threshold. "I'll be sure to consider all your worldly wisdom."

"Do that," Lord Viggo said. Though clearly reluctant, he took his cue and departed the chamber. As the door closed, Koel returned her eyes to Asta.

It was evident that Elias had commissioned a new wardrobe for his niece. She was wearing an elegantly cut dress in the same silvery shade of gray as her eyes, with matching shoes. She looked smart enough, but Koel sensed that Asta felt constrained by the dress—in spite of her good looks, Asta Peck had the air of the wild about her. Koel imagined she'd be far more at home in breeches and boots.

Koel now turned her attention to the Physician. In his left hand, he appeared to be clutching his postmortem report. For now, though, it wasn't the papers that drew her interest so much as the way his hand shook slightly. It was a subtle movement but Koel Blaxland was adept at picking up on such things. It was what came from attending innumerable functions but never being asked for her opinion. *If you are intelligent,* Koel thought—and she knew without being overly arrogant that she had been blessed, or very possibly *cursed,* with a fair degree of intelligence—*then you have to devise your own ways to engage and sharpen that intelligence, even if others around you seem to have little use for it.*

"I've brought you the notes from my examination of Prince Anders's body." The Physician offered his papers to the Captain of the Guard.

"You didn't have to bring this to me yourself," Axel said, taking the folder from him and dropping it onto his desk. "I'm sure your little apprentice here could have done a perfectly adequate job."

Koel watched Asta bristle at Axel's words. He, of course, did not notice. She felt a moment's kinship with the Physician's niece.

"Given the importance of this case," she heard Elias say, "I wanted to deliver the notes myself." He cleared his throat. "And to talk through my findings with you."

Axel sat down at his desk and gestured for the Physician to take the chair on the other side. Asta and Nash remained standing. Axel riffled through the sheaf of papers, glanced at it and then lifted his head again. "So tell me, Elias, what *are* your findings?"

The Physician clasped his hands together. Koel noticed that his head twitched slightly as he spoke. "It's all there in my report, for you to read. I trust I have been sufficiently thorough."

Axel smiled at the Physician. "You always are most thorough, Elias," he said, the small smile swiftly fading. He tapped the papers. "I assure you I will read this from cover to cover. But why don't you fill us in on your main findings?"

Elias took a moment to gather his thoughts, and then began. "Prince Anders was poisoned," he said. "That much is certain."

Axel looked appropriately somber. Standing at his shoulder, Elliot Nash wore an expression that mirrored his commander's.

"I believe I have narrowed the poison employed by the assassin to two possible toxins," the Physician continued. "Savin or ergot."

Axel nodded sagely. Koel had little doubt that it was the first time he had ever heard of either substance.

"The Prince's body was blistered in patches. And his feet were gangrenous. As I'm sure you'll know, either of these poisons could have caused such an effect."

The Physician's words conjured up a vivid image in Koel's

imagination. Cousin Anders had always projected such an image of flawlessness; it would be intriguing, to say the least, to see her perfect cousin with his newly deformed feet.

"If we know the assassin employed poison, are we saying someone tampered with the Prince's food?" The question came from Elliot Nash.

Not for the first time, his voice caught Koel by surprise. To look at him, you would expect him to speak in a coarse, thuggish tone, but his voice was rich and resonant. It was, she decided, a voice for declaiming poetry rather than military commands. Perhaps he had missed his true calling.

"Poisoning by food is the most likely scenario," the Physician said. "But it's not the only possibility. The poison might also have been administered intravenously or even as some kind of bogus medicine."

"But poisoning by food *is* the most likely?" Axel leaned forward as he spoke.

"Yes." Elias nodded.

Axel's fingers drummed on the pages of Elias's report. Koel could see that her brother's mind was racing, his eyes brighter than ever.

"If there's a strong possibility that Prince Anders was poisoned by food, then we must act fast. We need to close down the risk of another attack. If someone managed to tamper with the Prince's food, any one of us could be targeted by the same means." He pushed back his chair and rose to his feet. "We have to send out a very strong and swift message that we're on to this assassin."

"What do you have in mind?" the Physician inquired.

Axel lifted his hand. "We'll get to that, presently," he said. "There's no need for us to further detain you or your apprentice. I'm sure you both have other important work to pursue." He gestured toward the door.

In spite of Axel's very clear dismissal, Elias remained sitting in the chair, hands folded across his lap, reminding Koel of one of the statues in the village chapel.

"I wonder," the Physician began hesitantly, "if I might have just a moment of your time...in private."

Behind the carved oak screen, Koel couldn't help but smile. This was getting even more intriguing.

"Just us?" Axel appeared thoughtful. It was evident that the Physician's request had successfully hooked his interest. "Yes, yes, of course." His eyes signaled to Nash, who made for the door and opened it to allow Asta out first.

Axel leaned back in his chair, waiting for the door to close, then leaned forward again once it had done so, his forearms resting on the desk. "Well, now we are quite alone, Elias." Koel held her breath as her brother continued. "Talk to me."

Elias shifted uneasily on the chair. "It's a matter of some delicacy," he said. "It is with reference to the poisons I mentioned before."

"Go on," Axel encouraged him.

"As I'm sure you know, ergot is a form of mold that grows on cereal grains, whereas savin is a plant. A blue-green shrub, reminiscent of the trees in the forest. Indeed, you could say that it has the appearance of a forest in miniature…"

Koel could see her brother's interest already waning. She could imagine what he was thinking. *I've got an assassination to solve and you're wasting my time with a lesson in botany.*

"To the best of my knowledge," the Physician continued, "savin grows in only one place in Archenfield." He coughed, then continued hoarsely, "In the Physic Garden."

Axel drew himself upright. "*Your* garden!"

Elias nodded. "I used to employ it as a remedy. A rather specific remedy." He paused. "I haven't done so for some time, but still it continues to grow there."

"I see." Axel's expression was grave. He was clean-shaven, but Koel noticed he stroked his chin in the same manner his father was given to.

"I felt I should be direct with you on this matter," the Physician said. He leaned forward. "Axel, I had nothing to do with Prince Anders's poisoning. You must believe me."

For a moment there was silence within the chamber. Koel tried not to breathe.

"Of course I believe you!" Axel exclaimed at last. His

eyes were wide. "Elias, did you think I was going to arrest *you*?"

"I...I didn't know what to think." Relief flooded into the Physician's voice and it occurred to Koel that he might be about to cry. She really hoped not.

"Elias," Axel said, rising from his chair and walking around his desk to stand right at the Physician's side, "I could never think ill of you." He reached out and took Elias's trembling hands in his own. "Was it not these hands here, which delivered Prince Anders into this world and gave him life? And Prince Jared and Prince Edvin too? And myself of course..."

And me, Koel thought, not at all surprised to be omitted from her brother's list.

"You are a bringer of life and health and remedies." Axel bestowed a bountiful smile upon his companion. "You don't have a destructive bone in your body or an evil thought in your brain."

"Thank you," Elias said, his voice cracking with emotion. His body trembled with evident relief. "Well, I must say that is a great weight off my mind."

Axel placed his hands on Elias's shoulders, massaging them gently. "Thank you for everything you have done," he said. "Your work in this matter is, for the time being, concluded. Mine, I fear, is just beginning."

Elias rose from his chair and Axel escorted the Physician

to the door, intoning further words of warm reassurance as he propelled him through it. He then addressed Nash over Elias's head. "Wait there for me. I'll be out in a minute."

"Yes, sir."

Koel watched as her brother closed the door and walked back into the chamber, alive with a new purpose. He came to stand by the mullioned window, turning his back to her as he gazed out into the palace grounds.

Koel rose from the chair and walked out from behind the screen. In her stockinged feet, she was virtually soundless. She had almost made it to his side before he turned around.

"What are you doing here?" he asked, eyes wide. "Where did you spring from?"

"I've been here a little while," she said.

There was a plate of fruits—untouched of course—on Axel's desk. She hadn't seen that before. Reaching out, she lifted an ebony grape to her lips.

Axel frowned and shook his head. "You can't just sneak into my quarters, like a cat, whenever the fancy takes you," he said. "There is such a thing as privacy."

The sweet grape juices exploded inside her mouth. She reached forward for another. "Privacy or secrets?"

He shrugged. "It amounts to the same thing." His frown had subsided. She knew, though he might growl like a bear, he could never stay angry with her for long.

"Well, now you have had your fun," he said. "It's time for

you to go and commence work on a new tapestry or some such."

"While you stride out to make safe the Princedom? What's your next move?"

He smiled indulgently at her. "Much as I would love to satisfy your insatiable curiosity, sister dearest, I have a job to do. What you and our father fail to understand—you with your spying and questions, he with his rallying speeches—is that I'm the one in the family who shoulders all the responsibility." His tone grew mocking. "And I'm the only one in a position of true power and influence. Need I remind you that while I sit at the Prince's Table, the rest of you aren't even permitted to observe meetings of the Twelve?"

Koel bit down her annoyance and stepped closer. "I *could* help you," she said. "Why don't you tell me your grand plan?"

"I don't think so," Axel said. His eyes were directed toward the door, his message abundantly clear.

Koel shook her head. "If I didn't know better, I might think you're rather enjoying yourself."

Axel looked aghast. "Enjoying investigating our cousin's cold-blooded murder? How could you say such a thing? How could you *think* that? It's simply that I am the Captain of the Guard and..."

"You have a duty to make safe the Princedom." She nodded. "Of course you do," she finished softly. She could have said more but one of her many talents was knowing when it was best to curb her tongue.

"I'm going now," Axel said. "Fetch your shoes from behind the screen and, please, Koel, don't be here when I get back." Sighing, head down, he strode toward the door.

Hearing Axel's footsteps receding along the corridor, Koel Blaxland smiled. Her brother could talk big but sometimes he was such an amateur. She closed the door behind him, then considered her options. Her shoes were indeed safely stashed behind the oak screen. They could wait there. She sauntered over to her brother's desk and sat down in his chair. It was a little too low for her so she got up again and found a plump cushion—one she'd embroidered for him when she was considerably younger and less easily bored. It made her brother's chair far more comfortable. Reaching forward, she took Elias's report in her hands. Then she leaned back in the chair, lifted her stockinged feet onto the surface of the desk and began eagerly reading the Physician's confidential report. Well, she told herself, after the effort he had gone to, *somebody* ought to do him that courtesy.

ELEVEN

The Kitchens, the Palace

AXEL STOOD, FOR THE MOMENT UNNOTICED, ON the threshold of the palace kitchens, observing the scene with unusual interest. There must have been fifty people or more at work—men and women of all ages, engaged in a variety of tasks: chopping, draining and stirring the various components of the lunch dishes.

Axel glanced from one face to another. Any one of them could have been guilty of poisoning Prince Anders's supper the night before.

Was it that one over there chopping carrots? With the ruthless efficiency with which he used his knife, he'd have been handy in the army. Could he be the Prince's poisoner? It might just as easily be that harmless-looking older woman cracking eggs into a bowl. You didn't need to be young or strong to sprinkle a few grains of poison into a stew. Or that greasy-looking lad, there, sticking his finger into the mixing bowl, could equally well be the culprit. And what about that ugly brute lifting a heavy pot from the stove? Axel's eyes darted from face to face to face. It could be any of them.

But no, he told himself, that wasn't quite right. Because Prince Anders's food and *his* food alone had been tainted. So the savin or ergot, whichever it was, could not have been sprinkled into a pot or whisked into a sauce here in the kitchens. If it had been, they wouldn't be dealing with just one death but with a full-blown massacre at the palace. No, the assassin had to have gotten to the food on its journey *between* the kitchen and the dining hall. The assassin had to have had specific access to Prince Anders's plate.

The Huntsman's Bell chimed eight times as Jared arrived in the dining hall, accompanied by his mother and brother. There was the usual sound of chairs scraping back over the stone floor and the susurrus of low skirts swishing on the flagstones as the other royals and members of the Twelve— as well as the teams of subordinate staff who populated the outer tables—all rose to their feet. Then the vast cathedral-like chamber was uncommonly silent and Jared was aware of his own footsteps, along with those of his mother and brother—echoing, magnified, around the hall.

The central table for lunch—which accommodated the Twelve (with the exception, for obvious reasons, of the Cook) as well as the key members of the royal family—was in the shape of a horseshoe. Everyone's position at the table was carefully preordained. Jared would sit, for the first time, at the very center of the room.

The seat was not far from the chair he was accustomed to—currently empty, pending his decision of Edling—and yet it felt a million miles away. It was as if the stars in the heavens had reconfigured themselves and he now found himself at the heart of a strange new constellation.

The new Prince once again sensed that he was the focus of everyone's attention, as two hundred or so pairs of eyes followed his every step. He knew they were all looking for telltale signs. How had he taken the news of his brother's death? How was he handling his own accession? Were the palace and the Princedom in safe hands?

He could feel a flush of warmth rise up from inside himself and threaten to spread into his face. This often happened when he felt self-conscious—and he had never before felt so self-conscious. Determined to fight back, he sought out familiar faces in the crowd. Aunt Stella and Cousin Koel both bowed their heads graciously toward him. Kai Jagger, his first companion of the day, gave a brisk nod—no discernible emotion in his hard eyes. In contrast, Father Simeon's benevolent face was etched with pain, while Logan

Wilde smiled encouragingly from his seat at the horseshoe as Jared took his place. He noticed that two people were missing from the main table—Cousin Axel and Silva.

Cousin Axel's absence was easily explained—Jared knew that he was immersed in the investigation into Anders's assassination. Noticing now that Axel's deputy, Elliot Nash, also wasn't anywhere to be seen, Jared wondered if some important new information had come to light.

"You look distant," Elin said to him, as the others sat back down in their seats. "What are you thinking about?"

He turned to his mother. "I was thinking about the investigation and whether, instead of being here, I should be wherever Cousin Axel is, helping him."

Elin shook her head sharply and laid her hand over his wrist. "My son, you are Prince of All Archenfield now so it will not be *you* who helps Axel Blaxland, but *he* who helps you." Her eyes met his, knowingly. "And, frankly, whatever is happening with regard to the investigation, it will wait until after lunch. It has been a long morning and we all need to put something in our stomachs."

Jared nodded, smiling to himself. His mother had an unswerving belief in the importance of three square meals each day. Still, she never seemed to put on any weight. She had retained the same lean figure for as long as he could remember. She was an expert rider and huntswoman and her predilection for such activities perhaps accounted both for her healthy appetite and her ability to stay trim.

"I *can* smell food, but I see no sign of it," Elin resumed. "Where is our lunch?" Her eyes slid past him to the empty seat on Jared's other side. "And, while we're at it, where is Silva?"

It was hard to remain calm and coolheaded in the furnace-like heat of the kitchen. Spirals of steam rose up from the ranks of heavy pots that sat atop the iron stoves, while fresh blasts of heat emanated from the opening of the vast oven doors, as loaves of bread—sprinkled with aromatic fennel seed—were removed and crisp joints of pork were swiftly basted. The precise movements of each individual, and the frenetic interplay between them, brought to mind a night of country dancing. And there were few things Axel detested more than when the palace was given over to a night of dancing and its ghastly enforced merriment.

Axel's keen eyes darted through the crowd until he pinpointed, at its epicenter, the unappetizing form of Vera Webb, the Cook. Her doughlike face, poised over a steaming cauldron, was as red as uncooked meat from heat and exertion. She was shaking her head and giving a young lad at her side short shrift about something. Axel took a breath, then began weaving his way through the melee into the very heart of the kitchens.

"If I've told you once, I've told you a thousand times!" Vera was berating the lanky kitchen lad. "Yes, you do taste the foods for seasoning. But then you put the spoon in for washing—you don't just dip it back into the pot! I don't seem to recall your spittle being on the list of ingredients, do you?"

Axel reached out a hand to Vera's shoulder. At close range, her upper arms reminded him of plump hams. At his touch, Vera's head jerked around. Seeing who it was, she made no effort to disguise her displeasure.

"Axel!" she exclaimed. "What are you doing here? Can't you see how busy we are?"

"I need to talk to you," he said. "A matter of the utmost importance."

Vera frowned, lifting her hand to address the slick of perspiration across her forehead—but making decidedly little impact on it. "You'll have to wait," she said. "As you can see, we're in the middle of the final preparations for luncheon." She began turning back to the pot.

Did she really think he'd be so easily dismissed?

"This can't wait," Axel resumed calmly. "And I'm working on the assumption that you won't want me to say what I have to say to you in front of your many staff. So,

Vera, I suggest you step out into the gardens with me for a moment."

Something in his tone of voice must have persuaded her. When she turned around, he knew he had her attention.

"All right," she said. "I'll come with you. But this had better not take more than a minute or two. At this point in the proceedings, time is of the essence."

It would take as long as necessary, but he felt no need to share that thought with her. Head aloft, Axel maneuvered his way through the hectic kitchen, aware of Vera waddling in his wake, throwing out haphazard instructions left and right: "Smaller slices, Jutta! I said add some pepper, not salt! For God's sake, Fritha, get the rest of those loaves out of the oven and onto serving platters *now*! And, you two, start decanting the soup into tureens. It must have been ten minutes already since the Huntsman's Bell. We're late!"

Axel tuned her niggling voice down until it was just a dim babble in his ear. When the babble momentarily ceased, he glanced over his shoulder at her. "It's a good thing I don't run my army the way you do your kitchens," he observed pointedly.

"The kitchens are my domain and I have run them for many a year, without cause for complaint," Vera said. "You'd do well to stick to your job and leave me to mine."

"Oh, Vera," Axel said, unable to prevent a hint of pleasure creeping into his voice. "I only wish that were possible."

"There she is, at last!" Elin pinched Jared's arm as Silva appeared in the dining hall. She lingered near the doorway, in a jet-black dress, unadorned by embroidery. Jared was used to seeing Silva in light colors—pale blues and corals, with gold and silver threads. In her traditional mourning garb, with no trace of makeup, she seemed more fragile than ever and, perplexing though it was to think it, even more beautiful.

She looked unsure of her surroundings, as if she were entering the room for the very first time. Or, Jared thought, as if she had only just surfaced from a deep sleep and was not yet fully engaged in the physical world. As Silva stood there, he found himself unable to draw his eyes away from her. Had her skin always been so pale, her eyes so wide and blue as summer cornflowers, or were these the physical effects of Anders's death?

Elin nudged him. "Go and escort her over to her seat. She barely looks capable of making it on her own."

"Mother!" Jared exclaimed, reluctant to make himself the center of attention again.

"Jared, people are starting to stare at her. For goodness' sake, go over and bring her to the table—even if you have to throw her over your shoulder and carry her."

He realized he had no choice in the matter. He rose from

his seat and strode over to his brother's widow. As he stood before her—almost as if asking her for a dance, he suddenly thought—she scrutinized him curiously. He felt a fresh wave of panic pass through him. She wasn't about to mistake him for Anders again, was she? Please not here, in front of the whole court.

"Silva," he said softly. "We were concerned that you might miss luncheon."

"I almost didn't come," she replied. "I'm not at all hungry."

He saw the telltale red rings around her pretty eyes. "I'll let you in on a secret," he said. "I'm not that hungry myself." Smiling encouragingly at her, he extended his arm. "May I escort you to your seat?"

After a moment's hesitation, she returned his smile and nodded. As he led her to the table, he had a sudden memory of the one time they *had* danced together—at her wedding feast. She had seemed so brimming with life and light then. Was it possible that that was only one year ago? Was it possible it had ever happened at all?

Aware of the sea of faces watching him and Silva, he had a renewed sense of unreality about all of this. *I'm in the depths of a dream*, he told himself—*a nightmare. But soon, I'll wake up. I will, won't I?*

"You look shocked," Axel said, breaking the silence between himself and the Cook.

"Of course, I'm shocked," Vera said. Her usually sonorous voice was reduced to the soft rustle of the autumn leaves, stirring in the breeze.

"Shocked that Prince Anders was poisoned?" he inquired. "Or shocked that one of your staff is culpable?"

Vera flushed red from her chest to her forehead and glared at him. "Now, wait just a minute before you start throwing around accusations of guilt..."

Axel leaned closer, his breath on her face. "I can't wait," he asserted calmly. "You said yourself that time is of the essence. Only I'm not talking about lunch—I'm talking about the security of the Princedom."

"All right," she said, raising a hand as if in surrender. "All right. I understand. Just tell me what you intend to do about this."

He was pleasantly surprised at how swiftly she had become subservient to him.

"My first thought was to shut down the kitchens altogether, and have each and every one of your staff questioned," he told her, enjoying the impact of his words on her stricken face.

"You can't shut down the kitchens! People need to eat, especially at a time like this. It's impossible."

"No," he corrected her. "By no means impossible. But perhaps, I see now, unnecessary."

Her shrewd eyes were fixed on his. She was hanging on his every word. It was time.

"Look, I was thinking this through before," he continued, in a more measured tone. "We know that Prince Anders was poisoned at supper last night. But we also know that he was the *only* fatality. That tells us that the poison was not added to his food in the kitchen, but *between* the kitchen and the dining hall. I need you to think—and think fast—who had access to the Prince's plate at that point."

Vera did not hesitate. "That's simple," she said. "It's the stewards who take the trays of food from the kitchen up to the dining hall."

Axel nodded, assimilating the information. "Is one steward specifically charged with serving the Prince?"

"I don't think so," Vera said.

"Or the head table in general?" Axel inquired.

Vera hesitated.

"You don't seem at all sure," Axel continued. "And yet the stewards fall under your authority, do they not?"

When Vera resumed speaking, her voice was once more confident. "I leave the running of the stewards to the head steward, William Maddox. He does report to me, but I'm not up there in the dining hall when the food is served. You, of course, are. Perhaps you yourself might just have noticed who was serving you your breakfast, lunch and dinner?"

Axel shook his head, dismissively. "I can assure you,

Vera, I have rather more important matters to contemplate than who puts my plate of grub before me."

He regretted the words as soon as he had spoken them, as Vera was swift to seize upon his slipup.

"But it seems that the question of who serves you is perhaps the most important matter of all." Vera smiled at her little victory. *Let her*, thought Axel—*it will only be a fleeting one.*

"This Maddox," Axel continued, "the head steward—you say he reports to you?"

She nodded. "He certainly does."

"I need you to summon him to my office, to discuss this matter further. But be discreet. I don't want any of the other stewards getting wind of this. I'm sure I don't need to remind you what a deadly threat one of them may now pose to us."

Vera looked freshly troubled. "I can't get to William now without alerting the other stewards," she said. "Didn't you hear me, on the way out here? I gave the orders for them to take up the first course."

"What?" Axel was incredulous.

"I told them to go ahead and serve the soup. We were already running late. I didn't know how long you were going to detain me…"

"You stupid, stupid woman," Axel said, his voice all the more menacing for being so quiet. Already, he was moving away from her, striding, then running toward the kitchens. "Do you know what you've done?" he called back to her.

Vera Webb stood in the Palace Gardens, trembling at the thought. How had it come to this? How could it be one of the stewards, one of *her* stewards, who had committed such a terrible act? As long as she lived, she would never forget this day. Axel might as well have arrested her. Standing there, on the fringes of the Kitchen Garden, she felt suddenly weightless—as if the autumn wind might scoop her up with the rest of the falling leaves and carry her away.

Axel, meanwhile, charged through the kitchens. "Get out of my way! Move aside! Put that down. MOVE!" He left a trail of chaos and confusion in his wake as he shoved his way through to the stairwell on the other side of the room.

Leaping up the first few steps, he turned around to address his stunned audience.

"Listen! No more food leaves this kitchen until further notice. Do you understand me?"

"But, sir, what about luncheon?" This from the lad Vera had verbally bludgeoned before.

"There will be *no* luncheon today." The sea of blank faces looked questioningly at him. He had no more time. "Vera will explain further," he said, turning away.

Axel propelled himself up the rest of the stone staircase to the long corridor above. He saw that the last steward was at the other end, striding toward the dining chamber, tray held aloft. Axel took a quick breath. He might, after all, still be in time.

He ran onward, grateful for a level of fitness unrivaled within the court—even by Hal Harness and his team of bodyguards. But fast didn't necessarily mean dexterous and, at the threshold of the dining hall, he only narrowly missed a collision with the steward and the tureen of soup he held balanced on his tray. Pausing to glance inside, Axel took a quick reading of the scene before him.

The stewards had almost completed serving the soup. Across the serried ranks of tables, brimming bowls sat waiting to be drunk, curls of steam rising into the air.

Mercifully, there was a strict etiquette to the way food was served and eaten at court—so that the Prince's food would always be the freshest from the kitchens, the ruler was served *last* but ate *first*.

Axel watched as the steward he had almost collided with moments before proceeded to ladle out soup to those at the main table who had not already been provided for.

He had no time to think this through further; he had to act before any new tragedy afflicted the court. A nasty vision of the assembled falling from their chairs as one flashed before his eyes. He marched into the center of the room.

"Prince Jared, Queen Elin and members of the royal

household, fellow members of the Twelve and all those of you who serve at court...I must insist that you do not let a drop of the soup you have been served reach your tongue."

There was a moment of stunned silence, followed by a delayed reaction of whispers, swiftly rising in volume and intensity.

"Axel, what is the meaning of this?" Elin asked him.

"I cannot vouch for the safety of the food," he called across the length of the table to her. "So I must urge you not to drink."

"But why?" Kai Jagger asked, looking up from his bowl. "What exactly are you saying, Axel?"

Axel frowned—he didn't have time for a lengthy explanation. Why couldn't they just do as they were instructed? He needed to find William Maddox and get him to round up his stewards.

"Axel." It was Nova Chastain who addressed him now. "Are you saying that Prince Anders was poisoned?"

He nodded—thank goodness someone else on the Twelve had a keen intelligence. His eyes ranged across the room, frantically trying to locate the head steward.

"Is this true?" Emelie Sharp, close by his side, inquired. "Prince Anders was killed with poison?"

"Ask Elias! It was all in his report."

"Well, yes," he heard the Physician, now the object of everyone's attention, say. "There is little question that Prince

Anders was killed by means of poison. But it is not *absolutely* certain that the poison was delivered via his food..."

"Most likely," Axel shouted over the increasing babble, noticing his own sister watching him with something akin to amusement. He glared at Elias. "*You* said it was most likely that the poison was in his food. Whoever put it there had easy access to the Prince's plate. Just as he, or she, may now have had to each and every one of your soup bowls."

Elin spoke once more. "You think we are all now in danger?"

"Yes," Axel replied. "I do." Why couldn't they just do as he told them and stop detaining him with this unhelpful volley of questions? "I need to speak with William Maddox, the head steward." He turned and called above the rising hubbub. "Maddox! William Maddox, where are you?"

He felt a huge sense of relief as a vaguely familiar white-haired man raised his hand aloft, then began weaving his way through the tables toward him. Seeing Maddox's receding hair and beard, he nodded, recognizing him after all.

Axel turned from the others, who were still firing inane questions at him, to address Maddox directly.

"I need you to come with me," he said. "It's a matter of grave importance."

Maddox did not object. Was this an indication of guilt or simply someone demonstrating some rare understanding of the gravity of the situation? "Follow me," Axel said, turning to make his way back out of the hall. He could hear the rising tide of panic behind him and was grateful to make it out into the relative quiet of the corridor.

Back at the main table, Kai Jagger lifted his spoon. "Prince Jared, I apologize for breaking protocol but, under the circumstances, I find I have no choice but to begin my meal before you." They all watched, with horror, as Kai dipped his spoon into the soup bowl and brought the spoon of chestnut broth to his mouth.

"Is that wise?" Elin asked.

Wise or not, the Chief Huntsman had now supped and swallowed and was already filling his spoon again. Before any of them could object further, he took another mouthful. Having done so, he set down his spoon momentarily.

"It is our duty, wouldn't you all agree, to encourage calm throughout the court, rather than to instill panic as the Captain of the Guard appears to have done?"

There were some hesitant nods around the table.

Kai lifted his spoon again. "It is delicious soup, my friends. I would heartily encourage you to try some."

As his spoon plunged into the soup again, Nova Chastain raised her own spoon and filled it. Now Logan Wilde did the same. They each drank a spoonful. Logan smiled and nodded. Nova dipped her spoon again.

Around the central table, the rest of the room had fallen quiet as the members of the court watched them.

Elias watched helplessly. "This doesn't prove anything. These poisons do not have an immediate effect."

If the others heard his words, they chose not to register them. Now Hal Harness too brought a spoonful of soup to his lips.

The royals themselves had yet to be served. Elin beckoned over the steward, who still held the tray bearing the final tureen. "My family and I are hungry," she declared loudly. "We would very much like to partake of this delicious soup."

Jared leaned toward her as the steward came over to serve them.

"Is this really a good idea?" he asked her quietly. "What if Axel and Elias are right?"

Elin addressed him sharply. "Your impetuous cousin Axel is closing the stable door after the horse has bolted," she said. "And Elias has made a career out of being overly cautious. Of course, you can make your own decision, but I for one came here for luncheon and I am not leaving again without some food." Seeing Silva staring at her, she smiled. "You should try to eat something too, dear. You look fit to drop."

Silva opened her mouth as if about to speak, then evidently changed her mind. She pushed back her chair and, stifling a sob, stumbled out of the dining hall.

Jared turned to his mother once more. "Should I... should one of us go after her?"

Elin shook her head, turning to nod her gracious thanks at the steward who had just finished ladling soup into her bowl and was now turning his attention to Prince Jared.

"No, my dear son. I'm sure that Silva simply needs to rest. You stay here and have your lunch. We can have a tray delivered to her chamber later."

Jared turned and looked down at his brimming bowl of now tepid and potentially fatal chestnut soup. He had rarely felt less hungry but could feel all eyes upon him once more. The soup didn't seem to have done the rest of them any harm—yet. But, as the new Prince, he was the most logical next target.

"You need to show strength of character," Elin told him. "Don't look at me like that! I'm not asking you to don your armor and ride off into battle. Just put a spoonful of broth in your mouth and a smile on your handsome, if troubled, face. Make each and every one of them believe it's quite the most delicious thing you have ever tasted. Even if, in truth, it is as bland as Vera's standard fare."

Prince Jared lifted his spoon and, moving swiftly so that no one would see how his hand trembled, dipped it into his bowl.

TWELVE

The Cook's Office, the Palace

"I JUST CAN'T BELIEVE THAT ONE OF MY TEAM would be responsible," William Maddox told Axel.

"I understand that. None of us would wish to believe that we harbored the assassin on our team." The Captain of the Guard's words were not devoid of warmth. "What matters now is swiftly identifying the guilty party so that we can lift the threat of further attack and claim the Blood Price."

Maddox paled at the mention of this. He managed a faltering nod.

"The Cook told me that you have a team of twenty-four stewards." Axel said. "Is that correct?"

Maddox nodded. "Yes, twenty-four of them. I've known most since they were young lads and lasses."

"Most," Axel echoed. "But not all?"

"It's not unusual for staff to move into different teams within the court, as you know, sir. I've always thought it's rather a credit to the system in Archenfield that you aren't born into one role and forced to stay with it until your death."

Axel grimaced. Perhaps things would be a sight easier, if that were the case. He glanced out of the small casement into the Kitchen Garden, where Elliot Nash and his support team had assembled the stewards for questioning.

"I'd like you to join me for this," Axel told Maddox, gesturing toward the door.

⁓

Sunlight streamed into the Kitchen Gardens, the scent of sage and rosemary carried on the breeze. It made Axel momentarily hungry, but he dismissed the sensation. He had work to do before he could allow himself the luxury of food.

The stewards stood in a confused gaggle, surrounded by Elliot Nash and his team. As Axel and William Maddox strode toward them, the group fell silent. Nash broke off and came to meet his commander.

"I take it you'd like to handle this yourself, sir?"

Axel nodded. "Yes, but first ask your men and women to stand aside." As Nash gave the order, Axel cast his eyes over the group of suspects. Like those he had observed in the kitchen before, there was little to suggest that one rather than another was guilty. Perhaps the answer would lie in what Maddox had told him before—by separating out those who had served as stewards since childhood from the others who had transferred from other positions.

As Nash's guards peeled away to the side, Axel immediately saw that something was wrong. He turned to Maddox. "You said you had twenty-four stewards," he said.

"I do," Maddox said, squinting in the sunlight.

All previous kindness filleted from his voice, Axel pointed. "Try counting them."

Maddox began doing so.

"Let me fast-track this for you," Axel interrupted, feeling the familiar acid tang of impatience rising from his chest to his throat. "There's only twenty-three of them. Someone is missing."

Maddox frowned. "Yes, you're right." He stepped forward to address his team. "Where's Michael?"

"He said he wasn't feeling well this morning," a young woman answered. "Don't you remember..."

"Michael, eh?" Axel cut through the woman's unnecessary blather, addressing Maddox again.

"Michael Reeves," Maddox said. "But it couldn't be Michael. It just couldn't..."

"Take me to his quarters," Axel commanded, glancing over his shoulder at Elliot Nash. "Not that I hold out the least hope of finding him there."

Maddox knocked on a small door. Axel had had to bow his head in the low corridor that led to it. He wondered whether Archenfield had always had short stewards or if the size of the stewards' quarters had latterly dictated their hiring policy.

"No need to knock!" Axel said, kicking open the door with his boot. "He's hardly likely to be in here."

Leaving a dazed Maddox at the door, Axel crossed the threshold, beckoning Nash to join him. The attic room, bisected by a thick beam, was as lacking in decoration as it was in proportion. Pathetic really. Still, on the plus side, it wouldn't take long to search.

There was a slender bed and a nightstand, on which rested a candle burned low in its holder. There was a small wooden trunk that Axel employed his boot once more to open. The lid flew up and Axel crouched down, rummaging through the dull, rough clothes contained within. If they had been neatly folded before, they no longer were now.

"Sir, look at this," Nash said. He was propping up the thin mattress that lined Reeves's bed. In his hands was a small, linen-bound book. "I found this right here."

Axel snatched the book out of his deputy's hands. He could hardly believe his eyes. *A Book of Poisons,*" he read. Turning the pages, he saw the insignia of the Physician.

"The little bastard must have stolen this from Elias's library."
He slammed it shut and turned sharply to leave. As he did
so, his head made contact with the roof beam. The impact
was hard and painful, but the shock was only fleeting. As it
receded, Axel felt renewed with energy and purpose.

"It seems we have found our man," Axel told his deputy.

Nash nodded grimly, letting the gray, fibrous mattress
slump back onto the wooden bed frame.

Axel addressed William Maddox, who still hovered in
the dim corridor outside.

"When was Reeves last seen by you or one of your team?"

"We never served breakfast today, you see," Maddox
said in a dazed, disconnected tone. "It was all such a shock.
Those hours after the news of Prince Anders was brought
to us, everything was confused. I sent the stewards back to
their quarters to gather themselves and say a prayer..."

"Yes, yes," Axel cut in. "Forget the prayers for Prince
Anders's eternal soul, my friend. You are my best chance of
capturing his cold-blooded assassin."

Maddox nodded. He was shaking, eyes moist. "According to Jana, he complained of feeling ill when she and the
others made their way back to the kitchen complex."

"When was that?" Axel barked.

"That would have been around the time of the Groom's
Bell."

"The Groom's Bell." Axel turned his attention from Maddox to Nash. "That's over three hours ago."

"He'll have been running all that time," Nash said. "You can get a fair distance in three hours."

Axel's face was ignited with fresh purpose. "He'll be in the forest," he said, striding out of the bedchamber. "It's the shortest route to our nearest border, as the falcon flies." Leaving William Maddox—no longer of use—trailing in his wake, the Captain of the Guard barked fresh orders at Nash.

"Send word to Lucas. I want our best horses saddled and ready. Find Jonas Drummond—I want the Woodsman's assurance that the forest traps are all set—we'll see how our little steward copes with them. And Kai Jagger, fetch him too! The Chief Huntsman could come in quite handy, I'm sure. Tell him to bring his hatchets."

THIRTEEN

The Forest

MICHAEL REEVES WAS STILL DEEP IN THE HEART of the forest when he heard the first dog bark. The sound shocked him; it signaled the endgame. He knew he should have been farther ahead, much closer to the border, by now. He paused, surrounded by a cluster of giant sequoias, waiting to hear again the hound or one of its fellows. He didn't want to hear them—of course he didn't—and yet doing so might enable him to pinpoint just how far away they were. He would be able to make some quick calculations.

He glanced down at the map he clutched in his left hand. The hand was now shaking. He brought his right hand across and gripped his left wrist, pretending—an old trick—that he was someone else, someone calmer, telling him that everything was going to be all right. *Just look at the map*, he told himself. *You're very nearly there. Even if the dogs and riders are on your trail, you can still make it.*

Time had been on his side all day until now. He'd left the bounds of the court as the Groom's Bell was sounding. Close by the campanile, he had felt each of the five chimes reverberate through his body. And he'd already made good headway into the forest when he heard the subsequent striking of the Poet's Bell—pausing, he had glanced back in the direction of the palace, then turned to stride on. Later, he thought he could just make out the seven chimes of the Falconer's Bell—soft and sweet as birdsong. He'd been too deep in the forest to hear the next bells in the sequence, but his escape had seemed to be proceeding exactly as planned.

He'd done his best to track time by checking against his map to see the distance behind and, more crucially, the distance ahead. But the further he continued on his journey, the more he understood that though the map was rich in detail and kept him moving in the right direction, it was not quite as scientific as he had anticipated when it came to distance. Nor did it make any allowance for elevation. There were several points, as now, when the forest floor steeply rose and he had no option but to intensify his physical effort and climb.

He still hadn't heard a second bark and now he began to wonder if perhaps he had only imagined the first. Could it even have been the rumbling of his stomach? How long had it been since he'd had something to eat? He reached into his pocket, worming his fingers around until he found a dried pear. It was the last one. He'd planned to save it for the continuation of his journey, the other side of the gate. But something now compelled him to eat it. Even as he felt its sweetness on his tongue, the fleeting pleasure was pushed aside by an ominous voice—an all-too-familiar voice—inside his head. *You're going to need every last bit of the energy this food will give you, Michael. Any advantage you might have had is about to run out.*

He banished the disdainful voice. It should have no mastery over him here. He was in the sanctum of the forest, far from the whispering corridors of the court. His surroundings were soft and tranquil and silent. He glanced down at the map again, telling himself that he was still on track. But, in his heart, he knew he was running out of time and against all his better instincts, he felt the first stirrings of panic. Then, like the fulfillment of a dark promise, he heard the dog bark a second time. There could be no mistaking the sound for a stomach rumble or even distant thunder. It was the dog. It wasn't close, but it was closer than before.

Now he had two options. Stay here and give way to panic. Or start running—like he had never run before.

The momentum of movement tamped down his fear. He had always known that the task ahead was a daunting one. Now the fact that he'd made it to this point—both to this day of judgment and so close to the border—fueled him with new energy. As the blue-green forest flashed by on either side, his feet flew over the mossy ground, his head pulsing with memories of moments earlier in the day: Closing the doors to his cramped quarters for the very last time. Beginning his long journey, at a regular pace—not too fast, nor too slow—through the palace grounds. Getting stopped, at the line of beehives, by the iron-faced guards and being subject to their bored litany of questions. His relief, when it had become abundantly clear that they were on alert for a stranger trespassing in their midst—rather than someone familiar with, and to, the court. His elation as he walked on, beyond the last of them, toward the dark, pine-perfumed embrace of the forest.

He smiled to himself as he ran. It truly felt as if the forest was on his side. Now that his heart was working harder and harder, his senses were heightened. None more so than his sense of smell. He felt himself inhaling deep lungfuls of clean forest air. It was as if he were drawing the very greenness and sweetness of the forest deep down inside him, becoming a part of its ecosystem.

Then he heard a third bark. Closer than before. Alarmingly close. The dangerous illusion that the forest was his sanctuary was ripped away. *Just keep running*, he thought. *It's all you can do now.*

The forest floor continued to climb, gradually at first

then more sharply. He was aware of it not only from the strain in his leg muscles but from the shortness of his breath. When he paused, only for an instant, to glance back the way he had come, he saw—with a momentary frisson of vertigo—that he had indeed climbed swiftly to much higher ground. And then, to his horror, he saw a blur of movement below. Hunters, horses and hounds.

Heart racing, he turned and pushed on, trying to block out the discordant music of the advancing search party: the drumming hooves, the barks—more frequent now, the urgent shouts of men and women.

The tree trunks were a coppery blur on either side. He told himself to focus on good thoughts—like the welcome he'd get on the other side of the border. How pleased they would be to see him after all this time. Even this happy thought was swiftly undermined as he anticipated the unavoidable interrogation at the gates. Without slowing his pace, he brought one hand to his chest, reassuring himself that the folded papers were still in place. He had a well-practiced story to accompany them and there was no reason to think they wouldn't let him through. Why had he even bothered to run if he didn't believe he could convince them? Why had he so diligently forged the letter from the head steward, on the stolen paper with the official crest and seal of the palace? Why doubt himself now, when he was so very close to the moment of his liberation?

It was then that he saw the forest was beginning to thin. He felt light, almost giddy, seeing the first sign of the gates up ahead. And he felt his feet suddenly give way.

At first he thought he'd stumbled on a sweet root and missed his footing. Then he saw that the mossy forest floor itself was moving, a hole opening up, and felt the beginning of an inevitable fall into the yawning chasm beneath him. With a lithe, desperate movement born of fully fledged panic, he lunged to one side, fingers scrabbling desperately for purchase on a root, a rock...

He had known there were traps scattered throughout the forest. The map had alerted him to which areas to steer clear of and, in addition, he'd been warned that the closer he came to the gates, the more careful he needed to be.

He realized the truth of that warning now. He had only grazed the edge of the trap, but it had been enough to make him lose his balance and send him toppling onto the fir-needle-strewn ground.

Glancing across at the gaping hole, he saw just how much worse it could have been. The hole burrowed down deep beneath the forest floor. There would be no way a man could jump or claw his way back out from there. The hell hole hadn't claimed him but still it sent fresh waves of panic through him.

Drawing himself determinedly back up onto his feet, he fixed his eyes on the path ahead. *No looking back*, he thought. *No more fear.*

Running onward, he noticed that the trees were thinning out even faster now. He realized he had lost his map. Had it been sucked down into the hole beneath the forest floor? It didn't matter. It had served him well.

Ahead he saw the size of the vast wooden gates, bleached almost silver by the sun. Attached to the gates was a metal plaque with a capital *W* for Wynyard, the ruling family of Archenfield. The plaque was a potent reminder that this marked the extent of the Wynyards' domain. To Michael Reeves, the plaque also told him that he was almost beyond that domain. He could see three guards patrolling the high walkway above the gate, the shapes of their crossbows silhouetted against the Archenfield sun. No, he told himself, with a quick smile. Another sun altogether. For, at last, he was about to leave Archenfield far behind.

He could hear the drumming of hooves behind him. The hunting party was close, but he could still make it. He had to believe that. There was still a chance that they'd take a wrong turn and, in the time it took to correct their mistake, he'd have spoken with the guards and continued on his way. He had to keep calm and remember his story. *I'm visiting my dying mother.* But how could you leave on the day of Prince Anders's assassination? *I set off at the rising of the sun, you see. This is the very first I have heard of the Prince's assassination. Such terrible news. May the Princedom endure!*

Of course, I could turn back—though my mother might have only one more night, perhaps only a few meager hours. My overseer has given his written permission. It's all in this letter he drafted last night...

He slowed his pace now that he knew he was in the sight of the border guards. It was important to seem nonchalant, unhurried. Should he raise his hands to greet them—or would that seem too cocksure?

The three guards had all turned toward him. Their crossbows were in their hands but not trained upon him. Good. They must have sensed from his demeanor that he posed no danger. He thought of the sharp dagger, strapped to his shin, just in case of trouble. He knew he could take down three in a fight. He'd done so before.

He was close enough to discern the features of the guards' faces now, as he approached the last tree of the forest—a majestic Archenfield oak. Perhaps he *should* greet them after all. One of the guards raised her hand. That decided the matter. Michael Reeves raised his own hand above his head as he took another step forward.

Something closed tightly around his ankles and he found himself suddenly flying upward, his head scraping painfully against the bark and branches of a tree. When his precipitous journey had come to an end, Michael found that he was suspended upside down on a rope, from the higher branches of the oak. He must have fallen prey to the last of the Woodsman's traps. The guard's wave had not been one of welcome but rather one of distraction.

There were new sounds close by, then directly beneath him, as the pack of hounds broke from the undergrowth and, at last, found their prey. Michael felt sick from being the wrong way up and from raw fear, sicker still as the hounds reared up on their hind legs, bringing their hot, foul-smelling breath close to his face. Their barks reverberated in his ears just as the chiming bells had done earlier in the day.

He heard a creak and felt himself drop down a bit lower, dangling closer still to the mouths and teeth of the excitable hounds. Was the branch above about to splinter and send him down into their slavering jaws? For now, it simply spun him slowly around. He felt like some kind of attraction at the May Fair.

Now he saw the guards—the one who had waved still above the gate, the others on the ground beneath him. Where before they had been three, now suddenly there were seven. All now had their crossbows drawn and trained on him.

"Don't shoot! I want him alive!"

He knew that voice. The branch sent him turning around again, just in time to see Axel Blaxland, the Captain of the Guard, dismount from his horse and stride purposefully toward him.

FOURTEEN

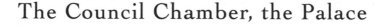

The Council Chamber, the Palace

"I KNOW YOU'RE TIRED," LOGAN WILDE TOLD Prince Jared. "I understand what a long and difficult day this has been for you. But we *have* to get this right. In little more than twelve hours, you'll be standing on the palace balcony and giving this speech for real. Your vocal projection has improved significantly, but you're still not speaking with the necessary conviction. Let's try again from the beginning!"

Jared frowned. He was frankly terrified about having to give the speech the following day but, even so, he was finding it harder and harder to focus on anything other than what was going on in the interrogation chamber in the Dungeons. Had Axel really caught his brother's assassin?

Aware of Logan's eyes upon him once more, Jared took a fresh look at the words on the paper, written in the Poet's meticulous script. His words were as elegant as his hand-writing. Maybe that was the problem. Glancing back up, Jared addressed his companion. "You have done a wonderful job, Logan." He sighed. "I just don't know if I can deliver this speech."

Not for the first time, Logan smiled reassuringly. "You have doubts. I understand that. But I know you *can* do it."

Jared jumped down from the dais and wandered over to where Logan was perched amid a single row of chairs—standing in for the audience of thousands who would gather to hear him the following day. Sitting down beside the Poet, Jared carefully set his script on the empty chair between them. "It just doesn't sound like me or the kind of thing I'd say."

"You say that like it's a bad thing!" Logan laughed. "Of course it doesn't sound like you! Don't take this the wrong way, but when did you last craft a speech for a state occasion? Never, right? I, on the other hand..." He paused and winked at Jared.

"Thanks," Jared said, "for the timely reminder of how much better qualified you are than me."

"I'm qualified to write the speech," Logan said. "No question about that." His bright eyes met Jared's. "But please don't be in any doubt that you're perfectly qualified to be Prince."

"Am I though?" Jared felt a fresh shiver of panic work through his insides. "Just because my brother and father were princes before me."

Logan shook his head. "You're forgetting," he said, "that isn't how it works in Archenfield. Prince Anders chose you, after much careful consideration, as his Edling. Just as you, in the coming days and after the same due thought, will select your own Edling. It's one of the many things I celebrate about our Princedom—that the right to rule is bestowed upon an individual, rather than it being a birthright."

For a moment, Jared felt buoyed by his companion's words. Then he felt the fragile house of cards that was his confidence begin to waver on its foundations once more. "How could my brother have known? I was fourteen when he chose me to be his Edling. How could he have possibly felt certain that when the time came, I'd be the best choice to succeed him?"

"Anders knew his mind," Logan said. "I'm sure you are aware that there were others within the court petitioning to be Edling. There was pressure from within your own family."

Jared smiled ruefully. "Of course. Axel wanted to be my brother's Edling, just as now he wants to be mine. It's his route to power."

Ignoring this last assertion, Logan's eyes met those of the young Prince. "Prince Anders was utterly certain from the very beginning. He had not a moment of doubt. He knew you were the one."

"I want Edvin to be my Edling," Jared told Logan.

"Edvin!" Logan made a grimace. "But he's only, what, fourteen? How can you possibly have confidence in him and his abilities?" The Poet's grimace transformed into a grin.

Jared smiled. "Very funny. And point taken. So Anders was right to put his faith in me. But when am I going to start feeling like the Prince? How long will it take? Will it happen at my coronation when they place the crown on my head?"

Logan shook his head again. "Jared, you are the Prince already. Your coronation will be a glorious moment in our history. People will speak of it for generations to come—you can trust me on that score. As to the matter of when you will truly feel like you are the Prince, who can say?" The Poet's eyes met Jared's, as he leaned in confidentially. "You may just have to act the part until you can feel you truly inhabit it."

Logan reached over and picked up the speech script. "You may not think these words are written in your voice, but you haven't found your voice yet. I will help you to find it, just as I helped Anders before you."

The Poet looked suddenly tired. Jared felt pangs of guilt. "You've been such a support to me today," he said. "Both practically and emotionally. I really couldn't have gotten through the past twelve hours without you."

"Of course you could have, Your Highness." Logan was quick to brush away the compliment.

"No, I *couldn't*. I've learned more about the Princedom in these past twelve hours than in the past twelve years."

He stared into Logan's eyes. "I know how much my brother depended on you. After today, I understand that all the better. I know how close the two of you were, Logan, but you have had to put your own feelings on hold to take care of me. I'm sorry."

Logan seemed initially to be at a loss for words. "You're a very kind person, Prince Jared. And you're right. There was a close bond between your brother and me. I'm going to miss him very much. But, at times like these, perhaps the best thing is to keep busy." He paused. "I'll have time enough to contemplate my loss once the business of the next few days has passed."

The Poet fell silent again. Filled with renewed purpose, Jared retrieved the speech from his companion's hands and strode purposefully toward the dais.

"People of Archenfield," he began once more. This time, Logan smiled encouragingly and gave a nod and, as Jared continued with the Poet's fine words, it was as if he had suddenly discovered a new language. It felt as thrilling and as exhilarating as if he had opened his arms and found he was now able to fly.

He was interrupted by the door to the Council Chamber creaking open.

"The Captain of the Guard," announced Hal Harness, stepping outside again as Axel swept into the chamber—his face a coalescence of elation and exhaustion. In his right hand, he clasped a roll of parchment.

"Apologies for the interruption," he said, coming to a stop between the dais and the row of chairs. "I know you are busy preparing for tomorrow, but I have important news to share with you both."

Before Jared could move or ask what he meant, Axel continued, his tone darkly triumphant. "I have solved Prince Anders's murder."

"You have?" Jared felt a fresh shiver of emotion move through him. "So soon?"

"We had to move fast," Axel asserted. "And we have done so. The assassin's name is Michael Reeves—at least that's the name he goes by in Archenfield. He works as a steward, right here in the palace. That's how he was able to poison Prince Anders's food."

Jared heard the words but struggled to absorb them. He realized he was still reeling from the news of his brother's death. It seemed too soon, somehow, to shift his focus from Anders's murder to his murderer. But Axel was unrelenting. "Reeves is originally from Paddenburg. He came here four years ago. I'm afraid he must have been a sleeper." Seeing Jared's puzzled expression, Axel elaborated. "An enemy agent who has been given time to settle in our state while he awaits instruction for his mission."

Jared felt breathless, as though a boulder was crushing his insides. "So you're saying there was a long-term plot to assassinate my brother?"

"It would appear so. I'm very sorry, Cousin. I know this can't be easy to hear."

Jared's hand made a fist, his knuckles white. He wasn't sure if he would be able to remain standing on his own two feet unsupported.

Logan spoke next. "If Paddenburg is behind this plot, what are you planning in terms of a revenge attack? Is it something we should be factoring into Prince Jared's address tomorrow?"

Jared felt a fresh flush of panic. Just as he was finally coming to grips with the Poet's words, was Axel about to change the script? Would he have to tell the people that, on the second day of his reign, he was taking the Princedom to war?

Axel turned to address the Poet. "I don't think the Prince should refer directly to Paddenburg or a revenge attack in his address. Keep it broad-brush while we consider our options and continue the investigation. What he can say is that the assassin has been apprehended and that the Blood Price will be paid." He paused. "I think that's what the mob needs to hear, don't you?"

Logan nodded, already reaching for his bundle of papers and making notes. "Yes. Yes, I agree. It's easily done."

Axel lifted the roll of parchment in his hand. "I have the death warrant here." He began walking toward the dais. "Prince Jared, I just need your signature."

"Has he confessed?" Jared asked, as his cousin presented him with the warrant and pointed out the two places where his signature was required.

"There can be no doubt it was him," Axel said, with utter confidence. "The postmortem report confirmed that your brother was poisoned, and that the most likely means of transmission was through his food. To poison Prince Anders, and Anders alone, the poison had to be added to his plate after it had left the kitchens. It's the stewards, as you know, who carry the plates from the kitchen to the dining hall. When we rounded up the stewards for questioning, one was missing. We apprehended the dirty fugitive in the forest. Within spitting distance of the Paddenburg Gate."

"Why?" Jared asked, as Logan handed him a pen. "Why did he go there?"

"To cross the border, of course," Axel said. "It's possible that he had accomplices on either side of the gates. Jonas and I have search teams stationed at key locations within the forest. The traps have been activated. If there's another assassin out there, he or she doesn't stand a chance."

"That's some comfort," Logan said.

Jared's fingers closed around the neck of the pen, glancing up at his cousin. "You really think there could be *another* assassin?" He froze. "If there is, then this one will be coming for me."

Axel nodded. "It's possible." There was nothing reassuring

in the words he spoke or his tone of voice. "I tried to get it out of the suspect, but he refuses to talk. Which only makes me more certain that he is an enemy spy whose part in this plot is successfully concluded. He'll have been trained not to crack under pressure. And, believe you me, I have applied quite considerable pressure."

"I have no doubt of that," Jared said. "He really won't tell you anything?"

A shake of the head. "He seems intent to go to his death as some kind of martyr." Axel's eyes met Jared's. "It's all under control, Prince Jared." He tapped the warrant. "All you have to do is sign your name. Leave the rest to me."

Jared's pen nib hovered above the parchment. "You are in absolutely no doubt that this man is my brother's assassin?"

"None whatsoever. I forgot to mention before that we found a book of poisons in his quarters, stolen from the Physician's private library. Evidently, he tried to hide it under his mattress before fleeing to the forest."

"A book of poisons?" Logan said. Jared realized that the Poet had risen from his chair and was now standing beside the Captain of the Guard.

"A book of poisons," Axel confirmed. "With ugly little scribbles and greasy fingerprints all over it."

Jared's hand began to shake. It was too much to take in. He could feel each shock he had experienced during the course of that day reverberating in his mind and body. The pen slipped from his hand and fell to the floor.

As the Poet knelt down to retrieve it, Jared felt Axel's hand firmly grip his arm. "I'm so sorry. If there was anything I could do to shelter you from this, I would. You need to get some rest, Cousin. Put an end to this day of horrors with a good sleep." The words hit home.

Logan rose up and extended the pen toward him. Jared found himself trembling again. "I don't understand it," he said. "After everything you've told me...after what that... traitor cold-heartedly inflicted on my brother, why can't I commit him to death? What is wrong with me? Why can't I just sign my name?"

Axel looked to Logan for support. Logan nodded. "As your cousin says, it has been a long and difficult day. For all of us who knew and loved your brother, but above all for you. Your mind is still racing to catch up with everything that has happened, with everything that has changed. But the ordeal is almost over. If you just sign the warrant, Axel can set the necessary action in motion—"

Axel cut him off, impatiently. "Your brother's killer will be put to death at sundown two nights from now. As ordained by Father Simeon and his predecessors, the prisoner will have two days and two nights to make peace with his tortured soul." His tone turned nastier. "Of course, if it was up to me, we'd do it right here, right now—with a rusty blade."

Jared turned back to Axel. "How will you kill him?"

"Beheading," Axel answered coolly. "It's the most efficient way, Morgan tells me. My only regret is the bastard won't suffer for very long."

Jared's eyes sought out the Poet's once more. "You think I should sign, don't you, Logan?"

The Poet nodded. "You said it yourself. This man coldheartedly planned and executed your brother's death. The Blood Price must be paid. Archenfield demands it. Your family demands it. Your brother..."

"All right," Jared said, needing no further persuasion. He seized the pen and swiftly inscribed his signature in the two places required. It was only as he returned the pen to the Poet, he noticed how he had signed his name.

Jared, Prince of All Archenfield.

After a day of body blows, seeing those five words before him—in indelible black ink—was in certain ways the greatest shock of all.

Jared had woken up a mere mortal. He was going to sleep in command of the Princedom. And sending his brother's killer to his death.

DAY TWO

FIFTEEN

The Physic Garden

ASTA FELT THE EARLY MORNING SUN ON THE back of her neck as she unlocked the door to the walled Physic Garden. Once inside, she closed the door behind her. She was surrounded by its four high stone walls. Opposite was the only other entry or exit point—the door that led to the walled Kitchen Garden, of equal dimensions, on the other side.

It didn't take her long to find what she was looking for. Uncle Elias was meticulous when it came to labeling his plants. Before long, she was crouching on the gravel path, bending down before the blue-green shrub named savin. It looked innocent enough, thought Asta. Boring even. It certainly wouldn't have drawn her eye had she not been looking for it. And yet, this innocuous-seeming plant harbored a dark power. Every part of it was toxic.

Even from where she crouched, she could smell its bitter leaves. If this was indeed the poison used to take Prince Anders's life, it must have taken some work on the assassin's part to disguise its pungent taste. But, Asta reminded herself, savin was only one of the two possible poisons referred to by Elias in the postmortem report.

Of the two poisons, savin would have been harder to get a hold of, Asta knew. It was not native to Archenfield and, according to Uncle Elias, this one shrub in the Physic Garden was the only plant in the Princedom. If savin had indeed been employed to assassinate their Prince, Asta could well understand why her uncle felt agitated about the presence of the plant in his own garden beds.

Access to the garden was prohibited. The most direct way in was via the path from the back of the Physician's House, through the door that Asta had earlier unlocked. But there was only one set of keys for the door, and Asta and her uncle were the only two people with straightforward access. That didn't get her anywhere. Asta knew that her uncle could not possibly be involved in Prince Anders's murder. Could someone have temporarily stolen her uncle's keys to unlock the door? To do so, they would have to be very familiar with the layout of the Physician's House and the place where he kept his keys.

Asta glanced across at the other door in the garden wall. Was it possible that someone had come into the garden from that direction? According to Elias, the door between the Physic Garden and the Kitchen Garden was kept locked at all times and, again, only he possessed the key. There were, he explained, very good reasons for this. In the event of a medical emergency at the palace, the route through the two gardens provided a shortcut from the village. The time saved could, he had told her, make the difference between life and death.

Could anyone have entered the garden other than through the two doors? Glancing up at the height of the walls, Asta shook her head. It might just have been possible if the walls had been covered with ivy or some other plant thick enough to cling to as an ascent and a descent were made. But all four walls were, perhaps intentionally, bare on both sides. The only realistic way over the top would be by means of a high ladder and Asta couldn't conceive how anyone could have propped a ladder against the outside of the wall, whether during the daytime or after nightfall, as one of the palace patrols would have been sure to notice and investigate this activity.

No, she decided, if someone had come to harvest a sprig of savin, with dark intent, they *must* have used her uncle's keys. The thought led Asta in a difficult direction. Though all and sundry, from the court and the settlements, had access to the Physician's surgery, only a very small circle of trusted colleagues enjoyed the same access to the Physician's House and garden. In effect, it came down to the Council of Twelve. And it was unthinkable, wasn't it, that one of them could have done this?

Why would one of the Twelve want to kill the Prince?

Asta turned her eyes back to the savin bush. Like the rest of the court, she was still in shock from the arrest the night before of the steward. The case against him had been well constructed but, to Asta's way of thinking, it didn't quite add up. For a start, there was no way the steward could have come into the Physician's House, her own new home, unnoticed and borrowed her uncle's keys.

Asta thought once more of the discussions she and Elias had had over the supine body of the dead Prince. The two poisons Elias had named triggered certain similar effects. In particular, both could have caused the gangrene she had seen on his feet. The case for savin was strengthened by the fact that the Prince had, according to Silva, suffered from convulsions and vomiting before he died. On the other hand, Silva had also told them that in his last hours, the Prince had experienced vicious hallucinations of wild animals stalking his bed and blood running down the palace walls. Such vivid fantasies might certainly have been caused by ergot.

Asta kept weighing in her mind the properties of the two substances. From what she had gleaned from her research, savin was a relatively fast-acting poison—capable of bringing about death in a matter of ten hours—whereas ergot was slower acting, and more likely to be fatal if administered on a cumulative basis.

These thoughts swirled around her mind, leading her up all kinds of dark alleys. Was it possible that a combination of the two toxins had been used? Then again, much of the information on which they had based their conclusions came from Silva. Was it possible that she was not telling the whole truth? The very thought felt treasonous. Asta thought of her own conversation with the Prince's widow and Silva's fear that the poison had not been destined for Anders at all but for her. As Asta now knew, savin had powerful abortive properties. So it was still entirely possible that the Prince had been killed by accident and that the assassin hadn't intended either Anders or his consort to die—only the royal couple's unborn child.

Shaking her head again, trying to break free from this maelstrom of thoughts, Asta kneeled down to inspect the shrub more closely from its tip to where the roots disappeared into the loamy Archenfield soil. Doing so, she could barely believe her eyes. Close to the base of the plant, she could see that one of the branches had been neatly snipped away.

As her pulse raced, Asta told herself that the small snip was not conclusive proof. Uncle Elias had said that he'd not used the plant as a remedy for a long time now, but that didn't mean he hadn't taken time to prune it. But Asta knew that when you pruned a plant—certainly when he'd instructed her on how to do so—you were supposed to take off an even number of branches on either side, to keep it in balance. Asta looked more closely for signs of further cuts but found none.

She was torn—she wanted to go and wake Uncle Elias to share her latest thinking with him, but at the same time, she knew he was opposed to her conducting her own investigation into the murder. *It is not for us to contemplate who was the intended victim or what provoked the attack. My job is to establish cause of death...* He had been very clear. But wasn't that all she was trying to establish too—what had caused Prince Anders's death and *who* was responsible?

It was vital to pinpoint the true path of the events that had led to Prince Anders's assassination. Doing so would not only solve this murder but also prevent further attacks on the court, attacks that might already be in the planning stages. In the first instance, uncovering the truth might exonerate Michael, but Asta knew that the ultimate effect of her investigation could be to save Prince Jared's own life. Such thoughts made her all the more determined to pursue the truth, wherever it led her.

"Elias! Elias Peck—is that you?"

A woman's shrill voice made her start and, in the low

sunlight, it took Asta a moment to place exactly where it was coming from. She turned toward the door that joined the Physic Garden to the Kitchen Garden. On the other side of the metal grille stood the formidable figure of the Cook.

"Oh, it's you," Vera Webb said, with undisguised disappointment, as Asta rose to her feet.

"My uncle is still sleeping," Asta said.

"Well, bully for him," Vera said. "Some of us have jobs to do at this hour." As she approached the grille, Asta could see that Vera was holding a trug filled with freshly cut herbs. "How come you are up and about this early then?" the Cook asked, surveying her with suspicion through the iron grille.

"I couldn't sleep," Asta lied. "My uncle is always testing my knowledge of the plants here, so I thought I'd get some early work in today."

"How nice to have time on your hands," Vera said sharply.

"You've been busy too," Asta observed. Didn't the Cook have underlings to send out for herbs?

As if reading Asta's mind, Vera's eyes met hers. "I thought it best to come and pick the herbs myself this morning. Just in case they arrest another member of my team before I get lunch under way."

Asta nodded noncommittally.

"I take it you know all about the arrest?" Vera continued.

"One of my stewards. Michael Reeves. The sweetest, kindest boy you could ever hope to meet. But thanks to Axel Blaxland—and *your uncle*—he's locked up in the Dungeons."

"What part did Uncle Elias play in that?" Asta asked, defensively.

Vera rolled her eyes. "Because of the postmortem report," she said. "Your uncle told the Captain of the Guard that Prince Anders was killed by poisoned food."

Should Asta remind Vera that Elias had offered up *several* possible ways in which Prince Anders could have been poisoned? There seemed little point in that.

"I wonder what Prince Jared thinks about all this," Asta mused instead.

"The new Prince signed the death warrant," Vera shot back. "So I'd say he's pretty sure about it. But really, that boy has so many people whispering in his ear, he can't know if he's coming or going. This is all Axel Blaxland's doing. He wanted a quick resolution to this investigation and Michael will be killed tomorrow night while the real killer goes free."

Tomorrow night? So soon?

Asta didn't like what she was hearing. She was very familiar with the postmortem report. Surely it wasn't conclusive enough to condemn a man to his death—unless there was evidence she, and perhaps Vera too, didn't know about.

"You seem very certain that the steward is innocent," Asta said.

Vera nodded. "You're right there," she said. "I run a tight kitchen. It's damn near impossible for food to be tampered with."

Perhaps she could see the lingering doubt in Asta's eyes.

"Sometimes," the Cook continued, "you can know things in your gut before you do in your head. Do you understand? And I know that my boy didn't kill the Prince. But I can't prove it. And now he'll lose his head by nightfall tomorrow." The Cook had worked herself up into such a state that her face was as purple as beetroot, but now she sighed, defeated.

"Well, I'd better go and oversee the breakfast preparations," she said. "I'll leave you to your 'studies.'"

As the Cook disappeared from view, Asta turned and pressed her back against the connecting door, surveying the four walls of the Physic Garden. Sometimes it was good to look at things from a fresh perspective. Her head was still full of the noise of Vera's protestations—her assertions of Michael's innocence and her anger with Axel and Elias.

Vera was not the most likable of creatures, but that didn't mean she wasn't worth listening to. In certain ways, the Cook had given voice to Asta's own doubts.

There was no denying that the steward had had direct

access to Prince Anders's supper plate. Nor that Michael had run to the forest before being apprehended. His behavior was, to say the least, suspicious. But still, things did not quite add up.

Asta looked around the garden again more convinced than ever that Michael could not have broken in there. Certainly not alone. He'd have needed some high-level help.

The Cook seemed certain that Michael was innocent. As certain as Axel was of his guilt. But in the postmortem report, Uncle Elias hadn't said that poisoned food was the definite method of murder, only that it was the most likely one. He had also raised another strong possibility, to which no one seemed to be paying attention—that the poison had been inserted through the wound on Prince Anders's leg.

The Cook might well be telling the truth. Michael might have no part in the plot. But, for whatever reason, Prince Jared *had* signed the young man's death warrant and he'd be executed at sundown tomorrow. Vera Webb was right—there could be no halting or reversing of this decision without hard evidence. Asta determined then and there to find some. She needed to find out more about Prince Anders's hunting wound and she knew exactly who she needed to ask.

SIXTEEN

The Grand Hall, the Palace

THE FIVE CHIMES OF THE GROOM'S BELL ECHOED
about the palace.

"It's time," Logan told Prince Jared.

Jared nodded. He had heard the crowd gathering in
the palace grounds during the past few hours and Edvin
had brought back reports from upstairs where he had been
covertly observing proceedings. Jared had listened to his
brother's descriptions, with a growing sense of doom and
nausea, declining the offer to come and take a peek for
himself.

"Do *you* feel ready?" his mother asked him.

"I'm not sure I'm ever going to feel ready for this," he
admitted.

"You'll be fine," Logan said. "Trust me. It will be over before you know it."

His mother kissed him sharply on the cheek. "Just stick to Logan's script, my darling, and you won't go wrong."

They walked out to join the others on the balcony. Jared was flanked on one side by Logan and on the other by his brother and his mother.

As the crowd below the balcony caught sight of the new Prince and his entourage, the hubbub that had preceded their arrival dwindled to an expectant hush.

Edvin and Elin walked off to the side, to join the other royals and the waiting Twelve. Meanwhile, Logan and Jared continued side by side toward the edge of the balcony.

Seeing the crowd down below, Jared felt a sudden sense of vertigo. They covered every last inch of the palace grounds. Their faces were a blur.

As Logan began speaking, making formal confirmation of Prince Anders's death, Jared remembered some advice the Poet had given him earlier.

"Find one face, somewhere central in the crowd. Focus on that one face alone when you make the speech. Forget about however many others are out there; just imagine you are speaking to one person."

Suddenly, he heard the sound of clapping. He turned and saw that Logan had finished speaking and was now gesturing to him to come forward. His throat felt parched and his limbs heavy as he took the few remaining paces to the front. There was no turning back now.

He looked out into the crowd, searching for that one face. With relief, he found it. It was the Physician's niece. He'd have zeroed in on her arresting gray eyes and copper-red hair within any crowd. She smiled at him—just as she had when he'd seen her helping her uncle with Anders's body. Now, as then, there was something reassuring in her smile.

Jared took a breath, then began speaking.

"Citizens of Archenfield," he said, "it is good to see so many of you here today. This is a sad day in Archenfield's history—the saddest certainly that I have known—and it is good, I think, that we should gather together like this and help each other through our grief."

He could feel the crowd hanging expectantly on his words. He kept focused on that one face, which was still gazing intently up at him.

"My brother, Prince Anders, is dead. My family and I, and all the court, are in a state of shock at this, as I know you are too." He paused. "Prince Anders was only at the beginning of his reign. In two short years, he achieved much for the Princedom, as well as finding deep personal happiness with his wife, Silva, who is very much in my thoughts today and, I'm sure, in yours too." He glanced across the balcony at Silva, noting that Elin had taken her daughter-in-law's hand and was holding it tightly. Nodding, Jared turned back to the crowd, finding the girl.

"We, all of us in his family and the court, thought that Prince Anders would rule over Archenfield for many glorious years to come. Sadly, this has turned out not to be the case. But even though his time here was much shorter than we would have wished for, his impact was great. Anders, my dear brother, Archenfield will never forget you."

Jared broke off. Although he was speaking words crafted by the Poet, still he could feel the emotion cutting through his voice. His eyes were now wet with tears and he knew he needed to take a breath to steady himself.

As he did so, he became aware of cheers ringing out from the ground below. The gathered citizens of Archenfield were showing him their support, telling him it was all right to be upset. The noise was soon like a waterfall, completely engulfing. It was as if every man, woman and child in Archenfield was cheering in support of the two princes, Anders and Jared.

When Jared resumed his speech, his voice was clearer than he had expected. "I want you all to know that the investigations into my brother's murder have already begun. Be under no illusions. The Blood Price will be paid. And soon. But while we await the results of the official investigation, I do not want our Princedom—this wonderful Princedom of Archenfield—to live under the shadow of fear. Yes, for now there are unanswered questions, but the answers are being sought and we will tell them to you when we ourselves know them. The truth matters to me and I will stop at nothing until I discover the truth of what happened to my brother. When I do, you may be assured, I will share it with you."

He paused, seeking out the girl. As he did so, a fresh—unscripted—thought occurred to him and it seemed right to give voice to it. "This is a difficult time for all of us. My family and I truly appreciate you coming here and showing your support." He paused, then smiled and continued: "I know, thanks to my younger brother who was spying on you all from one of the turrets above, that many of you have been here since the early hours. You must be tired and hungry and I hope you will take advantage of the food we have laid out before you journey back to your homes." He paused. "There is no immediate cure for the grief we all feel now, but it will come—for us all."

There was another burst of cheering. Eventually, Prince Jared lifted his hand to stay the noise. "You are very kind," he said. "There is just one more thing I want to say to you." Now he lifted his head, so that when he next spoke, his voice seemed to take flight up into the sky and out across the realm. "There was a Princedom. Its name was Archenfield. There is *still* a Princedom. Nothing and no one will threaten the future of Archenfield." Another pause. "There was a Prince and his name was Anders. His deeds were many and great and he died with so much promise unfulfilled. There is still a Prince. My name is Jared. And I pledge to continue my brother's work and to serve you and Archenfield to the end of my days."

As he finished speaking, the cheers were deafeningly loud and long. Looking back into the crowd, Prince Jared saw that the girl was once again smiling at him. Daring to look beyond her at other faces, he saw that many there too were smiling at him, while those who were not were lost in tears.

Moments later, when the cheering showed no sign of abating, Prince Jared lifted his hand to acknowledge the people's response. As he did so, some of the people began throwing flowers up toward the balcony. It was a magical sight—the sky in front of the palace suddenly dancing with garlands of leaves and early autumn flowers. Jared looked out as the petals fell like confetti, uniting them all for one glorious moment.

Jared glanced over his shoulder and beckoned to Edvin to come and join him. His brother marched over and stood at his side. Both young men lifted their hands to acknowledge the crowd. Jared glanced to his side, seeing Elin and Silva and the others watching from the side. Were they pleased with his words? And the crowd's response? He hoped so. All he could say was that he had done his best.

At last, Logan Wilde stepped forward and gave the signal that it was time to go back inside the palace. But not before some ambitious members of the crowd had been hoisted aloft on the shoulders of their friends to offer garlands of flowers to the two princes. Jared saw the nervous glances exchanged between the Poet and the Bodyguard. The Prince himself answered these with a smile and a shake of his head. Within minutes, his arms—and Edvin's too— were full of flowers and the two older men had to admit good-natured defeat.

Jared's eyes ranged across the crowd one last time, then he turned and began walking with his brother back to the main palace doors off the balcony. He and Edvin followed Logan inside, weighed down by their posies of flowers.

Elin and Silva, Uncle Viggo, Aunt Stella, Cousin Koel, and the members of the Twelve were waiting to greet them there.

When the doors were closed behind them, muffling the cheers still emanating from the crowds outside, Logan was the first to speak. "Well," he said, "I don't think that could have gone much better, do you?"

Elin nodded and Jared saw that his mother was smiling. She was still holding Silva's hand. Now Silva too gazed over at him, her face wreathed in a tranquil smile.

Uncle Viggo stepped forward. "I don't wish to appear

churlish," he said. "But Prince Jared did not entirely stick to the Poet's script." He paused. "Unless some final changes were made of which we were not informed."

Jared opened his mouth to respond, but Logan beat him to it. "No, you are right. Prince Jared did improvise a little. But the script was only ever intended as a guide. I think what the people wanted was to hear their new Prince speak from the heart and connect with them." He turned and nodded at Jared. "He certainly achieved that."

"Nonetheless," Lord Viggo said. "The script was there for a reason."

"He's right," Emelie Sharp, the Beekeeper, said. "We all have our jobs to do, and there are reasons we are entrusted to do them. Prince Jared, I mean no offense by this, but you were not just speaking for yourself and your family out there. You were speaking on behalf of the entire court."

Jared nodded, feeling the euphoria of finishing the speech and experiencing the crowd's ecstatic response drain away.

As other members of the Twelve and the royal party waded in with their own opinions, Prince Jared turned to Logan. "I'm sorry," he said. "You wrote me a great speech and I'm truly grateful for that. I hope you know that I did not depart from it for any reason other than . . . it just seemed the right thing to do at the time."

"I do know that," Logan said, as they watched the others

bickering. "And I can say without any hesitation that you did absolutely the right thing." He lowered his voice. "Some of the others can be terribly literal about everything." He cleared his throat and spoke normally again. "And now, may I suggest that we stop debating what was, by any standards, a wonderful performance, and help free the two young princes from the burden of these rustic garlands?"

SEVENTEEN

The Palace Gardens

ASTA FOUND KAI JAGGER IN A SECLUDED GLADE in the palace gardens, which bordered on woodland. The Chief Huntsman was standing on a grassy hummock, a willow basket at his side. The low sun made a silhouette of him, standing as still as a statue, as if in a warrior pose. Gripped in his left hand was what at first looked to her like a multiblade weapon. As she stepped a little closer, out of the immediate glare of the sun, she saw he was in fact holding a clutch of small hatchets. She counted five of them, their sharp blades glinting menacingly in the light.

A piercing whistle sliced through the air, making Asta jump. At the same moment, the Huntsman sprang into motion. "Blues," he called. A second later, he threw the first of the small axes.

Facing them, at a distance of perhaps a hundred feet, was a line of birch trees. Asta watched as the Huntsman's four remaining axes flew through the air in quick succession, each finding its mark in the trunk of one of the trees. She noticed that there were targets painted at varying levels on each of the central five birches—colored circles of blue, green, red and yellow. And, sure enough, each one of the hatchet blades was embedded within one of the blue circles.

She watched as two members of the Huntsman's team shinned up the trunks of the trees to remove the blades. She was tempted to approach Kai Jagger then and there, but something compelled her to wait.

The young man and woman made fast work of retrieving the hatchets. Asta saw that Kai was already poised with a fresh clutch of axes in his hand. The willow basket must be full of the small but deadly weapons, she realized. His colleagues had retreated to the edge of the row of birch trees. Now one of them gave another shrill whistle. "Reds," Kai called in response. Asta watched as he sent the next five blades flying down the clearing and toward the tree trunks. Once again, each one hit its target—this time the red circles, painted at varying levels on each of the central five trees. There was no doubting his precision, and Asta felt that she would not have liked to be an animal trying to evade the Huntsman's aim.

As Kai's subordinates moved into action again, Asta came forward.

"Mr. Jagger," she said, walking over to join him on the hillock.

Kai did not respond at first. It was as if he were in a trance. He already had a fresh collection of hatchets in his hand.

"Mr. Jagger," she repeated, slightly louder.

"Yes." Suddenly his eyes were upon her and she felt as though she were staring at a wild beast. Asta remembered someone telling her once that when a wolf caught your scent, it would make an instant decision about whether you were a friend or an enemy, and would never deviate from that judgment. She noticed that the Huntsman's eyes were as violet as the waters of the fjord, their color made all the more striking by their contrast with his tanned skin and long silver hair.

"I'm sorry to disturb you," Asta said. "I'm Asta Peck, the Physician's niece."

"I know who you are." She felt him appraising her as he spoke. It was not a comfortable sensation.

"I make it my business to know everyone who enters the court," he continued.

Kai shifted the hatchets in his hand slightly. Asta wondered whether she might have strayed into danger.

"Why did you seek me out?" he asked.

"To ask you a few questions," she said. "But, if you are busy, I can wait."

He nodded, raising his free hand to her. The message

could not have been clearer. *Stay there!* There was a fresh whistle. Now Kai Jagger turned his searing gaze from her and called out again. "Yellows."

He sent the hatchets soaring toward the line of birches. His movements were so fast, so subtle, that Asta was unable to fully appreciate his mastery. Still, it was no surprise to look down through the glade and see that yet again, each blade had found its intended mark.

Unhurriedly, Kai Jagger turned back to face her. "All right, Asta Peck. You say you have some questions."

"I'm helping my uncle with his investigations into Prince Anders's death," Asta began.

"You?" His eyes bored into hers. "You are only a child. What help can you give?"

"I'm Elias's apprentice," Asta said. "He's training me."

The Huntsman's eyes narrowed. "The murder investigations are being conducted by the Captain of the Guard. An arrest has been made and the death warrant signed." Asta's thoughts turned to the steward, trapped in the Dungeons, as Kai continued his rant. "The Physician's work was complete when he delivered his postmortem report."

"There are some lingering questions," Asta replied. "And we thought you might be able to help us with them."

Kai continued to stare at her. "The facts seem very clear in this matter—to me, if not to you."

Asta held her nerve. Before the Huntsman could raise

a fresh objection or, for that matter, a hatchet, she plowed on. "The day before Prince Anders died, he was out hunting with you, wasn't he?" ·

Kai Jagger did not, at first, respond with words, but held her instead in his penetrating stare. "Yes," he said at last. "Hardly an unusual occurrence."

"We observed a wound on Prince Anders's right leg, during the postmortem examination. It looked to us like a wound the Prince might have sustained while hunting."

She waited as patiently as she could for Kai to respond.

"Do you have a question?" he asked.

"Yes," she said, beginning to grow exasperated in spite of herself. "Do you remember if the Prince was wounded during that final hunting expedition?"

"No," Kai said. His head and body remained perfectly still.

"No, he wasn't wounded or no, you don't remember?" Asta pressed him.

He was silent for a moment and she thought for sure she had offended him. But then he responded. "The former."

Asta felt deflated. She had been so sure. She had seen the wound for herself and heard Uncle Elias talk about that same wound as a possible means of transmission for the poison. If that were the case, it would change everything.

Kai turned away and reached down into the basket at his side. He lifted five more hatchets from inside. "Greens," he called. Asta could feel the movement of the air as the

Huntsman sent the next five axes flying toward the trees. Four of the five hit their targets but, to her surprise, the fifth missed and sailed through the gap between two of the trees. She could see from the Huntsman's expression that he was displeased.

"I'm sure that doesn't happen often," she said.

If he'd heard her, he gave no indication of it.

"What's this game called?" she inquired now.

That caught his attention. "It's not a game," he said. "It's important to keep my eye trained for hunting."

"Of course." She frowned. "But which animals would you catch like this?"

Kai Jagger's violet eyes met hers. "These weapons are not used on animals," he said.

She trembled. The implicit threat of his words was clear enough.

"I'd better get going," she said. "Thank you for your time." She stepped down from the mound, feeling his eyes still burning into her back as she walked away. But she hadn't gone more than a few paces when, to her surprise, she heard his voice again.

"Prince Anders *was* wounded. But not on that final hunting expedition. It was over a week ago."

Asta stopped dead in her tracks. If Kai's information was accurate, this could still impact their findings. From what Uncle Elias had said, the wound could have been used for a slow buildup of the poison—and ergot was known to be significantly more potent with regular dosage.

Asta turned to face the Huntsman again. "Can you remember who was part of the hunting party that day?"

Kai nodded. "Myself, Prince Anders, Hal Harness and a couple of the other guards, Axel Blaxland, Elliot Nash, Jonas Drummond and Lucas Curzon. They were the main ones. And a few of my own team of course."

Asta nodded, making a mental note of each of the names.

"The Prince had shot a stag. But it wasn't a clean kill. I was surprised and I think he was too. Prince Anders usually had impeccable aim."

Asta drank in his words. Was it mere chance that the Prince had been off his game? Or might it suggest that something had been preying on his mind?

"The creature was badly wounded," Kai continued. "It was flailing about and Prince Anders ran over to it, intent on putting it out of its pain as swiftly as possible. When he got close, however, the creature had a sudden final surge of adrenaline. This sometimes happens, but it took Prince Anders by surprise. The stag charged at the Prince and one of its antlers made a shallow gash on his leg, before I was able to catch up and finally send the creature to its death."

Asta nodded. "According to Elias, the first he saw of the wound was during the postmortem. Wasn't the wound serious enough to need medical attention?"

"No," Kai said reflexively.

"Who made that assessment?" Asta inquired.

Kai narrowed his eyes once more. "I did. You don't need to be the Physician to apply a bandage to a wound. What next? Should I seek out your uncle's attention if I prick my little finger on a rosebush?"

Asta ignored this barb and pressed on. "Did you apply any form of remedy before you applied the bandage?"

Kai shook his head. "No. There was no need. Prince Anders didn't want to make a fuss."

"Do you think any of your hunting companions might have offered a remedy?" Asta asked. "Perhaps a salve of some kind?"

Kai shook his head. "I really wouldn't know," he said.

Asta could tell from his tone of voice that he had decided to shut down this line of inquiry. She frowned. His information had been useful but, for now, it had led her to a dead end. And if she was to further the theory that Prince Anders had been poisoned by a substance applied to his wound, then she needed to find more answers from another quarter. And she had to do it fast, now that there had been an arrest and the death warrant issued and signed.

"Asta!"

This time it wasn't the Huntsman who addressed her, but Uncle Elias. Her blood ran cold. How had he found her? She had no right to be in this part of the palace grounds and she could tell his level of anger was high, even though so far he had only intoned the two syllables of her name.

Hesitantly, she turned around to witness Elias marching toward her but was surprised when he was intercepted by the Huntsman.

"Peck!" Kai Jagger cried. "I was just answering your questions." Asta watched as her uncle's eyes darted across to her, then back toward the Huntsman. "I'd appreciate it," Kai continued, "if next time you dare to emulate Axel and question another of the Twelve, you are man enough to do it yourself rather than sending in your apprentice!"

Asta watched to see how her uncle would respond. He did not fight fire with fire but merely nodded in a placatory fashion. Asta had no doubt that she would receive the full force of her uncle's fury as soon as they were alone. She felt her own anger toward Kai Jagger rising.

"I'm very sorry that you were troubled," Elias said. "It will not happen again." His voice sounded cold as he turned. "Asta, you will accompany me back to the village now."

She was aware of Kai Jagger watching her discomfort with evident amusement. Fine. Let him feel smug and superior. Whatever he thought of her, she had managed to obtain some very useful information from him.

"Come on, Asta!" Elias said, reaching out for her arm, but she slipped out of his clutches. She'd go with him, but she wouldn't allow herself to be dragged away like an errant child.

Seeing this, Kai Jagger smiled and shook his head, then reached into the basket of hatchets and took up a fresh bunch of glinting weapons.

Asta felt Uncle Elias's hot breath on her ear as he hurried her out of earshot. "Remember your place, Asta Peck. If you ever embarrass me like that again, I'll send you straight back to the settlements—without so much as a second thought."

She nodded, shivering at Uncle Elias's dark warning. She couldn't return to the settlements—not now. There was far too much at stake.

"Blues," she heard Kai Jagger call out once more. Moments later, she heard the sound of the axes whipping through the air.

Asta could not resist glancing back over her shoulder. This time Kai Jagger had succeeded in hitting all of the targets. She was not surprised. In the brief time she had spent with the Chief Huntsman, she had formed a picture of someone who was rarely deterred from getting exactly what he wanted. A fresh thought floated into her head. Just how many creatures had the Huntsman sent to their deaths? And did these include a Prince?

EIGHTEEN

The Long Gallery, the Palace

JARED MADE HIS WAY THROUGH THE PALACE, Hal Harness five steps behind him. It was curious how quickly he had grown used to having the Bodyguard attached to him at all times, as if by an invisible string.

Through the leaded panes of the windows, Jared observed the light fading from the sky. His second day as Prince was drawing to a close. Already, he felt he had come on a momentous journey. Getting accustomed to being followed everywhere he went was only a small part of it.

As he continued on his way, a bell began to chime. He counted each chime in turn, all thirteen of them. It was hard to let go of such childish habits. He and Edvin had always teased each other about the Executioner's Bell—the penultimate bell of the day. But he found he could not return to that lost innocence. Now, when he thought of the Executioner's Bell, he thought of the death warrant he had signed the night before. And of the execution of the assassin, scheduled at the striking of the very same bell the following evening.

The past two days had given him a keen sense that the Princedom was a machine and each member of the Council of Twelve a key component within that machine. From the outside, it appeared as if the Princedom ran itself—but this was only because of their expertise and diligence. It had all passed him by as Edling. He had sat in meetings of the Twelve, often lost in daydreams, feeling the discussions to have little bearing on his own life and preoccupations. He had submitted to the rigors of his training—from archery to celestial navigation—with varying degrees of interest and enthusiasm. There had been moments of satisfaction and understanding before. But truly it was as if, in the past two days, a veil had been lifted from his eyes. Jared was also painfully aware that as much as had already been revealed to him, he was still only at the beginning of this journey of discovery.

He had reached his destination. His mother's quarters were protected by her own bodyguard—who, seeing the new Prince approaching, inclined his head in a bow and opened the first of the two doors he would need to go through to announce Prince Jared's arrival.

Jared turned to find Hal, of course, at his shoulder.

"You can wait out here," he told him. Seeing Hal hesitate for a moment, he added, "I'm not likely to come to any harm at my mother's hands."

Hal stepped dutifully back into the corridor as Prince Jared proceeded into the Queen's suite. It was Elin herself who had chosen the title of Queen, and not Prince's Consort, at the outset of Prince Goran's reign. Neither Goran nor anyone else had seen fit to challenge her. She had retained the title throughout Prince Anders's reign and was now poised to do so with Jared as ruler of Archenfield. This seemed entirely appropriate, he reflected; through all the turmoil and changes undergone by the Princedom, Queen Elin was its one constant—as steadfast and unyielding as the toughest Archenfield oak.

He found her, as he had expected, in the first of her rooms. It served as a combined office and parlor for her. She had a desk there—somewhat smaller and more elegant than the one in his own quarters—and was often to be found sitting behind it, writing carefully crafted letters in her immaculate handwriting. Now though, Elin was seated across the room, close by the windows, in front of her easel. It was her custom, every evening at this time, to take the same position and devote the hour or so preceding the evening meal to painting. A choice selection of her canvases covered the wall above the fireplace. They were, on the whole, bucolic scenes—depicting Archenfield in its rich and diverse natural beauty.

Elin was currently engaged in grinding pigment to a fine powder with a pestle and mortar, in preparation no doubt for making up another batch of paint.

"Jared," she said, acknowledging his presence without looking up from her task. "Thank you for coming to see me. Take a seat."

He assessed his choices and began moving toward an inviting-looking wingback chair by the hearth.

"No," she said. "Sit here, where I can see you. In the window seat."

He retraced his steps, hovering in front of the window. "Won't I block your view?" he asked.

"No," she said decisively. "I'm painting from memory." She glanced up at him, then went back to what she was doing. She began pouring a slow stream of linseed oil into the newly ground pigment powder.

"You look tired," she said, though surely she had had only the briefest opportunity to make this assessment.

"I suppose I am," he said, trying to make himself more comfortable on the window seat. "It's been another long day..."

"But you got through it," she said, stirring the paint pot vigorously. "You did what was asked of you. And you did it well."

"Thank you, Mother," he said. "I know that some of the Twelve thought I should have stuck closer to the script."

"Oh yes, you never know when one of them will throw the rule book at you. Or, indeed, which one it will be." She carefully teased out a portion of the paint she had made—a livid red—onto her palette. "Don't take it to heart, my dear," she continued. "Remember, *they* are here to serve *us*. As much as it might sometimes appear to be vice versa."

She smiled at him, her wide eyes radiant in the candlelight. He was struck by the way she made people feel when she deigned to bestow her full attention upon them— blessed somehow, as if they had the power to conquer new worlds or fly with the ease of one of Nova's falcons. In Jared's young life, there hadn't been many occasions when he had been granted his mother's full attention. She had, out of necessity, kept her focus squarely on Anders. But she was nothing if not a pragmatist and with Anders gone, he supposed he could expect her to take a keener interest in him.

"The trick," she said, applying her brush to the palette, "is to take one step at a time. But it pays to be a step ahead of the Twelve." Dabbing the new color onto the canvas, she continued, "Tomorrow, for instance, you must announce your choice of Edling."

"I have made my decision," he told her, leaning forward with purpose. "It will be Edvin."

"No," she said, with the same decisiveness as when he had selected the wrong chair. "Though your motives are laudable, Edvin won't do. He won't do at all."

"I know he is young," Jared began, "but so was I when Anders picked me."

"It's not a question of Edvin's youth," his mother said, swirling her brush in a pot of turpentine, its pungent smell instantly permeating the room. "It's not about what your brother has, or does not have, to offer the role. The fact is that there is only one viable candidate for Edling." Her brush stilled, and she met his eyes once more. "Your cousin Axel."

"Mother!"

"Don't adopt that tone, Jared." As if he were a child again, protesting at having to go to bed.

"But I don't even like Cousin Axel, and I'm not sure I know him well enough to trust him."

Elin smiled indulgently. "I *do* know Axel Blaxland and I'm not sure I trust him entirely either. That's rather the point." She wiped the turpentine off her brush, then dipped it into another pool of color—a rich blue—on her palette. "There has been a tension within Archenfield for some time now. My brother and his clan are desperate to get their hands on the Princedom."

Jared was confused. "So your answer to this is to cede power to them?"

Elin shook her head. "My answer is to give them a sign— to make them think that they are being brought closer to the table. We did it once before, when your father made Axel his Captain of the Guard. Now we need to pull your cousin in even closer, make him feel that his hands are in touching distance of the crown."

"If he becomes my Edling, then his hands *are* in touching distance."

"Only if you die," Elin said matter-of-factly. "Which you're not going to." Her eyes met his again. "I certainly don't intend to lose two sons in quick succession. No, you are young and healthy and you have a long reign in prospect. We will put Axel into position for the time being; then in ten years, maybe less, we shall reconsider. There are means at our disposal. Then, perhaps you *can* move Edvin into position so that we consolidate the Wynyard line. Or, of course, we may wish to consider Silva's child in order to renew the alliance with Woodlark."

Jared listened to his mother's machinations. "You talk about all this—about all of us—as if it is a game of chess."

"Do I?" she said, holding the thought briefly. "Well, I suppose it is in a way. Only much, much more important." She surveyed her canvas, paintbrush in midair. "So, we are agreed, Axel will be named your Edling."

"I suppose so," Jared said slowly. It was one thing standing up to the Council of Twelve but quite another taking on the force of nature that was his mother.

"This has to happen," Elin said. "And it has to happen tomorrow."

"All right," he agreed. "There's a meeting of the Twelve tomorrow morning. I can announce *my* decision then."

"Excellent," she said, dipping her brush again and continuing her work on the canvas.

"I'm curious," Jared said. "What are you painting?" He leaned closer toward her.

"No," she said, raising her free hand. "I've not quite finished."

He wasn't sure if she was talking about her picture or their conversation.

"How is Silva today?" Elin asked now. "Have you seen her?"

"Not since the speech," he said. In truth, he had not paid much attention to her there, having other things and other people pressing more centrally on his mind.

"The poor creature is badly shaken," Elin said.

"Understandably," Jared rejoined.

His mother seemingly declined to engage in this volley, busily daubing at her canvas again.

"I'm sure she feels utterly alone," Elin said, after a pause. "She's never really taken to Archenfield as her home. Have you seen how wistfully she looks through the windows up at the mountains? Thinking, no doubt, of what lies beyond."

"No," he said. Jared realized that he had never paid sufficient attention to his sister-in-law to make such an observation. He was surprised that his mother had, but he was starting to recognize that very little escaped Elin's notice.

"Well, I can assure you, Jared, that is what she does. And if she was feeling homesick before she lost her husband, imagine how it is for her now. That baby growing inside her will only make it worse. She'll be pining for Woodlark, mark my words."

"Perhaps it would be a kind gesture to allow her to visit her family?" Jared said.

"I don't think so." Elin shuddered at the thought. "Not at this time. They will, of course, come to Anders's funeral and stay to attend your coronation. But there is no question of Silva crossing state borders—not with the latest addition to our family tree growing inside her."

She spoke, Jared thought, as if Silva were only a vessel for Anders's child. He found himself pitying his sister-in-law. He made a mental note to seek her out at dinner and ask how she was bearing up. Someone had to show her some basic human kindness.

"You should marry her," Elin said.

"What?" Looking up in shock, Jared saw his mother's eyes twinkling above the rim of her canvas.

"You should marry her. That way, she remains the Prince's Consort and we keep the baby secure in our midst."

Jared's eyes narrowed. "That's very romantic," he said. "But I'm confident, when the time is right, I can make my own choice of bride."

"Your own choice?" Elin laughed at that. "Really? Is

that what you think your brother did? I know Logan Wilde excelled himself at seeding the story of Anders and Silva's fairy-tale romance, but I had no idea that *you* had believed it so wholeheartedly."

Jared was unnerved. "You're telling me it *wasn't* a fairy-tale romance?"

Elin shook her head. "I'd *never* say such a thing. When your brother laid eyes on the beauty of Woodlark, how could it have been anything but a fairy tale?" She smiled. "Does it really matter whose pen was writing the narrative?"

Once more, Jared had the sense of his mother's deft hands hovering over a giant chessboard. He and his brothers and Silva and Axel—they were all just pieces to be shuffled around to satisfy her power play.

Just when he thought he was at last getting to know her, he wasn't so sure that he wanted to.

"I can see you are morally outraged," Elin said. "Don't try to deny it! Your face is easy to read, Jared. That's something we must work on too. I shall talk to Logan."

"No," he said, rising to his feet. "Don't talk to Logan! Stop trying to manipulate me...I'll do your bidding as regards Axel, but it stops there. I'm not your puppet."

"Of course not, darling," his mother said, calmly setting down her brush. "You're tired. You said so before. That's why you're overreacting. I'm certainly not trying to manipulate you, just hoping to share with you the benefit of my experience. After all, you are not the first Prince of All Archenfield I have put on the throne. If *I* can't offer you informed advice, who can?"

Perhaps she was right. Maybe he was overreacting due to tiredness. Maybe she hadn't even been serious in suggesting that he marry his dead brother's wife.

She couldn't have been, could she?

"I've finished," she announced. "You may give me your verdict."

It took him a moment to realize she was referring to her painting. She was surveying it with a critical eye. He walked over and, at last, the picture was revealed to him. Elin's painting was of a stag. The animal had been wounded— Jared could see the hunter's arrow deeply embedded in its side and the trail of blood as it lumbered away.

"What do you think?" she asked him now. "Be frank. I'm always receptive to criticism."

"It's very good," he said. Though the subject matter was questionable, there was no doubting the technical artistry behind the scene.

"Do you really think so?" She rose from her seat. "It commemorates the moment when you first learned you were to be Archenfield's new Prince. Kai Jagger was kind enough to describe the scene for me. Though it's not as if I don't know how a wounded stag looks! I've shot enough of them in my time." She turned her gaze from the painting to Jared. "But this isn't intended as a nature scene," she told him. "It's symbolic. The stag represents the court of Archenfield. He has been wounded very close to his heart, but he is still moving. Though he is in pain, and bleeding, he knows that he has no alternative but to struggle on."

Jared's eyes were assaulted by the vivid red she had mixed up for the stag's blood. It took him back to that defining moment. But, of course, it hadn't been his arrow that had felled the stag. He wondered who had embroidered the truth—the Chief Huntsman or Elin herself.

"I painted it for you," she told him, looping her arm through his. "I hope you will find it an inspirational gift."

"Thank you, Mother," he said automatically. He would have to find somewhere suitable to hang it. Somewhere where he would rarely have to set his eyes on it. Both the image and his mother's explanation of it made him uneasy.

Elin seemed oblivious to his reaction. "Well," she said. "All of a sudden, I'm famished. Sometimes painting really drains me of my resources. If you'll excuse me, I'm going to wash up and change for dinner."

She kissed him, her lips fleeting as the wings of a butterfly on the side of his cheek. Then she was gone into the next of her chambers. Jared was left alone, with only his mother's grim artwork for company.

NINETEEN

The Dungeons

MORGAN BOOTH SMILED AS THE LAST CHIMES
of "his" hour faded away. He always felt a particular sense
of peace and homecoming as he descended the cold, stone
steps to the Dungeons below. Yes, this was the starkest area
within the palace complex. It was not the place to come
if you valued placing your feet upon richly embroidered
carpets—or indeed any kind of carpet. Nor, he reflected as
he continued his descent—lantern in hand—would you find
in the subterranean dankness fine artworks or elegantly
inlaid wooden furniture, such as you certainly would in the
rooms, suites and corridors above. Such fripperies mattered
little to the Executioner. The Dungeons were the one part
of the palace he could call his own. And though it was as
true down here as up above that every brick and beam was

property of the Wynyard clan, still he knew that the humble Booth family could also lay its own claim to this place.

At twenty, Morgan was undoubtedly young to be on the ruling Council. He had succeeded in the role of court Executioner after his father, Atticus Junior—who had assumed it in turn after the death of his own father, Atticus Senior. The passing of the role from generation to generation down a single family line marked out Morgan Booth as unique within the current Council of Twelve, but he had not inherited the position in any passive way—far from it.

He had claimed the position by virtue of one of the final decisive battles in the war against Eronesia. The battle had laid claim not only to the life of Prince Goran but also to Atticus Booth Jr. It was a battle in which Morgan, then only eighteen years old, had distinguished himself. The coolheadedness and appetite for violence he had demonstrated on the battlefield had, so Prince Anders later told him, made his succession to Executioner a clear-cut matter.

Though his father and grandfather were both now deceased, still Morgan often felt their presence here in the Dungeons. It occurred to him that they too had felt such a strong sense of belonging here that they had opted never to leave.

Perhaps for that reason, he liked it best when the Dungeons were empty, save for these jovial family ghosts. No one would say that Booth was an out-and-out loner.

He might be found sharing a joke or a smoke with the Captain of the Guard, the Woodsman or members of the night patrol, but still, he valued the hours of quietness and solitude. They enabled him to think—and to read.

He had, within two short years, amassed quite an extensive library down here. This was thanks, in no small part, to Queen Elin. At the beginning of his tenure, Elin had invited Morgan into the Queen's Library, high above, in the East Wing and, after questioning him closely about what subjects might be of most interest to him, had sent him away with his heavily tattooed arms loaded down with volumes.

The Queen had been delighted a few weeks later when he had returned, telling her he had read not just one but all of her recommendations. They had entered into lively debate on their merits. She had insisted that he keep his favorites among the books, telling him that she was constantly fighting a losing battle for shelf space in her own library.

In a short period of time, the Executioner had become a firm favorite of the Queen's. Over tea in her library, she quizzed him about what he had just read and what he might like to read next. Her choices rarely failed to intrigue him— though in spite of her best efforts, he was never quite so gripped by novels as by histories, biographies and, best of all, journals of adventure and expedition.

Morgan kept his growing collection of books on a wooden

bookcase he had crafted himself from a felled Archenfield oak. It was positioned against the wall to the right of his workbench. Pausing in front of it now, he ran his hand across the books' familiar spines. In a way, it was like greeting old friends. There was one in particular he was keen to seek out. The light from his lantern illuminated the titles across each spine. There it was! Reaching forward, he took the thin volume in his hand and, moving back toward his bench, he set the book down. It would come in useful later, once his labors were complete.

Now he utilized the lantern he had brought in with him to light another at his workbench so he would be able to see clearly what he was doing. It was none too clever to mess around with axes in poor lighting. There they were, his beauties! As the second candle took its flame, the array of different-sized axes above his bench was illuminated. Another row of friends, he thought, reaching out and making his selection.

Enjoying the familiar touch of the worn hickory wood handle, he placed the axe carefully down so that its convex blade jutted out just over the edge of the workbench. He gently pressed the pad of his thumb against it. Sharp but not sharp enough. No matter. He knew exactly what to do.

First he scanned the blade for signs of damage. There was one small blemish and he picked up a piece of coarse sandstone to attend to this. He was very gentle, as if he was one of the grooms, brushing the napes of the horses or dogs in the stable complex. After he'd been at it for a brief time, he paused, glancing down at the blade. The blemish was gone. Satisfied with his work, he set down the piece of coarse stone.

Next, the sharpening of the blade. He took another piece of stone in his hand for this, running his finger across its surface to satisfy himself that this was indeed a finer grade of sandstone. Whether it would do the job better wet or dry was a matter of preference. Booth opted for wet, submerging the stone circle in a basin of water for a moment or two.

Shaking off the excess liquid, he then applied the stone to the blade of the axe in a practiced circular motion, just as he'd seen his father and grandfather employ on the very same bench. Down and up, down and up with the stone. As he made the gentle circles, he remembered the very first time he'd done this, his father's large hand guiding his own as he circled the sandstone against the cold metal.

"Be gentle, Morgan. Gentler even than that." When his father's hand had released his own and allowed him to finish the job himself, he had almost burst with pride.

This blade didn't need any more work. It would be sharp enough to trim his neat mustache and beard. He set down the stone and finally picked up a worn leather strop. He ran the strop back and forth across the blade, where the stone had traveled before it, until he had dispersed every tiny burr of metal from the blade's edge.

Setting down the strop, he inspected his work. A perfect job. The axe was ready. Satisfied, Morgan thought he'd pour himself a nightcap and settle down with his book.

As he was pulling the stopper from the flagon of aquavit, he heard a sound from along the corridor. It must be the prisoner. The Executioner shook his head—he'd been so busy in his work and lost in his own thoughts that he'd forgotten he had company.

He withdrew his hand from the aquavit and took up instead the first of his lanterns, walking away from his work area and over to the cells. Booth could remember times when every one of the cells had been inhabited. That seemed a long time ago now. Peace had come to Archenfield under Prince Anders and it had proved a lasting peace. Until now. Tonight, there was but one prisoner, but if Axel was right and one of their neighbor states was on the offensive again, the Dungeons were likely to become crowded once more, as they had been in his father's and grandfather's days. It was not a prospect Morgan relished—the sounds, the smells of so many others in *his* domain—but he'd live with it if he had to.

And, on the plus side, he'd get to use his axes a bit more often.

The layout of the Dungeons paralleled the floors above, opening out from an alleyway to a circular area where above them the West Tower of the palace began. Beneath this tower was a central pod of cells, segmented like an orange. And within one of these segments was the prisoner.

The light within the cell was poor—the candle in the prisoner's lantern had burned low since Morgan had last checked. The Executioner set his own lantern on the floor in front of the cell door, then turned the key and let himself inside.

Michael Reeves was sitting on the stone shelf that served, if desired, as a bed. He had wrapped himself in the coarse wool blanket provided. Nonetheless, he was shivering.

"Can I have some water?" the prisoner asked.

Booth saw that the earthenware pitcher he had left there earlier was empty. He nodded. Taking up the pitcher, he walked back out of the cell without bothering to lock the door again. There were guards on the doors to the Dungeons, easily summoned by a whistle. Michael Reeves had nowhere to run. And if he tried anything clever, Morgan Booth was very quick when the occasion demanded.

He filled the pitcher with fresh water, then, on a whim, picked up the flagon of aquavit and a beaker for himself. When he arrived back in the cell, Michael was sitting in the exact same position. Booth set the pitcher of water down at his side. Leaving Michael to sort himself out, Booth pulled the stopper from the bottle and helped himself to a slug of aquavit.

"You look like hell," he observed. "I'd have thought your masters in Paddenburg would have prepared you better than this."

Michael took a gulp of water. "How many times do I have to tell you? I have no masters—other than the head steward. I had nothing to do with the Prince's assassination."

Morgan smiled wryly and took a sip of his drink. "'Course not," he said.

They remained in Michael's cell, neither one initiating further conversation for some time.

"You know what," Morgan said, at length. "I'm going to do something for you."

He returned to his desk and picked up the book he had earmarked earlier. He walked back over to Michael's cell and handed over the volume. Michael was taken by surprise.

Morgan shrugged. "Some people make a great fuss about their last meal. My view is—what does it matter what food you shovel into your mouth in the hours before your death? You'll only shit it out again." His eyes met the prisoner's. "But the last book you read, well, that just might have an impact on your eternal soul."

Without waiting to hear the prisoner's response, he took up his flagon of aquavit and, closing and locking the cell door behind him, headed back to his desk. Another book was on his mind. This book was not kept on his bookshelf but in a drawer just above his workbench, where it was always close at hand. He reached across and opened the drawer now, lifting out the precious volume as he hooked a leg around his grandfather's old stool behind him, dragging it forward and sitting down.

The clothbound book was a notebook, filled with hand-written names that told their own particular history of Archenfield. Morgan continued turning the pages, smiling as he once again made the acquaintance of his grand-father's, and then father's, own script. Then he came to the pages completed in his own hand. Finally, he came to a blank page.

He reached back into the drawer for his grandfather's pen and casket of ink. He dipped the pen in the ink and brought its scratchy nib to the current page of the book. There he wrote the following day's date and then just two words:

Michael Reeves

Morgan Booth poured himself another slug of earthy aquavit, promising himself that would be his last of the night, and waited for the ink to dry.

DAY THREE

TWENTY

The Palace Gardens

ASTA PAUSED FOR A MOMENT, LOOKING UP IN wonder at the palace. It truly was a stunning building and looked all the more beautiful in the morning sun. The stone of the walls seemed to glow with an orange light, deepening into the flame-red expanse of Virginia creeper that enveloped much of the front. The East and West Towers, with their crenellated rooftops, rose up high above the palace roofs, punctuated by mullioned windows and narrower loopholes. Asta's eyes lingered on the balcony, curving out from the terrace, from where Prince Jared had made his impassioned speech the day before. The balcony was empty now, but she could picture him there still, a shiver running through her as she thought of his stirring words and the intense connection made between the new Prince and the crowd gathered below.

Yesterday, there hadn't been more than an inch of free space as people had jostled for position to hear him. Now Asta was almost alone as she made her approach to the steps leading up to the palace terrace and entry.

Acknowledging the guards as she continued on her way, she couldn't help but think of the journey she had made in the last year. It was as if Uncle Elias had stretched a well-meaning hand right across the fields and the fjords and allowed her to jump from her rustic home right into the beating heart of the Princedom. Asta felt keenly that she was indebted to him. Which made what she was about to do all the more inconceivable.

She had come this morning to request a private audience with Prince Jared himself, to talk to him about the official inquiry into his brother's assassination and to share her conviction that the murder investigation had taken a wrong turn.

Her earlier confidence began to drain away. Who was she—a person of no rank or title—to question the official investigation? Suppose Prince Jared asked her for hard evidence? As yet, she had none. All she had were her thoughts and feelings. And Elias's postmortem report, she reminded herself. For it was Elias who had raised the possibility of the two poisons and the multiple means in which either poison could have been administered. She wanted to be clear that Jared knew all this, that he knew how hard it would have been for a steward to obtain savin when the only place the plant grew was in the locked, walled Physic Garden. She also thought it important that he knew about the hunting wound sustained by Prince Anders a week before his death and that someone—someone higher-ranking than a steward, with better access to the Prince—could have administered poison via that very wound. She knew the names of those members of the court who were on the hunting expedition with Prince Anders and, should his brother ask for that list, she would not hesitate to supply it. So, when all was said and done, all she was really doing was checking that the Prince was aware of the detail of the postmortem report. Surely, Uncle Elias couldn't be angry with her for that?

She winced at the very thought. She remembered how flushed with anger Elias had become when he'd discovered her putting her questions to the Huntsman. This was ten times, make that a hundred times, worse.

The first challenge, of course, was whether the Prince would agree to see her at all. She was unsure of the finer workings of palace protocol and, of course, she hadn't dared to question Uncle Elias, even indirectly, about this. In her pocket was what she hoped would prove her ticket to gain admittance to an audience with the Prince. To be more specific, in her pocket was a small velvet bag containing Prince

Anders's personal effects—his golden chain with three items attached to it, which they had removed during the postmortem.

She knew that Elias would have returned the chain to Jared at some point between the postmortem and the funeral, so she was just expediting the process, she told herself now, though she knew full well Elias would not see things in the same light.

She considered the three items—the vial containing a portion of Prince Goran's ashes; a tubular locket bearing the tiny, rolled-up love note from Silva; and the third item, the mysterious key. The first item was, she understood, a long-held Archenfield tradition. The second was a love token between the Prince and his wife. But the third, the key, was more of a mystery. Was this too merely a token—another gift from Silva perhaps—or did it have a more practical application?

Asta reminded herself that she mustn't become preoccupied with these items—they were useful to her only as currency with which to gain access to the Prince.

Indeed, she felt almost guilty at having them in her possession. This guilt was not because she had taken the items from her uncle's rooms, but rather because she was carrying such private and personal objects, which had until mere days ago been worn against the beating heart of the ruler of Archenfield. Reframing this thought, she told herself that it was entirely right that she pass the late Prince's precious belongings swiftly into the safekeeping of his brother.

With these thoughts swirling in her head, she realized she had reached the palace terrace. Looking across at the main entrance, she took a breath. It was now or never. She dipped her head and made for the doorway leading to the Grand Hall.

Before Asta could make her way inside, however, she was stopped in her tracks by a figure heading out of the very same doorway. Silva! She was dressed very differently from their previous encounter, two days earlier, but looked as otherworldly elegant as ever. This morning, her pale gold hair was pulled smoothly back in a modish chignon. She wore a fitted jacket—predominantly cream but embroidered in golden thread with outlines of butterflies and honeybees, pale jodhpurs and long riding boots. She was accompanied by two white lurcher dogs, who moved with the same grace as their mistress. Seeing Asta before her, Silva's face was instantly wreathed in a beatific smile.

"Good morning, my lady," Asta said, just about remembering the correct form of address.

"Well, this is too perfect! We're about to set out on a beautiful walk. Won't you join us?"

Asta hesitated. It would surely be an impertinence to decline such an invitation, but she couldn't bear the thought of being distracted from her intended audience with Prince Jared. It had taken quite some nerve to get this far. She wondered if Silva's sudden appearance might be a kind of sign—that it was a foolhardy idea to come in search of the Prince.

"I've decided to embrace a tradition of my mother's," Silva explained, striding out across the terrace as if she owned it—which, in a way, Asta supposed, she did. "Mother told me that, in the months before I was born, every day she took a beautiful walk through the landscape of Woodlark, in order that even before I left her womb I might feel something of the beauty of the world in general and Woodlark in particular." Her hands now lightly resting on the balustrade that ran along the front of the terrace, Silva gazed wistfully at the distant blue-tinged mountains. "I can't give my baby Woodlark just yet, but Archenfield has its own beauty." She spun around to face Asta once more. "So, you see, you must join us on our inaugural beautiful walk!"

As she said this, one of Silva's white hounds inclined its head to nuzzle against Asta's waist.

"You see?" Silva said. "Talitha wants you to join us too!"

"I would love to join you, my lady," Asta said. Inside her head, a voice told her to leave it at that, to accompany her new friend wherever she wanted to go. But that voice was displaced by another more insistent one and, before she knew it, Asta had added, "But I came here this morning to find and speak to Prince Jared."

She regretted the words even before they departed her mouth. But Silva did not seem offended. Petting Talitha's twin, she smiled prettily at Asta.

"You certainly won't have any luck at finding Prince Jared at this time. There's a meeting of the Twelve this morning and he's bound to be busy preparing for it."

"Oh," Asta said, instantly deflated. "Is there someone I could speak to about seeing him? I don't need very much of his time."

Silva's elegant head froze momentarily, her eyes locking with Asta's. "Jared is Prince of All Archenfield now," Silva said. "You can't have *any* of his time. That's how it works. Trust me, I was married to the last one."

"Of course," Asta said, her hand in her pocket, feeling the outline of the key as though it might prove some form of talisman. "But I really only need five minutes with him. Ten at the very most."

Silva shook her head. "Come along," she said, looping her arm through Asta's. "Goodness, doesn't the sunlight bring out the copper tones in your hair? I'd kill for hair that color! You and I are going to walk down to the fjord together. I'm simply not taking no for an answer. It's a glorious morning and..."

Before she could finish speaking, the Woodsman's Bell began to chime.

Silva frowned, raising a hand to her forehead. "The

incessant bells of Archenfield really grate on my nerves. In my homeland, we have clocks and, as a consequence, far fewer headaches." With a light laugh, she swept Asta away from the palace entry and down a flight of stone steps leading around the eastern side of the palace to the gardens at the back. The two snow-white lurchers followed enthusiastically.

Silva led her companion along a gravel path that was bordered on each side by small patches of well-tended lawn and topiary bushes in pyramid shapes. Following Silva through its stone gateway at the end of the path, Asta found herself in another larger formal garden at the back of the palace. Ahead was an elaborate ornamental fountain, its spouting waters iridescent in the morning light.

"Come along, ladies!" Silva declared.

Asta glanced around, looking to see if Silva was accompanied by her lady's maids that morning. She had hoped they were alone—and indeed this proved to be the case. Feeling rather foolish, Asta realized that the "ladies" Silva had addressed were her two dogs.

Silva sat down on the edge of the fountain, stirring her hand in small circles in the water and encouraging the twin lurchers to take a cool drink. Asta took advantage of the distraction to turn and look back toward the palace. She was not accustomed to seeing it from this angle.

"Which are the Prince's quarters?" she asked, trying to

make her inquiry sound as innocent as possible—but clearly failing, as Silva shook her head.

"I fear you are developing an unhealthy obsession," she said. Nonetheless, she pointed up toward a line of mullioned windows in the center of the first floor. "That's Prince Jared's suite there, if you must know. Though I wouldn't recommend throwing gravel up to attract his attention. Even if your aim is spot-on, that kind of activity is thoroughly frowned upon."

Asta gazed up at the Prince's windows, shielding her eyes with one hand to filter the intense sunlight that reflected off them. She wished she could see into the windows, but the light was so strong it made a mirror of the glass. She was about to turn away when the light suddenly shifted and a figure was revealed at one of the very windows Silva had pointed toward. Asta's heart began to race. It was none other than Prince Jared.

He was looking out into the gardens and his attention seemed drawn by the fountain and the small gathering in front of it. Before she could stop herself, Asta found herself waving up at him.

Behind her, she heard Silva stifle a laugh.

But, to Asta's amazement, Prince Jared waved back. She couldn't quite believe it. She stood, rooted to the spot, watching the window. Then Prince Jared moved away, as suddenly as he had appeared, to be replaced by another figure, whose attention had evidently also been drawn by the group.

"Is that Logan Wilde?" Asta asked.

"That's right," Silva said. "He's probably cursing us for distracting the Prince for a precious moment."

The Poet gazed at them for a moment or two more, then disappeared back into the room. A fresh ray of sunlight rendered the window mirrorlike. Asta turned back toward Silva, who had risen from her seat and was clearly ready to move on. "What exactly does the Poet do?" she asked.

Silva smiled. "It would be more apposite to ask—what *doesn't* the Poet do? He's the Prince's right-hand man. I often felt that he spent more time with my husband than I did."

"But what's his actual job?" Asta pressed her. "Not just writing poetry, surely?"

Silva shook her head. "Once, it was just that. But the role has evolved over time. It's very much about communications, now both within the court and to the world outside. The Poet writes the Prince's speeches—he'll have had his hand in the address Prince Jared gave yesterday—but his role is even more integral than that. He's more of a political advisor, a diplomat, you might say."

"Aha," Asta said, realizing there was still much about the court that she didn't know. Perhaps her fledgling friendship with Silva might help remedy some of that.

As they came to the end of this section of garden, they turned left and entered a long dappled avenue of saplings.

"This is pretty," Asta observed. "It can't have been planted long ago."

"A year ago to be exact," Silva said, some of the brightness departing from her voice. "It was for our wedding." She stretched out her arms. "To the left are lime saplings—native to Woodlark—a gift from my parents. To the right you can see Archenfield mulberries. The idea was to plait the two kinds of trees together as they grew—representing the strengthening bonds between my homeland and that of my husband. Eventually, it will form a shaded walkway."

Quietly cursing herself for raising the subject, Asta struggled for a suitable response. "What a lovely idea!" she enthused.

"In principle," Silva replied curtly. "It's just a shame my husband didn't live long enough to see these trees grow above shoulder height."

"No, of course," Asta said quietly, wishing she could erase all traces of the conversation and that it wasn't such a long avenue.

Silva shrugged and sighed. "Anders didn't live to see the trees reach maturity but at least his son will."

"His son?" Asta turned to her companion. "How do you know for sure your baby is a boy?"

"Archenfield needs another prince," Silva said, her eyes

as blue as the mountaintops. "And I am nothing if not a good servant of Archenfield." She smoothed a stray strand of flaxen hair behind her ear and continued on her way.

They walked along the line of saplings in silence; Asta desperately thinking how to restore her companion's earlier cheerfulness. Silva seemed lost in thought and, from the set expression on her face, they were not good thoughts to be lost in. Asta felt a huge sense of relief as they at last emerged from the row of saplings and Silva opened up a gate that gave onto a path along the riverbank. As they stepped through it, Silva turned to Asta.

"I'm glad to have run into you this morning. The last time we met, I fear I may have given you an inaccurate impression of my marriage."

"How do you mean?" Asta was instantly intrigued.

"I think I gave you the sense that it was a marriage of political expediency, rather than romantic love. But while there was an element of pragmatism to our union, certainly in the beginning, there was much more than that. Anders and I did love each other, very deeply as it happens." Silva shook her head. "It's strange trying to explain your marriage to a third party."

The two young women had reached a short wooden bridge that crossed over the stretch of river. They came to a standstill on it, while Silva allowed her two hounds to gambol in the waters below.

"Somehow I feel as if I must explain things to you," Silva told Asta. "It's as if you were apprentice to the Priest rather than the Physician. You are my confessor, Asta Peck." She smiled softly.

Asta shook her head. "You don't have to explain anything to me, my lady," she said. "You are the Prince's Consort. I am nobody."

"Don't say that!" Silva responded. "You are my friend. At least I hope you are." She reached out and took Asta's hand in her own.

"Yes," Asta said, surprised but pleased by the show of affection. "I am your friend." As Silva withdrew her hand, she added, "But I already knew that your husband loved you very much."

"You did? How?"

Asta took a breath, debating whether to follow her instinct or not. She decided that she must. Silva had opened herself up to her—Asta owed her this much. Reaching into her pocket, she took out the velvet bag she had brought with her.

"What's this?" Silva inquired as Asta set the bag on the wooden balustrade.

"The reason I wanted to see Prince Jared this morning was to give him these three items," Asta said, editing the truth just slightly. "They belonged to your husband. My uncle and I discovered them when we conducted our examination of the Prince."

Silva nodded, her attention fixed on Asta's hand as she lifted the chain with its three attachments—the vial, the locket and the key—out of the bag.

Silva's pale finger touched the vial. "His father's ashes." She wrinkled her nose. "That's a particularly gruesome Archenfield tradition, in my opinion."

"I agree," Asta said with a nod.

"They'll make me a vial of Anders's own ashes, you know, after the Burning."

"Will you wear it?" Asta inquired.

Silva shook her head. "No, I don't think so. Though his mother will shoot daggers at me for not doing so." Her attention drifted. "What's this key?"

"I don't know," Asta said, a little disappointed. "I thought perhaps you might."

"No," Silva said. "I haven't seen it before. It doesn't look like one of the palace keys."

Looking back, Asta realized she should have known at that moment to have gone no further. Because if Silva had never seen the key that Anders wore on a chain around his neck—the key that must have rested, as he walked, over his heart—then perhaps he was keeping other secrets from his wife too? But Asta did not have the presence of mind to stop there. Her conversation with Silva, her new friend Silva, was like the waters of the river flowing beneath them. Unstoppable.

"You said before that you knew my husband loved me, very much," Silva said. "I don't see how this collection of objects proves that. Unless I'm missing something?"

Asta tapped the tubular locket.

"The locket? It was a gift from Queen Elin, I think. What does that prove?"

Smiling, Asta took the locket into her hands and twisted the top until it was released. The roll of paper was revealed inside. Asta eased it out carefully, placed the note on the velvet bag and unrolled it for Silva to see.

"He carried this with him always. It's a love note from you. Surely you must agree that the fact he kept this with him, so close to his heart, proves how much he loved you?"

Carry this note with you and remember how I carry your heart with me.

It was as Silva gazed at the note, her tiny fingers unconsciously smoothing out its curled edges, that Asta knew what a terrible mistake she had made. Even before she spoke, she could see in Silva's eyes the wound she herself was responsible for inflicting.

"I...I don't understand," Silva stammered. "I didn't write this."

"If you didn't..." Asta began. Why—*why* was she even giving voice to this thought? "Then who did?"

TWENTY-ONE

The Council Chamber, the Palace

"AND NOW, THE MAIN ORDER OF OUR BUSINESS today." Axel Blaxland once more had the floor of the Council Chamber. "I refer to the execution tonight of Michael Reeves, the assassin of Prince Anders."

The mood in the chamber was more businesslike than during the previous two days, as the Twelve had struggled to absorb the shock of Prince Anders's murder. The deep grief experienced by the Twelve seated around the table and by the royals up on the dais was still raw; nonetheless the business of the Princedom could not wait. It was a time for action.

Kai Jagger raised his hand before taking the floor. "Are we making a mistake by not having a public execution?" he asked.

"Has it come to this?" Vera Webb exclaimed. "Are we barbarians once more?"

"It's a fair question, Kai," Axel said, ignoring the Cook's outburst. He turned to the Poet. "What do you think, Logan? *You* are our expert in such matters."

Jared could see that Vera was fuming and muttering under her breath to Father Simeon, who sat beside her. The Prince was gratified to see that at least the relationship between the Captain of the Guard and the Poet seemed to be back on a more workable footing.

"I confess I'm of two minds," Logan said. "There's no question that the populace needs the assassin to be executed—and fast. The people of Archenfield, Prince Jared's subjects, need to know that the Blood Price has been paid for Prince Anders's murder. Only then can they move on with their lives—and allow us to do so, too."

"But do they need to witness the beheading?" Nova Chastain said.

Logan nodded at the Falconer. "I share your caution. This is a potentially combustible situation and there are so many deep emotions in play."

"I'm not being cautious," Nova briskly corrected him. "I just think some things are not for the public eye."

"Come on, Logan!" Axel said impatiently. "Give us a firm decision one way or another. You are, are you not, the expert on public opinion?"

The Poet resisted rising to this bait. "We need to strike a balance, in my opinion, between demonstrating strong and swift justice, and not risking tainting the palace and Prince Jared—at the beginning of his reign—with blood."

Jonas Drummond shook his head. "You're wrong. They need to associate the palace with blood and the payment of the Blood Price."

· "There's a danger," Logan resumed, "that you make the people fear *us* rather than the external enemy. We need to renew their trust in the court and consolidate their belief in Prince Jared. They are reeling right now at the thought that an assassin could venture so deep into the Princedom and kill their sovereign." Logan glanced at Jared. "Yesterday, the new Prince made a fine job of addressing the people's grief and confusion, but that was only the beginning. We need to reinforce the message that the Princedom is safe again, that *they* are safe and that no one is going to threaten Prince Jared. Remember, it's only been two years since they lost their own parents, their own children. War is a fire that touches every man, woman and child in the land."

Axel interrupted again. "I'm confused, Logan. Public or private execution? And I'll settle for a one-word answer. It'll be time for lunch soon, eh, Vera?"

Vera Webb shot Axel a dark look. There was laughter from Jonas Drummond and Morgan Booth. Prince Jared was beginning to see the division lines between the Twelve and to understand how this might influence them when it came to voting on any matters of governance. He would have to keep that in mind.

Jared was impressed by Logan's equanimity as he continued.

"The next time the people come together, it should be for Prince Anders's funeral and then, a day later, for Prince Jared's coronation. In this way, they come to associate the palace firmly with order, control and continuity. Holding a public execution here could, under the circumstances, prove distracting at best and unsettling at worse."

As Logan sat down, Axel rolled his eyes. "Thank you for that very *thorough* analysis."

Shaking his head, Jonas weighed in again. "I completely disagree with you, Logan. The execution is the moment of catharsis. There is no better way to demonstrate that the Blood Price has been paid than by showing the common man the assassin's blood."

Elias Peck spoke next. "I'm with Logan," he said. "As I understand it, what we are dealing with here is a potentially bigger threat from Paddenburg. So the people we really need to sit up and take notice are the court of Paddenburg."

"What better way to make Paddenburg sit up and take notice," Jonas rejoined, "than by slicing his head off?"

"Why stop there?" Morgan Booth suggested, a wicked glint in his eye. "Why don't we send the court of Paddenburg, and each of our other neighbors for that matter, a portion of the assassin's body?"

Axel smiled at his comrade. "No one loves a bit of theater more than you, eh, Morgan?"

The Executioner shrugged and raised his palms high. "I can't deny it."

Emelie Sharp nodded. "I have to say, I like that idea better than a public execution. It would make a crystal clear statement of our mood."

Logan stifled a sigh. "That is safe to say. But it's not good diplomacy."

"As far as I'm concerned," Emelie shot back, "diplomacy went out the window when Paddenburg decided to kill Prince Anders."

The Priest, Father Simeon, cleared his throat before joining the fray. "I think we are in danger of moving too fast and making rash decisions. There is not yet official enmity between us and Paddenburg." He looked imploringly toward Jared. "I know that, because of the assassin's origins, we suspect that he was merely the pawn in a much bigger game, but shouldn't we wait until we have unassailable proof of that before making such an overtly hostile gesture?"

"I agree." The Groom's words were softly spoken, easy to miss. Especially as Emelie's sharp voice cut across them.

"Fight fire with fire and blood with blood," she said. "That's my policy."

"Mine too," Axel said.

"That may be so," Father Simeon acknowledged, "but that is not at this time the official policy of this court. I certainly don't remember—"

Emelie cut him off again. "I rather thought you'd be in favor of it, Father," she said. "It's textbook Old Testament."

Father Simeon frowned and shook his head.

Nova addressed Emelie sharply. "Do you ever get tired of hearing your own voice?"

"Rarely," Emelie said. "And I do see it as my responsibility, in exchange for my seat at the Prince's Table, to make helpful contributions."

"Oh," Nova said, sotto voce. "Forgive me. I didn't realize that's what they were."

There were a few smiles around the table. It seemed that it wasn't just the Falconer who had grown irritated by the Beekeeper.

Jared decided now might be an opportune time to take control of the debate. "Let's try to keep this discussion focused," he said. He was conscious of all eyes turning to him questioningly. Holding his nerve, he continued.

"We've heard a good range of opinions around the table as to whether the execution is to be public or private. So that I know exactly what you all think, I would like to conclude this matter with an open vote of the Twelve. This will inform my own decision."

Out of the corner of his eye, Jared saw his mother, over on the dais, give a discreet nod of approval at the way he had taken control. Jared turned his attention back to the Prince's Table.

"Good idea," Axel said, turning to face the assembly. "All those in favor of publicly executing the assassin, please raise your hand and say aye."

Four hands and voices were raised—those of the Huntsman, the Woodsman, the Executioner and the Bodyguard. To these Axel now added his own.

"Five of us are in favor of a public execution," Axel noted. "Now all those in favor of a private execution."

A flurry of hands was raised and there was a second, louder, chorus of "aye."

"That's seven in favor of the private execution," Axel said. "A majority." He turned to Jared.

Jared nodded. "My decision is made in accordance with the majority. Prince Anders's assassin will be executed in private." Axel did not, Jared noticed, seem overly perturbed to be on the losing side of the vote. The Captain of the Guard turned to the Executioner. "I suggest we meet separately after this assembly has dissolved to confirm the details."

"What about the Executioner's suggestion?" Emelie persisted. "That we deliver parcels of the body to our neighboring courts?"

Axel met her gaze. "I'm not saying I don't find the dramatic gesture rather appealing," he acknowledged, "but I think, as the Poet outlined—at considerable length—we need to move the investigation to the next stage before risking such a provocative gesture."

"It's unlike you to be so cautious," Jonas observed.

"There's a difference," Axel observed, "between decisive action and inflammatory action. The next few days will prove critical to how Archenfield is perceived both internally and externally. I'm certainly not opposed to making some very tough decisions and making some extremely strong gestures, but I think it's prudent to have more facts at our disposal before doing so."

"I agree," Prince Jared said. "Let us hear fresh reports from our spies abroad."

"Yes!" Logan said. "What is taking them so long? We need their reports."

"And we will have them," Axel said, clearly irritated. "But remember that I am dependent on horses and falcons. I can't just click my fingers and accelerate the process, much as I would like to."

Logan shook his head. Jared could see that the old enmity was back—with a vengeance.

"I agree with the Captain of the Guard," Nova Chastain said. "We should wait until such time as we have more information at our disposal."

"Hear, hear," added Elias.

Lucas simply nodded.

Emelie Sharp sat back in her chair, defeated for now but shaking her head to demonstrate her ongoing disagreement.

Axel turned to Jared. "Well, we have reached a majority decision over the execution. I believe that our business is concluded for the day."

"Not quite," Jared said, pleased to see the expression of surprise on his cousin's face. "There is one additional order of business."

"No one informed me of this," Axel said, consulting his papers.

Prince Jared rose to his feet. "I have decided it is time to appoint my Edling."

Axel was not the only one taken aback by the Prince's surprise announcement. Suddenly everyone sat up a bit straighter and became more alert, both around the Prince's Table and up on the royal dais.

"My choice was a very simple one," Jared continued, aware once more of his mother watching him from the dais. "And I'm delighted to proclaim that my chosen Edling is Axel Blaxland."

At these words, there was a brief ripple of applause—

but it did not, unsurprisingly, emanate from all quarters. Undeterred, Axel rose to his feet as Jared extended his hand toward his cousin. Smiling with undisguised delight, Axel fell to his knees and kissed his hand. It was, Jared knew, the traditional response from Edling to Prince, but nonetheless it was a shock to find the usually cocksure Axel kneeling before him.

Jared glanced over Axel's head to the dais. His own mother was smiling serenely—why wouldn't she when he had done her precise bidding? Beside her, however, Edvin's expression was harder to read. His younger brother's eyes seemed locked onto the middle distance as if he were gazing out to some distant shore only he could see.

Turning back, Jared seized the opportunity to address his new Edling and the assembly.

"Cousin Axel, I know you will do me personally and the court as a whole proud in the role of Edling. You have been an unswervingly loyal and effective Captain of the Guard to both my father and my brother and now also to me. No one has worked more tirelessly to make safe the Princedom. Though we are all still in shock about what happened here two days ago, let your appointment be a clear sign— to you and to all others—that neither I nor my family hold you in any way responsible. Indeed, when I speak of family, I want to say that there should no longer be any division between the Wynyard and Blaxland clans. I hope that your appointment will show you that I see you more as a brother than a cousin."

Jared had turned toward Axel as he spoke the final part of the speech that Logan had coached him in earlier that morning. The Prince saw how much impact the Poet's words had. Axel's face often seemed set with ambition and determination to achieve his goals, but now that one of his deepest, most long-held ambitions had at last been achieved, there was a decisive shift in his features. He looked almost lost in his own strong and sudden emotions.

"I won't let you down, Cousin," he said.

Jared reached out his hand to Axel's again. "I know you won't," he said.

He was distracted by movement on the dais. He saw that Edvin had risen to his feet and, in spite of his mother's best efforts to dissuade him, was stepping down from the platform. Edvin met Jared's eyes with a distant, wounded gaze, then turned and walked out of the chamber.

Jared was torn. He wanted nothing more than to follow him, but he couldn't. Not yet. There were other pressing matters he needed to conclude.

Doing his best to shut out his younger brother from his thoughts, he turned back to the Twelve. "You may be wondering how Axel is to occupy two chairs at the Prince's Table." As anticipated, this comment got everyone's attention. "Under normal circumstances, in becoming my Edling,

Axel would be replaced immediately as Captain of the Guard. But these are not, by any means, normal circumstances and I am sure I speak for all of you when I say that in my view Axel should remain as Captain of the Guard—at least until the present danger has lifted."

There were nods and a few "ayes" from around the table. "I'm pleased to see that you seem to agree with me," Jared continued, sticking closely to Logan's script. "But, once again, I think it is important to ask you to vote." He took a breath before continuing. "All those in favor of Axel continuing as Captain of the Guard in combination with his role as Edling, please say aye and raise your right hand."

Around the table, most hands shot up at once, but there were three waverers—the Cook, the Beekeeper and the Falconer. Jared exchanged the briefest look with Logan.

All this was, as the Poet had anticipated, a useful fact-finding exercise. It wasn't hard to reason why Vera Webb was hesitant to support Axel. Evidently, she had decided to use her vote to take a stance—such was her right and Jared couldn't blame her under the circumstances.

That just left Nova and Emelie, whose hands remained lowered. Although the vote was not required to be unanimous, only a majority one, still Prince Jared wanted to understand what objections there were. There were too many unhealthy undercurrents in this chamber.

"Emelie," Jared said, turning to the Beekeeper. "Do you

have concerns you would like to share with the rest of the Twelve?"

She nodded, needing little encouragement to share her thoughts. "Each chair at the Prince's Table comes with one vote. I want to know, while Axel occupies, albeit temporarily, two chairs, does he also carry two votes?"

Jared nodded, aware that Emelie's perceptive question had unsettled some of her previously more relaxed colleagues. "Thank you," the Prince said. "I'm glad to have the opportunity to address this. There is no precedent in the Book of Law because this situation has never before arisen." His eyes skimmed from Emelie's to Axel's, then back again. "What I am proposing here is that, for now, Axel retain just one vote."

"In that case," Emelie said, "aye." She lifted her hand to join the others.

Jared turned his attention to Nova Chastain, whose hand was still not raised. "Nova, does what I've told Emelie provide the same reassurance you are seeking or is there another matter for us to address?"

Nova's eyes met Jared's. She held his gaze for a time before speaking. "I can't endorse your choice of Edling," she said.

"I'm sorry to hear that," Jared replied.

"I know there were good reasons that Prince Anders did not make Axel his Edling."

This bold comment caused a ripple around the table. No one looked more shocked than Axel himself.

Jared held the Falconer's gaze. "Is there something more you would like to say?"

She considered for a moment, then nodded slowly. "I suppose I just want to be clear that you made this decision independently and that you are not merely bowing to pressure from your family." She glanced across to the dais and Jared knew that Nova was not only making reference to his mother now, but also to Axel's parents, Lord Viggo and Lady Stella, who did not have access to meetings of the Twelve.

Prince Jared did not turn around. "Nova," he said, "I am new to this position and, though I have sat at this table for two years, you and I do not know each other well yet. But I can assure you that the reason—the only reason—I have made Axel Blaxland my Edling is because I think he is the best person for that role."

His conviction seemed to take her by surprise. Jared was, in turn, surprised to hear the applause building around the table. As it faded, Nova addressed him.

"Prince Jared, you are our ruler now," she said. "If this is, in your opinion, the best way forward for Archenfield, so be it." A moment passed after she had finished speaking before she at last raised her hand.

"All right then," Jared said, keen to bring this meeting to a close. "This vote is endorsed by the majority of the

Twelve. Thank you all. I confirm that Axel Blaxland is now my Edling as well as my Captain of the Guard and retains one vote at the table."

There was another burst of applause. Jared cast his eyes around the table and saw Logan wink quickly at him, giving his approval at the way he had handled Nova. Then Jared glanced over to the dais, where Elin nodded discreetly. So the matter was concluded. Jared had done what he had needed to do. And, hopefully, he had managed to convince the Twelve that it was what he had wanted.

Seeing his mother alone on the dais, his thoughts returned to Edvin. He had to go and find him and explain to his brother the true state of things.

But as he turned, he was met by Axel.

"Cousin," Axel said. "*Brother.* I thank you for this honor. The Blaxlands thank you too. Today, you have ushered in a new epoch in Archenfield's history. Together, we will rule this nation as it has never been ruled before."

Jared was not surprised by Axel's words. He had no need for confirmation of his cousin's hunger for power. It was an insatiable hunger, but one which he—and perhaps he alone—must now control. Smiling at Axel, Jared shook his head. "There can only be one ruler of Archenfield. I am Prince and your main responsibility is to advise and support me." He smiled. "But I am confident, Cousin, you will prove to be a very satisfactory *second*-in-command."

TWENTY-TWO

~~~

The West Tower, the Palace

WITH SOME EFFORT, JARED PUSHED OPEN THE door and stumbled out onto the wind-blown circular roof of the West Tower. He saw, with relief, a figure standing up on the ramparts. Dressed in his dark greatcoat, Edvin looked like a giant version of one of Nova's falcons—perched on the very edge of the palace, contemplating the world spread out before him.

Hal Harness remained in the doorway. "Should I come out or wait inside for you, Your Highness?" he asked.

"Please wait in the stairwell," Jared shouted over the noise of the wind. "I need to talk to my brother in private."

The Prince turned and, head bowed down against the gale, made his way carefully across the blustery rooftop. Edvin did not turn around. Surely he must have heard his shouts or registered the footsteps on the gravel, strewn here to make the slippery roof more secure underfoot? Perhaps he was too preoccupied by his own thoughts. Or was he simply intent upon punishing his brother?

Edvin was lean and tall for his fourteen years—a little taller already than Jared. The youngest surviving Wynyard looked decidedly fragile standing there, up on the ramparts, his long pale-blond hair and steel-blue greatcoat buffeted by the wind.

As Jared climbed up to join him, he was possessed by the sudden fear that Edvin might suddenly propel himself over the edge. As the fantasy became all the more vivid in his mind, he reached out a hand toward his brother in a last desperate effort to save him. Just then, Edvin turned to face him and the stupid fantasy was revealed for just that— another sure sign that Jared had an unhealthy amount of adrenaline pumping through his veins. His brother might be tall and occasionally clumsy in his new height, but he knew the palace ramparts as intimately as the features of his own face; his footing, in his heavy winter boots, was rock steady.

"Found you!" Jared said, smiling with relief.

"What makes you think I wanted to be found?" Edvin didn't return his brother's smile. After a moment of scrutinizing Jared's face, he turned and gazed out again into the distance.

Jared tried another way in. "I should have known you'd be up here. If only I had stopped to think for a minute." This time, he was met by silence. Still he wasn't ready to give in. "Remember the time we made our camp right here? How old were we? Maybe seven and nine? We were forever making camps in one part of the palace or another, but I think this was our personal best." This time, his words, and the memory carried by them, succeeded in igniting the flicker of a smile.

"I was six and you were eight," Edvin corrected him.

Jared nodded, plowing on. "We were gone for hours, completely wrapped up in our game. Father had the guards out combing the palace borders for us. We saw the patrols from up here, but this was the one place they didn't think to look."

"He was incandescent with rage!" Edvin remembered, his eyes wide. "Said it was 'highly irresponsible.' That we were not *ordinary* boys; we were princes and we ought to behave accordingly." He smiled, but only briefly. He shook his head. "It's a wonder he even noticed we were missing. He was out with Anders—Anders the Golden. Training him in hunting or archery or whatever part of his princely apprenticeship was on the cards that day."

Jared nodded. "Poor Anders never had a moment to call his own, did he? While you and I had the run of the palace and its grounds for all our games of spies and soldiers, allies and assassins." He put his hand on Edvin's shoulder, caught up in fond memories of their shared childhood and feeling the need to rekindle that closeness.

Edvin turned his face toward Jared. It was a shock, seeing once again how similar Edvin's face was to their dead brother's. Anders and Edvin were like two shoots from the same tree. And yet it was Edvin and Jared who had always been so close, brought together by age, proximity and circumstance. Anders had always been the outsider in this most exclusive of clubs.

"That's all changed now, hasn't it?" Edvin's voice cut through his thoughts. "Now we have real assassins to contend with. Anders is dead and it's no game. And you are the Prince, with not a moment to call your own."

"You sound angry," Jared said, removing his hand from his brother's shoulder. "Edvin, are you angry with me?"

Edvin shrugged. Though he remained silent, his body language gave Jared a clear answer to his question.

"I needed to see you," Jared told his brother. "You left the Council Chamber so suddenly after I announced Axel as my Edling, I wanted to make sure you were all right with it and to make you understand my reasons."

Edvin shrugged again. "Why should I care?" he asked.

"I would understand if you did care," Jared said carefully. "It was my intention to tell you *before* the meeting—but I never got the chance. I was holed up for hours with Logan Wilde, preparing for the assembly. Edvin, you were always the one I wanted as my Edling—the only one. I'm pretty sure you know that. But, last night, I was summoned to our mother's rooms and she told me in no uncertain terms that I had to choose Axel. For the good of our family and to minimize an incipient threat from the Blaxlands."

Edvin smiled with no trace of humor. "'An incipient threat'? Listen to yourself, Brother. How quickly you've become one of them."

"That's not fair!" Jared said, flushed with anger. Edvin had no idea what he'd had to contend with in the crowded days since Anders's death. "You know what? Maybe you *are* too young to be Edling."

"I'm the exact same age as you were when Anders chose you."

"Yes." Jared couldn't argue with that. "And that was too young. I wasn't ready for the responsibility. How many times have you heard me tell you that?"

Edvin ignored this question and asked another. "Are you ready now to be Prince?"

It was Jared's turn to shrug. "I don't have much choice about that, do I?"

"I suppose not." Edvin pursed his lips. "I really don't care about you choosing Axel. Surely, you know such things don't matter to me."

"Well, that's what I thought," Jared said, confused. "But when you stormed out of the council room..."

"I didn't *storm* out. Don't be melodramatic!"

"Edvin, you marched out of the room the minute I spoke Axel's name. And then you fled up here and I've been looking all over the palace for you since. And now that I've found you, well, you don't exactly seem pleased to see me."

"Maybe I just wanted some time on my own." Edvin turned away again from him.

Jared followed his gaze. It was ages since he'd stood up there and he'd forgotten what an amazing view it offered—out across the palace grounds and to the diverse landscape of fields, fjords and mountains beyond.

"For your information," Edvin resumed, "the reason I left the room had nothing to do with you or Axel or who gets to be your Edling. The truth is, I didn't even hear you make the announcement. I was thinking about Anders and about how none of this really matters. All I heard in that room was jarring noise. All I saw was people pretending that they are important when in fact none of them are. None of us, none of this, matters one iota. We're all going to die—whether by natural means or by the assassin's blow—and until then, we're just killing time. We've got no more of a stake in our own fate than the drones in Emelie's hives."

Jared frowned. "I'm not sure I completely agree with that."

"Agree or don't," Edvin said. "It's all the same. I'm entitled to my views and if you don't like them, well, you can piss off and find your own turret."

For some reason, this made Jared laugh. He couldn't stop

himself. And the strange thing was that although initially his laughter made Edvin look even angrier, he then started to laugh himself. Soon, the ramparts were ringing out with the sound of the brothers' blended laughter.

"Piss off and find your own turret!" Jared repeated.

"There are enough of them," Edvin said, with a grin. "Take the East Tower. The views from there are rubbish compared to this one."

The brothers' laughter ended as suddenly as it had begun. Once more, there was silence between them.

"You asked me before if I'm angry with you," Edvin said. "So, I'll be honest. Yes, Jared, I'm angry."

Jared was growing impatient. "But you said you didn't care..."

"Not about the Edling thing," Edvin broke in. "Forget everything about the Edling! I'm angry with you because you don't seem to be upset in any way that our brother is dead, that he was assassinated. I know you weren't close to him, Jared, but even so. He was our flesh and blood."

"Is that what you really think?" Jared was stunned. "That I'm not upset?"

"You don't show any sign of it. You're like an automaton. Prince Anders is dead. No problem. Send for Prince Jared to pick up the crown and carry on running the Princedom."

Jared shook his head, profoundly shocked. "You know me so much better than that."

"I thought I did," Edvin said sadly. "I thought I knew you like a favorite book, cover to cover, but in the past forty-eight hours, I've been forced to revise my opinion."

Jared was silent in the face of his brother's latest, deepest attack.

"At least you don't try to deny it," Edvin said.

Jared felt a tidal wave of anger building up inside him. "Deny it?" he spat. "What good would that do when you've already made up your own mind? You who claim to know me better than anyone in this palace, anyone in this world!" He shook his head. "Do you have any idea what the past forty-eight hours have been like for me? The things I've had to get my head around—from giving a speech to thousands of people from that balcony down there to running meetings of twelve people, many of whom, it transpires, can't stand each other, to contending with Cousin Axel's ambitions and our mother's somewhat different agenda and signing a death warrant and accepting that the peace our brother brought to this nation might be coming to an end? Do you have any idea what it's like to have not one waking minute to call your own? And then to lie awake all night because you're so fearful that you've made the wrong decisions the day before and even more fearful of the decisions you'll be asked to make in the day ahead? And you can't even think about how bad you really feel deep down, how much you are crushed by the loss of your brother, because if you give that thought oxygen for even a second, it might just send everything else crashing down around you and stop you from doing what small good you can to honor your brother and your father and the Princedom to whom you swore your service." Jared swiftly drew breath before continuing. "And while I'm swimming through all of this excrement, you just sit at the side and judge me! You of all people!"

"I'm sorry," Edvin said and, for the first time, his voice faltered.

"Those are just words," Jared said angrily, storming away.

"Jared, I really am sorry," Edvin repeated, his voice becoming shaky.

Feeling hot with fury, Jared jumped down from the ramparts.

"Wait!" Edvin followed him. "Please, let's talk about this."

"There's nothing more to say," Jared barked. "I've wasted precious time coming to find you. I've got a thousand and one more pressing things to do and you've made your position abundantly clear." His anger flipped into sadness. "You know, I thought I'd lost one brother two days ago, but now I see I lost both of you. Thanks." He sighed. "Thanks very much. Now I know what it feels like to be utterly alone."

TWENTY-THREE

The Forest

Jared was surprised to find himself already in the heart of the forest. He realized his feet must have made their way through the palace grounds and out into the forest quite automatically, as his head processed all the pernicious thoughts that had built up inside it over the past few days. He realized too that, for the first time in three days, he was completely alone.

"Hedd!" he called. "Come here, boy!"

Jared stood perfectly still, eyes and ears alert for clues as to where his canine companion had gotten. Suddenly, there was a rustle of leaves, followed by the crack of a twig, and a blur of silver fur. The Irish wolfhound came bounding toward him.

"Good boy!" Jared said as the dog careered to a halt at his

side. He knew he could trust Hedd—he would dart off and explore all the hidden scents of the forest that were so fascinating to him but would always sprint back, in response to a call or a whistle. Especially on days like today, when Jared's pocket was filled—thanks to Vera Webb—with strips of cooked chicken. Hedd knew exactly how the system worked and was already sitting in front of his master, wiry tail swishing the leaf-strewn ground expectantly.

"There you go," Jared said, offering Hedd a nice plump gobbet of meat, which the hound licked enthusiastically off his hand. "All done!" Jared told him, when he lingered in hope of a second treat. "You can have another piece later. On we go!"

Jared couldn't believe how liberated he felt here. Perhaps it was something to do with the height of the sequoias. They enfolded him in their color and scent and made him feel dwarflike in comparison to their size. Jared realized someone might enter the forest, feeling a sense of importance because he was a prince, but he only had to stroll among those truly majestic trees for a short time for him to gain a true sense of perspective.

As he moved on, he became aware of the low afternoon sunlight slanting through the trees. He remembered walking with the Woodsman through this very stretch of his beloved forest sometime before. Jonas had told him then that some of the trees here were more than three thousand years old. They had seen many rulers come and go, Jared mused, and he wondered how many other new princes had found much-needed sanctuary here within the green shade of the forest.

As he reached the next sequoia, he pressed his palm flat against its bark. There was something deeply calming about making a connection with the strength and age of the tree. When he withdrew his hand, he was pleased to see the imprint the bark had left on his flesh. It spoke of a kind of brotherhood, albeit a temporary one, as he watched his flesh become smooth again.

Hedd darted off to pursue a fresh scent, leaving Jared alone. Or was he? He heard a twig snap, but it came from the opposite direction from which Hedd had gone. Jared paused, engaging all his senses. Sure enough, he heard Hedd snuffling through the undergrowth to his left. The twig had very definitely broken to his right. Still, there was no further sound. Perhaps it was simply another forest creature, or one of Jonas's team. The Prince moved on.

He hadn't gotten much farther when he saw a shadowy figure move between the trunks of two trees. He might not have noticed it were it not for the fact that the low sun had suddenly assailed his eyes through a gap in the foliage directly ahead, making him turn away instinctively. Of course, he had been followed! The Poet might have allowed him to leave the confines of the palace, but he wasn't about to let the new Prince wander freely. Jared couldn't find it in himself to be angry.

"Hal!" he called. "I know you're out there. Stop lurking in the shadows and show yourself!"

He waited. He could feel with certainty that he was not the only human in this part of the forest.

"Hal! Stop playing games!"

Surely his bodyguard would have come out at his first summons, let alone his second? Jared felt an icy shiver pass through him. If it wasn't Hal Harness skulking in the shadows, then who was it? He realized how rash he had been to venture out on his own like this—not that he went anywhere, these days, without a dagger. Giving a whistle to summon Hedd back, Jared reached for the hilt of the weapon, which jutted up above his belt.

Frustratingly, Hedd did not return on cue this time. Had something—or someone—detained him? With a sudden paralyzing dread, Jared watched as the shadowy figure emerged from around a tree to his right. He held himself in readiness, adrenaline rising once more, his dagger solid in the firm grip of his hand.

The figure moved closer. He saw, from its silhouette, that it was a girl. She was wearing a long coat, its collar turned up against the autumn chill, and boots. As she stepped into the light, Jared caught sight of her flame-red hair, and he knew immediately who she was and that she posed him no threat. Her gray eyes met his as she walked toward him.

"I'm not Hal, Your Highness," she said, running a hand through her untamed hair.

He nodded, smiling softly with relief. "Indeed you are not."

She nodded tentatively toward his hand. "Could you please put that dagger away, Your Highness? You're not in any danger from me."

As he slipped the dagger back into its sheath, he glanced back up at her. "You were following me, weren't you?"

She nodded guiltily. "Yes, I'm afraid I was. All the way from the palace gardens."

"Why, may I ask?"

"You didn't leave me much choice, Prince Jared. I needed to talk to you and it was proving impossible to gain an audience at the palace."

"It seems we're at a disadvantage. You know my name but…"

"Oh, yes, sorry, Your Highness," she said. "I'm Asta Peck." She extended her hand.

She should really have curtsied, Jared thought, as they shook hands, but he was actually relieved that she hadn't. It would have felt much too formal, especially in this setting. The flesh of her hand was pleasantly cool, like the stones in the fjord.

"It is I who should apologize," he said, looking into her

eyes. "I should have known your name. I seem to be seeing you with increasing frequency." He thought how her reassuring smile had twice guided him through moments of pressure. "You're Elias's niece, aren't you?"

She nodded. "His niece and his apprentice. I've been at court only six months."

He smiled. "Well, it seems you and I are both fish out of water, Asta Peck."

She seemed surprised by his words, but she smiled back at him. Just then, Hedd came hurtling back from his latest travels. But to Jared's surprise, in spite of the ongoing lure of more chicken treats, Hedd bypassed his master and instead made a beeline for Asta.

"Hello!" Asta said, ruffling his neck, just where he liked it. "What's your name?"

"Asta, meet Hedd."

"Hedd?" She wrinkled her nose. "That's a curious name for a hound."

"I know," Jared said. "I named him after one of the grooms. I sort of idolized him at the time."

Asta stared up at him, still tickling the delighted Hedd. "You…a prince, idolized one of the grooms?"

Jared shrugged. "I was young and this groom seemed able to make all the hounds do amazing tricks. My brothers and I were deeply impressed." He tapped his nose lightly. "Keep that to yourself, though."

"We'll see," Asta replied, daring to hold his gaze.

Jared felt suddenly awkward. He was just about growing accustomed to being stared at by the members of the court; somehow the gaze of this one, extremely pretty, girl was far more unnerving. "So you wanted to see me?" Jared said, moving things onto more certain ground. "Why don't you join us on our walk?"

She nodded enthusiastically, releasing her hold on Hedd and falling into step with Jared. The Prince noted that instead of bounding off to investigate fresh scents, Hedd chose instead to trot along at Asta's side. He shook his head at this show of instant, obvious devotion. On the other hand, he could see the dog had a point.

"So what was so important that you chose to trail me to the forest?" Jared inquired.

Asta took a deep breath. "It's about the investigation into your brother's murder," she said.

Of course it was. Though he had hoped with every fiber of his being that what the pretty stranger wanted from him might prove a distraction, somehow Jared had known that this wouldn't be the case. It seemed that the sanctuary offered by the forest was illusory. Every last corner of the Princedom was tainted by his brother's murder.

He turned to Asta. She took this as an invitation to proceed. "I've been doing some investigating myself, as it happens. And, well, I have some doubts I thought I should raise with you before you execute the wrong man."

This was a lot to take in. "You've undertaken your own investigation? How? Why? And how can you be sure that the wrong man is about to be executed?"

"I can't be sure," Asta admitted, ignoring the Prince's first questions and jumping straight into the last. "Not yet. But I can certainly prick significant holes in the case against him. And, after what you said in your speech yesterday morning, well, I knew I had to find you and talk to you..."

For a moment, Jared was back on the palace balcony, gazing out nervously at the populace but seeing her, only her. Her copper hair and wide gray eyes had seemed like a beacon to him then, just as they did now.

"I came to the palace to try to gain an audience with you this morning, but I was waylaid by the late Prince's Consort and she told me—in no uncertain terms—that there was no way I'd succeed in gaining access to you."

Jared's mind was racing. He barely knew where to begin. "You talked to my brother's wife? Of course you did—I remember you waved up at me from the fountain." He paused. "How long have you known Silva?"

"Not long," Asta said, realizing how immediately at ease she felt with Prince Jared, in spite of the gaping differences in their rank. She brushed a wayward strand of hair out of her eyes as they walked on. "Uncle Elias offered my services to sit with her two days ago, during the meeting of the Twelve." She blushed. "I think he, and others too, were concerned for her personal safety. Not only because of the harm someone might inflict upon her, but that she might inflict upon herself."

Jared's eyes widened at this. Asta continued, "She seems to like my company. When our paths crossed this morning, we ended up going on a walk together. And there are things she told me then, well, not *told* me exactly, but things I really think you need to know. Assuming, of course, that you don't know them already."

Jared drew to a halt, raising his hand. "All right," he said. "You need to slow down."

"You can match my pace," Asta replied.

"Not your pace of *walking!*" Jared exclaimed. "Your talk! It seems like you have an awful lot to tell me, but you need to help me find a way in here. Start at the beginning. Let's focus on the assassin, the steward..."

"The *supposed* assassin," Asta corrected him.

"All right," Jared said. "But the case against him does seem pretty conclusive."

"In certain ways, yes," Asta agreed. "There's the unholy trinity of evidence, right? One, he had access to your brother's dinner plate. Two, my uncle's book of poisons was found in his quarters. Three, he fled to the forest. Oh, and added

bonus, he just happens to be an immigrant from Paddenburg, the nation that may or may not have launched a fresh
attack on Archenfield."

Jared nodded. "It does seem pretty conclusive."

"Of course," Asta allowed, "but it might well feel that
way because someone has gone to great lengths to distract
us from the true state of affairs."

"You think the steward has been set up by the real
assassin?"

"I think it's a possibility we have to consider," Asta said.
There was an utter fearlessness in the way she said "we."
Jared rather liked it, in much the same way he'd enjoyed
her failure to curtsy. "It all goes back to the postmortem my
uncle and I prepared. Have you read it?"

Jared did not reply instantly. She took his silence as her
answer. "That's all right," she said. "I mean I wasn't entirely
sure how these things work. Though I assumed you'd be as
anxious as anyone to know what led to your brother's murder."

"I am," he said, bristling with sudden anger. "Of course I
am! But the investigation into the murder is being handled
by the Captain of the Guard. I was told that he would read
the postmortem on my behalf."

"That makes complete sense," Asta said, realizing she
had overstepped a boundary. "I mean, in one sense, you are
too close to all this to be objective. That's why I hesitated
before coming to you. But now I'm glad I did."

Jared nodded, his earlier anger draining away. "I think I am too. Tell me about the postmortem."

Asta didn't waste any time. "My uncle has identified two possible poisons that may have been used on your brother. It could have been either one of them or it could have been a combination of both. According to the case against Michael Reeves, the poison was conclusively savin, a plant not native to Archenfield. It only grows in the Physic Garden, which, in spite of its proximity to the Kitchen Garden, is not easily accessible to a kitchen steward." She came to a sudden halt, gazing at Prince Jared, giving him a chance to catch up.

"All right," he said. "So are you saying that the poison used wasn't savin? Or that it would have needed someone else to get into the Physic Garden—someone who had easier access?"

"I'm putting both of those down as possibilities," Asta said. Seeing Jared's look of frustration, she added, "Just like my uncle did in the report. He did not say definitively that the poison used on your brother was savin. I fear they have seized on that to make the case against Michael Reeves stronger."

"It was pretty strong to start with," Jared rejoined. "You can't argue that he did not have access to my brother's food, nor that he didn't have the book of poisons in his possession. Nor that he didn't flee, before anyone had put him into the frame."

"I certainly won't argue that he had access to your brother's food. Of course he did, but so did countless others who work in the kitchens, including the Cook. And it's possible that your brother wasn't even poisoned by food—I'll come to that. As for the book of poisons, that could easily have been placed there by the true culprit. And while Michael didn't help his cause any by fleeing, isn't it possible that he knew that the fact he was from Paddenburg would be uncovered and what was likely to happen when it came to light?"

"I suppose it's *possible*," Jared said, none too keen on the picture Asta painted of Archenfield's judicial system. One thought swiftly chased away another. "What do you mean that my brother may *not* have been poisoned by food?"

Asta nodded once more. "I spoke to the Cook..."

"Of course you did!" Jared interjected.

"She doesn't believe that the poison could have been administered in her kitchen," Asta finished.

"Sure," said Jared, "but you can see why she'd think and say that."

Asta gave a quick nod. "Another possibility raised in the postmortem was that the poison was admitted through a patch of broken skin. Last week, your brother went on a hunting expedition—"

"Nothing unusual in that," Jared observed.

Asta glared at him, wondering if she could dare rebuke a prince for interrupting too much. "During that expedition, your brother had a run-in with a stag and was wounded. Though the wound was only light, it could have been the ideal channel for someone to poison him, little by little, perhaps by means of a salve."

Jared felt as if his head was about to explode. "Have you found this salve?"

"No," Asta said. "I'm still looking for it. But when I spoke to Kai Jagger..." She paused, perhaps expecting him to interrupt again. He did not. "When I spoke to the Huntsman, he told me who was with your brother in the hunting party. It included the Huntsman himself, the Prince's Bodyguard, the Captain of the Guard and his deputy, the Woodsman and the Chief Groom."

Jared shook his head. "You have certainly been busy!" Though his words were light, they belied his true feelings. He was thinking how many of the Twelve were on that hunting trip—including the very man he had made his Edling earlier that day. "If only I'd been on that hunting trip myself," he said, "I might be able to shed some light on what happened."

Asta didn't miss a beat. "Why *weren't* you part of that hunting party?"

"I've had more than my share of hunting expeditions of late. Yes, I know I'm supposed to embrace each of the courtly pursuits, but there is a limit!" He smiled again. "Instead I brought the dogs here, into the heart of the forest, making sure I gave Anders and his party a wide berth. We had a great time—didn't we, Hedd, eh boy?"

He ruffled the fur under Hedd's chin, then glanced up

as Asta absorbed what he'd told her. He wondered if she would press him further, and if he would continue to feel compelled to answer any query she put before him. To his relief, she simply smiled. They continued their walk in companionable silence.

Prince Jared stopped dead in his tracks. He had realized where all Asta's questions were leading. "Are you saying that, in your opinion, my brother was assassinated by one of the Twelve?"

Asta's face was level with his own. "Yes, I believe that is what I'm saying."

"Do you have any idea what a treasonous thing that is to think, let alone say?"

Asta was flushed, but she did not recoil. "I'm new to the court," she said. "Protocol doesn't come easily to me."

"You're not joking!"

Asta looked somber. "My uncle is always telling me I should be more careful. But the truth matters to me. And I think it does to you too. That's what you said up on the balcony." She paused. "I took you at your word. Was that a mistake?"

He let out a sigh. "No. No, you have done the right thing coming to find me and telling me what you know. But, Asta, you need to listen to me. For your own safety, you must not share these thoughts and theories with anyone else. Only with me, understand?"

Asta nodded. This time, she allowed herself a small

smile, born of relief. "Who else would I need to talk to, now that I have the ear of the Prince?"

Jared smiled at her joke. Then his thoughts grew clouded again. "You said you had spoken to Silva," he remembered. "That you wanted to tell me something about her?"

"Yes," Asta said, brow furrowed. "It's all rather confusing. During that first meeting with her, she was emotional. Understandably, given what she was dealing with. But she told me that her marriage to your brother was—" Asta broke off, staring into the distance.

"Well?" Jared pressed her.

"I think I'm about to really overstep the mark," she said.

"I think so too," he agreed. "But time isn't on our side. If you think I need to know this, tell me. Don't try to find ways to pretty it up."

She nodded. "Well, Silva told me that their marriage was not the fairy tale it was painted as being. Then this morning, she was very keen to take that back and tell me that they *were* in love—that although their relationship started out as a political union, they came to develop deep feelings for one another."

"Perhaps she was simply talking out of grief when you first saw her?" Jared suggested.

"No." Asta shook her head. "I don't think so."

Jared was taken aback by the force of her response. "You seem very sure of that," he said.

"During the postmortem, we removed the chain your brother wore around his neck. The chain had three items hanging from it—a vial of your father's ashes, a key and a tubular locket. When we opened the locket, we found a love note, which we assumed was from Silva to Anders."

"What do you mean you assumed it was from her? Who else but my brother's wife would send him such a note?"

Asta shrugged. "That's the question," she said. "When I showed Silva the note, she was shocked. She told me that she did not write it."

Jared was briefly speechless. "Do you have this note? May I see it?"

Asta shook her head. "Silva took it from me. Along with the key. I still don't know what that key was for."

Jared nodded ruminatively. "That's a shame about the note," he said. "But tell me, did the key look anything like this?" Reaching under the collar of his linen shirt, he lifted out a chain of his own and revealed a vial—identical to that worn by his brother. Nestling against it, glinting in the sunlight, was a key.

"It's a perfect match," Asta said. "What does it unlock?"

"It's not a perfect match," Jared explained. "But it *is* very similar. We were each given one—Anders, myself and Edvin. They are keys to our own bathing houses down on the fjord. It's a tradition dating back to my great-great-grandparents' day. The thinking is that there are few places in the Princedom where a member of the royal family can enjoy true privacy. So we were each given a bathing house. They are only small but they are a place, by the fjord, where we can go to be alone, away from the noise and watchful eyes of the court."

"Or to be with someone you can't be seen with at the palace." The words fell from Asta's mouth before she had a chance to edit them.

Jared did not contradict her. "I suppose so," he said, letting the chain fall back beneath his shirt.

"Are there duplicates of these keys?" Asta asked. "I think it might be useful to take a look in your brother's bathing house."

"There are no duplicate keys. That was all part of the plan— to keep them private." Jared frowned. "But I'm lost. What has the bathing house to do with my brother's poisoning?"

"It would seem that your brother's personal life was far from straightforward," Asta said. "Whatever his true feelings for Silva, it seems certain he was romantically involved with someone else. Why else would he have carried the love note in the locket, always close to his heart?" Asta's eyes met Jared's. "I can't help but wonder with this evidence if your brother's murder was, in fact, a crime of passion, rather than a politically motivated attack. Could Prince Anders have been killed simply because someone found out about the affair?"

Jared now put a question of his own to Asta. "I know it's a dreadful question to ask but...do you think that Silva could have murdered Anders?"

"Yes," Asta said slowly, wondering why she hadn't arrived at this possibility on her own. "But remember, she only found out about Anders's betrayal this morning—when *I* stupidly showed her the note."

"Not stupidly." Jared shook his head. "It was rather a brilliant move on your part, even if it wasn't intentional. But what if Silva was putting on a show, reacting—*overreacting*—to the note when you showed it to her? It sounds, from what you told me before, that she knew her marriage was far from perfect. She seized on the opportunity today to try to change what she'd said about that. The note gave her the perfect opportunity to act surprised, but we can only guess at her true feelings. Maybe that note only confirmed what she already knew—what she has known for quite some time."

"Oh dear," Asta said. "I don't think I'm a good influence on you. I thought I was breaking every code of the court, suggesting that your brother's murderer might be one of the Twelve. But now you yourself are pointing the finger at members of the royal family, *your own family.*"

Jared nodded. "You're making me question everything I thought I knew, it's true—but not in an unhelpful way." He paused, thinking. "Silva would have had plenty of opportunity to poison Anders, whether via his food or by rubbing salve into his hunting wound."

Asta gasped, her face pale.

"What is it?" Jared asked, wondering if he could ever keep pace with her quick mind.

"I've just remembered something else Silva told me the first time we met. She said that, on account of her pregnancy, she was unable to eat much. And so, because she and Anders wanted to keep the pregnancy a secret, he offered to eat her food as well as his own."

"It would have given her the perfect opportunity," Jared agreed.

"But, in that case, why would she have told me?" Asta wondered.

Jared shook his head. "I can't answer that," he said. "But if everything you have told me is true, and I see no reason to disbelieve you, then I fear my brother and his wife were caught in a tangled web. Albeit of their own making."

"What on earth do we do next?" Asta asked.

"We don't have enough evidence to accuse Silva," Jared said. "I need to think further on all this."

"And I should get back to my uncle, before he grows suspicious," Asta said.

Jared nodded. "It's time I made my return to the palace." He checked to see that Hedd was still at his side. "Good boy, come along then!" He slipped him another scrap of chicken to reward his good behavior.

"And when do we meet up again, Your Highness?" For the first time, Asta sounded unsure of herself. "I mean, I'm assuming you would like for us to meet up again?"

Jared nodded. "Of course I need to see you again. What Silva told you about access to me is nonsense. You only have to come to the palace at any point, and request an audience..." Jared blushed a little and hurried to correct his own pomposity. "Just come to the palace and say you would like to see me."

"Might it be better if I have a way to get to you, without making our association widely known?" Asta said.

Jared nodded. "You're a step ahead of me, again. When we get back to the palace, I'll show you a private way of reaching my rooms." He smiled. "Of course, you'll still have to contend with my bodyguard. He never leaves my side."

"Except now," Asta said. "His name is Hal, isn't it? You thought I was him. Where is he now?"

"Probably lurking in the undergrowth," Jared said. He still couldn't quite believe that the Chief Bodyguard had not followed him into the forest. But, if he had, he hadn't made a sound and Hedd hadn't sniffed him out. A dark thought crossed Jared's mind. Was there a chance that Hal had been

there and had overheard some of their very private, potentially incendiary, conversation?

His thoughts were interrupted by the chimes of the
Priest's Bell.

"Come on, Asta," Jared said, with renewed urgency. "We
need to get going. The steward is due to be executed one
hour from now. I need to find the Captain of the Guard and
tell him things might not be what they seem."

Asta's face broke with relief. "That's wonderful news,"
she said. "But how will you tell him what you know, without
giving away where the information came from?"

"Leave me to work that out," Jared said. "And trust that
I will."

"I do trust you," she said.

"And I you, for some reason," Prince Jared told her. He
was gratified to see that his words brought a smile to her
lips.

The light was beginning to fade from the sky when they
made their return to the palace.

Jared bid Asta farewell. He was surprised how alone he
felt, as he watched her disappear down the path toward the
village. Though she had come to talk to him about his brother's murder and much of their conversation had strayed into

very dark territory, what he held on to from their meeting was a sense of fellowship. They had both been thrown into new worlds. Maybe they could help each other find a way through them. It was also good to have the chance to talk to someone of a similar age. And it didn't hurt that she had the most bewitching gray eyes.

His meeting with Asta had certainly restored his confidence; Jared realized that he was going to need every bit of it to tackle Axel. No time like the present, he thought with a small smile. He wondered where Axel might be at this time. In his office at the palace, or at the Captain of the Guard's villa in the Village of the Twelve?

He didn't have to wonder for long, because as he stood in the palace grounds, Axel soon strolled into view. He was coming from the direction of the Dungeons, Jared noted.

"Cousin Jared," Axel called. "Where have you been? I was about to send out a search party."

"I went for a walk," Jared told him, unwilling to dwell any further on his temporary disappearance. "But I'm very glad to see you now. I need to talk to you about your investigation."

"Of course," Axel replied. "Shall we decamp to your quarters or mine?"

"What I have to say won't take long," Jared said. "I want you to stay the execution. I have reason to doubt that the steward was my brother's assassin."

Axel's face paled. "What reasons? The case against him was watertight."

Jared shook his head. "I don't believe that to be so," he said. "But before I go into detail, do I need to sign something to delay the orders on the death warrant?"

"I'm afraid you're too late, Prince Jared," Axel said.

"Too late? Surely the papers can be drawn up at any time? I will talk to Logan."

"No, Prince Jared, you need to listen to me. You can't sign anything to reverse the death warrant because the prisoner was beheaded an hour ago. I was there when the Executioner swung his axe."

"What?" Jared felt his whole body begin to shake.

"That's why I was looking for you. I decided to bring forward the execution."

"You decided...*why*?" Jared's face flushed. "That wasn't your decision to make."

"Actually, it was," Axel said. "The Executioner and I made the decision together. Of course, we looked for you, but you were nowhere to be found."

"And so you just elected to press on with the execution anyway."

"I'm sorry," Axel said.

"No, you're not." Jared shook his head, anger coursing through him.

"You need to tell me what you think you know," Axel

said. "Why have you suddenly decided that the prisoner, whose death warrant you yourself signed, was not in fact guilty?"

"You're the one who owes *me* an explanation," Jared said firmly. "Not the other way around."

Axel's face grew clouded. "I'm constantly making allowances for you," he said. "You're a sixteen-year-old boy with precious little understanding of how this Princedom works. I keep giving you the benefit of the doubt, Cousin, but I fear you are starting to try my patience."

"Don't talk to me like that," Jared shot back. "Remember I am your Prince and start treating me accordingly."

"I'll treat you like a prince when you start behaving like one!"

Shaking his head, Axel Blaxland turned and walked back in the direction from which he had come.

Jared realized he was absolutely powerless to do anything about it.

TWENTY-FOUR

The Prince's Quarters, the Palace

JARED WAS SITTING IN THE CHAIR AT HIS DESK, his head cradled in his hands. Tufts of dark hair poked up between his long, rather graceful fingers. He had been sitting that way for ages, as still as one of the marble renderings of his ancestors in the statue garden.

Logan had long since given up trying to draw him into conversation. The only sound within the chamber was the muffled drumming of the persistent rain on the other side of the mullioned casement. It was a filthy night and one on which to be grateful indeed to be inside the palace walls and close to a lit hearth.

Jared thought back to what Asta had told him of his brother's hunting expedition. Axel had been there. Axel had had access to the wound. Jared shuddered. How did he know that Axel Blaxland—his cousin, the man whom he himself had made Edling, against his own better instincts— was not the real assassin? If so, it was no wonder he had been intent on serving such swift "justice" to the prisoner. Michael Reeves might have been nothing more than a scapegoat.

Jared's right elbow abutted an untouched tray of food sent up from the kitchens, at Logan's request, more than an hour before. The bread had been torn into pieces, morsels of it rolled into tiny doughy balls, thanks to a flurry of nervous energy. The meaty soup remained untouched, an unappetizing film of fat now congealing on its surface. It made Logan's thoughts turn to winter ice that would lay similar claim to the fjord during the coming months.

Logan walked around the edge of the broad oak desk and, brushing past Jared's side, approached the double mullioned casement behind him. The Poet lingered there for a moment, watching the teeming rain and feeling the chill that permeated the closed glass, then reached up and drew across the heavy curtains to shut out the darkness, cold and damp. Turning back again, Logan saw that the Prince still hadn't moved a muscle.

Logan gave Jared's shoulder a gentle squeeze. It was the smallest of gestures, but it seemed to bring the Prince back to life.

"Just answer me one thing, Logan. Am I or am I not

Prince of All Archenfield?" Jared drew his hands away from his face and gazed at Logan through troubled, red-rimmed eyes.

"Yes," Logan answered. "Of course you are the Prince. It's a strange question, if I may say so."

"No, it's not," Jared said. "For, if I am truly Prince here, how can it be that my cousin, the Captain of the Guard, has the right to act without my say-so?"

Logan's head tilted toward the Prince. "Can you be more specific?"

Jared nodded, his anger easily perceptible in the set of his jaw even before he spoke. "How come I came back from my walk this afternoon to find that Axel had proceeded with Michael's execution?"

"The kitchen boy?"

"The *steward*. And he had a name."

"Yes, that's right," the Poet conceded calmly. "You knew he was to be executed. You signed the death warrant two nights ago..." He reached into his pocket. "With this very pen."

"I know that! Though I'm equally aware that I signed it under duress from Axel, and actually from you." Logan frowned, poised to respond, but Jared went on. "My point is that Michael wasn't due to be executed until sundown tonight. What gave Axel the right to bring forward the execution?"

"Well, Axel is Captain of the Guard. It certainly falls

within his and Morgan Booth's responsibilities to determine such matters. I'm sure there were practical reasons for this decision and I can look into them if you wish. But you must realize, now that you are Prince, you can't simply disappear for hours on end."

"Yes, thank you," Jared said. "That has been made abundantly clear."

Logan's eyes met the Prince's. "Why is this so important to you?"

Jared gazed at the Poet with evident frustration. "It's important to me because I went to Axel to defer the orders on the death warrant. But I was too late. *Michael* was already dead."

"You wanted to stop the execution while the Executioner was sharpening his blade?" Logan's eyes narrowed. "That's *unusual*, to say the least." His voice dropped a register. "What, I wonder, compelled you to this new course of action?"

Jared waved his hand. "That's a whole other story. What I'm trying to understand here is where my powers end and those of the Captain of the Guard and the rest of you, the Council of Twelve, begin."

The Poet nodded. "I do appreciate your confusion and your understandable frustration. I suppose we all thought that, as Edling, you would have observed the workings of the Twelve. But, of course, the perspectives of Edling and

Prince are significantly different. For instance, you are now charged with making decisions about life and death."

"Am I though?" Jared asked, genuinely confused. "Am I really? Or am I merely the Council's puppet?"

"The Council is here to support you," Logan said. "In good times but especially in times of crisis. And, Prince Jared, Archenfield has surely never seen such a moment of crisis as we are experiencing now. The way you have coped these past few days has been nothing short of miraculous. If anyone had any doubts about your capacity to rule, then you have swept them away in the most decisive fashion."

"That's very flattering," Jared began but found himself interrupted.

"Credit where credit is due. Whatever the dubious reputation of the Poets, my business is not to flatter you." Logan paused. "My job, like the rest of the Twelve, is to empower you to be the best ruler you can. But it works in both directions. You need to trust in us and in our experience. We all have roles and responsibilities. And so, in terms of this investigation, you would do well to allow the Captain of the Guard to handle things his way."

As the Poet finished, the Prince stared silently at his companion for a time before speaking again. "Logan, can I trust you?"

The Poet frowned. "Prince Jared, I would hope you know the answer to that question by now."

"Yes, of course. But I need to be sure. I need to tell you something in confidence."

Logan nodded.

"This cannot go beyond these four walls. Not to any other Council members, nor my mother or Edvin..."

The Poet nodded. "Whatever you tell me will remain solely between us two."

Jared paused before speaking. "I'm not sure I trust my cousin."

Logan let out a sigh. "But you just made him your Edling."

"Yes," Jared said. "I'm painfully aware of that."

"Well, I'm sorry to hear you feel that way. It's not helpful for you to have doubts to contend with, on top of everything else. But let's be very clear about this—are you saying you don't trust in his ability to investigate your brother's murder or simply that you do not trust him?"

Jared considered the distinction carefully. "Perhaps both."

Logan nodded. This was explosive information and needed to be handled with due caution. "I'm going to need some time to reflect on this."

"Yes, fine."

"And I'm going to need to know why you have lost faith in Axel's handling of your brother's murder. What made you want to stay Michael's death sentence?"

Jared's eyelids flickered. "We'll talk about that, but not

tonight. I'm dog-tired, to be honest with you, and suddenly I'm really hungry."

This at least was something to which Logan could provide a ready solution. "Why don't I take that tray of food away and have a fresh one sent up?"

"Thank you," Jared said. "But perhaps they can find something other than another ladle of this greasy soup? I've seen more tempting pools of mud on the moors."

The Prince and the Poet exchanged a smile. Logan lifted the tray and carried it toward the door. Balancing it on one hip, the Poet used his other hand to turn the doorknob, a maneuver at which the chamber servants always showed great proficiency. He repeated the operation with the second of the two doors, stepping out into the corridor.

As the second door opened, a figure shot past him into the Prince's suite, tripping Logan off balance, the contents of the food tray coming perilously close to falling to the floor.

"Who was that?" Logan asked Hal Harness, as the Prince's Bodyguard joined him at the threshold. "How could you let that happen?"

"It's the Physician's niece. Asta Peck. She was arguing with me to let her in, but I said no—as per your instructions that no one was to disturb the Prince. Certainly no one of her standing."

"Well, she's in with the Prince now," Logan said, with clear disdain.

"She can just as easily be removed," Hal said, stepping to the closed door. His broad shadow fell across the Poet's slighter frame.

"You stay here," Logan said. "I'll handle this. Please send for another tray of food. And no more of that fetid soup! It's supper for a prince, not slops for a sow!"

Passing the unwanted tray to Hal, Logan opened first one door, then the second. Returning to the room, he found the tableau of Asta standing in the center of the rug, angrily confronting Prince Jared, who had risen to his feet. The thick oak desk formed a barrier between him and the girl.

Her face was red and wet. Logan's first thought was that she had been crying, but then the Poet noticed that her hair and clothes were wet too. Of course, the rain. Clearly, she had been caught unaware by the torrents on her way to the palace.

"How could you?" she asked Jared, her voice raw with emotion. "You said you'd show him mercy! How could you?"

Logan registered the impact of the girl's words, of her presence, on the Prince. Jared could not have looked more floored if she had punched him in the stomach. What was she talking about? And how dare she address the Prince in such a fashion?

"I said I'd talk to the Captain of the Guard about the things you told me," Jared said, glancing from Asta to Logan.

Logan was impressed by the Prince's calmness in the face of this uninvited guest. He seemed to have transformed himself in the time the Poet had stepped out of the room.

Asta's gaze was locked on the Prince. "Yes. And I, foolishly, took you at your word. I thought you meant you would actually think about it and come to the only decent and honorable decision." Her face blazed with fury and she wasn't yet finished. "I see I had you all wrong, Prince Jared, didn't I?"

Jared walked around the desk, until he was standing directly in front of her. "Asta, it's more complicated than you understand."

Logan nodded approvingly. Jared was acting every inch the Prince.

Asta, however, seemed resolutely unimpressed. "It's not in the least bit complicated, Your Highness," she said quietly. "It's the simplest thing in the world. It's the truth."

Her words hit home. It was plain to see as the veneer of control slipped from Prince Jared's face. Suddenly, he was a boy again. Logan was disturbed. What history did this girl share with the Prince? How did she possess this power to make him so vulnerable? And, more important, how had she been allowed to escape the Poet's notice until now?

"Your silence," Asta told Jared, "speaks volumes."

That was enough. It was clear to see that Jared was now stripped of all his defenses. Logan stepped forward.

"You've had your say," the Poet said. "Now it's time for you to go."

Asta's feet remained stubbornly rooted to the spot.

"Should I summon the Prince's Bodyguard to carry you back to the village?" Logan asked her.

Asta glared over her shoulder. "That would be very dignified for all concerned, wouldn't it?"

In answer, Logan gave a casual shrug, moved past Asta and started busying himself with some papers on the Prince's desk. Surely, she would understand the message. *We have business to get on with—business far beyond your understanding or importance.*

Logan registered her sigh and then the stamping of her boots as she made her way to the double doorway.

The next sound was the gruff voice of Hal Harness. "No, you don't get to slam it. Off you go!"

The door closed quietly but firmly behind the intruder.

Logan dropped the papers he held onto the desk and turned back to Jared, who stood motionless in the center of the room. "What was that all about?"

"I'd have thought it was self-explanatory."

"That girl seems to be unusually involved in matters of the state. Is the reason you changed your mind about Michael Reeves because of something she has said?"

Jared couldn't deny it. "She has some ideas about my

brother's murder, which she shared with me. Not all of them wide of the mark, in my opinion."

There was a pause. "You need to be very careful," Logan said. "It's not a good idea to let an outsider into an investigation of this magnitude."

"No," Jared snapped back. "Because the rest of us are doing such an outstanding job of it, aren't we?"

"She's got under your skin," Logan said. "I'd suggest you steer clear of her path for the time being. Let others deal with her and her hypotheses."

"I really don't think we have anything to fear from Asta."

"All the same..."

"All right! You've made your point." Jared brought his clenched fist down on the desk. The force of its impact made the papers and other items on its surface jump.

Prince Jared seemed surprised by the force of his own temper. When he turned back to Logan, his face was drained of anger. "I'm sorry. I'm tired and, right now, I probably just need to be alone with my thoughts."

Logan nodded. "There are some matters I should attend to myself. If you need me, call for me. Whatever the time, whatever the matter, I am here for you."

"I know," Jared said. The Prince reached out his hand to the Poet's shoulder and rested it there. "Quite frankly, Logan, I don't know what I'd have done without you these past few days."

"That's what I'm here for. It's what we are all here for."

Jared nodded. He walked back to the chair behind the desk, sat down and closed his eyes wearily.

Logan stood for a moment, in the center of the room, observing Prince Jared, just as he had often watched Prince Anders sitting at the very same desk. Logan knew that the new Prince still felt as if he was trespassing in his brother's quarters. He suspected that might be the case for some time to come. Archenfield's new Prince was considerably more sensitive than his past two predecessors.

Though the Prince's eyes were closed, his face looked far from peaceful. It was clear that the girl's visit had unsettled him. It was time to do some digging on her. And then to assess whether it might prove necessary to take preventative measures.

The Poet hastened toward the chamber door, opening it soundlessly, then glancing back at the Prince in repose. Logan smiled to himself—as if he had conjured up a piece of artwork for the palace walls. *The Prince in Repose.* Well, as long as it wasn't painted by Queen Elin! Logan shook his head as he walked softly away, careful not to rouse the Prince from his much-needed slumber.

DAY FOUR

TWENTY-FIVE

Prince Anders's Bathing House

ASTA WAS SURPRISED TO FIND THE DOOR TO
Prince Anders's bathing house ajar, banging to and fro in
the morning breeze. Silva must have come here ahead of
her—perhaps soon after taking the key from her the previous morning. The fact that she hadn't bothered to lock up
the place again, after departing, spoke volumes about her
state of mind. As Asta stood on the threshold of the little
wooden house, feeling the frigid air rising from the fjord
cool the back of her neck, she wondered how long it had
taken Silva to deduce what the key from Prince Anders's
chain was for. Maybe she had known all along and it had
simply been a matter of retrieving the key from Asta's possession.

Asta felt that, in the past twenty-four hours, her ideas

about everything connected to the Prince's assassination had been turned upside down. She had sought out Prince Jared to share with him her developing theories but, through talking to him, had come away with other, still more disturbing, possibilities. Could Silva herself be the murderer? Worse—if it was possible to conceive of a "worse" in this instance—could Silva be a coldhearted assassin at the heart of a complex and ruthless plot from Woodlark?

Asta had slept fitfully after leaving Prince Jared's quarters and walking home to the village in the rain. She knew she hadn't handled that second meeting with the Prince well, but she had been so shocked to learn of the steward's execution, especially after the assurances Prince Jared had given her. He'd acted differently toward her in his rooms at the palace than during their earlier meeting in the forest. Of course, at the palace, they had not been alone and, doubtless, Jared had not felt quite as free in the way he might talk to her.

She knew in the cold light of morning that she had overreacted—and very possibly wrecked their fledgling bond—but she could not easily get past the fact that an innocent man had been executed. With the new Prince's consent. Lying awake, hearing the dawn birdsong, Asta realized that, at the first opportunity, she must not only resume her investigation but start turning up some more conclusive proof to take back to Prince Jared.

Seized with fresh purpose, she pushed open the bathing house door and stepped inside. The place comprised one main room, with a smaller washing chamber adjoining at the back.

The main room was set up as a simple living room, with a wide chaise—offering ample room for two—and two further armchairs. There were a couple of tables too—a high one behind the chaise and a low one in the center of the room over a patterned rug. Evidently, a vase of deep red roses had stood until recently on the more central of the tables, but the vase now lay on its side, most of the heavily scented roses strewn over the table, in a pool of water that, for some reason, made Asta think of tears.

On the wall were some paintings—mostly watercolors by the looks of it—as well as a pair of antlers and a glass case containing a stuffed fish. Asta noticed that, behind the chaise, a large urn containing fishing rods had also fallen over. Against one wall was a small but elegant bookcase, crowded with volumes—though now she noticed that a number of these were scattered across the floor. The overall effect was of affluent, comfortable simplicity. The room lacked the scale or formality of the chambers at the palace but nonetheless, it was far from a rustic dwelling—Asta knew what it was to grow up in a genuinely rustic home.

The room was also definitely an intimate space. Prince Jared had told her that the idea behind the brothers' bathing houses was to give the royal princes a place of privacy and tranquility, away from the court. But, looking around, Asta was sure now that Prince Anders had used his house to meet with whoever had sent him the love note. There was something about the place that, in spite of all the emphatically masculine touches, spoke of femininity. Perhaps it was the woven throw, draped over the chaise, for added comfort and the vase of roses, even if it was now lying on its side.

The roses made Asta think of her mother. Few things brought more delight to her mother's face than when Asta's father gave her a bunch of wildflowers to remember her birthday or the day they had been wed. Thinking of her parents in this way, Asta felt a sudden tug of loneliness and fatigue.

Fighting these emotions, she forced her attention back to the room.

At first glance, she had thought that the small signs of disarray—the spilled vase, the scattered books—might simply have been due to the door being left open and the wanton destructiveness of the wind coming off the fjord. Now, as she looked more closely, she suspected that this was not the full story. The areas of mess were somehow too contained.

She stepped across the room, closing the door to shut out the insistent sound of the wind in order to get a better sense of things.

Ever practical, she looked around for something with which to mop up the spilled flower water. She decided that the throw was probably her best bet, though it seemed almost sacrilegious to use the fine cloth in this way.

She cleaned up the water and set the roses back into the vase, where a minimal amount of water remained. As she did so, she caught the musky perfume of the wild roses. The scent was so strong, it filled the small room—and not in an altogether pleasant way. She realized that though the blooms were still vibrant, they were on the verge of decay.

Next she turned her attention to the fallen urn containing the fishing rods. She righted this, realizing that it might easily have been knocked over by accident as someone—Silva?—had moved between the chaise and the bookcase.

Moving carefully in this direction herself, she crouched down over the pile of books, fanned open on the carpet. It pained her to see books mistreated like this. Silly, really, because books were only inanimate objects, weren't they? All the same, she began taking each book in turn and closing it properly, then stacking the books in a neat pile to her side.

As she lifted away the books, however, she noticed that hidden among them were narrow slips of paper, bearing familiar handwriting. She picked one up, her hand trembling. It was another note, in the same hand as the one she had retrieved from Prince Anders's locket.

One day, we will be together—in public as we are in private.

The note was almost identical in size and appearance to the previous one. The only significant difference was that, where the first had been curled to fit inside the locket, this one lay flat.

Setting the note carefully on the low table, Asta cleared away another couple of books, revealing another note lying beneath them.

You call me your mystery, but I will share all my secrets with you, my love.

Asta's heart was racing, but not from any romantic notion. On a sudden impulse, she made her way over to the bookcase and selected a book at random. She lifted it up and let the pages fan open. As she did so, just as she had expected, another slip of paper fluttered to the rug below. It was another similarly sized note.

She reached for another book and upended this too. Another note fell to the floor. Same size, same handwriting. She didn't bother reading it before choosing another book at random. Same procedure. Out came another note, in the very same hand. No wonder the notes were so smooth. They had been used as the most intimate kind of bookmarks.

She sat down on the floor, resting her head against the arm of one of the chairs. Things were starting to come together. This was Prince Anders's secret space—a place where he could not only meet his mystery woman but also safely stow the evidence of their relationship, away from the prying eyes of his wife. Until now.

Asta realized from the increasing chill that the door to the hut was open again. She knew she had shut it securely and that, however strong, the wind could not have twisted the handle. There could only be one explanation and, indeed, as her eyes turned toward the doorway, she found Silva standing there, at the threshold, her face cold with fury. Asta could not restrain the shiver that came not only from the fresh gust of outside air but from Silva's sudden arrival and obvious distress.

Silva's face was contorted with pain, her usually perfect skin streaked with tears. When she spoke, her voice was raw and husky, as if she had been out too long in the cold. "This was the place he came to—to be with her."

Asta rose slowly to her feet. "Yes, I think you're right. But do you know *who* he came here to meet?"

"I don't know for certain. But I have my strong suspicions."

"Who?" Asta asked.

Silva opened her mouth but then seemed to think better of speaking. She smiled at Asta instead, but it was a bitter smile. "Someone whose traitorous lips are as red as those rose petals." Her eyes lingered on the few petals that were still strewn across the floor.

Asta waited, barely daring to breathe, hoping Silva would say more. When she did not, Asta heard her own voice, reaching out as tentatively as a cat's paw.

"You know you can talk to me, don't you?" she said. "We haven't known each other long, but perhaps it would help to share your thoughts with a friend?"

Her words were intended to gain Silva's confidence, but they seemed to have the opposite effect.

"How can I be sure you *are* my friend?" Silva asked, shaking her head slowly. "How do I know who I can and cannot trust in this godforsaken place?" The poor woman seemed utterly broken.

Asta decided that bluntness might prove the best means of getting to the heart of the matter. "Silva, did you know when I showed you the Prince's key that it would open the door to this bathing house?"

Silva nodded. It was a very small movement and her expression called to mind a child caught in a mischievous act. "I always wanted to come here, but he would never let me. He said it was his one private place." Her cornflower-blue eyes glistened, as if with unshed tears, as they absorbed the room and its contents. Asta knew her companion was torturing herself, conjuring up all the betrayals—some small, others large—that might have happened within the flimsy wooden walls.

"You knew your marriage was politically motivated

to forge the necessary alliance between Archenfield and Woodlark," Asta said. "You're nobody's fool, Lady Silva. I'm fairly certain you knew exactly what you were getting into here."

She felt she was dancing on a knife-edge with these words and was grateful when Silva gave a nod.

"Of course, I knew. My mother and my older sister spelled it out for me. I was under no illusions. I had a duty to perform."

It was Asta's turn to nod. She indicated the chaise and was pleased when Silva picked up on her cue and sat down. Asta took her own seat, close beside Silva, and waited for the Prince's Consort to resume.

"Duty is important to me. The notion was drummed into me from an early age." Silva paused to straighten the folds of her skirt. "I take my own duties very seriously. Which makes it hard when others fail to do theirs."

She sighed, her shoulders dropping a little, her small hands unclenching. It seemed to be doing her some good to talk. Asta remembered at a previous meeting Silva saying that Asta was akin to her confessor. This thought sent a new frisson through her. What exactly might Silva Lindeberg Wynyard now be about to confess to?

"So you entered into this marriage knowing just what to expect. Your eyes were wide open." Silva nodded as Asta continued. "But somewhere along the way, Anders cast a spell on you. I remember you telling me, when we first met, how kind he was toward you."

Another nod, then the flicker of a smile. "We were always good friends," Silva said. "Right from the beginning. We joked about being soldiers of fortune, thrown together for the good of our nations. We made a pact to see one another through this unusual, but not unprecedented, situation by virtue of our friendship."

She broke off, her eyes falling to the floor. Asta had the sense that Silva had traveled back into her past, to the beginnings of her marriage. She knew she needed to pull her back, but gently.

"But you grew to have greater expectations of him," she said. "Perhaps it came from his own actions or simply from his charisma. But I've no doubt the fairy tale the court wove around you seduced you as much as anyone else." Seeing Silva's eyes fix on her again, Asta paused. "I'd have been exactly the same. I would have begun to lose the ability to distinguish between what was real and what was artfully constructed fantasy."

"I have no doubt that Anders loved me," Silva said. "But it wasn't a deep enough love." She paused to correct herself. "No, that's not it. It wasn't the *right* kind of love. How could it be? You can't be in love with two people at the same time, can you?"

Asta shook her head, in part because she knew that was

the response Silva needed. She was desperate to ask, "So, who was the Prince in love with?" but she knew that so overt a question might break the fragile bridge of trust between them. She saw Silva looking at her. She could not remember seeing such sadness in a face before. It was not simply the face of someone feeling grief, but of someone who had given up on all hope.

"You must have felt so frustrated," Asta said, desperately seeking for words to fill the silence. "And lonely. You were asked to give up so much more than he was. You did everything that was asked of you—from maintaining the image of the perfect marriage at all times to carrying Prince Anders's child."

Silva nodded. Her eyes moved to the low table between them and the note that Asta had carefully placed there before. As Silva's hand reached forward, Asta read the note again.

You call me your mystery, but I will share all my secrets with you, my love.

Following Asta's gaze, Silva reached down and snatched up the note. She read it again, wrinkling her nose as if it were assailed by a horrible odor, then she screwed up the note and tossed it across the floor. "Amoral bitch!" she declared.

Silva's tone was as shocking as dipping a hand into the cold waters of the fjord. Asta felt that the Prince's Consort had somehow crossed a line—was it due to grief or something more? She was behaving more and more erratically. Asta tried to keep track of everything she had told her.

Nothing that Asta had seen or heard in the bathing house gave credence to the thought that Silva Lindeberg Wynyard might be a cold-blooded assassin. But a murderer, propelled by deep, unexpressed hurt into a crime of passion? That now felt possible.

"Did *you* kill Prince Anders?"

Asta was almost as surprised by the question as Silva. Their eyes locked together, then Asta turned away, ashamed at her words.

The next thing Asta knew, Silva's hand had made contact with her face and sent her reeling out of the chair. She fell to the floor. Her face was burning with pain and her vision was momentarily blurred. Numbly, she lifted her hand to her cheek, checking to see if Silva had drawn blood. It appeared she had not.

Asta remained lying there for a moment, to regain her equilibrium. She was aware of Silva standing over her, watching her with cold, curious eyes. Then, without saying another word, she turned and walked out.

A moment later, Asta's ears were assailed by one of the most disturbing sounds she had ever heard. Silva let out a keening cry. It sounded at once inhuman and saturated with pain—the kind of sound you might expect a wild animal to make.

Asta stumbled out of the bathing house and found Silva, crouched down by the edge of the fjord. She hesitated, unsure whether she should try to comfort her or if this would only further enrage her. Asta decided she simply couldn't leave her like that and, with some trepidation, made her way to join her at the water's edge.

"I need you to go now," Silva said, rocking on her heels.

"I can't leave you like this."

"You can and you must," Silva said. "I will not be subjected to any more of your questions."

"I won't ask any," Asta assured her. "I'm sorry. I was impertinent and insensitive and—"

"Stop!" Silva cried. "Stop the noise!" She brought her hands to her ears. "Leave me in peace!" She drew herself up to her feet, then turned to face Asta. She saw, with apparent shock, the redness of Asta's cheek. "Did I do that to you?" she asked.

"It's all right," Asta said. "I deserved it."

Silva looked at her again, then nodded. "Yes, I rather think you did." She continued to stare at Asta for a moment, then hung her head sadly. "Please go," she said. "I really do need to be alone."

"Are you sure?" Asta asked. "Because I think that's the last thing you need."

Silva folded her arms. "Please do me the respect of accepting that I know my own mind." There was a faint renewal of strength in her voice now. Perhaps the slap and the scream had both served as some form of catharsis.

Asta remained unsure but, as she took her leave of Silva, she realized that her cheek was starting to throb and she could feel a dull headache taking hold of her skull. She knew she ought to get back to the village and either take a rest or apply some salve to her raw skin—hopefully, she would be able to slip back into the house unnoticed by Uncle Elias and thereby avoid an interrogation.

She felt more light-headed than ever as she made her way back along the path that edged the fjord and she realized that she was badly in need of some breakfast. The heady brew of emotions—both her own and those she seemed too easily able to absorb from others—combined with her lack of sleep had done nothing for her constitution. And the force of Silva's slap hadn't helped matters. A ray of morning light from across the fjord pierced her eyes so that she had to close them and she felt herself stumble on the uneven path. She took a deep breath, wondering if she might be about to faint.

"Hey! Are you all right?"

It took her a moment to come to her senses and open her eyes. She looked up to see Lucas Curzon at the head of a string of horses. Their manes were ruffled by the breeze coming off the water; steam spiraled from their gaping nostrils. Lucas himself was in the saddle of a large bay horse, its reddish-brown coat slick from sweat and shiny from the reflected sunlight. Despite her state, Asta couldn't help noticing that Lucas's shoulder-length hair was only just a darker shade of brown.

Asta had seen the handsome Chief Groom out exercising the horses before, though more often the task seemed to fall to lowlier members of his team. She wondered if there was a reason why he had chosen to take the horses out himself today but was soon distracted by the scrutiny of his piercing gray eyes. She gazed up at him, still feeling giddy, shielding her eyes from the sun with her hand.

"Asta, isn't it?" he said. "I asked, are you all right?" When she did not answer him, he jumped down from the saddle and, keeping hold of the reins, walked toward her. Her eyes fell to his worn boots as they pounded over the ground.

"Look at me!" He reached out with his free hand and gently turned her face toward his. He was so close, she could smell the shaving soap he had used that morning and see where he had missed a few stray hairs on his neck.

"What happened out here?" She realized he was staring at her cheek. "Did you see who did this to you?" Lucas glanced around, then returned his gaze to Asta. "He can't have gotten far."

She was confused by his questions. No one had tried to attack her, had they? He wasn't making sense. Why was she even here? She felt so hot and giddy. She really needed to get home. Seeing the concern in Lucas's eyes, she reached her own hand to her cheek. Her touch brought back the memory of the slap.

"I'm fine," she told Lucas, making a quick decision not to blame Silva. "Just a bit light-headed. I've been out longer than I intended and I haven't eaten breakfast yet." Seeing his still-furrowed brow, she added. "No one attacked me. I think I might have slipped, back along the path, and grazed my cheek."

His brow remained furrowed and, for a moment, she was unsure if he was going to accept her explanation.

"I don't understand," he said at last. "If nothing happened, why did you scream?"

Her eyes met his. "I didn't scream."

"I heard it from over the other side of the woods. I came as fast as I could."

What should she say? She felt tongue-tied.

"Asta, I heard you scream." He wasn't going to let this drop. "What the hell happened?"

She shook her head, slowly, aware that her options were reducing. "It wasn't me. It was Lady Silva."

Instantly, his expression changed. "Lady Silva is here? Where is she? Did someone attack *her*?"

"No!" Asta cried. "No one attacked her either." She lowered her voice. "She's just a little upset."

"A little upset?" He rested his hands on his hips. "The

scream that brought me galloping here was more than just 'a little upset.'"

In spite of what had happened at the bathing house, Asta did not want to betray Silva's confidences. She remembered what Prince Jared had told her the previous day. *"For your own safety, you must not share these thoughts and theories with anyone else. Only with me..."* But the intensity of Lucas's gaze was disconcerting and she knew she had to give him some information. "She found out something terrible about Prince Anders this morning." As she said it, she noticed how guarded Lucas's expression suddenly became. She sighed. "She feels things very deeply. Perhaps because she has to put on such a public face at all times. And especially now, of course, her emotions are all over the place."

Lucas's eyes scanned hers curiously. "Because she is new in grief?"

"Well, yes, and also because she is pregnant."

There was no more guardedness in Lucas Curzon's soft gray eyes. Now they were as open as the door to the Prince's bathing house had been. "Silva is pregnant!"

"Yes," Asta said. Waking out of her strange reverie, she suddenly realized that she had broken a major confidence. "In time, I'm sure it will be a comfort to her to bring Prince Anders's child into this world. But, right now, I think she is feeling very overwhelmed with everything."

There was a strange expression in Lucas's eyes. "In the

middle of life, there is death," he said. "And in the middle of death, there is life."

Asta hadn't expected such a poetic turn of phrase from the Chief Groom. She found herself smiling and nodding.

"I'll go and check she is all right," Lucas said, nodding, full of purpose. "And take her back to the palace."

"She said she wanted to be alone," Asta told him. "That's why I left her."

"You shouldn't have left her," he said. She was surprised to hear a note of anger creep into the Groom's usually gentle voice. "I have no intention of leaving her here when she is so clearly in distress."

Asta wanted to protest that she hadn't had much choice in the matter of whether to leave Silva or not—for all his talk, Lucas could have no idea what Silva was like when her passion was high.

And then it hit her, like the sun skimming off the waters of the fjord. Maybe he *did* know. Maybe handsome Lucas, with those gentle gray eyes, knew the Prince's Consort far better than the Chief Groom should.

Maybe Silva Lindeberg Wynyard had her own secret.

TWENTY-SIX

The Prince's Quarters, the Palace

"THE CAPTAIN OF THE GUARD," LOGAN announced. The Poet stepped back into the Prince's study, closely followed by the taller, more imperious figure of Axel Blaxland. Jared had the curious sense that his quarters had been invaded, even though the invasion had happened at his own command.

He had to make it clear to his cousin that he would not tolerate being addressed again in the manner that Axel had used at their last meeting. And that he needed the Captain of the Guard to renew the search for Anders's killer, if only to eliminate the possibility that it could have been someone other than Michael Reeves.

"Cousin Axel," he said, rising from his seat. "Thank you for responding so swiftly to my message." He gestured to the chair on the other side of the desk from him, then continued with well-rehearsed formality. "Please take a seat. There are urgent matters we must discuss."

Axel remained standing. And now his face moved through a strange series of contortions, light suddenly retreating in much the same way it did from the peaks of the hills when the weather changed. "Prince Jared, there has been a confusion. I did not receive any message from you. I sought you out of my own accord. I have grave news to impart."

"What are you talking about?" Jared asked Axel.

"You might want to sit down for this."

Jared remained standing—if his cousin wouldn't sit at his bidding, why should he do so now at Axel's behest? "Tell me your news, Cousin," he said gruffly.

Axel glanced over his shoulder, checking that the doors to the Prince's quarters were shut. Reassuring himself that they were, he turned back to Jared. The Prince was aware of Logan, who remained close by, watching them both closely.

"Believe me when I say that I'm deeply sorry to bring such news to you," Axel told them now. "Silva is dead."

"Silva!" Logan exclaimed. "No!" He closed his eyes.

Jared felt as if the ground was about to give way beneath his feet. He slumped down into his chair.

"She was discovered an hour ago in the river," Axel continued. "She was not long dead, by all accounts, but quite beyond anything the Physician could do."

"Was she murdered too?" Jared asked.

"It's too early to say for sure," Axel answered. "Elias has her body now. It was Jonas Drummond who found her, tangled up in weeds, in a tranquil pool, at the point where the river opens out into the rapids. She had sustained some wounds to her head. It seems as if she might have been dragged along by the current for some distance and acquired these injuries on the way."

"Surely it was an accident, then?" Logan said, then paused. "Or, do you think, suicide?"

"Suicide seems the most compelling explanation," Axel said. "I'm sure we can all imagine the intense upset she experienced in the wake of Prince Anders's death. And this scenario is certainly supported by the physical evidence." He approached the desk and unrolled a large square of parchment on it. "This, as you can see, is a rudimentary map of the fjord and the stretch of river that connects to it."

Jared reached out his hands to keep the paper from curling up again. "I know this stretch of water very well."

"Of course," Axel said, his tone becoming darker. "We all do." His finger tapped a point on the map. "This is where the wooden bridge crosses the river, at its narrowest point.

We found this key here." He reached into his pocket again and produced a medium-sized key, setting it down on the edge of the map.

The key, of course, was immediately familiar to Jared. He picked it up and turned it between his fingers. "The key to Anders's bathing house," he said, setting it back down again. "Why would Silva go there?" He suspected he already knew the answer to that question. The combination of the key and love note on Anders's chain would surely have been motivation enough.

Axel shrugged. "Perhaps in an effort to be close to Anders spiritually? Or perhaps she was in a more heightened state of emotion."

"What makes you say that?" Logan inquired.

Axel turned to acknowledge the Poet's question. "The bathing house has been burned down to the ground. It was the smoke that first attracted Jonas's attention. It's too early to be sure about these things, but it looks very much like Silva set the bathing house alight—for whatever reason— and then jumped from the bridge, upstream, propelling her body into the strong current there. Whether she dropped the key accidentally or left it there as some kind of message for us, we don't know. There was no suicide note."

Logan nodded. "Perhaps the key was a convenient substitute."

Jared rose to his feet. "We cannot just assume this was suicide. I know that Silva was deeply distressed about Anders's murder. How could she not be? And, though I'm no expert in these matters, I'm sure that, being pregnant, her emotions were heightened still further. The sad truth is that I really didn't know my sister-in-law—perhaps in truth none of us did—but still I find it very hard to believe that a pregnant woman would condemn her unborn child to death, however strongly she might desire to end her own life."

"What are you suggesting?" Logan asked.

Jared met Logan's gaze. "I'm saying we are now looking at the strong possibility of three murders in the court. First Anders, and now Silva and their unborn child. Three murders within three days, striking right at the heart of the court and right at the heart of my family."

There was a long pause. "It's possible," Axel acknowledged.

"It's more than possible," Jared retorted. "And I'm guessing that since Michael Reeves was executed yesterday afternoon, you can't pin this one on him."

"Of course not," Axel said, seeming shocked by the very suggestion. "But we must rely on the evidence before us. Silva has exhibited marked signs of instability since her husband's death. Her behavior has been noted by others within the court. The destruction of Anders's bathing house

302 · JUSTIN SOMPER

is further testimony of Silva's state of mind. And then to leave the key where she did..."

"It sounds like your mind is made up," Jared said. "Will you not even consider any alternate possibility?"

"Prince Jared is right," Logan broke in. "We must keep an open mind about all this. We don't know that Michael Reeves was working alone. A second assassin may have come into play..."

Axel frowned. "I know you trade in matters of the imagination, Logan, but I'd like to keep this investigation rooted in reality rather than fantasy."

"Don't be so quick to dismiss Logan's thoughts," Jared said, struggling to contain his impatience. "We need to gather the Twelve. I will hear everyone's thoughts on this matter."

Jared felt like he was beginning to gain control again. The feeling did not last long.

Axel raised his hand. "With respect, Prince Jared, I am Captain of the Guard. The inquiry into Silva's death is already under way. And the investigation into the assassin from Paddenburg continues. I'm asking for you to let me and my team handle this in the best way our experience advises."

Jared shook his head. "Not this time, Axel. You've already had three days to pursue my brother's murder and I am far from convinced that you've made any significant headway—I believe that last night you executed the wrong man. And now you've got two more deaths on your hands. From now on, I want to be kept informed of every move you make in these investigations."

"Cousin Jared!" Axel could not keep the note of protest out of his voice.

"That's Prince Jared, to you." Surprised at the vehemence of his response, Jared continued in a more measured tone. "I am Prince of All Archenfield and if there is an assassin or, as you have suggested before, that Paddenburg is hell-bent on threatening the peace of this Princedom in the most profound way, then I need to be at the center of the retaliation." Refusing to entertain any further argument, he met Axel's eyes. "Summon the Twelve, Elias permitting. I understand that he has a more important job to do at this point. But I'll see the rest of you in the Council Chamber within the hour."

Jared observed Axel glance briefly at Logan. Was he looking for support from his fellow member of the Twelve? If so, he did not receive it. Logan's eyes remained fixed on the middle distance.

Axel exhaled deeply, then nodded.

"I understand, *Prince* Jared. I shall summon the remainder of the Twelve, as you command." He turned on his heels and left the Prince's quarters.

After he had gone, Jared felt himself trembling, and he was unsure whether it was a result of the exceptional strength he had had to summon to face down the latest challenge from his cousin, or if it was the well of his emotions at the heartbreaking news about Silva and her unborn child? Whichever it was, the physical effect was profound and he retreated back into his chair, shuddering.

He found Logan at his side, the Poet's hand resting on his shoulder. "Just breathe," the Poet said with a gentleness bordering on tenderness.

Jared shook his head. "It's so hard," he said. "Silva didn't deserve to die. Nor her child." He felt a new wave of cold fear snake through his insides. "I know it wasn't an accident, or suicide. I can feel it. They were assassinated, just as Anders was assassinated." He glanced up at Logan.

"Perhaps you're right," the Poet said. "But you should try to keep an open mind, at least for now."

Jared shook his head. "I can't," he said. "I can't think rationally about this. It's too much and too close. It feels like my family is under attack. Who will be next? My mother? Edvin?" He paused. "Me?"

Prince Jared glanced up at the Poet. More than anyone else, it was the Poet who had enabled him to get through the past few days. He had never needed a friend's reassurance more. But, on this occasion, Logan Wilde did not have a reassuring answer, or indeed any kind of answer at all.

TWENTY-SEVEN

The Council Chamber, the Palace

"AND SO," AXEL WAS CONCLUDING HIS ADDRESS to the Council of Twelve, "once Elias completes his post-mortem, we should have a better indication as to whether Silva's untimely death was an accident, suicide or murder."

"It wasn't suicide." The outburst came from Lucas Curzon. All eyes turned toward him.

"Lucas," Jared said, taking control. "You sound very sure about this."

"I am," the Chief Groom said. "I think I was the last person to see her alive." His face was red and, as much as he wanted to speak, he seemed short of breath.

"Tell us what you know, Lucas," Prince Jared said.

"I was out exercising the horses this morning," Lucas recalled. "I ran into Asta Peck, down by the fjord. She had been talking to Lady Silva, close to Prince Anders's bathing house."

"Asta Peck?" Logan Wilde repeated. "The Physician's niece? That girl is turning up everywhere. Someone needs to..."

"Lucas, please continue." Jared was keen to move the focus away from Asta.

"Silva was really upset. She told me she had set off on a walk this morning. It's become her habit of late. She had acquired the key to the Prince's bathing house and decided to go there and look inside. I think she thought it would be a way to connect to him, for her and her baby..."

"Such sentimental superstitions," Emelie Sharp interrupted. "Prince Anders is not to be found in his old bathing hut."

Father Simeon cleared his throat softly. "Perhaps not for you, Emelie. But maybe his grieving widow found some presence of him there. Something to comfort her."

The Priest's soothing tone was swiftly shattered by Lucas. "What Lady Silva found in the place was proof of her husband's betrayal."

The word ricocheted around the room. "What do you mean exactly?" Axel asked the Chief Groom.

Lucas looked deeply uncomfortable. "I don't want to go into details—it's not my place—but there were notes there. Love notes sent to the Prince by someone other than his wife."

Once more, the room was united in stunned silence.

"Did you see these notes for yourself?" Jared asked.

Lucas shook his head. "No," he said. "Nor would I have wanted to. And, before you ask, she didn't tell me what was in them—only the gist. What I did see very clearly was the effect they had on her." He sighed. "It wasn't pretty."

"The notes upset her?" Axel spoke again.

Lucas met his comrade's eyes. "They left her quite distressed," he said. "And who could blame her? It was the ultimate betrayal."

"Distressed." Axel savored the word. "Distressed enough, in your opinion, to burn the bathing house to the ground?"

"Absolutely," Lucas responded, with a nod. "It was the best thing for it, if you ask me."

"But Silva was not, according to you, of a mind to take her own life and that of her baby?"

Lucas recoiled at Axel's latest question but took a moment to consider. "She was angry. And yes, she was upset. I'd have said she might have done harm to someone else—the person who had written those notes, for instance. But to herself? No."

"Did she know who had written the notes?" Logan asked. "Do *you* know?"

There was an uncomfortable silence as all eyes turned to Lucas.

He shook his head, but Jared couldn't help wondering if

he was being truthful. "All I know," said the Chief Groom with renewed vehemence, "is that Silva was not in the frame of mind to harm herself. I'd lay down my own life for that."

Nova Chastain shuddered.

"Don't say such a thing, Lucas," Emelie Sharp said. "Don't summon any more death into this chamber."

"It does feel," Morgan Booth observed, "as if we are being picked off, one by one."

"No." Jared shook his head. "Anders was the Prince, but Silva wasn't one of the Twelve. It's not the court but *my family* that is under attack here."

"It amounts to one and the same thing," Axel said. "Either way, someone has launched an attack on the leadership of Archenfield. But, for now, let's focus on specifics." He returned his attention to Lucas. "When and how did you leave Silva? If she was so distressed—as you put it—wouldn't it have made sense to stay with her and try to calm her down?"

"I agree," Father Simeon said, lifting his hands. "What were you thinking, leaving her alone when she was clearly in such a fragile state?"

"I did try to calm her," Lucas insisted. "But she was very adamant that she wanted to be alone." He paused, took a breath. "It was what the girl, Asta, told me when I came across her. I gave her a talking to about leaving someone in such a state. I'd heard Silva scream, you see. It was a scream that carried right across the fjord. The girl had heard it too and was obviously shaken by it, but Silva sent her on her way." Lucas's face spoke of defeat and dejection. "And then she did just the same to me."

"So the last you saw of her"—Emelie Sharp rejoined the interrogation—"she was in the bathing house?"

"No," Lucas corrected her. "Close to the bathing house. But she was sitting on a rock, by the edge of the fjord."

"And, to be clear, what time was this?"

"It was very early. There was still mist on the surface of the fjord. The Captain of the Guard's Bell had not long sounded."

Axel's eyes swept across the company. "And no one else saw Silva after that, until Jonas noticed the smoke coming from the burning hut and, journeying there to see what had happened, discovered Silva's body—not at the edge of the fjord but back along the river?"

He was met by a further stunned silence. "Is that right?" Axel pressed them. "None of you, no one in your teams, saw her in the intervening time?"

Their continued silence was answer enough. "Well then, Lucas, it appears that you were indeed the last person to see Silva alive."

"Except," Emelie spoke again, "the murderer."

"I understand, Lucas, that you don't *believe* she killed herself," Axel said, ignoring the Beekeeper. "But your own testimony convinces me otherwise. It's clear she was very angry and distressed. Let's suppose that, not long after you took your leave, she got the idea to set fire to the place— to destroy, as she saw it, every last trace of her husband's betrayal. As the bathing house burns, and it would burn swiftly, she turns back in the direction of the palace. Perhaps she moves at speed now. I suspect that her progress was erratic, for now her mind is not only filled with thoughts of Anders but also the act of destruction she has wrought. Perhaps she regrets her actions or, at least, feels conflicted about them—in torching the house, she has destroyed the very place where she might have experienced some lingering sense of connection to her husband. Now she reaches the wooden bridge and, having exhausted herself physically and emotionally, pauses to take a breath."

All eyes were fixed on Axel as he continued his hypothesis. "We know she was there because she placed the key on the low wooden rail, where it was found later this morning. I considered that she might have slipped, but there was no sign of this, no marks on the planking and no threads from her clothing, snagged on the rough wood. And then there is the key—perfectly positioned like a sign of her intent. If she fell, would that key not have been dislodged?"

He paused, letting the question take seed with the others, before continuing.

"The current would certainly have carried her back in

the direction she had come. And the combined shock of the cold water and the still-fresh discovery of those notes would have made for a hellish journey. Even though the current spared her a battering in the rapids, it was too strong for her fragile body. The undertow dragged her into the tranquil pool to die."

He took another breath. "That is what I believe happened to Silva. There is no evidence of anyone else having been there. No one was seen leaving that area after Lucas."

Morgan Booth raised his hand. "You're assuming, of course, that Lucas is not our killer."

Lucas paled at the Executioner's words.

"That's correct," Axel said. "Negligent in his actions concerning Silva, yes, but Lucas does not strike me as the killing kind."

"Nor me," Prince Jared said, with conviction.

Morgan Booth turned to Lucas with equanimity. "I didn't mean to imply anything. I was just posing a necessary question."

Lucas did not return the Executioner's gaze, let alone voice a response.

Prince Jared took the floor once more. "Cousin Axel, the case you lay out for us is indeed persuasive. I, for one, have been skeptical from the outset about suicide. As I said to you, when we spoke of this before, I do not think it likely that a pregnant woman would choose to end her child's life, however despondent she feels about her own. But, from what Lucas has told us, in her final moments, Silva sounds to have been at the very end of her tether."

"But..." Lucas protested.

"Moods can change as suddenly as the direction of the wind," Vera Webb, never short of a proverb, observed.

Jared glanced now at Axel. "Obviously, we are all waiting to know what Elias has to say, on completion of the postmortem. But I think you should pursue the investigation into death by either accident *or* suicide."

Axel nodded. "Yes, Prince Jared." He turned to the others. "Well, if no one else has any further business..." He rose to his feet, clearly more than ready for the meeting to dissolve.

"There *is* one additional matter we need to discuss." It was Logan who spoke. "It concerns Silva's body and her funeral."

There was a sharp intake of breath from Vera Webb. "I'm not sure how much more of this I can stomach."

Prince Jared nodded. "I'm sure we all feel the same but we have very little choice. Logan, please continue."

Logan nodded. "I understand it's not a pleasant subject but firstly we need to send word to Woodlark."

"By a rider? Or by one of Nova's falcons?" Axel asked.

"A rider would be more sensitive and certainly better received," Logan acknowledged. "But a falcon would be the swiftest means of communication. And I do feel that time is of the essence here. In two days' time, we have Prince Anders's funeral. What I'm wondering is if we should make this a double funeral for Anders and Silva? The people are still new in grief for Prince Anders. When they hear of his Consort's death, they will be further...unsettled." His eyes swept across the rest of the company. "That's why I feel a joint funeral would be useful. It would bring Prince Anders's reign definitively to an end and clear the path for Prince Jared's coronation and a new beginning for Archenfield."

Emelie Sharp let out a low breath. "Could you be any more callous?"

But Axel came to the Poet's defense. "Logan is simply doing his job," he said. "It's no different from you dividing the hives when your queen bee dies..."

"That's not how it works," Emelie said crossly.

"I'm sorry," Axel said with a dismissive shrug. "But I don't know your job and I don't tell you how to do it. Perhaps you can extend the same courtesy to Logan."

Emelie's face flushed with anger, but she said nothing further.

Jared turned to Logan. "Shouldn't we ask Silva's parents, Queen Francesca and Prince Willem, what their preference would be regarding Silva's funeral?"

"That's a laudable sentiment," Logan agreed. "But, strictly speaking, once Silva married into your family, she became subject to the laws of Archenfield. It's far more important how her death is received by *our* people than by those of Woodlark."

Jared frowned. "Can that really be true? Aren't the people who matter most in this her parents and her siblings?"

Logan shook his head, with visible sadness. "No. The people who matter the most are your subjects. They are already deeply shaken at the news of your brother's murder. Reports of Silva's demise will push them further to the brink. The fairy tale of Archenfield is over. Of course, we will usher in a new era of history with your coronation. Nothing must overshadow the joy and hope embodied by that ceremony."

Jared looked at Logan with new eyes. He hadn't realized until this morning how hard-hearted the Poet could be.

TWENTY-EIGHT

The Physician's Ice
Chamber, the Village

ASTA FOUND IT A CONSIDERABLE CHALLENGE TO
remain detached from the bruised and battered corpse
lying before her on the slab. The last body she had been
confronted with like this was Prince Anders. That had been
different somehow because she had only ever known him
from afar. But over the past few turbulent days, she had
gotten to know something of the psyche of Silva Lindeberg
Wynyard—from their first meeting only hours after the
Prince's death to their final painful encounter at the bathing house that morning. It made her uncle's request for her
presence in the Ice Chamber challenging, to say the least.

There was no question that Silva had been a difficult
and even disturbed individual, whose moods and mind-set
seemed to change as often as her clothes. One minute, she

was squeezing Asta's hand and telling her she was a true friend; the next, she was taking her own hand to Asta's face—albeit, not without certain provocation. And it wasn't only in relation to Asta that Silva had proved inconsistent. The same was true of the way she had talked about her complex relationship with Anders.

Asta suspected that Silva's ever-changing moods were the result of grief—exacerbated by her pregnancy on the one hand and the torment of Anders's betrayal on the other. But who was the real Silva? Thinking it over, Asta concluded she was probably a rather vulnerable young woman, who had been dispatched to a foreign land to make a new life with a man who did not love her—or, at least, did not love her enough. Silva had been complicit in selling a royal fairy tale, but along the way, she too had come to believe in a fairy-tale ending, which had not come to pass.

"Asta!" Her uncle's voice cut sharply through her thoughts. "I asked you to make a note."

"I'm sorry," Asta said, raising her eyes from Silva's water-pale body.

"You seem distracted," Elias said, without looking at her.

"It's more difficult, isn't it," Asta observed, "when you know the person?"

"You didn't *know* her," Elias said, prodding Silva's exposed shoulder. "You sat with her for a few hours on the day her husband died. Please don't overdramatize this or make out you knew her better than you did. I have a job to do."

Uncle Elias was wrong. Asta had begun to know Silva far better than that. Her uncle could be so cold and clinical about people. She doubted she could ever be that way. Might that prove a barrier to her success as his apprentice?

Now his eyes met hers. He stared at her impatiently. "Well?" he asked.

"I'm sorry, what?"

"I asked you to make another note," he said, with a frustrated sigh.

"I'm sorry," Asta said, determining to become more businesslike. "What did you want me to write down?"

"Bruises to both shoulders, consistent with her body being dragged downriver by the current."

Asta made the note. Looking up again, she saw Elias had now turned Silva's head to her left side and seemed to be checking her scalp. Despite his gruffness with the living, she noted that he was very gentle as he cradled Silva's skull, smoothing her flaxen hair first one way, then another.

"Take a new note," he instructed Asta. "There are four wounds in close proximity on the upper-right section of her skull."

Asta obediently wrote down his observations. When she glanced up, what she saw made her gasp. Elias had reached for a measuring implement—a long needlelike object—and had inserted this into one of the wounds. "Top left wound is a one point eight," he said, removing the measure, then inserting it into the next lesion. "Top right measures one point five." Once more, he withdrew the measure and then appeared to skewer Silva's head a third time. Asta winced, as Elias announced, "Bottom left is one point seven." Again, the measure was removed and reinserted. She was starting to feel really nauseated now. "And bottom right is one point six." Elias set down the measuring needle. "Can you make a sketch, showing clearly the positions of the four puncture wounds?"

Asta moved around to where her uncle stood, and applied her pencil to a fresh page in her book. She started sketching deft strokes on the page, but soon found her hand was trembling. She really had to pull herself together. This was a rudimentary part of her job and she was failing at it. She tried again but, once more, her fingers shook.

This time, the pencil fell through them and tumbled to the floor. The noise made Elias turn.

"Hand me the notebook," he said with a sigh. Asta did so, then reached down to retrieve the pencil and offered that to him too.

"What could have made those marks?" she asked, trying hard to make up for her momentary weakness with an incisive question.

Elias did not answer for a moment, intent on finishing the sketch to his satisfaction. Then, when his pencilwork was done, he spoke. "The body was dragged through treacherous waters. Any number of jagged rocks could have been responsible."

"But the stones in the riverbed are so smooth," Asta thought out loud.

Elias handed the notebook and pencil back to her. "Asta, there's a reason the Captain of the Guard does not conduct postmortems and I do not investigate crime scenes. Try to remember you are apprentice to me, not Axel Blaxland, and apply your focus to the job at hand."

Asta frowned. "But surely we have a duty to explore all the possible scenarios that might have led to Silva's death?"

"Such as?" Elias rejoined.

"Well, for instance, that she could have been murdered. Like I said before, the stones on the riverbed are typically very smooth."

Elias gazed at her questioningly. "You seem remarkably well-informed on this subject. How on earth can you speak with such authority?"

"I saw Silva by the river this morning," Asta told him. "And, as I walked back along the riverbank, I was struck by how smooth the stones were…"

"Never mind about the stones." Elias stared at his niece.

"What were *you* doing by the river in the first place? And why do you only tell me now that you saw Silva only shortly before her death?"

Asta felt herself flush. "I wanted to tell you, but I thought you might be angry." Elias's face was now also flushed, but Asta continued. "Silva was upset when I left her, but I don't believe she was suicidal. We were talking about Prince Anders's murder…"

Now Elias's temper erupted. "First I catch you questioning the Huntsman, then I hear from the Cook that you have also subjected her to your wild theories and pontifications. Now you tell me that you were chasing after the Prince's Consort! You have no right to talk to any of these people— no right at all, unless specifically instructed to do so by me." His gray eyes, the perfect match for hers, narrowed. "And I recall expressly forbidding you from pursuing these ridiculous flights of fancy of yours."

"Yes, I know," she argued, "but—"

"No!" Elias raised his hand. "I've heard enough and I've seen enough here too." The anger subsided from his voice as he continued in a more clinical, detached tone. "I am satisfied we may conclude that this death was a suicide, brought about by the unbearable grief of a young widow."

Asta shook her head, determined to make her uncle see her point of view. "I just don't believe that. Shouldn't we at least consider the other possibilities?"

Elias gave a sharp shake of his head. "You said yourself that she was upset when you saw her."

"Yes," Asta said, pausing before she continued. She knew what she was going to say next would probably only inflame him further. Still, she had to tell him. "It is possible it was my own fault that she was upset."

Elias did not speak, but his face was thunderous. Somehow, Asta was compelled to continue.

"It all started when I gave her Prince Anders's chain and she..."

"You did what?" Elias roared. "That's it. This arrangement is not working out," he said. "I need you to leave."

"I'm sorry," Asta said, realizing that yet again she had pushed her uncle too far. "But please let me stay and help you finish the post—"

"You misunderstand me. I'm sending you back to the settlements."

They were the words she had always dreaded. He couldn't send her away! Her cheeks burned and she felt fresh waves of nausea.

"I would suggest you go upstairs and pack," Elias told her. "You will leave first thing in the morning."

Asta stood on the riverbank above the shallow pool where Silva's body had been recovered earlier that day. The Captain of the Guard's team had marked the spot with flagpoles, evidently to help inform their investigation. She noticed that none of Axel's men seemed to be in evidence now.

The pool was only a short walk from the charred remains of Prince Anders's bathing house. The air, usually so fresh in such close proximity to the fjord, was acrid with the aftermath of the smoke. The pool of almost perfectly tranquil water was circled on three sides by boulders, which formed a natural dam.

Asta looked across to a ridge of rocks that divided the shallow pool from the rapids on the other side. The river roared and churned beyond, coursing around half-submerged boulders before dropping down through a series of treacherous rapids that would effortlessly tear a small boat to shreds—and do untold damage to human flesh and bones. Asta watched as the water at the edges of the main current lapped against the bank and washed into the tranquil pool, causing only the slightest movement among the silky weeds beneath its surface.

Now she looked upstream, toward the wooden footbridge, which crossed the river at its narrowest point. This too was marked by the guards' yellow flags. It was on this bridge that the key to Anders's bathing house had been discovered. That was where they said Silva had jumped—or fallen—into the river below and embarked on her final, watery journey.

It was curious how one part of the river could remain so tranquil when, close by, the current was so strong. Her ears were filled with the sounds of the water gushing and crashing. Spray from the heart of the rapids carried on the breeze and spattered her face. Wiping her face dry, Asta returned her attention to the flow of the river. She watched as a medium-sized branch, carried along by the current, was sucked down by the hungry rapids on the other side of the rocks. The branch then hurtled down over the larger rocks on the other side. The power of the water forced it against the rocks and she watched it break into pieces, just as she knew it would.

Asta stared back at the bridge, a thought forming in her head. She knew a body was heavier than a branch. Even so, wouldn't Silva have been carried along with the current and been thrown against the boulders before being swept down into the swirling, hungry rapids? It just didn't make sense, when you watched the flow of the water closely, that her body could have ended its journey there, in the placid grave-yard of the shallow pool.

Adrenaline suddenly surging through her, Asta walked back along the riverbank until she reached the bridge. She climbed up onto the wooden structure and looked back in the direction she had walked. She dropped her eyes to the rushing waters beneath her. There was something utterly mesmeric about them. Before she knew it, she had marched back to the bank, removed her shoes and set them down on the lush grass. Then she slid down the bank until her feet dipped into the frigid waters of the river.

A voice inside her head told her to stop, that this was madness, but another voice urged her on. Keeping one hand stretched up to the lower planking of the bridge to help her balance, Asta felt the cold water seep through her clothes as she waded out. By the time the water level was at her waist, she could feel the current tugging at her legs, drawing them out from under her. She gasped at the icy kiss of the water against the back of her neck. Thinking of Silva jumping—or slipping—from the bridge, she made her decision. Letting go of the supporting struts of the bridge, she swam forward, toward the midpoint of the river, and was immediately carried away by the current.

Although the water was very cold, the speed at which she traveled—and the thought of what she was about to discover—brought a certain exhilaration. Asta tested her theory by relaxing her body, allowing the undertow to carry her. Noting her course as her body was propelled toward the rapids, she knew now that there was no way Silva could have washed up in the shallow pool. Seeing the mist above the rapids ahead of her, Asta, satisfied, began to swim over to the left bank of the river.

At first, she thought she had made some headway, but then the current pulled her mercilessly back to the center of the river. She tried a second time, but the same thing happened. Feeling a rising sense of panic, she gave it another try. Once more, the undertow proved too powerful. It kept propelling her down the right-hand side of the river, toward the rocks and the churning white water on the other side. Then, for a moment, she was pulled under. The icy water was forced down into her lungs as she tried to breathe. Kicking frantically upward, as her face crested the surface, her body convulsed with coughing and she tried desperately to draw breath.

"Hey!" She heard the cry from the riverbank, but she couldn't turn. It took all her strength just to resist being pulled back under.

With rising dread, she realized that the pace of her movement downstream was increasing all the time. She had known that this was a risky thing to do but now she was starting to fear the worst. As strong a swimmer as she might be, there was just no way she could overcome the strength of the current—it continued to sweep her along toward the white water and certain death on the rocks below.

TWENTY-NINE

The River

THE CURRENT SEEMED TO GATHER PACE WITH
every inch of the river. Asta was temporarily blinded by
white spray as she was sent hurtling toward the rocky channel that marked the beginning of the rapids. She felt completely out of control, her legs and arms bumping against
submerged boulders.

Then everything seemed to happen in a blur of speed.
She saw a figure propel itself from the riverbank onto the
rocks that formed the boundary between the shallow pool
and the rapids. It was the Huntsman, leaping from one boulder to another as though they were giant stepping stones.
Her first instinct at seeing Kai Jagger was fear. She had a
vision of him throwing his axes, with ruthless precision, at
the birch trees and remembered too his ominous words.

"These weapons are not used on animals." But she realized he was attempting to rescue her.

In one lithe movement, he slid down a boulder a little way in front of her until he was chest high in the water. Just in the nick of time! But now, surely, Kai had placed himself in the same path of danger?

As Asta hurtled toward the same rock Kai was braced against, he reached out and caught her, pulling her to him and encircling her in his strong arms. The force of her body and the rush of water behind her pinned him against the boulder.

"Don't speak!" he cried. His usually strong voice was almost drowned out by the din of the waters coursing around them. "Just wait and do as I say!"

She nodded, her heart racing with the fear she had somehow managed to contain until then.

"I'm going to lift you up," he told her after a moment or two. "Just onto the top of this boulder. Hold on to it and stay there, whatever it takes, until I get myself up again. All right?"

"Yes!"

"Ready?"

She nodded again. As she did so, she felt herself being lifted up over him, two thirds of her body already free from the water. She reached out to the smooth surface of the rock, as he had instructed, working out the best way to gain purchase. He guided her knees onto his shoulders to aid her exit from the merciless current. She knew he would not be able to support her for long.

"All right, you can let go!" she cried, feeling herself secure on the rock.

Kai let go, the force of the water pushing him back against the rock. Now he faced the harder challenge of getting himself out of the water. Looking around, Asta saw him take a breath, then allow the water to carry him the short but crucial distance to the next rock. It was a major gamble, but it seemed to pay off as he reached it and managed to get a grip on it. Asta watched, her heart in her mouth, as he struggled to pull the rest of his body to safety. She wished she could help, but she knew she was powerless to do so. She was exhausted, pummeled and frozen by the water.

Asta watched as Kai's muscled body rose from the water until he was able to pull himself up onto the rock; he must have found some kind of foothold. Asta let out a sigh of relief. Kai, however, remained utterly focused as he gathered his strength for a moment or two. Then he raised himself and jumped over onto the next rock—the one close to hers.

"Can you stand up?" he asked her.

She tried. She was unsteady on her feet and the surface of the stone was slick with water. As she began to slip, Kai reached out a hand to help her. She took it gratefully. He then led her back, stone by stone, until they had removed themselves from the churning rapids.

As they reached the ridge of stones above the shallow pool, Kai grabbed her and held her tightly. She was grateful—she found herself trembling.

"What the hell were you doing out there?" he asked.

She barely had the strength left to speak. Still she managed to rasp, "I was in search of the truth."

Kai Jagger's intense eyes bored into her own. He shook his head—but she could tell somehow that he wasn't angry with her, merely bewildered by her actions. The Chief Huntsman, she realized, had risked his life for her.

"Thank you!" she said falteringly. Then she felt her body shaking uncontrollably from the cold and her knees beginning to weaken.

Once more, he caught her. She felt her body grow limp, but Kai had taken enough rest to support her weight. He carried her across the ridge of rocks toward the edge of the shallow pool.

"All right," he said. "Let's rest a minute. But we must get you home to dry out."

He set her down on the riverbank and sat down himself, his eyes locked on the rapids that had so nearly consumed them both. They continued to spew and foam as if angry at being denied another human sacrifice.

The Huntsman raced over to his tethered horse and

returned with a wolfskin, which he wrapped around Asta's soaking, shivering body. Her tired eyes fell to the shallow pool, tracing the surface of the clear water. The riverbed here was covered in weeds—gold, copper and emerald, like silken threads. The pattern they made called to mind the kind of fabric Silva might have chosen for a dress. Only now, Asta reflected sadly, there would be no more pretty dresses for Silva. She thought of the Prince's Consort lying there, awaiting discovery. She must have looked rather beautiful in a way—her flaxen hair intermingling with the jewel-bright reeds, her eyes turned up toward the mountains, thinking perhaps of Woodlark.

As Asta's eyes followed the movement of the underwater plants, they suddenly alighted on something even more revealing. And everything began to make sense. Filled with a fresh surge of hope, she began sliding down toward the pool.

Becoming aware of her movement, Kai turned—just in time to see her slip into the pool. He rose to his feet again. "Are you completely out of your wits?"

Ignoring him, she reached down between the weeds and claimed her prize.

"What is that?" Kai asked. "A souvenir of your near-death experience?"

Asta gazed up at him, smiling softly. "Something like that," she said.

Asta felt the pressure on her hand—a light squeeze. As she struggled with the seemingly arduous job of opening her eyes, the thing of which she was most aware was a delicious smell. It made her think of springtime. Eyelids still closed, she smiled—thinking that spring was the very opposite time of year from now. Spring was when things were born; now it was autumn, season of death.

Once more, she felt pressure on her hand and heard a voice. "Try to open your eyes." She absorbed the words and, though it still took quite some effort to obey, she forced open her eyes.

She saw that she was in her own bedroom, in her uncle's house. From somewhere she remembered the last thing he'd said to her. *"Go upstairs and pack. You will leave first thing..."*

Asta saw that it was Elias himself who had squeezed her hand and, even now, kept hold of it. He was sitting close beside her bed, watching her carefully. His face was etched with deep tiredness, but there seemed to be no trace of the anger he had displayed when they had last been together. Over his shoulder, on her bedside cabinet, was a jug filled with purple hyacinths. So that was where the heady smell of spring came from.

"Prince Jared brought those for you," Elias told her now. "Wasn't that kind?"

Prince Jared had brought her hyacinths? Why would he have done that? Elias gave a gentle nod. She realized he was trying to convey something to her. Feeling a movement, she turned her head and saw that they were not alone. Prince Jared was here too—sitting on the edge of her bed!

"Hello," he said, smiling at her pleasantly. "How are you feeling?"

"I'm fine, thank you," she said automatically. "Thank you for the flowers too!"

He grinned. "I'd tell you that I picked them myself on the way over, but I'm afraid that would be a small lie."

"That's all right," she said. "It's the thought that counts." She pushed back the bedclothes. "I'm really warm," she said, distractedly.

She saw Prince Jared look past her toward Elias, his deep brown eyes wide with concern.

"Your temperature may be affected by your dip in the river," Elias told her. "By all accounts, you weren't in there for long, but the cold must have gotten to you."

His words brought it all back to her. Standing on the bridge, looking down the river. Slipping off her shoes. Wading out into the water. Feeling the undertow tug at her legs. The moment that the current began to take her downstream. The exhilaration. And then the fear. And Kai's rescue.

She frowned again. "If the cold got to me, shouldn't I be feeling cold rather than so warm?"

Elias shook his head. "It doesn't necessarily work like that," he said. "But I can give you some medicine. With that and rest, you should be back to normal in a short time. You're young and robust—thanks be to heaven!"

Asta was taken aback. It was the first time she had heard her uncle make any kind of religious pronouncement.

"Why on earth did you jump in the river?" Prince Jared asked her. "You must have known how dangerous it was... after what happened to Silva."

Asta met the Prince's troubled gaze. "I needed to know the truth," she said. "The truth is important to me. As I know it is to you."

He nodded, smiling softly in complicity.

For the first time, it occurred to her what a strange set of circumstances this was—to awake in her tiny, messy bedroom and have the new Prince sitting there on her bed. A strange situation made all the more weird by having her uncle in attendance.

Suddenly, she thought back to their earlier argument. "You told me you were sending me away," she said, her voice uncharacteristically vulnerable as she peered up at her uncle from her pillows.

Elias winced at her words, trying but failing to find the right way to respond.

"That's not going to happen," Prince Jared cut in. "While you have been sleeping, your uncle and I have had a good opportunity to talk."

"The Prince has told me how invaluable your help has been in investigating Prince Anders's death," Elias told her. "You have made me proud, Asta."

It was such a shock to hear those words. He'd never told her that before. "Proud but also rather anxious."

Asta still said nothing but took the opportunity to give her uncle's hand a squeeze.

"You do seem to have a reckless side to you," Prince Jared said. "Jumping from bridges and so on."

Asta shook her head. "I didn't jump from the bridge, actually. I waded out into the water from the riverbank."

"You wanted to retrace Silva's final journey," Jared said.

"No," she corrected him. "I wanted to prove that it was impossible for Silva to have died in the way it was set up to make us believe."

Jared nodded encouragingly. "I think you had better share your latest findings with us, don't you?"

Pleased by the request, Asta pushed herself upright. Elias reached over and helpfully plumped up the pillows behind her. All ready, she began to fill them in.

"As you know, the key to Prince Anders's bathing house was discovered at the bridge," Asta said. "So the guards assumed, naturally enough, that Silva either fell, or jumped, from the bridge. We know how unstable she has been these past few days. It is all too easy to believe that she could have had a terrible accident, or made the decision to end her own life." She paused.

"I'm guessing you have different ideas about what happened," Prince Jared prompted her.

Asta nodded. "I'm sure that she was murdered." She glanced at Elias. "Our postmortem, in addition to my own last encounter with her, convinced me of that." Eyes back toward Jared. "I went down to the river in search of proof. The first place I visited was the shallow pool where Silva's body was found. Supposedly, she was carried by the river from beneath the bridge into this pool, picking up the fractures to her head as she was crushed against the rocks and either drowning on the way or in the pool itself." She paused, finding her voice hoarse and dry.

"Here," Elias said, holding a beaker to her lips. "Drink some water."

Asta gratefully took a sip. "Thank you." She took her mind back to the riverbank. "I watched the river channel for some time. I could see that it was impossible for Silva's body to have gone on that particular journey. Whoever set up the scene to look that way did not think it through thoroughly. The current is too strong on the right-hand side of the river. It forces everything it carries down to the right-hand side of the ridge of rocks, away from the shallow pool and down into the rapids. It doesn't matter whether it is the branch of a tree or a human body; there is only one direction in which the river will carry it."

Prince Jared frowned. "So you knew this, but you still put yourself in certain danger, knowing that you, like Silva, would be swept away on the current. That's the part I don't understand."

"I'm a strong swimmer," Asta said defensively. "I had every reason to think I would be all right. I had my wits about me. My mental state was entirely different from Silva's."

"All the same, you *were* both swept away by the same current."

"No," Asta rejoined. "That's my point. Silva was not swept away on any current. She cannot have entered the river at the bridge. The only reason we even think she did is because someone put the key there, to mislead us. And I can't help thinking that whoever did that, and whoever killed Silva, also burned down the bathing house. In many ways, it was a remarkably efficient execution. The killer really only made one mistake."

"You seem very sure that Silva was murdered," Elias spoke now.

"I am," Asta said. Dimly, she remembered the piece of evidence she had plucked from between the weeds. Where was it? She looked at her bedside table, but there was no room for it there, not with the jug of flowers. She glanced across to her dressing table, but she could see that it wasn't over there either. She felt a cold panic. Had she lost it? Had someone taken it from her? Or had she only imagined that she had brought it with her? Everything now hinged on it.

"Looking for something?" Elias asked.

She nodded. "I brought something with me from the shallow pool."

"Yes, rather a curious object." He smiled. "You were clutching it very tightly, so I knew it must be important. I stowed it away, to keep it safe." Now Elias opened the door to her bedside table and Asta watched with relief as he removed a stone and placed it, smooth side down, in her hand.

"This is what killed Silva," Asta told them both. She leaned forward and offered the stone to Prince Jared, who took it and weighed it in his hands.

"One of the most noticeable things about the shallow pool where Silva was found is that all the pebbles there are incredibly smooth," Asta told him. "All except this one. Look how smooth it is, except for the four spikes on one side, where it has broken in half." She turned to Elias. "I'm convinced that these will match the four incisions on Silva's skull."

"So you're saying Silva didn't drown at all?" Prince Jared said. "Someone clubbed her to death with this stone?"

"There was water in her lungs," Elias informed him. "But it might have been a close-run thing between death from blood loss through the head wounds and death by drowning. Assuming the stone fits as well as Asta surmises."

"Let's see!" Asta said, flushed with a fresh surge of energy. "Uncle Elias, can we go down to the Ice Chamber and see if the spikes match up with Silva's wounds?"

Elias considered her suggestion, then nodded. "If you feel up to it. But your temperature is fluctuating. I'm not sure it's wise to go down there where it's so cold."

"I have to see this investigation through to the end," Asta asserted.

"Yes." Prince Jared nodded. "You've more than earned that right."

"All right," Elias agreed. "So long as you wrap up warm against the chill."

Asta felt a bit pathetic as the two men helped her up from the bed. Jared helped Elias wrap a heavy blanket around her. Then, the three of them made their way down through the Physician's house into his surgery and on toward the locked door that led down to the Ice Chamber below.

Elias unlocked the door and continued on his way. Asta felt Prince Jared gently squeeze her arm. "Asta," he whispered—it was strangely thrilling to hear him speak her name. "You showed such rare bravery today. I'm in your debt."

"Anyone would have done the same," she said softly. Nonetheless, she flushed with pleasure at his words.

As Elias lit the candles and the interior of the Ice Chamber came into light, Silva's body was revealed under its shroud on the central slab. Elias moved toward it and folded down the sheet, exposing the corpse's head, neck and shoulders. Silva's head was still resting on its left side—the four puncture wounds clearly exposed.

Asta saw that Prince Jared, seeing these for the first time, winced. "Poor Silva," he said, shaking his head.

The three of them clustered around the top end of the slab. Elias turned to Prince Jared. "Do you have the stone?" he asked.

"Yes," Jared said. He weighed it again in his hand for a moment, then placed the smooth side of the stone in the palm of Asta's hands. His intent was clear. Barely able to breathe, Asta lifted the stone carefully toward Silva's skull.

"You need to turn it around a little," Elias told her.

She did so.

"Now, back again, just a fraction."

As Asta brought the flinty points to just above Silva's head, they rested directly above the four wounds. Her heart began to race. "It's a perfect fit. So now we know for sure... I'm holding the weapon the assassin used on her."

"No." Elias shook his head. "It's a compelling explanation, I grant you. But we cannot be sure about this."

Ever the scientist, Asta thought. *Always weighing his words so carefully.* But, whatever caution her uncle espoused, Asta knew it was true. She knew it not only in her head but also in her gut—as if Silva had risen from the riverbed and told them herself the story of her death. Asta felt hot tears budding in her eyes, and was unsure as to whether it was out of sadness for the brutal end of Silva's wretched life or simply relief that her own ordeal had paid off.

Prince Jared let out a breath. "So, tell me then, how exactly do we think my sister-in-law was killed?"

"You can see the bruising on her shoulders," Elias said, pointing. "My initial assumption was that those bruises were sustained as she was buffeted along the river channel. But now I'm inclined to think these bruises were caused by the assassin's own hands—I believe the two of them must have struggled."

"I agree," Asta said. "I believe the murderer intended to drown Silva and perhaps thought it would be a straightforward murder. She was a petite woman, so it would have been easy to underestimate her strength."

Elias nodded. "Even the most seemingly fragile people may draw on inner resources we cannot fathom in their fight to cling to life."

"And so Silva's murderer reached for this stone in order to finish her off?" Jared said. "If that is the case, I don't understand why they didn't do a better job of getting rid of the evidence."

"I've been pondering that too," Asta said. "The murderer had a lot to do at that point, to set up the scene as if it were a suicide or horrific accident. I'm sure they had intended to get rid of the stone, but probably they ran out of time."

"Why didn't they just take it with them?" Jared asked.

"They could hardly have afforded to have it discovered in their possession," Asta said. "And the further it was from the river, the more suspicious that stone would seem. Besides, it is smooth on one side. They may have turned it under the water, thinking that no one would notice. Silva's blood would have been washed off it. It was only luck really that I happened to see it through the weeds. The pool is very tranquil, but there is still a gentle current at work there."

Prince Jared shook his head. "I don't think that was luck, Asta," he said. "I'm starting to think you have a rare knack for this kind of thing."

"I'm inclined to agree," Elias said, a distinct note of pride to his voice.

Asta's mind was already awash with fresh questions. "What we need to think about now is who might have killed Silva. And how is this murder connected to that of Prince Anders? It is looking to me less and less like a politically motivated assassination and more of a crime of passion. Don't you think?"

Elias looked blankly at his niece. She realized he was still missing some crucial information.

Jared frowned. "I feel so bad that we thought Silva herself might have been my brother's killer."

Asta shook her head. "Don't feel bad," she said. "And don't be so quick to dispatch that thought. It is still a possibility that Silva killed your brother. She could have murdered him and then been murdered by his lover in a revenge attack."

"His lover?" echoed Elias, clearly shocked at the talk, the information.

"My brother was involved with another woman," Jared told him. "But we don't yet know who."

"We have to renew our efforts to find out who it was," Asta said. "At the very least, she will be able to shed light on a hidden part of Prince Anders's life." She paused, letting out a soft sigh. "At worst, she's the one we're looking for."

Jared nodded, his face dark and troubled.

It was Elias who spoke next. "If Prince Anders was conducting an extramarital affair between the palace and the fjord, then it must have been with a woman of rank—either a royal or a member of the Twelve."

"I agree," Prince Jared said. "Those are the only people who could have passed by the various teams of guards, without questions being raised."

"All right," Asta said. "Well, that certainly reduces the possible suspects. I think we should start drawing up a list of names, don't you?"

Elias let out a sudden sneeze, swiftly followed by another. He drew the shroud back over Silva's broken head. "Let us return upstairs," he said. "It's too cold to think down here. And it doesn't seem right to me, continuing this conversation in Lady Silva's presence."

THIRTY

The Captain of the Guard's Office, the Palace

PRINCE JARED SAT PATIENTLY ON THE OPPOSITE side of the desk from Axel as his cousin took the time he required to process all the new information he had just been told.

Jared reflected on his decision to come to the Captain of the Guard's office for this meeting, rather than summoning Axel to his own quarters. He had wanted to make a gesture of conciliation. He smiled to himself—four days in the close company of the psychologically astute Logan Wilde appeared to be rubbing off on him.

Axel had now stood up and was pacing back and forth on the other side of the desk. At last, he came to a stop and reached out to pour himself a fresh slug of aquavit. He turned and gestured to offer Jared a refill, but the Prince held aloft his still-brimming glass. He had little taste for the stuff but hadn't wanted his cousin to think him rude. They had endured so many clashes over the past few days but now, more than ever, they needed to come together and work as a team.

In a nutshell, he needed Cousin Axel's help.

"All right," Axel said, sitting back down and setting his glass on the desk in front of him. "I'm prepared to concede that Silva's death may not have been either accident or suicide. There is, as you say, sufficient evidence to consider murder a very real possibility." His eyes met Jared's. "But you must acknowledge that Silva could still have been assassinated as part of a plot from the court at Paddenburg or any one of our neighbors—with the exclusion, I think we can agree, of Woodlark."

As he paused to take another swig of his drink, Jared seized his opportunity to respond. "So we are agreed that murder is a strong possibility here too. Forgive me, Cousin, but I don't understand why you won't consider the possibility that there was absolutely no political aspect to both of these murders and that they were crimes of passion?"

"Let me explain," Axel said, leaning forward across his desk. "In these past four days, Archenfield has lost its Prince and the Prince's Consort, right?"

Jared nodded. There was no argument with these cold, hard facts.

"Well, these two murders have achieved two—no actually *three*—outcomes. First, our ruler has been removed. The first murder achieved that. Second, our alliance with Woodlark is in jeopardy—given that Silva Lindeberg was very likely assassinated on our soil." Axel frowned. "Third, as a result of Anders's death, we now have a much weaker, less experienced Prince on the throne." He attempted to soften the brutality of his words with a smile. "No offense, intended, Cousin. I'm just telling the truth as I see it. In time, I'm sure you will dazzle us all and Logan Wilde will record your epic deeds for the history books."

Though it wasn't pleasant to be reminded of his youth and inexperience, Prince Jared couldn't take issue with Axel's assessment.

Axel leaned back in his chair. "So you must see how all these factors point very clearly to two politically motivated killings, murders, assassinations—whatever you choose to call them, the impact is the same." Axel reached forward, lifted his glass and drained its contents. When he had done so, he looked back at Jared. "You're still not convinced, are you?"

"Everything you have said rings true," replied Jared slowly. "But I think it is just as likely, given the evidently tangled love life of my brother, that these were murders motivated by deeply personal matters rather than by politics." Jared frowned. "I just don't want us to create a tense situation with one of our neighbor states when this might have nothing at all to do with them."

Axel granted him a nod. "It doesn't help your case that you don't know *who* your brother's *inamorata* was."

"I know that's the missing piece of the puzzle," Jared said. "That's why I came to talk to you tonight. I would really appreciate your expertise and insight."

It seemed that the last thing Axel had expected from his cousin was praise. It stopped him in his tracks and Jared could see fresh thoughts passing through his mind.

"All right then, if you want my expertise I'll tell you how I see this." Axel rose to his feet. "Motivation is actually of secondary importance here. The primary thing we must focus on is this—for both Anders and Silva to have been killed, the killer—or *killers*—must have been someone either of high rank *or* in residence within the court to have the necessary access."

Jared nodded. "That makes sense to me. Elias said the same thing."

"So now we're getting somewhere." Axel refreshed his drink. "Look, one of the most useful things you have brought to me tonight is this information about Anders's hunting wound..."

Jared was tempted to ask why, when this had been spelled out so clearly in Elias's postmortem report, Axel was treating it like fresh information. But he didn't want to wreck the amiable tone of the meeting—so he just nodded.

"As you say, Prince Jared, all those within the hunting party were of very high rank. I propose to question each of them anew, starting in the morning. My aim will be to flush out if any of them have a secret affiliation to Paddenburg. It seems unthinkable, but we have to face facts, I fear."

Jared sighed. "So, you persist in viewing these as political assassinations?"

"I do and I think that's the best next step in this investigation. I intend to have my team continue going through the immigration files to see what they can turn up." Axel smiled once again. "You still think it's important to discover the identity of your brother's mystery lover, don't you?" He shrugged. "Look, it certainly won't hurt us to know that information. And I have absolutely no problem if, while my team and I interrogate the hunting party, you—and your little friend—want to start questioning the women of the court. You never know—you might unearth something useful."

Could Cousin Axel be any more condescending if he tried? Jared doubted it. Nonetheless, it seemed like a reasonable division of labor—one team pursuing the political conspiracy, the other (he rather liked the idea of him and Asta being "a team") investigating the personal angle.

"Perhaps you would like my help in drawing up your suspect list?" Axel offered.

"Why not?"

Axel seemed to be enjoying himself. "Well, as I say, we need to think high level here. So members of the Twelve for starters." He made a face. "I think we can rule out Vera Webb. Let's credit your brother with better taste than that."

"The Beekeeper?" Jared said.

Axel nodded. "Yes, put her on your list. Though she is such a tightly strung shrew, I can't quite see her throwing herself into an epic romance."

"I'll talk to her," Jared said, noting down her name.

"The Falconer," Axel said, lost for a moment in his thoughts. "You should definitely talk to Nova Chastain. She's something of a mystery altogether. I'm not sure I can see her forming a relationship with anyone other than her birds, *but* she was certainly shaken up after your brother's death. That might prove significant."

Jared added Nova Chastain to his list.

"Those are the only women on the Twelve, so that's your suspect list..." Axel paused. "Unless you think your brother had a preference for his own gender?" Jared looked up, with a start, to find Axel grinning at him. "Now that would open up several more possibilities—Lucas, for instance. He's quite the pretty boy, is he not? Or Logan? Your brother and the Poet were practically joined at the hip."

Jared shook his head. "Don't you think I'd know if my brother's tastes ran to men?"

Axel shrugged nonchalantly. "It seems to me that, as the days march on, neither you nor I seem to know very much for certain about your brother. Who did? You must admit—good Prince Anders is proving to be more and more of an enigma." Axel's tone of voice changed. "Obviously, I'm not making any value judgments here—just sifting through the possibilities."

Jared frowned, reluctant to continue any further in this vein. He realized he didn't really care whether his brother was heterosexual, homosexual or asexual. What bothered him was Axel's barb that he hadn't really known Anders. It was the unassailable truth and it rankled. Suddenly, he had a fresh thought. "There is one possibility we have overlooked."

"Kai Jagger?" Axel shot back with a smile.

"No," Jared said. "Koel Blaxland."

Axel let out a laugh. "My little sister? You think your brother and my sister . . . . no, trust me when I say I think we can safely rule her out."

"On what basis?"

Axel's voice became huskier. "On the basis that I *do* know my sister. And, believe you me, I would know if she was in love with your brother—or anyone else for that matter."

Jared shrugged. "All the same, I think I will put some questions to her, if only to definitely rule her out." It was his turn to smile. "Assuming you don't object."

"Object?" Axel's eyes narrowed. "No, of course not. I know Koel would want to help. She feels as passionately devoted to Archenfield as I do."

Jared added Koel's name to his list. He'd talk to Asta in the morning and work out how best to divide up the three interviews. He rose from his seat. "Thanks for your help, Cousin Axel," he said. "I'm very glad I came to see you."

Axel nodded slowly. He seemed distant for a moment, lost in thought.

"I'll let myself out," Jared told him, heading for the door. As he reached out for the door handle, he heard Axel speak.

"You know," Axel said, "it would have made a lot more sense if Anders *had* waited a few years to marry Koel instead of rushing into the union with the spawn of Woodlark. There were other ways to achieve an alliance."

Jared frowned. "It's all very well saying that now. Maybe you should have made these feelings clearer at the time."

"You may rest assured that I did make my thoughts perfectly clear," Axel said. "But I was shouted down by your mother and Logan Wilde and others on the Twelve. They were all so utterly convinced they could pull off this political marriage and transform it into a fairy tale. But, as it turns out, they could not."

"Perhaps not," Jared allowed. "But Anders and Koel? I can't really see that having worked, can you?" He was surprised to feel protective, not only of his brother but of his young cousin too.

"Well, we'll never know now." Axel's eyes seared into his. "But such a union would have strengthened Archenfield from within, uniting more strongly than ever the Wynyard and Blaxland families. We can agree on that at least."

Jared fought Axel's fire with his own. "Now that you are my Edling, our two families *are* more closely united than ever. You and I may not agree on everything, but surely we can at least agree on that? I put you at the heart of the Princedom and I did so because I wanted you there, at my side."

Axel shook his head. "No, *Prince* Jared, you and your mother pulled me close and threw me a bone because you knew I was your biggest threat." His eyes blazed. "Can't we at least be honest about that?"

DAY FIVE

THIRTY-ONE

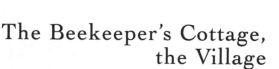

The Beekeeper's Cottage,
the Village

TO ASTA'S SURPRISE, EMELIE SHARP WAS WAITING
for her outside the cottage door. "Axel tipped me off you
might be paying me a little visit. I was about to brew some
tea. Won't you join me?"

Asta followed the Beekeeper inside her cottage, immediately liking the homey feel of the place. The narrow hallway
led into an open living area, with a small kitchen to the left-
hand side and comfortable places to sit by a small hearth
on the right. The comfortable throws and pictures, and the
air of cozy informality to which they contributed, reminded
Asta in certain ways of the Prince's bathing house. Had
Emelie also influenced the decor there? If so, then Asta and
Jared had their answer. But she knew she must resist jumping to conclusions. When Jared—she corrected herself—when

Prince Jared had come to find her that morning, and proposed this fresh interview strategy, he had made it clear that the time for guesswork was over; between them, they needed to pinpoint the truth.

Asta felt a new sense of mission, now that Prince Jared and she were working together. The fact that only they knew this—and it was obviously best kept that way for the time being—only made it more thrilling. She had no doubt that, working together, they would finally prove, beyond all doubt, the identity of Prince Anders's one true love. And, through that information, reveal his killer.

She watched as Emelie busied herself over the stove. The Beekeeper's movements were graceful, precise—but also charged with an underlying energy. Asta was aware of herself trying to get the measure of the woman and thinking already of how she would frame her thoughts to the Prince when they met up again later.

At the back of the living area, a pair of stable doors—the upper one open—gave out onto a small, well-tended garden. Asta opened the lower door and stepped out into the pretty cottage garden. Everything was on a small scale, but she could tell that there was, nonetheless, as much artistry here as in the more showy palace gardens.

"I'm afraid it's not looking its best," Emelie called, from just inside the doorway. "Blame that on too good a summer!

Everything came out early and died too soon." She marched away to attend to the boiling kettle.

Asta's attention was drawn by the row of hives, which dominated one length of the garden. She knew that the main hives were in a dedicated section of the palace garden and that it was from these that Emelie harvested the plentiful supply of honey and beeswax for the palace and its many residents.

"We've nicknamed that Beekeeper's Row," Emelie said, appearing in the garden with a tray of tea things, which she set on the table just outside the living room doors.

"I thought you lived here alone," Asta said, curious.

"Oh, I do," Emelie said, setting out cups and saucers. "Well, there's Chaucer, of course." She crouched down and stroked a cat that was dozing beneath the table. He luxuriated in his mistress's touch for a moment, then rolled over and stretched out his limbs in the sun.

After five minutes' small talk, Asta decided it was time to get down to business. "I came to talk to you about the Prince," she said, carefully setting down her teacup.

"Which one?" Emelie rejoined.

"Prince Anders," Asta said. "I'm interested to know what you thought of him."

"What did I think of Anders?" Emelie mused. "He was a natural leader. Well, no, that's not quite true. It would be fairer to say that he was perfectly groomed to be leader."

Her bright eyes met Asta's. "Do you know anything about queen bees?"

Asta shook her head.

"Well, you might think that a queen bee holds power over the rest of the bees in the hive. And so she does—in a way. But the queen bee is not born to rule. She is, at first, just a normal bee, but then she is chosen by the worker bees in the colony and fattened up on generous amounts of royal jelly."

Emelie paused to take a sip of tea before continuing. "Swap the gender and forgive the clunky analogy, but Prince Anders was rather like the normal bee who was chosen by the workers and stuffed with royal jelly. Suddenly, before our eyes, he transformed into something majestic, something otherworldly. Our Prince."

Asta nodded. "He became the all-powerful ruler."

Emelie shook her head. "That's not quite how this Princedom works. It's not dissimilar with bees. It might seem as if the queen controls the colony, but this is not the case. Her only function is to reproduce. Oh sure, she is surrounded by worker bees who service her every need—bringing her food, taking away her waste. As long as she does what is asked of her, her position is assured."

"And if she doesn't do what is asked of her?" Asta wondered aloud. "What then?"

Emelie's eyes met hers. "Very simple. The worker bees kill her and produce another."

Asta was shocked. "So to continue your analogy, it's as if Prince Anders failed to do his duty, so the workers—the Twelve in this case—killed him and replaced him with Prince Jared."

"Exactly!" Emelie nodded, eyes wide. "Barbarous, isn't it?"

Asta wondered if the Beekeeper was trying to tell her something.

Emelie smiled at her. "You may perhaps have heard," she said, "that I don't much enjoy beating around the bush. If you have a question for me, I'd much prefer that you just ask me directly."

"In that case," Asta said, taking a breath, "did you love Prince Anders?"

Emelie swallowed another sip of tea. "Did I love him? No. I respected him—greatly. I thought he rose to the challenge of being Prince marvelously. His metamorphosis was extraordinary and impeccable."

"But as a man?" Asta persisted. "Forget, for a moment, about his being Prince. Did you love him as a man?"

"No! You can't love someone you don't know. You can be dazzled by them, infatuated with them, focus all your dreams on that person—and no, before you ask, I felt none of those emotions with regard to Anders." She shook her head. "I'm a worker bee, Asta. It's my job to feed the royals, if you will. But to love them? That's very much beyond my brief."

Asta sighed. The Beekeeper could not have been more lucid, nor more believable. Asta felt convinced that Emelie Sharp was not Prince Anders's carefully guarded secret.

～～○

Prince Jared watched from a short distance away as Koel Blaxland pointed her bow to the ground and placed the shaft of her arrow on the arrow rest, attaching the back of the arrow to the bowstring by the nock. Holding the bowstring and arrow with three fingers, Koel raised the bow and drew her string hand toward her face, resting it momentarily on her right cheek. Jared held his breath as Koel released the arrow. It flew toward the target but, disappointingly, only hit one of the outer rings.

Koel shook her head, clearly displeased with herself.

"That was bad luck," Jared said, making his way toward her. "Your setup was near perfect. You just need to work some more on your follow-through."

"Cousin Jared!" Koel exclaimed, turning as he walked toward her. "What a heavenly surprise!"

Jared smiled, seeing her standing there, an eye patch placed over her left eye. "Is that really you, Koel Blaxland, or are you some wicked pirate queen who has taken my dear cousin's place?"

Koel laughed at that. "Oh, I forgot I was wearing this thing!" she said, raising her hand and pulling the eye patch and its string off her head, sliding it over her long, dark hair. "It's to help me focus on the target, but I'm sure it looks ridiculous."

"Actually, it rather suits you," Jared observed with a grin.

"I'm not sure I like the implication of that." Koel set down her bow in its stand, and gratefully received the glass of lingonberry cordial offered to her by her lady-in-waiting. "May we offer you some refreshment?"

Jared nodded. "Thank you, that would be nice." Koel's servant poured another glass and handed it to the Prince.

"Shall we sit for a moment, over there in the shade?" Koel led Jared toward a table and chairs, beside an old willow tree. "So," she said, taking a seat. "What brings you out here? Were you thinking of having some target practice yourself? Oh, but of course not, you haven't brought your bow!"

Jared sat down beside his cousin. "I'm sure I could do with the practice, but no, I came to find you."

Koel smiled and took a small sip of her drink. "I'm flattered that with all the people who are doubtless competing for your time and attention, you would choose to seek me out."

Jared turned toward her. "I wanted to check how you're doing after all the terrible things that have happened these past few days."

Koel shook her head. "That's so typical of you," she said.

"*I* should be the one offering *you* support. After all, you've lost a brother and now a sister-in-law too."

Jared nodded, feeling a cool breeze through the rustling leaves of the willow tree. "Anders's death is a source of deep grief to us all," he said. "Silva's too. We are one family—the Wynyards and the Blaxlands. We all bleed the same blood."

"Indeed," Koel said. "But let us hope that no more blood is shed for a long while yet." She reached across and squeezed his hand, just for a moment. Releasing it again, she asked, "What news of the investigation?"

"I'm sure your brother has kept you up to speed."

"Axel?" Koel laughed lightly. "Axel doesn't tell me anything. He thinks I'm far too young and frivolous to be interested in his serious man stuff."

"Then I think he does you a disservice."

"I think so too, Cousin Jared." She smiled again. "Thank you for saying so."

Jared took a draft of cordial before continuing. "Your brother and I met late last night to discuss the latest evidence and he and his team are pursuing some fresh leads this morning. It is possible Anders wasn't poisoned through his food but by other means. Forgive me for not going into too much detail."

"Of course, I understand," Koel said. "But that certainly

sounds promising." She paused. "And what is the latest thinking with regard to Silva—accident or suicide?"

Jared took a breath before answering. "Murder."

"No!" Koel's pretty face paled.

"I'm sorry but I fear so," Jared said. "And it seems that her murder was connected to that of Anders. Axel believes that Archenfield has been infiltrated by more than one assassin from across the borders."

Koel shuddered. "It makes me feel so powerless—dealing with an unseen enemy."

"Yes," Jared agreed. "I know exactly what you mean." He paused, anxious to get the conversation, flowing as it was, in the direction it needed to go. "Koel, I need to ask you something. Something rather personal. I hope you won't be angry with me."

She shook her head. "I could never be angry with you, Cousin Jared. What's on your mind?" She took another sip of her drink.

"It has come to light that my brother was conducting a romantic liaison with someone, outside of his marriage to Silva."

Koel's eyes locked with his. "How...how do you know about this?" she inquired.

Jared frowned. "Several factors have led us in this direction but, most of all, the discovery of certain love notes to

Anders. One in particular, which he carried in a locket, close to his heart."

"That is kind of romantic!" Koel said. "Well, it would be, if it wasn't under such tragic circumstances."

Jared winced as he asked the next question. "Koel, I'm sorry but I have to ask you this. Did you write the love notes? Were you in love with my brother?"

"Me?" Her brown eyes were wide. "No! I mean—don't get me wrong—I always liked your brother. But not in that way. No, absolutely not."

"That's a relief," Jared said, settling back into his seat. "I'm sorry. Please understand that I had to ask."

She shook it off lightly. "I do understand. You need to gather answers. And it's an intriguing situation." Her eyes met his. "But, Jared, if I were to send love notes to one of my male cousins, they would not be for Anders." She held his gaze a moment longer.

Jared thought he knew her meaning and it did not displease him. Suddenly, however, her brown eyes seemed to transform into gray ones and, for a moment, it was as if he were not looking into Koel's eyes but into Asta's.

As if Asta were warning him to stay on track.

Just then, one of Nova's falcons soared into view. Both Jared and Koel turned their eyes upward as the majestic bird flew overhead.

"I fear that is the envoy to Woodlark, informing Queen

Francesca and Prince Willem that Silva is dead," Jared said. He dropped his eyes again and sighed. "I should return to the palace, and let you get back to your archery."

Koel nodded, running a hand through her long dark hair. "I fear I need the practice."

Jared set down his empty glass, then leaned across and kissed her lightly on the cheek. "Just pay attention to your follow-through. You're better than you think."

She basked in his kind words. "Thank you for the vote of confidence."

Prince Jared strode away. Koel watched him, replaying their meeting in her mind even before it was fully over. After he had disappeared into the glade, she placed the eye patch back over her head and strode over to retrieve her bow from her waiting servant.

She loaded another arrow and locked into place the nock. Checking her stance, she raised the bow and appraised her target. She drew back her string hand to the very same spot on her cheekbone where her cousin, the Prince, had so tenderly kissed her. Then she released the arrow. It flew through the air and landed plum in the center of the target.

THIRTY-TWO

The Falconer's Cottage, the Village

ASTA KNOCKED ON THE DOOR TO THE FALCONer's Cottage. She waited, but there was no sound of anyone moving around inside. She knocked again, a little louder. No reply. She walked around to peer through one of the windows. The place seemed deserted. She went back to the door and tried to open it herself. It was locked.

Adjoining the Falconer's Cottage was its tower, on top of which was located the Falconer's Mews. Glancing up at the glass-domed structure, reminiscent of an orangery, Asta thought she discerned movement. Whether it was the Falconer herself, or merely her birds, she was unsure from that distance and in the gloomy late afternoon light. Still, nothing ventured, nothing gained.

The entrance to the tower was unlocked. Asta pushed

open the wooden door and began climbing the stone steps, already feeling a sense of anticipation. With each turn of the spiral stairwell, she knew she was rising higher and higher above the Princedom. There were no full windows on the main body of the tower, but there were narrow embrasures, used for looking out and—when the need arose—shooting arrows through.

Asta paused at one of these, gazing through the slim gap back toward her own home. Already, she had climbed high enough to look down upon the roof of the Physician's house. She continued her ascent. The next embrasure was on the opposite side of the tower and afforded her a view of the fjord and the mountains beyond. She drew her face away from the gap. The air was chillier now that she had almost reached the summit and the warmth had drained from the day.

She came to a stop before a second door. She suspected that this would not be locked either. Still, out of politeness, she knocked. After a short delay, the door opened and Asta found herself face-to-face with the Falconer. She was struck, at this close range, by the woman's rare beauty. Nova was unlike any of the other women in court—indeed unlike any woman Asta had ever seen before. Her long dark hair was not teased into intricate plaits; instead it hung loose and wild over her shoulders and down her back. Her skin was unpowdered but nonetheless flawless, burnished gold by the elements. Her lips were unusually full and deep red. They made Asta think of plump raspberries in the heat of summer.

Nova's catlike eyes scrutinized Asta coolly. She gave no pretense of being pleased at Asta's arrival. "Of course, it's you," she said. "I guessed you'd be up to bother me before long."

Asta was, unusually, lost for words.

Nova shook her head. "Don't you think we talk to each other, my fellows and I?" she asked pointedly.

"I'd very much like to talk to you," Asta said.

"No," Nova countered, still blocking the threshold. "What you want is to ask me questions. You've taken it into your head you are some kind of investigator. It seems you have mistaken your relish for prying for a qualification."

Asta felt flushed. She needed to get inside the Falconer's Mews but, with every passing moment, she feared that the door might be slammed shut in her face and the key turned in the lock.

"You're right," she said carefully. "I am helping with the investigation into the assassinations. At least I'm trying to."

"Assassinations?" Nova hesitated. "There has been only *one* assassination—that of the Prince. Silva committed suicide."

Asta shook her head. "No," she said, firmly, sensing she might be gaining the upper hand. "The death scene was made to look that way. But we now know otherwise."

Asta's ploy seemed to have worked. Nova drew back inside the room but, rather than slamming the door, left it ajar. Asta stepped inside, closing the door behind her.

She found herself at the foot of another spiral stairwell. Without waiting for her, the Falconer continued on her way. Asta followed. It proved to be only a short climb before the stairway deposited her in the circular room at the summit of the tower.

The room stretched across the entire top area of the tower. It was essentially a vast dome. Standing there, surrounded on all sides by metal and glass, Asta felt as if she were contained within a giant birdcage. This impression was driven home to her as one of Nova's falcons spread its wings and took flight above her—but not so high above that she couldn't feel the stirring of the breeze on her upturned face. It felt as if the bird had come to keep an eye on her, Asta thought—then scolded herself for being ridiculous.

Around the perimeter of the mews ran a balcony, accessed by one of four doors—which, judging by the letters engraved above each, marked the exact positions of north, east, south and west. This, Asta realized, made absolute sense as it would enable Nova to send her birds out in whichever direction she desired.

She glanced upward again, watching with fascination but also a certain nervousness, as the falcon turned perfect circles above her. On the opposite side of the dome, the bird's six companions were poised on a vast wooden perch.

Nova was making her way toward the perch, her low, rustic skirt skimming the stone floor. In her right hand was a small wooden pail. Dressed though she was in the most humble of clothes, Asta thought, still, Nova walked with the confidence of a queen. She realized she was falling a little under the Falconer's spell.

Not wanting to disturb her, Asta gazed once more around the dome. Though Nova lived in the locked cottage down below, there were signs that she might actually spend a considerable amount of her time up here in the company of her birds. There was a chaise (it made Asta think, of course, of the one in the bathing house) and a couple of other chairs and tables, a bookcase, a free-standing mirror and several candelabra. Further in the distance, closer to the perch, was a desk and accompanying chair.

The haphazard assortment of furniture gave the mews the feel of a human aerie. Asta had the sense that Nova had foraged about the palace complex, gathering up things that were useful—or, perhaps, simply appealing—to her. Asta couldn't help but wonder—had Prince Anders been foraged in a similar fashion?

But there was little to be gained by simply standing and staring, Asta decided. If she was going to learn anything of value here, she needed to draw out the Falconer in conversation, however challenging that was likely to prove.

Asta walked over to join Nova at the perch, just as the itinerant falcon returned to join her sisters. As Asta herself arrived in front of the perch, she realized that it was not, as she had first thought, crafted from wood but rather from a number of antlers, cleverly welded together. Seeing the cluster of antlers, she had another visual flash of Anders's bathing house and the pair of antlers fastened to the wall there. In her mind, another connection was made to the place, but she knew that she needed concrete evidence to determine if Nova really was the Prince's secret love. Antlers were not exactly a rarity in the environs of the court.

Ignoring her uninvited guest, Nova busied herself petting each of her falcons in turn and offering them food from her pail. Glancing in the metallic-smelling bucket, Asta saw blood-slick gobbets of dark, shiny flesh.

"Rabbit organs," Nova announced, as if sensing her next question. "Caught fresh in the woods this morning." She extended a slick piece of liver to the bird that had turned circles above them. Asta watched as the morsel was snatched up eagerly in the bird's small beak and swiftly devoured.

"She seems hungry," Asta observed.

The Falconer did not respond to this comment. It seemed that she was preoccupied, feeding and talking to her birds. Asta had often heard tell of the intense bond between the Falconer and her falcons; now at last she was witness to it with her own eyes and ears.

She felt rather bilious from the feeding display and was relieved when at last Nova held up her empty, blood-stained palms, signaling to the seven falcons that mealtime was over. The Falconer then turned and wandered over to a small washstand, cleaning her hands with soap and water. The pleasant smell of verbena filled the air for a moment.

Asta watched the Falconer scrubbing her bloody fingers—a jumble of thoughts running through her head—then returned her attention to the birds on their perch.

"Here!" Asta turned to find the Falconer once more at her side. Nova's right hand was now encased in a leather gauntlet and in it she held a spare glove, which she offered to Asta. "Put this on your strongest hand."

Asta took the gauntlet. She felt herself under scru-tiny, not only from the Falconer but also from the seven pairs of avian eyes, all reflecting the light from the nearest candelabra.

"Here, let me help you," Nova said, her eyes meeting Asta's as she tightened the straps on the glove. "Don't be scared. I can sense your fear. And if *I* can, you can be sure that the falcons can too. It unsettles them."

Asta glanced down at the gauntlet, willing herself to rise to this challenge.

"Watch!" Nova told her, resting her gauntlet-covered

hand and wrist alongside the perch. One of the falcons immediately extended one clawed foot, then the other, onto the Falconer's wrist. Nova took on the bird's weight easily and drew her wrist away, nuzzling the falcon tenderly against her cheek as she did so. Then she glanced across at Asta. "Your turn!"

Asta had no desire whatsoever to follow suit, but she realized she wasn't going to have any choice in the matter. The sooner she submitted to this test, the sooner it would be over. Taking a steadying breath, she placed her arm adjacent to the perch, just as Nova had done.

To begin with, nothing happened. The six remaining birds stood their ground. Asta imagined what they might be thinking—*Who is this amateur? Why would I want to travel anywhere on her wrist?*

But then it seemed as if one of the falcons deigned to take pity upon her. Asta watched nervously as its talons took a firm grip of her gauntlet. As the bird settled, she felt her arm begin to buckle under its surprising weight. The falcon began to stretch out its wings as if it knew it had to cover its options.

"Hold your arm steady!" Nova barked at her imperiously.

Asta did as she was told. The falcon appeared to calm down again.

"That's better," Nova said, with a fraction less severity. "Now follow me."

She walked to the nearest door—the one marked with a large *E*—and, opening it with her free hand while maintaining perfect balance, continued outside onto the balcony. Asta found it to be a considerable physical challenge to walk with an even gait with such a weight bearing down on one arm—especially as her falcon persisted in shifting from foot to foot on her wrist. Perhaps it could still sense her nervousness.

She made it out to the balcony, coming to stand beside the Falconer right at the edge. She found herself looking down at the village green. It soothed her somewhat to see the familiar locale, albeit from this new and unique perspective. The light was already draining from the day and it softened the shapes of the buildings below.

"Now watch!" Nova commanded. She gave a precise flick of the wrist and, receiving its cue, her falcon immediately spread its wings and took flight.

Asta felt the Falconer's sharp eyes upon her once more. She readied herself, then did her best to emulate Nova's elegant wrist-flick. Her movement was, inevitably, far less fluid but still her falcon seemed to get the message—or perhaps it had simply decided it was high time that the two of them parted company. It opened its wings and rose majestically away over the balcony, out across the village. Asta felt a body-rush of exhilaration as "her" bird turned a circle over the rooftops.

Nova placed a hand on Asta's arm. "I always envy them the moment of flight," she said. "Imagine taking to the skies and soaring over the Princedom!" As she said the words, Asta had a sudden vision of the Falconer stretching out her long, muscled arms and propelling herself off the side of the tower. She had no doubt that if someone could fly, fueled by willpower alone, then Nova would be the one to do it.

The balcony offered no defense against the strong, bitter wind and Asta felt herself shiver.

"Come on," Nova said, her hand on Asta's arm again. "Let's return inside before you catch a chill."

They walked back inside and past the perch of falcons. Nova now seemed at something of a loss, Asta thought, as though she wasn't used to human company. There would, she could confidently predict, be no offers of tea and honey from her. Nova hadn't even offered her a seat. Already, her attention seemed to have returned to—had it ever really left?—her birds.

Asta had failed to close the east door properly behind her and a gust of wind pushed it open again and whipped around the mews. Frowning, Nova marched back and reached for the door handle. As she did so, something fluttered before Asta's face. Something far smaller and whiter than a falcon.

At first, she thought it might be a kind of butterfly, though it surprised her to think of one so high up here. As

Nova closed the door and the breeze died down again, the butterfly drifted down to the floor. Asta realized that it was merely a fold of paper, animated by the draft. She crouched down to her feet to retrieve it.

As she grasped the folded slip of paper between her thumb and forefinger, she felt an electric shock of recognition. The paper was exactly the same size as the one in Anders's locket and those she had seen at the bathing house.

"Give that back to me!" Nova demanded now, hand outstretched.

Asta was reluctant. She had to see the writing on the note. The very moment she opened it, Nova snatched it out of her grasp. But not before Asta had the chance to confirm that it bore the very same handwriting as all the others.

"You have no right to read that!" Nova told her sharply. "That's confidential business of the court."

The Falconer turned and carried the errant note back toward the desk it had come from. Asta followed—seeing the pen and inkwell and the pot containing the narrow slips of paper, ready to write on and assign to one of the falcons.

Asta couldn't believe it had taken her until now to realize that the slips were the perfect size to be inserted into the falcons' messenger tubes. Now she not only knew who had penned the love notes to Prince Anders but also exactly how he had received them. Nova's clandestine love for the Prince had been borne on the Archenfield wind.

Having set the note back down on the table, Nova turned toward Asta. Her arms were folded, her beautiful face now flushed with anger and perhaps other emotions too. "Why did you really come here?" she demanded. "What do you want from me?"

"I think it's time we had a talk," Asta said. "About Prince Anders and the secrets the two of you were keeping."

THIRTY-THREE

The Falconer's Mews, the Village of the Twelve

"I DON'T NEED TO TELL YOU ANYTHING," NOVA said. "To the best of my knowledge, the Captain of the Guard is conducting the investigation into Prince Anders's assassination and now Silva's death. You're supposed to be the Physician's apprentice, aren't you? Not Axel's."

Asta nodded. "You're right. I'm not here in any official capacity and I'm certainly not here to judge you. I'm just trying to understand what happened." When this did not succeed in changing Nova's demeanor, she added, "The past five days must have been extremely hard for you. It has been a difficult time for everyone, but you alone of the court have had to grieve in secret." She shook her head, moved by genuine sadness. "I cannot imagine how painful it has all been for you."

She knew immediately that her last comment had hit home. The Falconer's face had changed and, when she spoke, so too had her tone of voice.

"I have grown adept at keeping my true emotions hidden."

"Yes," Asta said. "I'm sure you have. But you deserve to grieve for him. You, most of all, deserve to grieve for him."

She saw tears spring from Nova's eyes. Tears not only of grief, she surmised, but relief.

"Why don't we sit down?" Asta suggested, moving toward the chaise and seating herself.

"We never had enough time," Nova said, sitting down beside her. She turned toward Asta. "Do you know what it's like to love someone but not really have him? No, of course you don't. You're too young to have experienced such intense emotions."

Asta wondered if Nova was referring to loving a prince or loving a married man.

"At first," Nova continued, "it was so easy. No one knew anything. That was the beauty of my being one of the Twelve. A prince has to be versed in all the talents of the Princedom—falconry included."

Asta nodded, remaining silent so as not to interrupt Nova's flow.

"Deep down, at heart, Anders was a simple man. If he

hadn't been born to the Wynyard family, I think he might have been on the Woodsman's team. He loved the nature of Archenfield, as do I. He was never happier than when walking in the forest or climbing the mountains."

"Or spending time with you by the fjord," Asta ventured. Nova's eyes met hers and Asta pressed home her advantage. "I saw what a lovely home you made together there."

"Yes," Nova said, blotting her tears with the back of her hand. "Yes, we did. It was the one place we could be together, away from prying eyes." She smiled at the memory. "You know what we would do, on rainy afternoons? He would read to me. He read from the books on the bookcase there and sometimes he made up stories, using nothing but his imagination. I cherished every moment we spent together. But it was never long enough. There was always somewhere he had to be, someone he had to be with."

Asta nodded, taking another gamble. "And of course, there was always Silva."

Nova nodded. "Silva was not a bad person," she said. "But she was not right for Anders."

"But you were? Because you shared a love of nature?"

"We shared much more than that," Nova said. "But there are things that must remain between Anders and me. Until the day we are together again." She frowned. "You know, I would have married him. But then his mother and the Poet hatched the plot to marry him off to Woodlark, in order to secure the alliance."

Asta couldn't help but notice that Nova hadn't even deigned to speak Silva's name this time. Perhaps it was easier to think that way.

"We stopped seeing each other for a time—in the run-up to his marriage and a short while after. I tried my best. We both did. But can you imagine what it was like for me seeing them together at the front of the chapel, saying their vows? And afterward, sitting through those interminable speeches, suggesting theirs was the perfect love when I knew the lie of it?"

Asta nodded. "It must have been heartbreaking for you."

Nova's voice was stronger when she resumed again. "Ultimately our bond was too strong to break. He needed to see me, to be with me. He knew I was his true love. We were destined to be together." She nodded emphatically as she spoke.

"And then Silva fell pregnant," Asta said, watching Nova's face for her reaction. "I'd guess that felt like a terrible betrayal."

Nova shrugged dismissively. "I felt nothing. I always knew he had to impregnate her to secure the longevity of the alliance. That was all that baby would have meant—it certainly wasn't created out of love, only politics."

"I wonder if Prince Anders felt the same way?" Asta

reflected. "From what Silva told me, he was very caring to her once he discovered she was pregnant."

Nova frowned again. "He was doing his duty. He was very focused on that—his duty. His mother especially had drummed it into him at an early age." She sighed, then smiled serenely. "I knew he would come back to me, in the end."

Asta knew it was a risk, but she decided to push Nova still further. "I wonder. If perhaps things changed for Anders at that point? If Silva's pregnancy might have prompted him to take stock and think about the future? That it was time for him to draw back from you and devote his full care and attention to his wife."

Nova's feline eyes blazed with fury. "What do you know about Anders's thoughts and feelings? What do you know about anything?"

Asta's heart raced. She knew from Nova's reaction that she was onto something important.

"He did stop seeing you again, though, didn't he? Much like he tried to at the beginning of the marriage. Only this time, for whatever reason, it seemed like he was going to stick to his plan. And you knew that, with Silva carrying his child, things would never be the same again. There would be no more walks together through the forest, no more rainy afternoons down by the fjord…"

"No!" Nova exclaimed, but she had begun to tremble.

Asta pressed on. "That's why you came to such a difficult decision. The hardest, most heartbreaking decision, I'm sure you have ever had to make. You couldn't live with things as they were, and so you would have to remove the one thing that stood between you and Anders. It was the only possible way to return things to how they had been."

Nova seemed to be rendered speechless now, though her body shook—perhaps with the shock of grief or another kind of release. Asta knew she had to finish the story.

"It was clever in so many ways. You took savin from my uncle's garden and found a way to get it into Silva's food. Perhaps you persuaded the steward to put it in there—perhaps you found information with which to blackmail him—but even if he was guilty of that action, it wasn't his idea. It was yours. You know about nature and animals and plants. You knew savin would trigger a miscarriage."

Nova's eyes seemed locked on her own as she proceeded. "So, whether by your own hand or that of Michael Reeves, the savin was added to Silva's food and carried to her. Had she taken a bite, she would certainly have miscarried the baby. But, you see, Silva had been feeling so sick with the pregnancy that she wasn't eating. Not wanting others to know yet, Prince Anders, devoted husband that he was"— Asta noted the flicker of pain that crossed the Falconer's face—"ate his own food, then swapped his plate with Silva's and consumed hers too. He ate the poisoned meal. And now your simple plan took another wrong turn. You didn't know that you needed to use only a small quantity to achieve the intended outcome. You used much too much. Far more than was needed to kill a fetus—enough, as we now know, to fell a full-grown man."

"No!" Nova cried, rising to her feet. Her whole body was vibrating now, as if waves of grief were breaking through her.

Asta had gone much further than she had intended to, and yet she couldn't help herself. She rose up to her full height before the Falconer.

"You killed the man you loved more than life itself," she said. "I know you didn't mean to. Fate played a terrible trick on you. I understand what drove you to that point, truly I do. What puzzles me is why you went back and killed Silva. Did you really hate her that much? Why couldn't you just have let her live and raise Prince Anders's child? Wasn't that the least consolation you could have offered her?"

But now Nova shook her head defiantly. "I didn't kill him." Her face was contorted. "I loved him."

"Yes," Asta said. "I know that. You loved him so deeply that it made living without him impossible to bear."

"You know absolutely nothing!" Nova said, spitting her words into Asta's face. "You think you have this all worked out, but you don't. You're not an investigator—you're just a pushy piece of filth from the settlements." She leaned toward Asta, so close that her plump lips were almost touching Asta's own. "Get out now or I don't know what I might do to you."

"I'll go," Asta said, raising her hands in submission. She backed away hastily and went down the first flight of stone steps toward the door. Opening it—and closing it firmly behind her—she went quickly down the second stone stairwell. Her head was a jumble of thoughts.

As she pushed open the door that led back out onto the village green, she gasped for air, as if she had come up from deep water. She had thought that when she finally solved this twisted mystery, she would feel suffused with a sense of satisfaction and elation. So how was it that instead she just felt sad and empty and queasy?

As she closed the tower door, Asta had the sense she was not alone on the green, that she was being watched. If she didn't know better, she'd have thought that Nova had somehow made it down ahead of her—taking flight, perhaps, as she had spoken of, or sent one of her seven birds to monitor her.

Feeling a shiver, Asta tried to pull herself together. Dusk had come early, due perhaps to the dull weather of the afternoon. It was easy to trick herself into fear in the half-light. But she had accomplished her goal that day and now she had to find Prince Jared and tell him at last the terrible truth of his brother's murder. At least now they could be sure there would be no more deaths. It all ended here, where it had begun some years before, at the Falconer's Mews. It was not, by any definition, a happy ending. But it was an ending nonetheless.

"So it was Nova." Prince Jared looked dazed as Asta concluded her report.

Asta nodded. "Evidently, she loved your brother very deeply. So deeply that she intended to induce Silva to have a miscarriage. From that point on, she was set on a course she could not pull back from. Like a falcon pursuing its prey."

Jared sat, stunned, on the edge of his desk. "She killed my brother by accident and my sister-in-law by intent." He shook his head sadly. "I thought I'd feel lighter, somehow, once we knew the truth." His eyes met Asta's. "But I feel as heavy as stone."

She came over to sit beside him. A few days earlier, she wouldn't have dared make such a bold gesture but now it felt quite natural to do so. "I'm glad that you said that. I feel exactly the same way."

They sat there, for a time, in silence. Then Jared turned to her, with a new question.

"Did she actually confess to the murders?"

Asta looked at him. "Well, no. Not in so many words. But the way she talked—the way she let me talk—she didn't leave me with any remaining doubt."

Jared frowned, standing up again.

"You do believe me," Asta said. "Don't you?"

He nodded vigorously. "Of course I do. You've done a remarkable job here, Asta. You trusted your instincts and they have led us to the heart of this dark matter." He paused, a troubled look in his eyes.

"But...?" Asta prompted, folding her arms. "I feel like a 'but' is coming."

Jared was silent for a moment. "Asta, you're the Physician's apprentice, so you know how vital it is that we have something tangible to go on here. Nova has to confess to what she's done. We have to have her confession, or some other evidence. Though I don't know exactly what that would be."

Asta couldn't help but feel frustrated. After everything that had happened this day alone, after all their concerted work on the investigation—just when she had thought it was over, he was telling her there was yet more to be done.

"Look, I need to start dressing for dinner," Jared said. "A delegation from Woodlark will be here within the hour." He rested his hand gently on Asta's shoulder. "You won't thank me for saying this, but you look dog-tired. Why don't you go back home and get some rest? We can pick this up in the morning."

Asta shook her head. "It's Prince Anders's funeral tomorrow morning."

"Of course," he said, his words frayed with fatigue and frustration. "Come and see me first thing tomorrow, before the ceremony. We'll have time to talk more then. We can work out our next move."

His use of the phrase "our next move" more than made up for his momentary irritableness.

"If you like, I'll go and talk to her again now," Asta said. "Maybe I can get her to confess this time."

"I really don't think that's wise," Jared said. "From everything you've told me, you left her in quite a state. I think it would be dangerous for you to go anywhere near her again tonight. Besides, she's supposed to be coming to dinner with the Woodlark delegation. It's my belief she won't attend. She's not fond of ceremonial dinners at the best of times. Perhaps she just needs time on her own to reflect on her actions. Maybe she will come to her senses and realize what she needs to do."

Asta nodded. "That makes sense."

"I'm sorry, but I need to send you on your way now. But let me dispatch Hal or one of his team to escort you to the village."

Asta shook her head. "There's no need. I can take care of myself." Already, she was at the door.

Prince Jared frowned. "Sometimes, Asta Peck, you can be most infuriating."

Asta grinned. "I know," she said. "I work hard at that."

He shook his head, but he was smiling. "Thank you," he said. "For everything you have done. Please try not to feel frustrated. We really are close to the end now."

Though she knew it was far from his intention, nonetheless his words made her sad. She had enjoyed this sudden, brief intimacy with Prince Jared, not because he was Archenfield's new Prince, but because he was the first friend she had made in quite some time.

Not wanting him to witness her dismay, she slipped out of the chamber, leaving him to prepare himself for the arrival of the Woodlark delegation and all that came with it.

THIRTY-FOUR

The Village Chapel

FATHER SIMEON COULDN'T SHAKE THE FEELING that he had failed to serve the key members of his flock properly during the five days of crisis that had been visited upon the Princedom. If he had been another kind of man, he might have taken comfort simply from the fact that his door, both literal and metaphoric, had been open to them, whatever the hour. And, if he had been another kind of man still, he might have drawn further comfort from the fact that many people *had* come to him seeking answers to their shock and grief. But these people were those who had made the pilgrimage from one of the settlements. Of course, it was a legitimate part of his role to provide comfort to the common man—and woman. Still, it frustrated him that his fellow members of the Council of Twelve and the royal family itself had not consulted him in any meaningful way. But perhaps tonight would mark a significant change. With the arrival in Archenfield of Lady Silva's family, tensions would doubtless reach a new high.

Shutting the lych-gate was no inconsiderable feat with a storm blowing in from the north. Accomplishing this task, the Priest surveyed the road ahead. The Priest's Chapel was at the lowest point of the village, bordered by the fjord to the north and connected to the nearest settlements by the paths snaking out to the east and west. The chapel was the very last of the dwellings of the Twelve and Father Simeon was exposed to the raw brutality of the seasons first among the villagers. He had always drawn a certain stoic comfort from this fact. Bracing himself against the weather, he set off along the steep road that would take him through the heart of the village and up to the palace at the top of the hill. As he did so, he heard the chiming of the Edling's Bell— the final peal of bells each day. These bells represented the future. Usually, they filled him with a sense of hope. But not tonight.

It was a routine walk, which made it easy for him to absorb little of his surroundings and instead find himself sinking into an all-too-familiar morass of thought. What was the fundamental point of the Priest if he could not offer succor to his community in a time of unprecedented grief and confusion? True, he had an equal chair at the Prince's

Table and his title had been carved into the ancient oak, and made permanent with boiling metal, just like all the others. Father Simeon knew he had no rational basis to feel that he was becoming less important, less relevant, than had the Beekeeper or the Bodyguard or any of the others. But, rational or not, the feeling persisted as he continued on his way.

Prince Jared had been the most obvious candidate for his help: a sixteen-year-old boy forced to contend with the horror of his brother's murder and its corollary of propelling him into a position of unprecedented power and responsibility. Here was a young person, by certain definitions a child, whose world had literally been turned upside down. Yet, when Simeon had tried, on more than one occasion, to talk to the new Prince, he had been turned away—first by Queen Elin and later by Logan Wilde. They had both told him that the Prince had too much to contend with of a practical nature to devote time and focus to spiritual matters. Simeon had known better—given the people to whom he was speaking—than to argue the case that "such matters" were the true stuff of human life, and not speeches or meetings of the Twelve or murder investigations.

As he passed the Chief Groom's lodgings, Simeon's thoughts turned to the next likely candidate in need of his help—Lady Silva, the grieving widow. Had there ever been a more fragrant and delicate creature to grace the corridors of the court? Yet they hadn't let him speak to her either—saying she was too frail and that her overarching need was simply to rest. He should have asserted himself but, yet again, he had allowed the more forceful members of the court to push him around. Now Silva was dead and it seemed more than likely to him that the poor girl had taken her own life. If only he had been stronger, more persistent, he might have been able to help her. Now it seemed unlikely that he would even lead the prayers at her funeral. That honor would surely fall to the High Priestess of Woodlark.

Continuing up the hill, Simeon's thoughts turned to Michael Reeves, the steward turned fugitive. Simeon had visited him in the Dungeons. And, to give credit where it was due, he had received a warm welcome there—from Morgan Booth. It seemed that the young Executioner *was* a religious man. The two members of the Twelve had had a very engaging talk, over several glasses of aquavit. But when Simeon had approached the convict's cell and offered to help him settle his mortal soul, he had been told to go away in no uncertain terms, in language he did not care now to think of.

Such thoughts left him in a dark mood as he set foot on the green at the heart of the village. It was bordered by a cluster of buildings belonging to others of his fellows, from the high tower belonging to the Falconer to the Physician's dwelling on the opposite side. From there, he could also see the Captain of the Guard's mansion and the Poet's dwelling, with its unrivaled and inspiring views out onto the fjord.

Father Simeon couldn't help but feel a little envious of those who lived there at the heart of the village, when he thought of his splendid isolation down below where the waters crashed and the summer sun and winter winds were most harsh. He shook his head and decided to cross over the green itself, as opposed to walking around the border. It would buy him a valuable few minutes.

He had almost reached the far side of the green when the strangest event of his life occurred. As he moved over the soft grass, a figure fell down from the sky, landing right in front of him. It took him a moment to realize that, in fact, the figure had fallen from the top of the adjacent tower and another moment to confirm that the fallen woman was the Falconer, Nova Chastain.

She had dropped from her perch utterly soundlessly, no cry emanating from her deep red lips. As he dropped to his knees beside her, he thought distractedly how he had heard tell around the court that the Falconer enhanced the natural hue of her lips with a dye made from crushed berries, foraged in the woods. On taking a second look, he realized, with an unprecedented coldness, that what he had at first taken for dye was in fact blood. A trail of it ran from the corner of her mouth across her cheek to her exposed neck. It was as vivid as it was horrible.

Father Simeon reached out his hand to her neck, checking for a pulse. There didn't seem to be one, but he could not be sure as his own fingers were trembling so much that it made it hard to assess the state of his companion. He glanced up at the tower that loomed vertiginously overhead. There was no way she could have endured such a fall with her life intact.

As Simeon glanced up, he saw a dark shape moving at the top of the tower. His first thought, heart hammering beneath his overcoat, was that an unknown assailant was up there. But then the shape began to shift and descend toward him. Nova's cast of falcons were following in their mistress's wake.

"What happened here?"

At first, Simeon thought the bird nearest to him was asking the question, but then he saw, reflected in its glassy eye, the figure of a girl. The Physician's apprentice. He stood up. He saw her eyes, as quick as the falcons', home in on his blood-stained fingers.

Father Simeon opened his mouth to describe to her the sequence of events. This would have been the natural, rational thing to do. The direction from which he had entered the green. Where he had been when Nova had fallen. The fact that she had made no sound. The way her body had bounced, like a rag doll, on the long grasses at the foot of the tower. But, instead of telling Asta all these things, all he could do was emit a low moan. He realized he was shaking, out of control.

The girl looked shaken too, as well she might, but she pushed past him. Seemingly fearless of the birds, she reached out to Nova's neck as he had done before. He watched her go through the same thought processes he had been through until at last, despondent, she withdrew her hand, her own fingertips now stained with blood. A sense of fellow-feeling gave him the bravery to speak.

"I couldn't find a pulse before, but my own hand was shaking so. It was all such a terrible shock. To see her fall." He realized he was in danger of rambling. "What about you? Could you discern a pulse?"

Asta stared at him. "I'm not sure." Then she drew herself up to her full height. "Did you see anyone else in this vicinity? Either just before or just after she fell?"

"No," he said. "No. Why would you ask that?"

Asta frowned. "Because I'm trying to decide if she was pushed or if she jumped of her own volition."

He nodded weakly. "Surely, she must have been pushed. Why would the Falconer take her own life?" He thought of Silva, then Anders, then Nova again. What kind of maelstrom were they all caught up in?

Asta's eyes were as merciless as those of the birds gathered around them. "She had good reasons," she said.

Of course, he wanted to ask what she meant by that, to argue that there was *never* a good reason for such terrible action—but, before he could speak, she was already striding past him. Gone to seek the help of other, more practical men, he thought. Father Simeon slumped back onto the damp earth, staring in wonder and horror at the traces of dirt and blood on his fingers.

THIRTY-FIVE

The Grand Hall, the Palace

"THE DELEGATION FROM WOODLARK HAS ARRIved," Hal Harness announced to the party of royals assembled in the Grand Hall.

"Within the hour, our alliance will be in shreds," Lord Viggo announced darkly.

Jared's blood ran to ice at his uncle's words and all they portended.

"Don't be so sure," Elin said, squeezing Jared's hand as she spoke. Her touch was cold but firm. "But, even if it is so, we will forge new alliances. We have a new Prince now and, in his hands, a new world of opportunities."

What did she mean by that? Was she already hatching a plan to marry him off? Jared turned toward his mother, but he didn't dare to ask the question. His mind was racing, and so too was his heart.

"Just stick to the script," she said calmly. "It's the best chance we have to preserve the alliance. I know you'll do your utmost, Jared. All our hopes are with you."

Jared nodded but hated what he was about to collude in.

The main palace door opened and Queen Francesca and Prince Willem swept into the room. Their usually tanned faces were ashen at the news of Silva's death. They were followed by Princess Ines—Silva's older sister and heir to Francesca's crown—and other members of the royal delegation.

Prince Jared strode across the room to meet them. He bowed low before Francesca. "Welcome back to Archenfield, Your Serene Highness," he said. "I'm so very sorry for your loss."

He knew that protocol dictated that Queen Francesca return his bow with a curtsy, signaling the equality of their rank. The fact that she did not was no great surprise, but he was unsure if her breaking of protocol was simply due to grief or also indicative of anger.

Queen Francesca stared at him dispassionately.

"Your Highness, on behalf of my family and my people, I express my condolences at the death of Prince Anders," she said. "He was beginning to deliver on his promise."

"Thank you," Jared said, turning toward Prince Willem, who did bow before him. "Prince Willem, I'm so sorry for your loss. Please pass on our sympathies to Teresa and Javier. And to Rodrigo, of course." He saw the warmth and the grief in Willem's eyes and added, "Silva had become a dear sister to me this past year. We will all miss her greatly."

Queen Francesca snorted at this. "Not as much as her family will miss her. Where is she? We want to see her."

"Yes, of course," Jared said with a nod. "We will bring her to a viewing chamber for you."

Queen Francesca frowned. "Why has this matter not already been attended to? You knew we were coming. Surely, you can imagine how great is our desire to see our dear daughter?"

"I know," Jared said. "I'm sorry..." He realized he was at a loss for words and in danger of losing his grip. He was inordinately grateful when his mother came to his aid.

"Dear Francesca, of course we wanted to have Silva ready for you on your arrival. But you have made even better time than we anticipated. And, in addition, we wanted to talk to you about an idea."

"What idea?" Francesca's fiery eyes locked onto Elin's.

Elin, however, deferred to her son, the Prince.

"As you know," he said, "tomorrow is the state funeral for Prince Anders. We thought, if you were in agreement, it might be fitting for this to be a joint funeral for Anders and Silva." He paused, knowing he was going to hate himself for what he said next, but also knowing it was vital for the sake of the alliance. "Although Silva took her own life, there is no reason she should not be given a full state funeral."

He saw Prince Willem's kindly blond head begin to nod.

Francesca shook her head sharply. "Absolutely not!" she said. "For twenty-one years, Woodlark was Silva's home. She is greatly loved there and it is there she will be buried, and mourned by her people."

Prince Jared nodded. "As you wish," he said, somehow relieved. "Your wishes take precedence here. But though Silva lived in Archenfield only one year, I want to assure you how much she is loved here and how deeply she will be mourned."

Prince Willem nodded graciously once more, but Queen Francesca seemed unimpressed. "I cannot help thinking," she said, "that it's a shame you did not take as much care of her in life as you appear to be doing in death."

"Grief calls to the surface raw feelings," Elin said. "We understand why your choice of words may be harsh, Francesca. But please remember that we are mourning Anders as well as Silva. This is a very dark time for us all. Perhaps our two families, our two nations, may help to comfort one another?"

Francesca shook her head. "That is hardly possible," she said, "when I hold your family responsible for my daughter's death." Her velvet-brown eyes blazed with fury.

"I do not see how," Elin responded. "Her death was her

own decision. What could we possibly have done?" She had gone further than Jared could or would have.

"Her grief at her husband's murder was too much for her to bear," Francesca snapped. "And I hold you accountable for that. The assassination of a ruler in cold blood is unprecedented within the territories."

Axel broke away from his family group to respond to this. "Queen Francesca, as Queen Elin says, we understand your grief and anger. But please be assured that extraordinary security measures are in place here. We are facing a plot from one of our rivals to strike terror at the heart of our court and threaten the alliance with Woodlark. An assassination could just as easily have happened on your soil."

Francesca shook her head. "No, it could not have." She glanced across at Princess Ines. "*My* Captain of the Guard would never have been so lax."

Ines, every inch her mother's daughter, gazed defiantly at Axel. It was clear that she felt the same.

"We must agree to disagree, perhaps," Elin observed.

Francesca returned her focus to her. "Archenfield is weak," she said. "It has ever been a troubled patriarchy."

"That is not correct," Elin shot back. "Like all the territories, our history is marked by intermittent bloodshed. But my husband and my oldest son ruled over Archenfield in peace. The same will be true when Prince Jared takes the crown in a week's time."

Francesca shook her head dismissively. "A sixteen-year-old boy." She glanced dubiously at Jared, then directed her attention back to Elin. "What hope is there for Archenfield with him upon the throne?"

"There is *every* hope," Elin said, her voice more impassioned than Jared had ever heard it before. "Jared was Anders's Edling these past two years. He will make a consummate ruler."

Francesca laughed lightly. "I just don't understand it," she said. "It's clear to me, indeed to all of us in Woodlark, that Archenfield would have been far stronger under your rule as a matriarchy like ours. You took the title of Queen, but in truth, all you have ever been is the Prince's Consort or the Prince's Mother. No one would have made a finer, more potent ruler than you, Elin. Yet you have wasted your time and energy putting ill-equipped boys on the throne."

In spite of the element of flattery, Elin shook her head. "A woman or man may rule in Archenfield. Woodlark and Archenfield have different ways of governance. Please respect ours as we respect yours."

"I'm afraid that is no longer possible," Francesca said coldly. "Any respect we may once have had for you dwindled when we learned of our precious daughter's death."

"I'm very sorry to hear that," Elin said, standing her ground. "It does not leave our alliance in good stead, does it?"

Queen Francesca laughed once more—a deep, bitter

laugh. "There is no longer any alliance between our two states." She turned to Princess Ines once more. Her Captain of the Guard held out a scroll of parchment.

Francesca took it and walked over to the nearest candelabra. She dipped one end of the scroll into the flame of a candle. It quickly caught light. Everyone watched as the alliance between Archenfield and Woodlark burned away before their eyes. It took less than a minute before Francesca was brushing hot ash from between her fingers. The remnants of the carefully negotiated union now lay as ashes on the flagstones of the hall floor.

"We will not be staying for Prince Anders's funeral," Francesca announced. "I'm sure you will understand that we have a state funeral of our own to plan. And now, without further delay, please make Silva ready for us."

"Of course," Elin said.

"I'll handle this," Prince Jared said, desperate to get away. "Hal, come with me!"

"Ines will go with you," Francesca decreed.

"No," Jared said, meeting Francesca's gaze. "She will not. You hold no sway in this court, Queen Francesca. And now that our alliance is no more, you hold less influence than you did a moment ago. You have made your feelings very clear to us, so now let me make ours clear to you. We are deeply grieved by the death of Silva. She was a member of our family as well as yours. It would be nothing more than a courtesy to expect some forbearance from you that we have lost a brother and a son and a Prince ourselves."

Queen Francesca frowned, but Jared did not allow her to speak before continuing. "We are your hosts and we have prepared quarters for you and your delegation in the palace. A dinner has been cooked for you. I do not doubt you will turn up your nose at all our gestures of hospitality. That is your prerogative. But I am ruler of *this* nation. So, wherever you and your family decide you want to wait to see Silva, you may. But wait you will until I tell you she is ready for you."

He felt flushed as he finished speaking. He was unsure how the others—both from his own family and the foreign court—would respond to his outburst. Had he overstepped the mark?

He was met by utter silence. He took this to mean, if nothing else, that he had successfully asserted his authority. It was, if only they knew, nothing more than a charade. "Come, Hal," he said. "Let's lose no more time."

His bodyguard at his side, Prince Jared marched out of the Grand Hall. He felt flushed with anger, but it was only partly toward Francesca and the severity of her words and much more at himself and the abhorrent lie he had agreed to endorse. A lie designed to safeguard the alliance. Well, it hadn't worked and Jared couldn't help wondering if he and his court had paid a fitting price for their horrid deception.

As he departed, he heard Francesca address his mother. "That's your idea of a ruler, is it?"

"Yes," he heard his mother say. "He *is* our ruler. And, as he says, you are guests in *his* court. Now, shall we show you to your rooms or would you prefer to wait in the courtyard? It looks to me like it has begun to rain, but I'm sure that makes little difference to you." She smiled coldly. "As I recall, it often rains in Woodlark."

As Jared stepped outside into the courtyard, Axel's deputy, Elliot Nash, ran toward him out of the shadows.

"Prince Jared," he rasped, short of breath, "I came to find the Captain of the Guard. I'm afraid I have grim news."

"The Captain of the Guard is tied up with the delegation from Woodlark," Jared told him. "You had better tell me your news."

Axel's faithful deputy seemed to consider the matter for a moment, then nodded. "Yes, of course, Your Highness. I'm sorry to have to tell you this, but there's been another death."

Jared met Nash's eyes. "Nova," the Prince said. "It's Nova, isn't it?"

Nash nodded, clearly taken aback. "How did you know?"

"Just take me to her," Prince Jared told him, feeling the all-too-familiar knots of fear and grief and tension take possession of his stomach. When? When would this come to an end?

THIRTY-SIX

The Palace Ice Chamber

PRINCE JARED FELT THE CHILL WITHIN THE ICE Chamber and knew his shiver was not from the ambient temperature alone. This chamber brought him—sadly not for the first time—into unflinching proximity with death. All too vividly, he recalled coming here to see the bruised and bloodied body of his father, fresh from the battlefield. He remembered reaching for Edvin's hand as they gazed at their father's empty eyes and wondered where the light within them had fled.

Now Jared was alone as he walked through the chamber. *Yea, though I walk through the valley of the shadow of death, I will fear no evil.* Jared shuddered. In truth, he did fear evil. He feared it very much. After the conclusion of the war, there were those on the Twelve who had argued for the removal of the palace Ice Chamber—reserved as it was for members of the royal family and the Council of Twelve. They had argued that the Ice Chamber in the Physician's village residence was sufficient for the needs of the court. But the second Ice Chamber had not been removed. It was as if they had all known, on some level, that peace was only ephemeral and that the familiar twins—chaos and confusion—would soon return to stalk the Princedom. And so they had. Walking forward, his legs heavy as oak, Prince Jared wondered how much more death he would be forced to confront in the course of his reign.

He gazed at the three bodies that lay before him, each on a separate dais. Prince Anders, naturally, occupied the central platform. Anders was always destined to be at the center. His face looked quietly peaceful. Five days of death had done nothing to erode his handsome features. Indeed, with his flesh now tinged blue and violet, he had the appearance of a marble statue. Nonetheless, in spite of having been in cold storage for several days, his body now emitted a pungent odor of decay. Jared knew, from what Asta had told him, that beneath his gilded shroud, Anders's feet were shriveled and gangrenous. He wasn't brave enough to take a look; the stench alone was enough to contend with. It pervaded the room, in spite of the burning incense that had been lit to mask the smell.

To Anders's left was Silva, her fracture wounds almost invisible now that her pale golden hair had been plaited artfully across her forehead. After the Physician's examination, she had been dressed in her finest ceremonial robes, in readiness for Queen Francesca and Prince Willem to view their daughter's body. Jared imagined the hot tears in the eyes of Silva's maid as she had combed the weeds out of her mistress's silken hair, then dried and arranged it as carefully as if for a banquet. Laid out on the dais, Silva looked as beautiful—and as distant—as ever. Her tiny hands were clasped together, clutching a posy of wildflowers. Jared wondered if Silva's devoted maid had been responsible for this detail. If so, it was a thoughtful touch.

On Anders's other side was the newest addition to the ranks of the dead. Like her companions, Nova Chastain looked as if she were sleeping, though Jared knew that beneath her customary dark robes lay a body fatally broken and contorted by her fall from the tower. Unlike her companions, the Falconer had not yet been subjected to the Physician's blade. That would have to wait until morning. For now, her body had been hidden away as quickly as possible in case word of another death within the court reached the Woodlark delegation. Elias Peck, so Elliot Nash had informed him, had had the presence of mind to have guards rush Nova's body here with little more than a preliminary examination.

Jared's head was still spinning from all the mental adjustments he'd had to make as one day had chased away another, bringing fresh secrets to the surface. At first, Jared had thought Anders's killing was a political act. They had shut down the borders and launched a manhunt for an assassin or assassins, imagining crumbling alliances and a fresh descent into war. But there was no assassin, and no assassination. Anders's murder, Silva's too, had been a crime of passion.

The phrase hung uneasily in Jared's mind. For how could passion—something as pure and good as love—lead someone to take another life? Nova's calm visage yielded no answers. She looked at peace. And he hated her anew for that. He realized that, in truth, he had never before felt genuine hate for anyone, but Nova Chastain had taught him how to hate just as adeptly as she had schooled his brother in love.

Jared shook his head sadly at the three corpses laid out before him—together yet alone, in death as in life. He couldn't have asked for a more poignant visual depiction of the tragedy that had lately befallen Archenfield.

He was in no doubt that his brother had loved Silva. *In his way.* It was curious that he knew this less from anything his brother had ever confided to him in life, and more from the conversations Asta had relayed to him, following her own startlingly intimate encounters with Silva. But, whatever love Anders had felt for his wife, it had clearly been eclipsed by the magnitude of his feelings for the Falconer and, it would seem, by hers for him.

Jared glanced at Nova's masklike features. She had been an enigma all her life and, by removing herself from life at this juncture, ensured she would always remain one.

There was enough of a gap between the three daises for Jared to walk between them and stand at his brother's shoulder. Trying to keep from inhaling the pervasive stench of death, Jared looked down upon Anders, addressing his brother, face-to-face.

"Why?" he found himself asking. "Why wasn't Silva enough for you? You had the most beautiful girl in Woodlark and all of Archenfield in your hands. Why wasn't that enough?" He received no reply. Nothing had altered in his brother's face and Jared thought he detected there lingering traces of arrogance. Prince Anders had been born with a sense of entitlement. He had expected to have every last thing he wanted, failing to give sufficient thought to the consequences of his selfish actions.

Jared made a promise to himself then and there. When he married, it would be for love. He could imagine those, including his mother, who might find it a naïve notion. But that was how it was going to be. Perhaps he wouldn't deliver another strategic alliance to the Princedom but at least he'd save Archenfield another almighty mess like this.

Jared turned from Anders and caught sight, once more, of Silva's childlike hands, filled with the posy of wildflowers and resting on her belly. Now he understood. The flowers were not just for decoration—they were to mark her unborn baby's place of death. Feeling overwhelmed by sadness, Jared walked back to the feet of the corpses. He thought he might be about to vomit.

He was distracted by a knock at the door. He turned to see it open and Hal Harness enter the Ice Chamber.

"I'm sorry to interrupt you, Prince Jared, but the guards have come to collect Lady Silva and take her to the viewing chamber."

Jared nodded, feeling grateful at the sight of other living beings. "Come in," he told Hal, stepping aside as Hal beckoned the guards into the room. They worked fast and efficiently. Prince Jared stood to one side as Silva's body was borne away on a bier, on the shoulders of the guards.

"Would you like me to stay, Your Highness?" Hal asked him. Prince Jared wondered if he looked as queasy as he felt. He gritted his teeth. However hard it might prove, he had one more piece of business to conclude here in this chamber of horrors.

"Just give me another moment here. I'll be out shortly."

Hal nodded and exited the chamber. Jared heard the solid door close behind him. There could be no delaying the moment anymore. He came to stand at Nova's feet. In many ways, he reflected, everything that had happened over these past few days had been leading him to this point, this confrontation with his brother's—and sister-in-law's—murderer. He was filled with frustration and anger toward Nova. And not the least of it was that she had taken her own life and thereby denied him the chance of hearing her reasons.

"Damn you, Nova," he said, hearing the visceral fury in his own voice. "Couldn't you have waited one more day— until we had the chance to talk? Didn't you owe me that at least?"

He could feel the hot tears in his eyes. As quickly as he blotted them away, fresh tears took their place. His vision became blurred, but he stopped trying to fight it. At least he'd be spared the sight of Nova's beautiful, calm, mocking face. What was he even crying for? For his dead brother? For Silva's unborn child, denied the gift of even one Archenfield sunrise? For this whole horrible, unnecessary situation? For how it had turned his own life upside down? Perhaps for all these things. And none of them.

He took a deep breath and pulled himself together. Lifting his shirt cuff to his eyes, he determined to cry no more tears. Why had he even come here, to visit with the dead? His place was with the living. These corpses had no answers for him, only riddles. And he was sick and tired of riddles. He needed truth. It was the only possible anchor in this terrible storm they'd all been swept up in.

He turned his back on the dead and looked toward the door. He knew Hal was waiting for him just outside, in the shadow of the stone stairwell. He felt pathetically grateful for this.

As he stood there, between the platforms, he suddenly felt a touch as cold as the east wind on his hand. He jerked around. Was it his imagination or had Nova's left hand moved slightly? *Of course, it couldn't have*, he told himself. *I have to get out of this godforsaken place; its madness is contagious.*

Nova lay in the exact same position as before. It was nothing more than a trick of the candlelight and his feverish mind. He glanced briefly at her placid face. As he did so, he felt the same coldness as before on his wrist. It shot through him, like the shock from an electric eel, slipping through his limbs in the river. The shock now took hold of his whole body until he was trembling, eyes tightly shut.

When he dared to open them again, he saw that Nova's hand *had* indeed moved toward his. He calmed himself, remembering something Elias had once said about the erratic reflexes of the body in the hours following death. After all, Nova was barely an hour dead. Jared turned once more toward the door, renewed in his determination to rejoin the living and put these morbidities behind him. But walking to the door was like moving against the force of the rapids. Thinking of Asta, and what she'd put herself through for him—for the cause of truth—he proceeded with grim purpose.

As his hand made contact with the door—he was close enough to hear Hal's footsteps on the other side of the slab of oak—something compelled him to turn and glance back one last time.

His eyes were met by the sight of the latest twist in this macabre freak show.

Nova's head had turned toward him and her eyelids were flickering open. Was this another postmortem reflex? Jared stumbled back toward her. Her eyelids closed again, but now he saw her hand move, just as it must have moved before. Next her mouth opened and a low, terrible, animal moan was emitted from her lips.

"Good God!" Jared rasped. "You're alive." He felt sick and giddy.

Moments earlier, it was what he had wanted more than anything in the world. Now, seeing her looking helplessly up at him, he was filled with doubt. Maybe it was better never to know her dark secrets. But as he stood looking down at her in shock, Jared realized that it no longer mattered what was better and what wasn't. There was no getting away from her now. The Prince and the Falconer were bound together on this hellish voyage. The only way out of it was through it.

THIRTY-SEVEN

The Palace Ice Chamber

JARED WAS ROOTED TO THE SPOT AS NOVA'S LIPS emitted another low moan.

"Is everything all right?" Hal's voice came from the other side of the door.

"Yes," Jared called back anxiously. Then, with a more commanding note to his voice. "Wait there, Hal!"

"Yes, Your Highness!"

"Nova," he hissed, perhaps more loudly than was prudent. "It's Prince Jared. I know you're alive. It might not be what you wanted, but you *are* still alive."

She made another sound, softer now, and he could see the faint rise and fall of her diaphragm. The movement was minimal but there all the same. He glanced up and saw her eyes, half open, as if caught on the brink between death and life.

"Don't try to speak," he told her. "You're too weak." He hated himself for his natural inclination toward kindness.

Her eyes and lips closed and her diaphragm shuddered. Jared realized that simply mustering these animal noises had necessitated a huge effort on Nova's part. She might not be dead, but she was still far from a living, functioning creature.

"I'll send for help," he said, resting his hand on her robe. "Elias will know what to do."

These words had been intended to calm her, but they seemed to have the opposite effect. Her hand began to tremble. Reflexively, he took it in his own. "It's all right," he said. "But I think you need to stay still."

It was awkward for him to stand and maintain his grip on her hand at the same time, so he found himself making room on the dais to sit. Glancing across at his brother's corpse, Jared wondered if this moment could possibly be any more surreal. Here he was holding hands with the woman who had taken the lives of his brother and sister-in-law, a woman who herself had one foot in this world and the other already planted in the next. A big part of him wanted to just withdraw his hand and walk away, allowing her to die a second time. It didn't seem like she had much fight left inside her. But he knew he couldn't do anything but stay at her side. He had virtually prayed for her return. Now he had to deal with the consequences.

He withdrew his hand. "How could you do such terrible

things?" he asked her, angrily. "You are responsible for four deaths. My brother. His wife. Their unborn child. And the steward."

His words prompted another animal moan. Shorter than the previous ones.

"I told you before, don't try to speak. Save what strength you have. You're certainly going to need it." He stared down at her face. "I just can't believe you had such evil in you."

This prompted a fresh moan, more of a whimper. At the same time, her hand became agitated. Her mouth and eyes were closed tight, but her hand was trying to make contact with his. Against all his better instincts, he found himself making physical contact once more.

"Nova, are you trying to tell me something?"

He wasn't sure where his words had come from, but as he finished speaking, she gave a sharp squeeze of his hand. He was surprised at the strength she had been able to muster.

As her hand relaxed its grip again, he found himself trembling. "Is that it?" he asked. "Are you trying to tell me something?"

Once again, her hand squeezed his own, then released it again.

"Don't expect any pity from me," he said. "Or forgiveness. I know that you killed my brother and Silva, and I know why." He shook his head sadly. "Don't you feel any level of guilt for what you have done?"

He waited, expecting her to react to this. Her hand remained limply in his own.

"No," he continued, angrily. "Of course you don't feel any guilt. How could you have done the things you have done if you..." He broke off. "And I always thought you were a person of honor."

She squeezed his hand.

"Oh really? You think you are an honorable person?"

Nova squeezed his hand once more.

Jared shook his head. "Either your guilt or the fact your evil deeds were successfully concluded prompted you to take your own life. That's not my idea of honorable."

Nova's hand remained limp. Did her failure to respond mean she took issue with him? Or was this a show of defiance, even so very close to death?

"You jumped, Nova!" he said, feeling a certain exasperation.

Still, her hand remained limp. He realized that she was talking to him, but with her hand and not her tongue. Jared's head began to race.

"What are you trying to tell me? That you didn't jump?"

A pronounced squeeze.

"Nova, I need to be sure about this. Are you telling me that you did not jump from the tower?"

Another squeeze—so tight he felt it might crush his bones. *Think*, he told himself. This could be a trick. She could be playing for time. And yet, something told him she wasn't. He had to follow this, wherever it took them.

"Nova, did someone push you off the tower?"

She gripped his hand again. His insides flushed ice-cold.

"They did! Did you see who it was?"

Again, a squeeze.

"Are you sure you don't need me?" Hal called from outside. Had he overheard this strange one-sided conversation?

"No, Hal," Jared called back. "Wait right there. I'll be out very soon."

"Yes, Your Highness."

Jared turned back to Nova. He could feel his blood coursing through his body, his heart pumping with expectation. If she was saying she hadn't jumped but had been pushed, did that mean that she hadn't killed Anders and Silva? How did that square with what Nova had told Asta? Could she have been guilty of an illicit relationship with his brother—but only of that? He knew he'd have to work that out later. Time was of the essence.

"Nova, squeeze my hand if the person who pushed you was one of the Council of Twelve."

Her hand remained still. So, they had been wrong. It wasn't one of the...

But then came the squeeze. Softer than before, but still a squeeze. Why softer? Was she losing strength? He should send for Elias. But he couldn't leave it at this. Not now.

Should he send Hal to fetch Elias? No, it was too dangerous to risk his own protection—especially if the true assassin was still at large.

"Nova, I know you don't have much strength left. I need to know the truth. You owe me that. You owe Anders... squeeze my hand if the person who pushed you was one of the Twelve."

This time, she squeezed back immediately.

Jared let out a breath. "All right," he said, filled with fresh frustration. "How the hell are we going to do this? You can't speak and your eyes are shut tight. I guess there's no other way..." He lowered his voice. "Nova, squeeze my hand if it was Hal Harness who pushed you."

Her hand remained still.

"Nova, just so I know you still can, squeeze my hand again."

She did so—a small but discernible movement.

"All right, so it wasn't Hal. Was it Jonas Drummond?"

He waited, but she did not move her hand.

"Not Jonas either. Was it Kai Jagger?"

Still no squeeze. That put three members of the Twelve in the clear—four counting Nova herself. Assuming she was to be believed. Jared took a breath, thinking fast. Who else had been on his brother's final hunting trip?

"Lucas Curzon?"

No squeeze.

"Nova, was it Axel?"

He felt her hand begin to move. But it wasn't a squeeze as such. And then her hand separated from his and fell limply onto her body.

"Nova!" he cried, more loudly than he had intended. "Nova! Can you hear me?" He reached for her hand again, but it was now as limp as a rag doll's. Their time had run out.

"Hal!" he called, urgently. "Hal, get in here!"

His cry hadn't even faded before Hal had joined him inside the chamber.

"I need you to fetch Elias," Jared told his bodyguard. "Bring him here. Tell him Nova's alive, but do not tell anyone—*not anyone*—else about this. Do you understand?"

Hal nodded, "You can trust me, Prince Jared."

Jared's eyes met his bodyguard's. "I hope I can," he said. "For all our sakes."

DAY SIX

THIRTY-EIGHT

The Prince's Dressing Chamber

JARED TOOK A DEEP BREATH, THEN LIFTED THE black cloth off the mirror in his dressing chamber. Let the mirror try to claim his soul—with everything else that had happened in the past five days, it might be a blessed release. He folded the cloth into a tight bundle and placed it on top of the dressing table, then turned back to face the looking glass.

He barely recognized the visage that met his gaze in the mirror. In less than a week, his face had become lean, bordering on gaunt; the events beginning with his brother's assassination had chiseled away at his flesh with the dexterity of a sculptor. He looked older and not in a good way. Maybe it was fatigue, pure and simple. He had gone to bed late, after his surreal interlude with Nova and the tense evening that had followed with Queen Francesca and the Woodlark delegation. And though he'd been grateful beyond belief to finally bury himself under the covers, his sleep had been thwarted by racing thoughts of the assassin stalking the palace corridors. At one point, he had bolted upright in bed to find himself drenched in sweat, having dreamed of the savage beasts his brother had supposedly seen before his own death. It felt like an omen. All things considered, it was not the perfect preparation for his brother's funeral procession.

He thought again of Nova. The Physician was with her now. Elias had sent a messenger to inform him that the Falconer had slipped back into unconsciousness. She had to make it out of this alive. *Somebody* had to. There had been much too much death in the court. Filled with a sudden sadness, Jared closed his eyes and said a prayer for Nova. When he opened his eyes again, they were wet. It was too early in the day for tears. He swallowed down the emotion and wiped his eyes dry again. His mother would have been so very proud.

Jared purposefully disconnected from his own dispiriting gaze and turned his attention to his funeral coat, brushing a stray dog hair from its sleeve. In the mirror of his armoire, he could see the reflection of a small bureau that nestled against the wall of his dressing room. On its mahogany surface lay the sheet of paper bearing Nova's list.

That list was the one thing that gave him hope. It seemed to him the one sign that they might be making progress and that, with thought and logic, they might confront the looming chaos.

His thoughts were interrupted by an urgent knock on the chamber door.

"Who's there?" he called, bracing himself for the next piece of bad news.

"It's me," Asta called out. Of course, Jared thought, his mood instantly lifting—he had asked her to come the night before.

Jared smiled to see Asta's reflection in the mirror as she entered his dressing room. For an instant, the door was ajar and the mirrored door of the armoire revealed Hal, standing guard at the entrance. It was a reassuring sight—all the more so, since Hal's name had been the first to be crossed off Nova's list.

The sight of Hal's hulking body was lost to him as the chamber door closed. Jared and Asta were alone. He turned from the mirror but found looking into Asta's face an experience not dissimilar to seeing his own reflection. She too looked shattered, tired and pale.

In spite of this, she managed to raise a smile. "You look very handsome," she said. "If that isn't an inappropriate thing to say."

"Because I'm dressed for my brother's funeral?"

"No." She shook her head. "Because you're the Prince and I'm...well, I'm just a girl from the settlements."

"Asta," Jared said, walking toward her, "you're my... friend. You're one of the very few people I can trust around here. That means a lot to me." He surprised them both by hugging her. Her skin was cool to the touch, like marble. He drew back, disconcerted.

"Are you all right?" he asked, thinking again how tired she looked.

"I'm fine." As she spoke, she started to walk away but stumbled. They were self-evidently not the movements of someone who was fine.

Jared pulled over one of his broad-backed dressing room chairs. "I think you should sit down." He expected her to protest, but to his surprise, she nodded gratefully and did as he suggested.

"I have something important to tell you," he said.

Asta's cool gray eyes met his own expectantly.

"Nova Chastain did not jump from the tower," he said. "She was pushed."

Her eyes widened. "What? How do you know this?"

"I know because the Falconer is alive."

"No!" Asta gasped. "That's not possible, is it? Where is she?"

"She's in a makeshift surgery, set up by your uncle at the

palace. He's under strict instructions not to tell anyone else about this. For selfish reasons, I wanted to tell you myself, though I half suspected that he'd have told you, or that you would have found out by now."

Asta shook her head. "That explains why he was up earlier than usual this morning," she said slowly. "He left me a note, but no explanation as to where he had gone. The next thing I knew, I received word that you wanted to see me."

"That's good," Jared said, relieved that, so far at least, the plan was working.

"Nova was pushed?" Asta shook her head. "That can't be right! *She* killed Anders and Silva, and then tried to take her own life! She had the motive and opportunity for both of the murders. Everything points to her. I wouldn't use the term 'mad' loosely, Prince Jared, but I really do think she is mad. You should have seen the way she reacted when I visited her quarters. I'm sorry, but whatever she's told you now, I don't think you can take it at face value."

Jared frowned. "I know it blows a hole in your theory," he said. "But I think we've got to entertain the thought she could be telling the truth." He could see from Asta's expression that she remained unconvinced.

"Did she tell you who pushed her?"

"Not exactly," he said. "But she helped narrow down the range of suspects."

"How?"

"I asked Nova if she jumped from the tower or if someone pushed her. She was too weak to speak, but she squeezed
my hand to answer my questions."

"She squeezed your hand?" Asta shook her head again.
"Does she know who pushed her?"

He nodded. "It was one of the Council of Twelve."

Asta looked fit to burst. "Well, what are you waiting for?
Tell me who!"

Jared wished it were as simple as that and that he had
a definite answer for his companion. He knew that, next
to him, no one else was as intent upon learning the truth
about the multiple murder plot. Asta had risked her own life
by jumping in the freezing river. He had a sudden thought.
Was that why her skin was so cold now?

"Who is it?" Her question cut through his reverie.

"I'm afraid we don't know. Not yet." He picked up the list
from the bureau and offered it to Asta. "But we do know
who it wasn't. As I say, Nova managed to squeeze my hand
and, in doing so, I was able to eliminate these names."

Asta glanced down at the list, seeing the names of the
remaining eleven members of the Council, written in Jared's neat script. Four names had been struck through—Hal
Harness, Lucas Curzon, Jonas Drummond and Kai Jagger.

Asta lifted her eyes back to Jared. "So, if we believe Nova
is telling the truth—and it's a big if as far as I'm concerned—
then there are seven suspects remaining."

Jared nodded.

"Father Simeon. Logan Wilde." She took a breath. "Elias Peck. Emelie Sharp."

"I suppose we could cross Emelie off too," Jared said. "You talked to her and ruled her out before."

Asta came straight back at him. "I ruled her out of being Anders's lover and therefore of having no motive for a crime of passion. But, if we accept that Nova wasn't the killer, then we also have to accept that we're probably not dealing with a crime of passion at all."

"Of course, you're right." He realized how much he needed Asta to get to the heart of things. He had cockily thought he had made great progress on his own, but it was only now that they were together that he was starting to appreciate that the task ahead of them was still huge and daunting.

"If Nova is telling the truth," Asta continued, "then she was set up to look like the murderer. And whoever is really behind the murders wanted us to think it was a crime of passion. Or"—she frowned—"I led us down a blind alley with the notion of this being about Anders and his secret lover."

"Don't take the sole blame for that," Jared said. "You and I came to these conclusions together. And if we went down the wrong path, it was only because someone made it all too easy for us to go there. But maybe now we're finally getting to the truth."

"Or else Nova is a dangerous lunatic who failed to kill herself and is now changing her story in order to save her own skin."

Jared refused to believe this. He had talked to Nova. All right, so she hadn't talked as such, but somehow he knew she was telling the truth. After all, at this point, what did she have to gain by lying? "Please read out the remaining names on the list," he requested.

"Vera Webb. Morgan Booth. And, last but not least, Axel Blaxland." She caught Jared's expression as she read Axel's name. "Why are you frowning? You don't want to believe it could be Axel?"

Jared shrugged. "I don't want to believe it could be any one of them, but it's hard to think otherwise now. No, I frowned because Axel's was the last name I put to Nova before she became too weak to continue. Her hand moved slightly when I said his name, but I couldn't be sure if she was actually squeezing my hand or not."

Asta tapped the page. "Then Axel definitely stays on the list." Her eyes remained on it, her expression grim. "You'd have thought we'd have whittled it down to fewer than seven suspects by now, wouldn't you?"

"When I questioned Nova, I started with who we knew formed the hunting party when Anders was wounded. That list included Elliot Nash, Axel's deputy, but as he's not one of the Twelve, we can rule him out." Jared paused. "I wonder if we should also discount Father Simeon," he offered. "He does seem an unlikely murderer. In fact, we could rule out several of the names. Vera Webb, for instance..."

"No!" Asta exclaimed. "We can't eliminate anyone from this list until we talk to Nova again—assuming she recovers sufficiently to offer us that chance—or we find conclusive proof that it wasn't them. We can't make choices based on instinct or what we believe to be true. If we've learned one thing from this investigation, it's that whoever is behind the murders knows plenty about smoke and mirrors."

Jared nodded. "You're right." He sighed. "I'm afraid we are back to square one."

Asta glanced up. "Maybe it's not that bad. Tell me, who else knows that Nova survived the fall?"

At least he had a concrete answer to that one. "The only people who know she survived the fall are Elias and Hal— Hal helped your uncle take her away. They used the tunnel from Axel's village residence to the palace."

"Then, surely, doesn't Axel know too?"

Jared shook his head. "He wasn't there. He was with me, with Silva's family."

Asta nodded, clearly deep in thought. Jared watched as she rose from her chair and began pacing about his dressing chamber.

"You and Axel were on the way to solving these murders— on the basis that they were politically motivated. But then I waded in and persuaded you it was all about your brother's tangled love life. I'm so sorry, Prince Jared. I've wasted so much time and I'm responsible for Nova's terrible injuries." She shuddered. "I could easily have been responsible for her death."

"Nova's alive," Jared said. "That's what matters. Things are grim enough as it is—we can't start blaming ourselves for things that have *not* yet happened."

Jared saw a fresh wave of tiredness cross Asta's features. He knew that, just as he had been fueled by adrenaline, so too had she. And he could sense that they were both now very close to running on empty. He watched as she sat back down in her chair. Indeed, she did not so much sit as slump. She closed her eyes and lifted her hand to her temples.

Worried, he knelt down at her side.

"Are you sure you are all right?" he inquired.

For a moment, she did not say anything. This in itself concerned him. Then she opened her eyes. "I'm sorry," she said. "I've got a splitting headache."

Jared frowned, placing his own hand on her head.

Asta cried out as if he'd hurt her. "Your skin is so hot!"

"*Your* skin feels very cold," Jared said, alarm spreading through him. "I don't think you have a headache from mental exertion. Asta, I think your body is still in shock from when you were caught in the rapids. Do you think you might have caught something?"

Asta waved her hand dismissively. "I might have mild hypothermia, I suppose. All I know is I'm just so hot." She began fanning herself with her hand.

Jared shook his head. "Asta, we need to get you back to your uncle." He was filled with panic. "It could be serious. We need Elias..."

She shook her head, her eyes glazing over. "You have a funeral to get to and I'll be fine if I just rest. It's not a long walk back to the village."

He frowned. "You're in no condition to walk anywhere." He glanced at the clock. They were running out of time. In a matter of minutes, he was due to join the others for the funeral procession. "Anyway, I don't want you walking any-where unescorted. We've got to accept that the murderer knows you've been helping me with the investigation. And that means that you're in the line of danger now too."

Asta shook her head, defiantly. Jared wondered if he'd upset her pride when he'd said she was "helping" with the investigation. He knew it would be truer to say that she was leading the investigation, but he didn't want her to feel responsible for what had happened to Nova, or anything else for that matter.

"Hal!" he called.

As ever, the Bodyguard was quick to do his bidding. "Yes, Prince Jared?"

"I need you to look after Asta while I'm at the funeral."

"No, I'm fine," Asta protested.

"She's not fine," Jared asserted. "She's potentially in danger and I don't want you to let her out of your sight. I think, all things considered, it's best if you stay here during the funeral. Asta, you can use the bed if you like. And, Hal, I want you to stay right here and watch over her. Don't let anyone else in, you understand?"

Hal nodded, his fingers brushing the hilt of his dagger. "Completely."

Jared placed his hand on Hal's shoulder. "It's really good to know I can depend on you."

Hal nodded once more. "Always."

"There's one more thing," Jared said. "Asta has a headache. Do you know where we might find something to relieve the pain?"

"Actually I do," Hal said, brushing past them and toward the door. "I just need to step into the Prince's Office." He was only gone a matter of moments and, when he returned, he was clutching a small glass vial containing a reddish substance.

"Your brother was plagued by headaches in recent weeks." Hal lifted up the vial with its cork stopper. "A dose or two of this seemed to do the trick. You don't need much—it's strong stuff. You mix it with water." He removed the stopper. As he did so, a thin wisp of the powder stored inside was released into the air.

The powder had a very particular smell. Asta knew she had experienced it before. It took her a moment, as Hal busied himself mixing it with water, to place it. Then, as he offered her the glass, she shuddered and exclaimed, "Ergot!"

"What?" Jared was unsure how to respond. He and Hal watched as the glass trembled in Asta's hand, and neither was surprised when it slipped through her fingers and fell onto the rug beneath her chair. Asta's face was a vision of panic.

"Don't worry," Hal said gently. "I'll make you up a fresh dose."

"No!" Asta recoiled. Her expression had taken on a manic air.

"What's wrong?" Jared asked.

She pointed at the glass. "*This* is what killed your brother. Not poison mixed in with his food, nor poison administered through his hunting wound. This headache cure."

"What?" Jared dropped to his knees beside her. He was aware of Hal, standing over him, also frozen to the spot.

"When my uncle conducted the postmortem on Prince Anders," she said, "he identified two possible poisons, savin or ergot..."

"I know," Jared said defensively. "You and I have discussed

it over and over. Your uncle concluded that the toxin was most likely savin, but you suspected that it could actually have been both."

"Yes," Asta agreed. "But Uncle Elias was only going on the facts he had at his disposal. He told me, in passing, that ergot is sometimes used to relieve migraines. In low doses, it isn't harmful, but if used on a regular, cumulative basis, it can be fatal."

"What are you telling me?" Jared asked her. "That my brother inadvertently killed *himself* with a headache remedy? Even if I do accept that, how do you explain Silva's murder and the attempt on Nova's life?"

Asta was silent for a moment. He could sense her mind racing nonetheless. "No," she said at last. "Anders's death was not accidental. He was murdered."

Jared suddenly caught Hal's gaze and wondered, for a moment, if they should be having this conversation in his company. He tried to catch Asta's attention, but she was possessed of a new, urgent energy.

"Maybe Axel was right from the outset and this is a political attack—whether from outside or within Archenfield. It makes sense. First, you murder the Prince—to send the Princedom into shock and prove you can strike right at the heart of the court. Next, Silva, not because of the baby she is carrying but to break the all-important alliance with Woodlark. Then the Falconer—the one who controls communication with the borders and the other territories beyond. Don't you see? You're being picked off, one by one. The murderer *was* the one who gave Prince Anders this headache remedy. If we find out where he got this medicine, we have the name of our assassin."

"Where does anyone in the court obtain medicine?" Jared said, speaking before thinking. Seeing Asta's expression, he wished he could take back his words.

"My uncle."

"It can't be Elias!" Jared exclaimed, shaking his head.

"Why not?" Asta inquired. "Because he is my uncle? This isn't a game. There are no rules. Savin was a difficult substance to get hold of, because it only grows in the Physic Garden. But ergot is far more readily sourced..."

"It wasn't Elias." Hal Harness's voice caught both their attention.

They turned. The Groom's Bell began to sound. It was the last bell that would sound today—the one to summon all the mourners to the funeral.

"What's that you say, Hal?" Jared inquired, not waiting for the bells to cease. He couldn't wait any longer for the answers he needed.

"It wasn't Elias who supplied this medicine to Prince Anders."

Jared's eyes were wide. "You know this for a fact? You need to be very sure about this, Hal."

Hal nodded. "I understand."

"Well?" Asta's eyes implored Hal. "If Uncle Elias didn't give it to Prince Anders, who did?"

Hal paused for a moment, then he shook his head sadly. "Logan Wilde," he said. "The Poet."

THIRTY-NINE

Archenfield

EVERY LAST MAN, WOMAN AND CHILD IN ARCH-
enfield had turned out to bid goodbye to their beloved
Prince. At least, that's how it seemed to Prince Jared as he
walked at the heart of the funeral procession. Both sides of
the road were crowded deep with Prince Anders's mournful
subjects. Many held aloft the flag of Archenfield—creating
a sea of gold and blue and green. Those at the front of the
crowd reached out their hands as the horse-drawn bier
came near. Perhaps they imagined if they could only achieve
a physical connection with Prince Anders, the strength of
their united desire could work some alchemy and breathe
life back into his skin and bones. Jared had no doubts
regarding the depth of Archenfield's communal hunger to
resurrect its fallen leader, but he was under no illusions.

His brother was dead, as was his Consort and their unborn child.

Prince Jared walked a short distance behind the bier, assuming his position as Archenfield's new leader. As great an adjustment as it would be for his subjects, it was an even more momentous metamorphosis for Jared himself. He was Jared, Prince of All Archenfield. The days when he might race around the palace ramparts, or go running with Hedd in the forest or sit quietly daydreaming in meetings of the Twelve were long gone. This week's cruel events had initiated him into leadership and now there could be no turning back. *"One foot in front of the other."* He heard his mother's voice in his head. It had been her advice to him and Edvin on managing their pace during the funeral procession, but it was equally valid, he supposed, when it came to taking on the many responsibilities of rule.

He turned now, exchanging a glance with Edvin, who was on Jared's left-hand side. As Edvin returned his discreet smile, Jared was struck once more by how much his brother resembled Anders. He was sure the crowd must be affected by this too. It offered a certain kind of continuity, as if their wish for resurrection really had been granted.

Jared returned his eyes to the crowd, greatly moved that they had turned out in such numbers. It took him back to another September day, little more than a year before, when the Princedom had been swept up in Anders and Silva's fairy-tale romance. Anders had been the first Archenfield Prince in living memory to take a bride from outside the Princedom. This marriage had not only brought together the whole of Archenfield in a mood of warm optimism, but united Archenfield itself with its neighbor. Now that alliance with Woodlark was broken, as Queen Francesca had made abundantly clear the night before.

The royal wedding day had been at the same changing of the seasons. Prince Anders had sported a boutonniere of acorns and leaves of oak. Now acorns lay on the ground once more. Silva had been an autumn bride and an autumn widow. Today her broken body was on its way back to the homeland she had never truly been able to let go of. Jared hoped that her soul might find some peace and that, in time, her family might feel able to forgive what had happened to their daughter while in the foreign court. Somehow, he doubted that was possible.

He turned to his right, where Logan Wilde, the Poet, walked—of course—in perfect synchrony with him. Logan was too busy watching, acknowledging the crowd to notice Prince Jared's glance. *Good,* thought Jared. He would deal with Logan later. For now, all that mattered was keeping him close. He heard his father's voice. *"Keep your friends close, Jared, and your enemies closer."* Prince Goran's words had never assumed such potent meaning as now. Jared drew comfort from this. It was as if his father were there too, walking beside him, offering the support he so desperately needed.

Some distance behind Jared, Edvin and Logan, Queen Elin walked alone. It was little more than two years since the death of Prince Goran. He too had been beloved. The dead Princes of Archenfield were a tough act to follow. It was only the deep affection for, and belief in, young Prince Anders that had allowed Archenfield to move through its grief for Prince Goran. Jared knew that his mother's iron resolve had been a key factor in transferring the reins of rule from Goran to Anders and it was arguably Elin as much as Anders who was responsible for the mood today— the love, the grief, bordering on something more. Now Elin was faced with the challenge of transferring the Princedom successfully from the first of her sons to the second. And he had witnessed, firsthand, her bloody-minded determination to succeed at this.

Prince Jared lifted his hand to the crowds on either side of the road—acknowledging their grief, knowing that, for now, it must take precedence over his own. The duties of the Princedom were as unyielding as the oldest trees in the forest, the very forest into which the cortege was now heading, where it would at last leave behind the crowds as their fallen Prince journeyed on to his final resting place.

Jared closed his eyes for a moment, thinking grimly of

what lay ahead. Opening them again, he glanced over his shoulder and glimpsed Cousin Axel a short distance behind Elin. Jared saw to his brief amusement that Axel, with his long limbs, was having to exert some considerable restraint not to stride ahead of Elin and wreck the ordered procession of mourners.

As Jared's Edling, Axel was now heir to the Princedom. And, despite his initial doubts and their obvious differences, Jared was starting to see the wisdom in his mother's advice. Of course, Axel had failed spectacularly in his duties as Captain of the Guard when he had allowed the wrong man to be executed for Prince Anders's murder—that was something Jared believed would haunt him for the rest of his days. But, in the end, Axel had been there when Jared needed him and it seemed that, for now at least, they were on the same side.

The next two rows in the procession were made up of the remaining key officers of the Princedom: the Priest, the Beekeeper, the Woodsman, the Huntsman, the Executioner, the Cook and the Groom. The Falconer was, of course, missing from their ranks—presumed dead but, hopefully, slowly journeying back to life in the makeshift surgery in the palace, watched over by the Physician. Also missing was the Bodyguard who, on the Prince's command, was guarding Asta. And then there was the Poet.

Jared turned briefly to his right side again. This time, Logan caught his glance and smiled reassuringly. Jared gave a nod, then turned swiftly away.

It was, thought Jared, a sign of the mourners' respect that, in spite of their grief, none attempted to follow the members of the cortege. Instead, they hung back to the sides of the road. Only those within the Prince's family and immediate retinue would be present for the Burning at the edge of the fjord.

The sun was beginning to set, its rays seeming to ignite the trees of the forest. It was beautiful, but it made him think again of the funeral pyre that would soon come into view. He shivered. The air was cold, the wind more biting than ever. Jared's eyes stung and were now running with water. He wiped away the tears with the back of his funeral coat's sleeve and was horrified to feel Logan place what was clearly intended as a reassuring hand on his shoulder. It took every fiber of his being not to shrug the murdering fiend's hand away then and there. But he was hamstrung until they left the crowds behind.

Had Logan noticed the way Jared had reflexively tensed at his touch? If so, it seemed he had not read anything into it. His hands back at his sides, he was walking on, continuing to survey the crowds, who remained many rows deep even as the forest came ever closer.

Jared thought of Anders—of all he had been, of what had

happened to him, and what was about to happen. He felt the cold grief of saying goodbye to a brother he had never truly known. It tore through his insides, sharp as a hunter's knife. He vowed then and there not to make the same mistake with Edvin. They had always been close, but now there was a danger, as Edvin had said, that Jared's princely duties would create a distance between them. Jared would fight not to let that happen. He may not have been able to make Edvin his Edling, but he would find a role for him, a way to keep him close. That could all be taken care of in the coming days and weeks. After the merciless pace of the past five days, Jared might even find time to exhale. But not yet. There were important matters to attend to still. He would need every ounce of self-discipline to conclude things to his satisfaction. To honor his dead brother and father and all the other Princes of Archenfield who had come before him.

Now the funeral procession entered the forest. Finally they left the grieving crowds behind them. It was time to attend to business. Prince Jared turned to Logan.

"That went well, I think." The Poet's words, accompanied, as they so often were, by a reassuring smile, cut him off.

This time, for the first time, Jared did not bother to return it. There was no need to anymore. He could show Logan that the charade had finally come to an end.

"It's all worked out just as you wanted, hasn't it?" Jared addressed Logan as they ventured ever deeper into the blue-green forest. "When did you know you had such a talent not only for planning, but also for improvisation?"

Oblivious to the Prince's true meaning, Logan shrugged. "I'm not sure exactly. Perhaps I've always been that way." He smiled again. "It's in my blood."

"Yes," Prince Jared said, conscious of the edge in his voice. "But then again *no*. I tend to think you have worked quite hard to hone these skills of yours. You would have to have done, I suspect, in order to convince your superiors that you were capable of such an important and treacherous mission."

Now he could see a flicker of uncertainty in Logan's eyes. The Poet opened his mouth to speak but Jared interrupted him; the days of Logan Wilde writing the script were over. "You successfully positioned my brother's body on the bier for all of Archenfield to see. Tick. You dispatched the Prince's Consort back to Woodlark. Tick. There's only really one thing you messed up, isn't there?"

Logan frowned. "I'm sorry, I don't think I follow what you're saying."

"Let me spell it out more clearly for you," Jared said evenly. He took a breath. "You killed my brother and my sister-in-law and their unborn child. Those three murders all went swimmingly for you. But you failed to kill Nova

Chastain." He nodded, pleased to note the sudden look of horror in Logan's eyes. "Yes, *my friend*, against all odds the Falconer survived her fall and brought your evil house of cards tumbling down. The game—and I really think that's all this was for you—is over."

FORTY

The Forest

THE FUNERAL CORTEGE MAINTAINED THE SAME
even pace as it made its way along the main track through the
heart of the forest. Its green shadows washed over the members of the procession, broken only by the blue sky and the
shafts of golden light as the afternoon sun cut through the
gaps in the branches. Green, blue and gold, just like the flags
the crowd had waved. The ancient colors of Archenfield.

"It wasn't a game," Logan now told Jared. "Though, I will
admit, it had many entertaining moments."

Jared's jaw dropped. "What kind of sick mind do you
have? You've sent four innocent people to their deaths!"

Logan shook his head. "Innocent? My jury's out on that.
Anyway, I thought you said the Falconer is still alive? So it's
three, not four, by my reckoning."

450

"Anders, Silva, their unborn child and Michael Reeves—the steward you framed for my brother's assassination."

"Oh yes!" Logan said, his eyes bright with realization. "The steward. It's so easy to forget about him, isn't it?"

"For you perhaps," Jared said. "I doubt I ever will."

"No," Logan agreed. "I daresay you'll carry his unjust death on your shoulders all the days of your reign." He smiled. "Well, let me tell you, Michael Reeves may *not* have been guilty of Prince Anders's assassination, but he had amassed a few other crimes against the Princedom. Spying for his homeland, for instance. Word to the wise, Prince Jared—it's far easier to frame those who have something to hide."

Jared's blood ran cold at Logan Wilde's words. Glancing over his shoulder, he could see that others had now noticed that he and the Poet were talking. It was bad form, but he could see that it was not a source of alarm to them. For all they knew, he was reflecting upon the size of the crowd with his chief advisor, or discreetly being reminded of the next part of the funeral rites. He turned his attention back to Logan.

"It's of little consequence that you have betrayed me," Jared said now. "We hardly know each other. And, though I have gained valuable insights from you these past six days, I'm sure I'll do just fine without your help."

Logan rolled his eyes. "I wouldn't lay money on that.

You show every indication of being as inept a prince as your older brother."

Jared glowered. "Your betrayal of Anders is so much worse. You were his closest companion during the two years of his reign. He trusted you implicitly. And, all the time, you were plotting his downfall."

Logan laughed. "First, I assure you I was *not* his closest companion. I think we can safely award that title to the Falconer. If you only knew the number of times that your brother raced down to the bathing house to while away the afternoon with her. But, of course, you wouldn't know that. Because I covered it up. Like I covered up so much else." He was getting into his stride now. "Your brother was something of a simpleton, if truth be known—if he hadn't been born into your family, he'd have been fortunate to make the grade of assistant groom. Oh, he was extraordinarily handsome, no one can deny that. But he was not a natural prince, any more than you are, my friend. It was only thanks to the talents of those around him—your ambitious cousin, your scheming shrew of a mother and, most of all, yours truly— that he was able to dazzle as he did."

Jared shook his head. "That's what I don't understand. If that is the truth, why would you even bother to go to that effort when all you wanted to do was to destroy him?"

Logan smiled nastily at Jared. "Of course you don't understand. Because you're blessed with only a few more brain cells than he had. It was *never* my mission to destroy *him*. My mission was far bigger than that—to bring Archenfield to its knees. And, by the way, I think we can agree that I've been extremely successful at that." He paused, looking at Jared and shaking his head in exasperation. "Do you know how tedious it becomes watching the cogs turn in your head? I *had* to make Prince Anders seem like a demigod in order to achieve maximum devastation. Believe you me, I was working with base material—but somehow I got there, bringing in Woodlark's prize princess to complete the happy picture."

"Is everything all right?" Jared whipped around to see Edvin at his shoulder. He had walked up soundlessly beside them.

"Everything is fine," Jared told his brother.

Edvin shrugged and stepped away again. Jared returned his attention to Logan.

"So tell me, Logan, why did you do this? Who are you working for? Besides yourself, I mean."

Logan considered the question, then shook his head. "I don't think I'm going to answer that," he said. "But, Prince Jared, I believe I will do you and Archenfield one final favor."

One final favor? What did he mean by that?

The forest path now veered to the north, and the sun shone directly onto their faces. Temporarily blinded, Prince Jared instinctively turned away. As he did so, he saw Axel racing toward him, dagger drawn. He felt a cold shiver run through him, as everything seemed to slow down in an instant. Was Cousin Axel in league with Logan Wilde? Had they been in this together from the beginning? He could see Kai Jagger and Jonas Drummond pursuing Axel, daggers visible in their own hands. But they weren't fast enough. They wouldn't catch Axel.

Jared started to turn away, just as the dagger cut into his chest. Cold fear was replaced by a burning pain that tore through his chest like a hot poker. He fell to his knees, feeling blood pumping out onto his shirt and his hands.

It was only as he crashed to the ground that he saw Logan Wilde with a bloody dagger in his hand and Axel restraining the Poet, with his own knife, until reinforcements arrived in the shape of the Huntsman and the Woodsman.

Jared looked away, becoming aware of Edvin crouched at his side, tearing madly at his own clothes to find cloth with which to stanch Jared's wound.

Behind him, Jared heard voices—his mother, the other members of the Twelve. He could hear the confused commotion, but it sounded strangely distant.

Then he felt a sharp slap across his cheek. He looked up to see Cousin Axel crouching before him. "Sorry," Axel said, his eyes wide with concern. "But you have to stay with us, Prince Jared. That traitorous bastard cut you deep, but I'm pretty sure he missed a major artery. It looks worse than it is and believe me, it looks pretty damn awful."

"Where is he?" Jared asked faintly. "Did he run?"

"Fat chance," Axel said. "No, Kai and Jonas have taken him away. Tempting as it was to kill him on the spot, it seemed more prudent to throw him in the Dungeons—for the time being."

"He wouldn't tell me why he did all this...the killing," Jared said.

Axel nodded. "He didn't need to," he said. "This very morning, I received word from my spies that Logan Wilde has a sister who, not long ago, crossed the border to Paddenburg and is poised to marry Prince Henning." He frowned. "It seems clear that Wilde was anticipating that day and was already taking his orders from within the court of Paddenburg." He shook his head. "I don't know what precisely Wilde or his sister have been promised by the two demented princes of Paddenburg, but I'm going to make it my mission to find out."

Jared felt short of breath. "But that's it now. It's over?"

Axel frowned. "I wish I could say yes, especially with you dripping blood over my nice new boots, but I can't. Someone in the court of Paddenburg issued an order to Logan Wilde to assassinate Prince Anders. Did that order emanate from Prince Ven or Prince Henning, or is someone else out to create enmity between their court and ours? We need to find out fast and, even though we've now taken Wilde out of commission, we must still continue to be on our mettle against further attacks."

It wasn't the answer he had wanted, but Jared was nonetheless grateful for the truth. He nodded ruefully. "So, what you're saying is that I need to recover from this attack because I'll almost certainly be facing another before long."

Axel's tone and words were measured. "I'm saying that we need to get you back to the palace and into the Physician's care. You must focus all your energies on a full recovery at this point."

"But what about my brother's remaining funeral rites?" Jared asked. "We can't exactly pause the proceedings here." He looked up, seeing that the other side of the forest was in view. Through the gaps in the trees, he could glimpse the violet waters of the fjord and, in front of them, a wooden structure as terrible as it was beautiful. The funeral pyre.

"We have no alternative but to halt the funeral," Axel said. "You are the Prince of All Archenfield now. You have to be our main priority."

"You're right," Jared said. "I *am* Prince, so I suppose I have the last word in this." He turned to Edvin. "Help me to my feet, Brother!"

He saw Edvin exchange a glance with Cousin Axel.

"I said help me to my feet, Edvin!"

"We'll both help you," Axel said, moving swiftly to Jared's other side. "All right, Edvin? On the count of three, we lift, yes? One, two, three..."

Jared was lifted to his feet. The pain was excruciating and he had to grit his teeth not to cry out. But now that he had a better view of the fjord and the pyre—and his brother's bier, at a standstill between them and him—it was enough to renew his determination.

"We're almost there," Jared told his companions. "This is something I want to do, for Anders's sake. I think I can make it, if you'll just lend me an arm."

Edvin nodded, reaching over to support Jared's back. "I've got you," he said.

Jared turned to Axel. "Don't bother to argue with me. We *are* going to complete my brother's funeral rites."

"Yes, Prince Jared," Axel said, nodding, a new respect in his eyes. "If I have to carry you to the fjord myself, that's exactly what we are going to do."

SEVEN DAYS
LATER...

FORTY-ONE

The Fjord

THE PYRE WAS NO MORE. IT HAD TAKEN A DAY to burn, but it was gone now and only the scorched earth was testament to it ever having been there. Still, this would always be a sacred place to Prince Jared. The place where he had said goodbye to his older brother and felt the mantle of power being passed onto his own shoulders.

Standing there now, he thought back to that day a week before, when Edvin and Axel had supported him on his painful walk. The three of them had journeyed right inside the pyre to visit Anders one last time. Axel and Edvin had each said their goodbyes, then left Jared to say his. The words he had used were still fresh in his head.

"Grant me the strength to continue your work. I don't know where you are now, but wherever it is, watch me and

guide me if you can. Whatever your faults, you were born to be Prince of All Archenfield. I am second best. But I will do what I can to honor your name, and our father's, and all who came before us."

Stepping out from the pyre, Lucas Curzon had closed the gap in the structure behind him. Then, as Edvin had continued to support him, he had seen Cousin Axel walking toward him, a lit torch in his hands.

Jared had taken it into his own hands, immediately feeling both its surprising weight and the intensity of the heat emanating from it. There had been nothing to be gained by drawing things out. He had nodded at Edvin, who stepped aside. Staggering slightly, he had walked back toward the pyre and, before the painful thoughts could take hold or his strength simply give out, had hurled the torch at the structure as high as he could, turning away as flames began to lick their way hungrily over its dome.

Slowly, now, he came back to his senses, relieved that there was no more fire. He heard the lapping waters of the fjord and walked down the short way to them, leaving Lucas behind him to tend to the horses. Jared knew that his wound had started to heal within the week; even so, he still felt some discomfort as he walked to the water's edge. But at least this time, unlike seven days earlier, he was able to make this short journey alone.

As he stood there, gazing out over the purple-blue

waters before him, he became aware of footsteps behind him. He glanced over his shoulder—immediately regretting it. But the small twist of pain was worth it for the sight of Asta Peck, making her way through the glade and down to join him at the edge of the water.

He smiled as she drew level with him. "Are you following me again, Asta?"

"Of course," she said. "I have nothing better to do with my time." Though her words were ironic, he saw she was smiling—not only with her pretty lips but also with her arresting gray eyes.

"Well, it's good to see you," he said. "It's always good to see you."

She didn't meet his eyes, but she continued to smile, gazing out at the water.

"Are you better?" he asked.

She nodded. "Yes, Uncle Elias has given me the all clear," she said. "And strict instructions not to immerse myself in the river again until well after the May celebrations."

Jared laughed. "That seems like sound advice."

She turned to face him. "You'll be the Prince by then. I mean, I know you are already, but, after tomorrow, it will be official." She paused. "How are you feeling about it all?"

He shrugged. "Happy. Anxious. Excited. Confused."

She nodded. "You're going to be a pretty spectacular Prince, you know," she said.

"Is that so?" He felt the warmth of her words, even through the chill of the wind. "You know that, do you?"

"Yes," she said. "You know me, Jared...*sorry, sorry, Prince* Jared. I'm always right!" She smiled once more. This time, her eyes met his.

"I don't think I have ever said thank you," he said now, gazing into her eyes. "Thank you for being such a maverick. For not trusting the official version of events. For throwing yourself in the river and for, generally, watching my back."

She shrugged, seeming uneasy in the face of so many compliments.

"I meant what I said before," he continued. "You knew that the truth was important to me and you refused to rest until you uncovered it and brought it to me."

"I'm glad I could help with the investigation," she said. "If it doesn't sound crass under the circumstances, I enjoyed spending time in your company. I know we're from incredibly different worlds, but it was nice being around someone my own age for a change."

He nodded. "That goes for me too!"

She looked away from him and he thought he knew why. "Asta. Asta! You need to know—nothing has to change after tomorrow."

"Of course it does," she said, turning her face back to him so that he could see the tears welling in her eyes. "You'll be Prince of All Archenfield. And I'll be…well, I'll just be the Physician's apprentice."

"No," he said, opening his arms to draw her into a hug. "I will be Prince and you will be my friend. Even princes need friends, you know."

She shook her head, blotting away her tears, then—after only the briefest hesitation—stepped into his hug, reaching her arms around his shoulders.

As she did so, he cried out in pain. "Oh no!" she said. "I'm so sorry. I put pressure on your wound, didn't I?"

She tried to pull away, but he refused to let her. "You did," he said. "You're a horrible person, Asta Peck. A really bad and horrible person. But, in spite of this, I can't help being inordinately proud and grateful to call you my friend." He kept his arms wrapped tightly around her as the waters of the fjord broke gently on the shore in front of them and a breeze circled around them.

In the distance, they heard the chiming of a bell. Six chimes.

"The Poet's Bell," Asta observed.

Prince Jared nodded. "Come on," he said, releasing her from his arms but reaching out and taking her hand. "It's getting cold out here and I have to get back to the palace. Will you ride back with me?"

She nodded, daring to squeeze his hand tightly this time.

Morgan Booth turned to find an unexpected guest in his subterranean domain.

"Prince Jared," he said, his face breaking into a smile. "No one told me to expect you. How is that wound of yours?"

Jared nodded. "Getting better every day, thank you," he said, tapping the bandage gently. "Although you wouldn't believe how itchy it gets."

"Well, you're on the mend," Morgan said. "That's what matters." He paused. "So we're all set for tomorrow?"

Jared nodded. "Everything will proceed according to plan."

"That's what we like," Morgan said. "Everything running to plan again." His eyes met Prince Jared's. "I suppose I can guess what brings you down to my lair."

"I'd like to speak to the prisoner," Jared said.

"Be my guest!" Booth said. "Want me to make myself scarce?"

"No need to leave on my account," Jared replied. "I'm sure you have things to sharpen."

Booth grinned, his teeth snow-white in the candlelight. "I always have things to sharpen, Prince Jared." He nodded and turned back to his desk, as the Prince continued on his way.

Logan Wilde rose to his feet as Jared approached his cell.

"Well, well. To what do I owe this pleasure?" It seemed the former Poet was in fine spirits this morning.

"I wanted to see you," Jared said. "Before my coronation tomorrow."

"Still going ahead with that?"

Jared smiled. "Did you think the business of Archenfield would grind to a standstill with you out of the picture?" He leaned closer toward the bars that separated them. "Turns out you're not *quite* as indispensable as you think."

Logan smiled back, shaking his head. "Anyone can plan a procession," he said. "I'm sure you and Axel have been poring over my notebooks. My point is this—how can your coronation happen when the Blood Price for your brother's murder has not been paid? The people still have no sense of catharsis." His voice grew colder. "Your reign will be tainted in death and confusion from the very beginning. You'll never be able to break free from those shackles."

Jared stared at the prisoner. Logan spoke as if he were still making a valid contribution to the running of the Princedom. Had he forgotten that he had, by his own admission, attempted to wreak "maximum devastation" upon Archenfield? Jared wondered at the extent of the prisoner's delusions.

He could see Logan, arms folded, was still waiting for an answer.

"You're wrong," Prince Jared told him. "As far as the people know, the Blood Price *has* been paid. Prince Anders was assassinated by a renegade steward, Michael Reeves. It was a terrible crime, striking unexpectedly at the heart of our Princedom. There was no way it could have been anticipated, but the threat was swiftly addressed and swiftly eliminated. Our security is second to none."

"Ha!" Logan shook his head. "I see that I underestimated you—it seems like a week in my company did rub off on you."

"I hate to disappoint your superiority complex," Jared replied. "But we managed to work this out without your help."

Logan shrugged. "I wouldn't call it a 'complex.'" He paused. "All right, so you have successfully pulled the wool over the people's eyes regarding your brother. But what about *poor* Silva and the Prince's unborn child? That's not so easily explained away."

Jared's eyes met Logan's once more. "The death of the Prince's Consort is another tragedy; no one has any doubt about that. But she was terribly distressed by her husband's murder and it drove her to take her own life. As for the baby, well, she wasn't yet showing. No one outside the court need ever know."

As Jared stopped speaking, he felt quite nauseous from the lies at which, through repetition, he had already become so practiced.

"Well," Logan said. "Someone really has become quite the politician since last we met."

Jared continued, ignoring him. "So you see, Logan, the coronation will proceed tomorrow, just as we always planned. It will mark an end to the time of crisis and signal the return to peace and stability under a new ruler." He paused, allowing himself a small smile. "Me."

Logan shook his head again. "It's an admirable attempt to sweep the truth under the carpet—worthy of me, you might even say. But you and I both know that cracks will soon appear. The threat is still out there and, just when you think all is safe, the world will come crashing down around you all over again."

"Perhaps," Jared said with a nod. "And perhaps not. You took us by surprise, Logan. We won't let that happen again."

"Is that all you came to tell me?" Logan said. "Do you still need a pat on the back from me, even after everything? You Wynyards are all the same. Didn't Elin wean any of you properly?"

Jared shook his head. "I don't need or want anything from you," he said. "I just came to see you one last time."

"What do you mean by that?" Was that a note of panic beneath the cocksure retort? "Are you going to proceed with *my* execution? But how will you explain *that* to the people?"

Jared rested his hand casually on the bars of Logan's cell. "The Captain of the Guard and I have discussed three options in regard to you," he said. "One—extradition to Paddenburg." He shook his head slowly. "That's not going to happen so don't expect a reunion with your equally ambitious sister anytime soon." He noted with satisfaction Logan's shocked reaction, then continued. "Two— execution. Obviously tempting and I'm sure Mr. Booth would be happy to oblige." He glanced across at the Executioner, then back to Logan. "But, on balance, we've decided to plump for option three."

"Which is?"

"You're obviously a patient man," Jared said. "You waited until the time was just right to unleash your firebrand of chaos upon the Princedom. So, given that you are so patient, we're going to keep you down here for a good, long while. I'm sure it will be a considerable comfort to you that you will remain, symbolically at least, right at the heart of the Princedom."

Logan frowned. Then his frown shifted into a smile. Jared was starting to think his trusted advisor had finally succumbed to madness. But when Logan Wilde spoke, his voice was full of cold conviction.

"I was only ever the advance party. The fact I achieved as much as I did goes to show how weak the Princedom has become."

Jared's eyes blazed with hatred. "Perhaps you are right. Perhaps our defenses were down. But I told you before that won't happen again. Not on my watch."

Logan smiled once more. "Your words are a little simpler when I'm not scripting you, aren't they?" He shrugged. "No matter. They have a certain naïve power. But make no mistake, Little Prince, you will need every ounce of that power in the time ahead. You talk as if you are in control, but that is far from the true state of affairs. You'll see how things really are soon enough."

The Poet's words—for he couldn't yet stop thinking of him as the Poet—chilled Jared to the core. But he couldn't let his adversary see that. If he had learned one thing, in these past days, it was that as Prince he had to mask his inner thoughts and, most especially, his inner fears.

"Our time together is concluded," Prince Jared told Logan.

Logan Wilde shrugged. "It's probably a good thing," he said. "If I'm honest, compared to your older brother, you're a bit of a bore."

Jared let the latest barb fall away. "Goodbye, Logan." He turned away, then paused, glancing back. "Thank you for everything you have taught me during our time together. I'm sure I'll draw on your advice throughout my coming reign."

Logan shrugged. "We'll see," he said, retiring to the depths of his cell.

The Prince turned away again and walked back over to Booth's desk. The Executioner was busy working on the edge of his axe.

"Believe me, Morgan, when I say I'm sorry you won't get a chance to use that today."

Booth shrugged. "Never mind. It pays to keep them all nice and sharp anyhow."

"Don't let the prisoner give you any trouble. If he does, I want to know about it."

Booth nodded. "Don't worry yourself on my account. Just get yourself ready for your big day tomorrow. Archenfield is ready to welcome its new Prince."

Jared smiled. "I'll take my leave," he said. "But my mother asked me to pass on a message. She's expecting you for tea on the striking of the Physician's Bell. She's already picking out fresh reading matter for you."

Booth nodded. "I'll be there," he said. "It's about time things got back to normal around here, don't you think?"

Prince Jared nodded and took his leave. Yes, more than anything, he thought as he mounted the stairs from the Dungeons, he yearned for things to get back to normal. He couldn't bring his brother or Silva back from the dead, but he could honor their memories, and those of his ancestors, by committing himself to delivering a lasting peace to Archenfield. He knew this would be no straightforward matter. Logan's latest taunts were already spinning in his brain. He knew that Axel was far from convinced that the incipient threat from Paddenburg had been lifted. The Princedom was still on alert, but Prince Jared knew he was not alone.

He had his family and the Twelve and the Princedom as a whole to support him in the coming days and months. For now, they had rooted out the true poison at the heart of the court.

Coming up from the Dungeons into the light, Jared felt some sense of release as the noonday sun fell across his face and neck. Logan's threats and the pressure of the past two weeks were already beginning to lift from his shoulders. He knew that he'd feel better still when tomorrow's formalities were over, but he intended to stop and enjoy them—or, if not *enjoy* them, at least be fully conscious of them. It wasn't every day that you were crowned Prince, and the whole of your nation took to the streets to wave flags and chant your name. *Jared, Prince of All Archenfield*. It still sounded strange in his ears, but he had a feeling he'd soon become accustomed to it. He shrugged and continued on, enjoying the poignant warmth of the autumn sun.

~~~

"Ready?" Asta asked Nova as they reached the door at the top of the stone stairwell.

Nova nodded, smiling softly. "Ready."

Asta pushed open the door and began climbing the final few steps that led to the Falconer's Mews. It was strange to think that the last time she had climbed these stairs, she had thought Nova Chastain was the assassin. She glanced over her shoulder to check on Nova's progress. She could see that the climb had taken its toll on the Falconer, but also that its completion and the arrival back in her own domain had brought with it a sense of elation.

"How good does it feel to be back here?" Asta asked, reaching out her hand.

"So good!" Nova exclaimed, her eyes moist. She took Asta's hand and squeezed it gently. "Thank you for all your care and support this past week. We didn't get off on the right footing, you and I, but you have proved a true friend to me."

Asta smiled. "I'm just glad to see you make such a strong recovery."

"Do I hear voices?" A tall young man, with black hair and the beginnings of a beard, strode across the stone floor toward them, a falcon on his forearm.

"Adam!" Nova exclaimed. "Asta, this is Adam Marangon, my Deputy Falconer. Adam, this is the rather wonderful Asta Peck."

"The Physician's apprentice?" Adam said, reaching out to shake Asta's hand. "I've heard a lot about you around the court."

Asta shook his hand. "Good to meet you, Adam. And who's this?" She nodded toward the falcon that rested on his gauntlet.

"It's Pampero!" Nova exclaimed, a smile breaking across

her face. "She looks well. How are they all? How I have missed each and every one of them."

Adam smiled. "They have all pined for their mistress, but other than that, they are all fine. And now, I think I shall return Pampero to her perch and leave you to your happy reunion with them all."

"I should get going too," Asta said. "I'm sure Uncle Elias will have..."

Nova reached out her hand. "Stay just a little, would you?"

"Of course, if you'd like me to."

Adam led the way toward the perch, where Pampero's companions were waiting eagerly, having sensed the new arrivals in the mews. It was a clear, bright day and Asta could see through the glass panels far and wide across the palace grounds—up to the glen, over to the forest, out to the fjord. Archenfield had never seemed so beautiful to her before. Maybe it was the last of the autumn sunshine; perhaps it was simply the fact that things were getting back to order after the turmoil of the last two weeks.

Adam helped Pampero back onto the perch, alongside her companions, then began unstrapping his leather gauntlet. As he did so, he smiled at Asta. The way he smiled was so unguarded, it seemed to light up his whole face. She felt instantly that she liked, and could trust, Adam Marangon.

"Where's Mistral?"

They both turned around at Nova's question. The Falconer looked disconcerted.

Adam shook his head. "Oh, I'm sorry, I forgot to tell you. The Captain of the Guard asked me to send her with a message to the Paddenburg Gate." As he said the words, they heard the familiar bell begin to chime.

"The Falconer's Bell," Adam said with a grin. "Right on cue. Mistral should be back at any moment."

Nova did not return his smile. She pushed past him, out onto the balcony.

Asta approached Adam Marangon. "It's only natural she should be a little anxious. After everything she has been through, I think she just wants everything to be back to normal."

He nodded. "We all want that, Asta, wouldn't you agree?"

Before she could answer, they saw a bird swooping toward the balcony. They both turned as it landed right in front of the Falconer.

It was not a falcon but a great golden eagle. It was a huge bird with a vast wingspan.

Intrigued, Asta strode out onto the balcony, followed closely behind by Adam.

"I thought it was..." Asta began. She stopped speaking as she saw the stricken expression on Nova's face and then looked more closely at the eagle.

In its claws were the bloody, torn remains of a much smaller bird. And in its beak was the bird's head.

"Mistral!" Nova exclaimed, stumbling back toward the glass. Adam moved over to stop her from falling. He held her tight in his arms, though she writhed like a wild animal.

"I'm so sorry, Nova," he said, soothingly. "I'm so sorry. I know how much she meant to you."

Asta gazed at the eagle. She had the strange sense that the bird was scrutinizing her and her companions with disdain. Suddenly it moved one of its claws and, as it did so, she noticed that it was carrying a messenger tube, almost identical to those carried by Nova's falcons, only somewhat larger.

Without checking with the others, or donning a gauntlet, Asta moved toward the eagle.

"Asta!" Adam hissed. "Be very careful. A bird like that can kill with ease."

But she was beyond fear. And actually it seemed as if the eagle wanted her to reach over and disconnect the messenger tube.

She did so and, opening it, allowed a scroll of parchment, sealed with wax, to slide out.

"Who would use an eagle as a messenger?" Adam asked, frowning.

"What does it say, Asta?" Nova broke free, at last, of Adam's hold.

Asta unfurled the parchment and began to read the words, written in elegant but unusual handwriting:

> *To Prince Jared of All Archenfield,*
>
> *Your Princedom is irredeemably weakened. Paddenburg is ready to take over full control. You have seven days to surrender your lands and people to us.*
>
> *If you fail to submit by sunset on the seventh day, our armies will break through your borders.*
>
> *Should anything happen to Logan Wilde during this time, we will know about it and our armies will arrive even sooner.*
>
> *Enjoy your coronation and the fact that yours will be the shortest reign of any Prince in the history of Archenfield.*
>
>
>
> *Yours in ambition and anticipation,*
>
> *Prince Ven and Prince Henning of Paddenburg*
>
>

As Asta finished reading, she gazed up into the others' faces. She could see they were as shocked as she was; no one could find words to give voice to this new horror. Behind her, she distractedly heard the eagle's wings opening. She glanced back, just in time to see the bird take flight. As it did so, it let Mistral's decapitated head fall onto the stone balcony, then soared away on the Archenfield sky. Evidently, the dark courier had completed its mission. Now it could return home to its masters.

Acknowledgments

A note of thanks:

Writing a novel can appear to be a solo activity, but in reality, it is a team sport, and I am indebted to a number of people who helped bring *Allies & Assassins* to life. The list begins with Hedd ap Emlyn, an inspirational librarian who, one grim autumn day in Wrexham, told me about the Welsh tradition of "The Poet's Chair." The story of Prince Jared and his court began to take root that very day. Hedd, thank you for opening the gates to the premedieval Welsh courts to me, for your generosity of time and spirit in directing me toward sources of information and inspiration and perhaps most of all, for your forbearance when I played fast and loose with the source material. My next thank-you is to my wonderful literary agent, Philippa Milnes-Smith at Lucas Alexander Whitley, who guides my writing career with a strong but steady hand and always seems to know the next step on the journey, even when I'm less certain. Thanks to my dynamo duo of editors: Sam Smith at Atom in the UK and Kate Sullivan at Little, Brown in the U.S. I'm so grateful to you both for your enthusiasm about this idea and for all the energy and wisdom you have shared as the project has developed. Thanks to my niece Nadine Mahoney for guiding me—and Elin—through how to mix paint pigments and to Billy Taylor, resident falconer at Lainston House Hotel in Hampshire, for opening up the world of hawks, falcons and eagles to me. Last, but never least, thank you to Peejay Norman for championing this story from the first spark of an idea to the final edit, for being such an enthusiastic partner in research (from the glen to the fjord) and for helping me to find and keep my connection to Archenfield and all who live—and die—within its gates.

—Justin Somper